GHOST BLACK

DAUGHTER OF MARS BOOK 3

MATTHEW S. COX

DIVISION ZERO PRESS

Ghost Black
Daughter of Mars Book 3
A novel by Matthew S. Cox
© 2015 – Matthew S. Cox
All Rights Reserved

Cover art by Eugene Teplitsky

ISBN (ebook): 978-1-949174-40-3

ISBN (print): 978-1-949174-41-0

DIVERGENT FATES UNIVERSE

Division Zero Series
The Awakened Series
Daughter of Mars Series
Virtual Immortality Series
Prophet of the Badlands Series

CONTENTS

AUTHOR'S NOTE

At some points in the story, characters communicate via cybernetic implants in a manner similar to a holographic video phone call transmitted directly into their brains. Dialogue spoken over this link is not said aloud, only audible to the person on the other end of the call. To differentiate this from actual spoken dialogue, internal communications are contained in <> marks rather than quotes.

    <This is a character speaking over the comm link, no one near them can hear this.>

    "This is a character speaking out loud."

WHIRLWIND

F rayed wires draped from a gouge in the wall where a section of plastisteel panel suffered small arms fire. Risa held her breath for the moment it took her to hurry forward through the cloud of smoke. Air in the subterranean street still tasted like scorched plastic and flesh, though no sign remained of those involved in the shootout. Two figures in dull-crimson jumpsuits hovered by the damage; the white letters 'ECMA' across their backs identified them as city employees. One busied himself with a datapad while the other ran her hand around the damage. A small group of locals passed in the opposite direction; no one paid the workers notice, their presence merely another ubiquitous component in the great ecosystem of Elysium City.

Risa paused to stare at the technicians. *The Municipal Authority never shows up that quick. I can still smell the ballistic propellant.* She glanced back at Pavo, slowed by his effort to navigate the sparse mass of pedestrians without dropping a pair of steaming noodle bowls. *Nothing in this place ever gets fixed this fast without money changing hands.* She observed the workers for a moment more, but they didn't do anything to raise her suspicions further—other than arriving before the bodies had likely reached the morgue.

Pavo had an apartment on Tier 4, which put it four stories plus twenty meters of dirt and rock underground. Sure, Elysium City had a sizable surface footprint... but the rent down here was a quarter what it would've cost to live topside.

The female tech seemed to react to Risa's pointed look and made eye contact. Another Marsborn, she had snow-white skin stark under a violet bob. She returned a confused smile, as if some random citizen even acknowledging ECMA workers existed was a rare event—or more likely, those 'technicians' had been sent to watch her back... or watch her.

Or, perhaps ordinary workers had simply been fast today.

Risa offered a nod of acknowledgement, and the woman returned her attention to tinkering with some electronic device.

Pavo brushed past Risa and headed for his apartment door. "What?"

She walked after him, her attention still on the open panel in the wall spewing sparks. "Something's not right. They're not doing anything but standing there."

"They're ECMA. Standing there *is* what they do."

Risa hurried a step and poked him in the side. "I'm serious."

He stopped. "You're starting to sound paranoid. Those two are probably doing an initial site survey so they know what parts to bring for the repair."

"Bots are supposed to do that." Risa pulled her hair off her face and looked up at him. "Aren't they?"

Pavo grinned. "If there were a pair of orbs hanging there instead, would you suspect them of being spies too?"

"Probably." Risa folded her arms, and lowered her gaze. "I think my brain is fried. Too much, too fast."

He gestured with a soup bowl in the direction they'd been walking. "Everett did say we need to lay low for a while. You'll feel better inside."

Risa unthreaded her arms; the smirking grin on his face made her heart swell. She could only tolerate two seconds of gazing into his slate-grey eyes before shying away. Despite the haze of exhaustion, his feelings for her showed clear. *How could he brush off being abducted so easily?* The artificial orbs in her skull could offer only cold plastisteel and violet light in return. She laid her head against his shoulder, clinging, not wanting him to see her false eyes.

"Now what?" He managed an awkward hug while holding a plastic bowl in each hand.

She shivered. "I don't want to wake up. I know I'm back at the safe house, asleep... or maybe I didn't survive Bliss."

"You're taking recreational chems now?"

Risa chuckled. "No, ass. Bliss the city."

"What?" he yelled, then stammered a second before recovering his composure and continuing in a hoarse whisper-shout. "They sent you to the goddamned heart of Corp territory?"

She kept staring at the ground.

"Risa… Don't give me the silent thing."

"Yeah," she whispered. "I thought you were dead. I…"—she covered her mouth with one hand—"went out there not expecting to come back."

He prodded her with a bowl. "Inside. I need to hear this."

She walked backward for three steps. "I'm not sure I want to tell you." She waited for him to pass, then followed. "You'll never let me out again."

"Oh, as if you'd listen to me." He chuckled.

Risa glanced over her shoulder every so often as they walked down the subterranean street. Every fifty meters, crossing tunnels led off on both sides into various degrees of darkness, depending on how many lights had been shot out. The occasional person coming the other way nodded at them in greeting.

Pavo eventually took a right turn down the passage leading to the façade of his apartment. Four on-duty MDF officers coming the other way paused long enough to fist bump him as they went by. Cush job, patrolling the housing block one lived in. Since Risa learned C-Branch created the Martian Liberation Front, a sector populated mostly by Mars Defense Force people didn't quite scare the hell out of her like it once had. She shadowed him across the lobby to the elevator. The building extended down some forty more levels, like a skyscraper built in reverse. Elysium City stopped at Tier 4, but a handful of 'low-rises' kept on going. The elevator let them off on the -4th floor, where Pavo's living quarters waited nine doors down the corridor on the left.

He edged up to the door and grumbled when the panel refused to beep.

"Damn. I'm going to need a new 'mini."

"Uhh, about your apartment." She filled her lungs through her nostrils.

Pavo came about in a slow turn, eyebrow raised. "What did you do?"

"Oh…"—she smiled—"Nothing major. I just, uhh, let someone stay here."

He blinked. "You left Kree alone?"

"No." Risa cringed inwardly. *I still can't even get her out of the safehouse.* She waved her NetMini over the silver rectangle on the wall. The panel chirped, and the door slid to the side with a short *pfft* of air. "It's another long story."

The living room looked as tidy as a demo unit. Genevieve perched on the couch in a thigh-length pink T-shirt, bare feet up on the coffee table, attention glued to the holo-panel on which played one of the *Monwyn* fantasy movies. A two-inch orb-bot hovered around her toes, layering nail enamel into floral patterns.

"At least your friend cleaned..." Pavo walked in, looking around. "This is my apartment, isn't it? We didn't go into the wrong one?"

Risa slipped in behind him. "You can't tell anyone she's here."

Genevieve waved at the video display, pausing it. "Wow, Bit, where the hell did you find him? Is Maris recruiting the homeless now?"

"Gen... this is Pavo."

The redhead's eyes shot wide open. "Holy shit!" She tossed her bowl of pretzels on the table and ran over, leaving the tiny nail-painting orb spinning in midair. "You told me he was dead!"

Risa braced for impact seconds before a suffocating hug almost took her off her feet. "We landed twenty minutes ago. C-Branch was holding him in a remote camp."

"Bit? That's cute." Pavo smiled as he headed for the small kitchen. He flopped in a chair at the table and attacked one of the noodle bowls. "Genevieve, huh? Looks like Risa's gotten into the habit of collecting the supposedly dead."

Genevieve laughed. "Not her fault... I faked it."

He coughed, trying to laugh and eat at the same time.

Risa removed her weapons harness and plodded down the hall. Genevieve followed. The little bot tilted like a confused dog, waited a second, and landed on the table. A second later, its lights went out. Once in the back bedroom, Risa set her laser pistols on the small desk by a terminal, sat on the Comforgel pad, and bent forward to unfasten her boots.

Genevieve leaned on the doorway, arms folded. "Details, girl."

"Remember me talking about Shiro?" Risa pulled her feet out of her boots, adoring the relief of chilly air.

"Yeah."

Risa grabbed at the neck of her ballistic suit and pulled the MolWeave fastener down to her hip before peeling off her 'second skin.' "He's not a sympathetic executive from Earth." She gathered the material in two hands and pushed it down over her hips. "He's C-Branch."

Genevieve gasped. "Oh, shit…"

"It's not as bad as it sounds." She stood naked for a moment, fanning air over her sweat-soaked skin. "We all are. The Front is a puppet of C-Branch created for plausible deniability."

"Whoa… Are you playing with my head?" Genevieve grabbed her shoulders. "That's not funny."

Too tired to fight back, Risa tolerated the shaking. "No, Gen. I'm serious. The MLF was set up by military intelligence to allow them to run black ops against targets both Corporate and domestic while diverting blame to a 'terrorist organization' rather than have fingers point back at the government."

Genevieve let go of her and covered her mouth with both hands. She seemed about ready to either cry or stomp off to kill someone. After a moment of staring around in shock, she sat on the edge of the Comforgel pad beside her.

"That file you hid in the 'sem didn't have much dirt on Maris. Most of the data involved Garrison." She paced around to let perspiration evaporate in the air conditioning. "Maris, as much as I couldn't believe it, appears to be the reason they sent Shiro and his team in."

"What?" Genevieve clutched her knees, leaning forward. "*They* who?"

"Military intelligence command. Maris has been refusing orders to conduct false flag operations. He won't go after UCF civilian targets. Arden Settlement was supposed to have been us. When he refused, they used an official black ops team." Risa surveyed a pile of laundry against the closet door, picking among the garments with her toe. "Once they realized Maris had a mind of his own and wouldn't be their puppet, they identified me as the biggest threat. Shiro was sent in to 'neutralize' me if he thought I'd be a problem."

Genevieve cocked an eyebrow. "Didn't you say Shiro's been trying to talk you into going to Earth with him?"

Risa faced her and struck a cover-model pose. "Apparently, he couldn't handle the hotness."

"Hah." Genevieve laughed. "If you weren't like my kid sister, I'd totally jump on that."

Chuckling, Risa plucked an unwashed black T-shirt from the rug and slipped it on; one of Pavo's, it covered her like a short dress. "Yeah, well… Shiro fell in stupid for me and wanted Pavo out of the way. He arranged for his team to get rid of him, only somehow, Everett got wind of it and intercepted Pavo before they could kill him." She ran a hand up over her face, raking her fingers through her hair. *I just know Everett's going to call in that favor someday.*

"Eww. Bit, that's not clean."

"Neither am I." Risa smiled. "Just throwing something on while I eat. Gonna hop in the tube right after... then sleep for a week."

Genevieve took her hand. "You don't look okay. What's wrong?"

She pulled Genevieve to the kitchen, suppressing a shiver at the cold air invading her improvised dress, but reveling in the sense of freedom afforded by actual fabric. More and more, her ballistic suit felt confining, not the security blanket it had once been. Pavo looked up as she rounded the table and took the seat facing him. Genevieve sat on the end to her right. He fought with his soup, struggling to eat the too-hot meal faster than his mouth could tolerate.

Risa grabbed the pull-tab and tore her bowl open. "Crap, Gen. I should've got you one."

"I'm good." Genevieve smiled. "I ordered about an hour ago."

"So, what's 'Bit?'" asked Pavo.

"Garrison used to call her that when she was small." Genevieve grinned. "Because she was really small for her age."

Risa's heart sank. "Umm, Gen... I..." She stared into the morass of noodles, shrimp, and broth, appetite gone.

Genevieve put a hand on her arm. "No... Don't tell me he's dead?"

"Not yet, he isn't." Risa narrowed her eyes.

"I don't like that look." Genevieve squeezed. "That man is like your father. What the heck is going on in that head of yours?"

Risa couldn't bear looking at either of them. "The data you thought Maris wanted to kill you for... It was all about Garrison and some woman named Serena Var. He used to be Special Operations, Delta."

"So?" Genevieve tilted her head.

"The man's gotta be past fifty, and I *still* wouldn't want to mess with him," said Pavo. "Delta's some bad, bad dudes."

Risa's guilt and exhaustion succumbed to the smell of food. She twirled noodles around her chopsticks and ate a few bundles. "I'm not sure how that woman is involved, maybe nothing more than being caught in the surveillance. Her name sounds familiar, but I can't place it."

Pavo shrugged with his eyebrows while stuffing noodles into his mouth.

Genevieve exhaled. "Whatever it is you're trying to avoid saying must be bad."

"Garrison…" Risa made a fist, an onrush of anger energizing her to where she almost wanted to run off and kill him at that second. Rage survived the span of three breaths before she fought back the urge to sob and her sorrow settled into a lingering nausea. "He's the one who gave the order to kill my father."

Pavo set his chopsticks down and reached across the table to take her hand. "No wonder he took you in… he must've felt guilty."

Genevieve's cheeks flushed red. Her eyes hardened. She seemed angry enough to kill as well. "Son of a bitch! Why?"

"Corp agent, remember?" Risa muttered. "Told you about Andriy on the ride back from Araphel."

"Oh." Genevieve slouched. "Right."

"I…" Risa fumed. "For so long, all I wanted to do was find the piece of shit that ordered my father dead, and tear them apart… and I was living right next to him the whole time." She clenched both hands into trembling fists. "I can't believe he lied to me."

Pavo gripped her hand tighter. "He was responsible for the security of the UCF, and issued an order against a foreign intelligence agent. You can't think it was personal?"

Genevieve leaned back in her chair and wiped both hands down her face. "Wow… still, it's twisted taking her in and not telling her the truth. You were such an angry little thing."

"Still is." Pavo winked.

Risa continued staring into her soup. Scene after scene of her ranting at Garrison about how much she wanted to kill the people responsible for her father's death played by in her mind. Each time, he'd simply nod or murmur in agreement. His assurance of 'I'm sure you'll find them someday' took on a new meaning, one that made the sick feeling in her gut stronger.

"So…" said Genevieve. "If the Front is a giant pile of dustblow… now what?"

Pavo took a long drink from his bowl, tapping the bottom to chase a few stray bits of vegetable or beef into his mouth. He held a finger up in a 'give me a sec' gesture until he finished chewing and swallowed. "The PVM has been around longer. I have doubts a purely political effort will give control of Mars to her own people, but I can't fault Everett's logic that fighting both sides is pointless."

"I think Garrison also tried to kill you." Risa looked up, locking stares with Genevieve. "The Front got those rigged detonators from a different contact. This guy Heitzenroeder. The file you hid in the 'sem had images of Garrison meeting with him in person." She sighed at the table before glancing at Pavo. "That's why she's here. None of them know she's not dead. She can't go back."

"It's not an issue. She's welcome to stay as long as she needs." Pavo shook his head. "That Heitzenroeder guy's a real edgy sort. Started a gang, lives off the grid. Even the Syndicate stays out of his way. I guess they don't like their own methods pointed back at them."

"Huh?" Genevieve glanced at him.

Pavo set his bowl down and dropped the chopsticks into it. "Both react the same way to people who interfere with their business. Usually, it involves destroying anything the person cares for, piece by piece, while they watch... then killing them."

"They shouldn't be in bed with the Syndicate." Risa twirled her chopsticks around in her soup. "They're worse than any of the dustblow the NewsNet ever accused the MLF of doing."

Pavo blinked. "Sounds like you're talking about the MLF like you aren't one of them.'"

"Yeah." She splayed her fingers flat on the table, pondering her plastisteel bones and the synthetic diamond blades within. "I'm not going to be able to go back when I'm done."

Genevieve fixed her with a stare. "What are you gonna do?"

Anger bubbled up. Risa pictured her claws entering Garrison's neck, delivering her long-awaited revenge on the man who murdered her father. "I'm going to..." She closed her eyes. Upon the black of her eyelids, the sad face of the man she'd spent the past sixteen years thinking of as a protector appeared. The same expression he gave her whenever she did something foolish: disbelief tinged with sorrow... and hurt. Her heart thudded in her chest. "...talk to him."

For what he did to her father, she wanted to kill him, but couldn't. To get her revenge, she'd have to start an argument that would give her enough anger to lash out in the heat of the moment. However horrible she felt after the fact, well, she'd find some way to deal with that. Maybe she could convince herself he hadn't ever really cared for her like a father, believe he only became what she missed the most in order to control her. So what if he started taking care of her when she'd been nine years old, before any cybernetic augmentation? Intelligence agents play the long game.

Pavo stood, rounded the table, and offered a hand. "You look exhausted, and I am in dire need of a shower."

Risa let him pull her standing. "'Kay."

"Right. The holo-bar calls me. I haven't seen this one yet. Monwyn's taking on the Shadow Goblin king." Genevieve drifted off to the living room. As soon as she flopped on the couch and put her feet up on the table, the tiny orb leapt up with a happy chirp and resumed painting her toenails.

Risa trudged along behind him out of the kitchen, down a short hall decorated by drab grey carpet and slim silver light bands on the walls. A thin door of gloss-black 'glass' slid out of their way as they approached the bathroom. Like an assembly robot performing a rote task, Risa removed her shirt and stepped into the floor-to-ceiling autoshower tube.

He tucked in behind her and closed the door. "Standard cycle, start."

Machinery in the metal base whirred to life, and within seconds, the interior filled with warm spraying water. Risa turned and wrapped her arms around him, chest to chest. A mechanical ring descended around them, rotating as it coated them with a sudsy mixture. She kept her eyes and mouth closed, and basked in the reality of having him back. Steamy air in her lungs sapped the energy right out of her.

He kissed the top of her head. "You're not dreaming yet."

"Mmm." She tucked her face into the crook of his neck. All the emotional weight of having thought he'd died hit her at once. She didn't want to deal with any more surprises, any more deceptions. One more revelation that her world existed as nothing more than a series of intricate lies balanced on top of more lies would be too much. She thought of attempting to outrun an explosion on The Strand, a leap onto a tiny patrol flier... how many thousands of ways that could've gone wrong. Her stoicism, battered to shreds by Garrison's betrayal, gave out. Strength left her legs, and she clung to him, crying into his shoulder.

"Risa?" whispered Pavo.

"I was ready to stand there and die. I thought you were dead. I gave up."

He held her upright, swaying side to side. The gentle motion coupled with the rhythmic thrum of the machine lulled her into a half-awake calm. "You've got a guardian angel."

She chuckled and recovered her footing. "He's not real. You were right; I must've really sounded Cat-6. He's—" The rinse started; she clamped her mouth closed until the driving spray from the descending ring stopped pelting her in the face. "A synth. AI."

"A lot of things make sense now." He spun her around and pulled her back against his chest before the dry cycle started. "Restart program."

The console chimed a pleasant tone. Two seconds later, the initial rinse spray started. He stood behind her, clasping her hands and holding her arms up to expose her front to the following soap. She let her head drape back against him, wishing the massaging torrent of hot water would scrub her emotions clean. Again, before the dry cycle could start, he shifted around to face the spray and restarted the process.

Risa clung to his back, content to hold him while the shower did its job. After the third wash cycle, he let the hot air tornado run. Once dry, he faced her. They stood holding each other without speaking for a few minutes, breaths echoing in the plastic tube. She drank in his scent, wishing she could forget all about the Martian Liberation Front and spend forever holding him like she did right there.

Pavo kissed the side of her neck.

"I'm too tired to—"

He brushed a hand over her hair, staring into her soul with total sincerity. "It's more than I could've asked for to be with you right now."

She cringed inwardly at the reflection of her violet irises in his eyes.

Pavo backed out of the tube, holding both her hands. She stumbled after, drowsy gaze on the floor, and let out a muted squeak when he lifted her into his arms. Too tired to protest, she held on as he carried her to the bed. After he set her on the Comforgel pad, he glanced at the door.

"She won't mind." Risa stretched into the satin sheets, unable to keep her eyes open. "The safehouse isn't big on privacy."

He crawled in next to her. She rolled half on her side, arm across his chest, and slipped into a dream of free fall. Again and again, she saw herself leaping out over the Melas Chasma, missing the little aircraft, and plummeting down eleven kilometers to the ACC settlement below. Tired as she was, and with Pavo at her side, even that nightmare didn't wake her.

2

BEHIND THE CURTAIN

A few seconds after Risa realized she'd become conscious, her mind latched on to the reason for it—a conspiracy between an overfull bladder and the scent of bacon in the air. She emitted a weak groan and rolled onto her belly. As soon as she stared at the nightstand, a tiny holo-bar sensed her looking at it and projected a transparent clock: 11:14 a.m. She scowled at the lump of flexible armor on the floor. Confronting Garrison could go sour fast; she'd have to wear it again.

Risa dragged herself upright, intent on heading straight for the kitchen after a stop at the bathroom. In the hall, she caught a scrap of conversation between Pavo and Genevieve, and realized she hadn't put any clothes on. After a second or two of indecision, she doubled back for a clean shirt. Not that Genevieve would mind, but there *was* such a thing as *too* casual. She rummaged a shirt from the floordrobe and pulled it on, suppressing the urge to be annoyed at not being alone with Pavo. She'd spent years thinking her 'sister' was dead, and worried the tiniest scrap of resentment at her presence might cause fate to change its mind.

After a quick detour to the bathroom, she trudged into the kitchen. Pavo and Genevieve sat catty-corner at the table, both absorbed in their breakfast. Risa headed for the 'sem and dialed up scrambled eggs with bacon. While standing and watching the beige slime reconfigure itself into her meal, she lamented being unable to send her armor out like laundry. No one in their right mind would risk a two-million-credit set of quasi-legal armor to a delivery laundry service.

Grumbling, she took her plate and headed for the table. Pavo's hand intercepted her ass before it could touch down on a chair, and he guided her into his lap. Since he'd already cleared his plate, she pushed it out of her way and used him for a seat. He threaded his arms around her middle, pressed his face to her hair, and inhaled a deep sniff.

"You two are adorable," said Genevieve.

"Did anyone call Aurelia yet?" Pavo's voice vibrated over her.

Risa shook her head. "Not yet. I was so twisted up and exhausted, I never got to it. She's gonna kill me for not calling her from the flight in."

Genevieve collected her and Pavo's empty plates and carried them to the dishwasher.

"You're right. She's going to be upset," said Pavo. "But, Everett did ask me to stay out of sight until he had a chance to brief my superiors in the Defense Force. Hopefully, it won't take long. I figure each day we don't tell her roughly triples the nuclear response."

"You're going to kill Garrison today, aren't you?" Genevieve kept her back turned, leaning both hands on the counter by the sink.

Risa mulled it over while chewing a piece of bacon. Having had the real stuff from that hole-in-the-wall lunch counter, the OmniSoy variety amounted to pork-flavored snot. "It's possible. Finding the person who murdered my father and destroyed my childhood was all I thought about for years…"

"But for some reason, you can't make yourself angry enough to kill him." Genevieve shifted around to lean against the counter. "Or are you still numb?"

"I keep seeing him. Whenever I close my eyes, I see him. That same sad face he always made when I did something stupid. Almost like he cares."

"Maybe he does?" Pavo hugged her tighter. "You weren't an ACC infiltrator. He had to feel awful for you. Ever think maybe he lied because he was afraid you'd hate him?"

Risa squirmed, trying to move his squeezing arms off her stomach so she could eat. Her motion stirred his interest, and he poked her through his boxers. Awkwardness at having Genevieve so close bubbled over. She covered her mouth to avoid spitting half-chewed eggs on the table and laughed.

"Are you sure you're not Cat-6?" Genevieve's smile evaporated when she glanced at the clock. She hurried to the living room.

Pavo took a deep breath and let it out. "Oops. Guess she noticed." He kissed the back of her shoulder, an inch to the left of her neck. "You don't have to run off right away, do you?"

"You're unbelievable." She gasped and giggled as he tried to pull her shirt up. "Not here!"

He relented, letting his hands rest innocently on her hips. "You think Gen would mind if we locked ourselves in the back for a few hours?"

"I think she'd understand." Risa scooped the last forkful of eggs into her mouth.

She set the plate down and did a little shimmy, sliding her butt back and forth across his lap. He grunted. When she started to get up, Pavo's fingers dug in and held her down. Risa looked up, about to ask why, but stalled at the sight of Aurelia in the archway between kitchen and living room, in civilian clothes: a loose raspberry top and tight black leggings. Her normally medium-tan face darkened with a look caught between livid and about to burst into tears.

"How long?" Aurelia's voice came flat, detached, near lifeless.

Risa sat as still as she could manage. "Sorry. We got back late last night and basically went straight to sleep. And we had, uhh, orders to keep it quiet."

Aurelia ran over, arms wide. Genevieve appeared in the doorway looking guilty.

Pavo eased Risa to her feet and managed an ungainly hug with his duty partner that somehow managed to conceal his aroused state. Risa made herself a cup of coffee and took a seat at the table. Over the next hour, they brought Aurelia up to speed on how one faction within C-Branch attempted to have Pavo eliminated, but other operators loyal to the Pueri Verum Martis extracted him before he could be killed. Risa danced around specifics and names, giving Aurelia the abbreviated version: one part of the government wanted the Liberation Front to attack its own people, while the other did not.

"General Maris' continued refusal to basically commit war crimes caused them to re-evaluate the need for the MLF." Pavo sighed. "There's an internal war going on right now. One we can't afford. It could give the Corporates the upper hand."

"That's fucked up on an entirely new level." Aurelia accepted a refill from Genevieve, and smiled at her. "So the bastards that left me hogtied on the floor of my bedroom were ours?"

"More or less. The hardliners who are afraid of the PVM." Risa swirled her coffee around, staring into it like a fortuneteller. "The guy at Arden said they need the continued 'threat' of terrorism to justify large budgets for military operations."

"But there's an *actual* damn war going on." Aurelia grumbled. "Isn't that enough?"

Pavo shook his head. "Apparently not. It's not a traditional war. There aren't large groups clashing out in the Martian desert. I mean, yeah, there's small-scale engagements all the time, but when you look at it from a macro perspective, it's basically a planetary pissing contest. You've got maybe four million people on this rock. Full-scale war isn't something either side could survive. No matter who 'won,' we'd cripple each other into extinction. Humanity's grip on Mars isn't that solid yet."

Aurelia held her head in her hands, rubbing her eyes. "The MDF trains us to prepare for that moment when *something* happens out there. I always wondered if I'd be fast enough or strong enough to make a difference if anything went south... or if I'd be the one hoping you were fast enough." She sighed. "I never dreamed the moment would come when I was at home asleep."

"Hey, that isn't your fault," said Genevieve. "There aren't many people in the world who could walk away from C-Branch sneaking up on them while they're out cold."

Risa frowned at her empty mug. *If I could wish away the MLF and spend the rest of my life with Pavo, I'd do it right now.* After a moment of intense concentration, she felt pretty sure Garrison still existed. "I'll let you two catch up. I have someone to talk to."

Pavo shot her a longing stare. "Be careful." When she stood, he gathered her into an embrace. "Please don't do anything stupid," he whispered.

I already did. Risa shied away from his stare, not wanting him to see her metal eyes. "I won't."

FOLLOWING A TWENTY-EIGHT-MINUTE SHUTTLE HOP FROM ELYSIUM TO Primus, Risa lowered herself down a vertical shaft in the ventilation ducts as she had countless times before. The Martian Liberation Front safehouse existed well below the level of 'civilized' tiers, where even the gangs had little interest in going... not out of fear of what dwelled there, but being so far away from civilization made it boring—no one to mess with.

Plastic cups, cartons, and wrappers crunched under her boots as she settled into a junction in the conduit, down on what would've been the twelfth tier of the city had they continued building that deep. Night vision revealed the childish decorations still hanging on the walls in her 'safe place.' Old pillows and a blanket sat atop the trash in the left corner, the one farthest from the vent leading to Garrison's office. Three of her childhood dolls hung from loose rivets nearby. One still had char marks from where the flames reached under her bed. This chamber of thin plastisteel had been her sanctuary away from everything, a place where an angry little girl could feel protected from the world.

I should've stayed right here. She curled up with her chin on her knees and her arms wrapped around her legs the way she always used to. *Never should've trusted the MLF.*

The voice of her father, of Andriy Voronin, of an ACC spy, roared in her head, screaming at her to run. For the millionth time, her brain returned to the instant she'd watched the fire engulf his face. His death elicited somewhat different emotions now. Pure rage and a thirst for revenge had given way to nonspecific anger at the war in general. She couldn't call it a case of the military betraying its own any more. Andriy *was* a foreign combatant pretending to be a UCF soldier. An enemy infiltrator. Learning that he'd murdered her mother, Marisa Donnelly, when she tried to convince him to betray the Corporates, blunted the fangs of her rage at his death. Could Risa hate Andriy for killing the mother she never had a chance to know more than she wanted to hate Garrison for issuing the order that killed her father? To him, the man had been a foreign enemy.

She peered down the length of ductwork at the pattern of lines created by light in Garrison's office. After he'd found her on the street and brought her here, it took her two years to work up to sleeping out in the open, in the bed he'd set up for her. Two years to trust Garrison wouldn't hurt her. What did it mean that he allowed her to keep crawling back in here at night instead of forcing her to sleep in her 'room' outside? Did it mean anything at all? She sighed, remembering how she'd resented him and screamed when he tried to keep her from volunteering to be wired up. *I thought he wanted to 'protect the weak little girl' or keep me from getting my revenge.* She squinted. *Maybe he was afraid I'd find out the truth someday and come after him.*

Anger pushed guilt aside. She crept down the tunnel on all fours. No one would see her enter. She could get out before anyone found his body, but once they saw him, they'd know who did it; Nano claws were distinctive weapons. Would anyone in there possibly believe *she* would be able to hurt him? For so long... and even during her angriest years, Garrison had been the only person she'd allow close. With any luck, the others might think an outside agent tried to frame her.

The vent offered two routes into the office. Closer, a floor-level opening. Farther ahead and beyond a short vertical spar, a vertical duct led to a second exit nearer the ceiling at eye level. Risa opted for the nearer choice and crawled into a short section of duct between the feed shaft and the office where she crouched behind the slats, staring at the back of a man she no longer understood.

Garrison leaned over his desk, focused on something she couldn't see due to her low angle. A small, oscillating fan at the corner rotated back and forth, pushing small plastic bits around and sending sparkles of dust past his holographic terminal. She perched in place, watching the fan go back and forth for a few minutes, its rhythm offering an idle distraction from the conversation she dreaded starting. Her feelings toward him had been teetering between killer and father, but seeing this office, the place she had grown up in, filled her with guilt. Despite all the dustblow flying around, it sounded so ridiculous to suspect Garrison had been manipulating her since she'd been a little orphan on the street. Maybe he hadn't even known she existed when he signed the order. Much of her demand for revenge came from believing the UCF was so corrupt they murdered one of their own soldiers.

But Andriy had been a spy.

And he'd killed her mother.

Risa lost her urge to fly in and kill Garrison right away. She bowed her head and decided to let him talk, a part of her deep brain knowing it meant she'd already chosen not to hurt him—and hoping that proved to be true.

Opening the vent cover without making a noise had become an old game. At one point, she'd thought it funny to sneak up and scare him. Now, knowing he'd been Spec Ops, she bit her lip. Startling that man had probably been one of the more foolish things she'd done. *He never raised a hand to me. Did he know I was coming?*

She nudged the hinged flap of plastisteel open and crawled into the office she once considered her childhood home. Twenty meters past the desk, behind a portable medical partition, her cot sat beneath a wall covered in plasfilm posters. Risa smirked at the tanned bikini-clad blonde she'd envied so much as a tween. No amount of sun would change her skin color. Marsborn went from inhuman white to burned.

"How'd it go?" asked Garrison, without looking back.

Risa pushed the vent closed and rose to her feet before wandering over to the side of the desk. Two holo-panels hovered in front of him, filled with numbers: inventory of supplies and budget details. She wondered if any of these reports went back to the government. *I guess it makes sense now how we have money coming in. Hackers can only do so much.*

"Risa?" Garrison looked up at her.

Without even realizing it, she'd adopted her broken-marionette stance. Her unfocused gaze settled on some far-off point on the wall. The posture seemed to unsettle him, and his chair creaked. She tried to blot out the memory of flames devouring her father's face, at the same time fighting to ignore the true sorrow she remembered in Garrison's eyes whenever she yelled at him.

"What's wrong? Is it Pavo?" He reached out to take her hand.

She didn't move, suppressing a shiver as his coarse, warm skin touched hers. "What's APSE?"

"It's an administrative organization. Government management for Arcadia, Primus—"

"I know." She shifted her weight on to her left leg. "You worked for them."

"What's gotten into your head?" Garrison eased himself out of his chair.

He's afraid. Does he know I'd be able to kill him? She tightened her jaw. *Do I know I'd be able to kill him?* "The truth."

"I don't know what misinformation you've been fed, Bit, but I can't straighten it out if you don't let me in on it."

The nickname hit her in the gut. Her dissociative calm faded, and with it, she abandoned the posture of a smashed doll. She put her hands on the desk to steady herself, and locked eyes. "I know you're the one who ordered my father killed."

His cheeks paled. After a few seconds, he lowered his gaze to the floor.

Shit. It's true. "W-why…"

"I'm sorry. He was ACC—"

"I mean, why did you *lie* to me?" Risa swallowed. A sense of betrayal threatened to take her legs out from under her while anger rode wires down her arms into her claws. Ten shards of synthetic diamond sprang from her fingertips. She stepped toward him, arms out to either side, her deadly 'nails' gleaming in the light. "You watched me throw my life away trying to find the people who did it… and you knew the whole time."

"Risa…" He reached for her.

She jerked away. "Don't touch me right now. I trusted you. I… Why Genevieve?"

Garrison froze. "What?"

"I swear… Don't mindfuck me. I'm not in the best headspace right now for dealing with dustblow. I know you're the one who got the rigged detonator from Heitzenroeder. You're the one who tried to kill Genevieve." *Fuck!*

"Genevieve's death was an accident."

A slight uptick in tone toward the end made it seem almost a question. He'd noticed her slip up. *Tried* to kill. Risa clenched her jaw. That cinched it. Without an awesome answer, she'd *have* to kill him to protect her friend. "I know it wasn't."

Garrison's stance changed to one a person might adopt while attempting to talk down a hostage taker. He raised a hand in a cautioning gesture. "Calm down, Bit. How can you possibly know something that isn't true?"

Risa thought about the data tile, vindaloo exploding all over her, Raziel. "An… an angel told me." Her claws retracted, answering the doubt in her mind.

"You don't sound very confident."

The desk fan whirred toward her, rustling two empty plastic cups and an old fork.

"Raziel…" She took another step back. "He's not really an angel. I'm not quite done dealing with that yet. T-there's so much damned dustblow, I can't take another pound of it on my back."

"Not an angel?" Garrison tilted his head. "I guess you found him in Araphel. What else are you hiding?"

"Me? You've got a lot of balls asking *me* what I'm hiding." Risa scowled. "Genevieve found a file. She thought it had information about General Maris on it, but it didn't. I saw the orders. E-signed by Lt. Col. Garrison

Tanais of C-Branch, APSE. A kill order for my father. I thought you killed Gen to protect Maris, but you were trying to cover your own ass. You didn't want the guys to learn you used to be black ops. You're up to your eyeballs in this entire shitstorm." Her composure slipped, and tears flowed down her cheeks. "You tried to murder my only friend... over nothing."

"That's twice you said 'tried.'" said Garrison in a soothing, low tone. "Is Gen still alive?"

Risa let her arms hang limp and extended her claws. "I suppose there's no point hiding anything now. Yeah. Gen figured out the detonator had been rigged for an immediate explosion, and realized someone inside tried to kill her—but not who." Her voice fell to a half-whisper. "I thought it was Maris. I'd hoped..."

"Risa... Look at me." Garrison waited for her to regain eye contact. "I did not try to kill Genevieve. We had been getting materiel from Denmark for a little over a year, and then this new guy shows up offering us similar components at one-third the price. It was a rookie mistake."

Hairline circles superimposed over Garrison's eyes in her vision. Thin threads led back from his cheeks to sensor readouts of perspiration levels. A cluster of wavy lines created by her somatic response system hovered at the right of his head. They showed no trace of deceit.

"You're from the Special Operations Group. You don't make 'rookie mistakes.'" She leaned to the right, her brain poised to trigger speedware. "You're also good enough to fool a soma. If you're going to feed me dustblow, at least make it believable."

"Damn the machine." Garrison, in apparent disregard of her exposed blades, took a step closer. "What do *you* feel? Of course, I thought it was a load of shit. No one runs black market demo gear 'on the cheap,' but even someone like Heitzenroeder can be looking to score points with a potential major buyer. A trial sale to test the products, then the price goes up." He pointed at her chest. "I told Maris it stank to Hell and back, but all he saw was the goddamn credit counter."

Risa glared at him. He had the same frustrated sadness in his eyes she'd seen so often before. Garrison's voice in her head pulled her a few weeks back, standing in her room on Death Row after Tamashī said she'd found information on Pavo.

I can't lose you.

She'd called him 'Dad.' At the time, she had no doubt his concern for her was genuine. No longer able to look at him, Risa glanced to the left.

Pat. Boosted hearing picked up a droplet of blood hitting the floor, a side effect of her claws' emergence. Tingles surrounded the point at which synthetic diamond pierced her fingertips, thousands of nanobots working to seal the wounds.

"Bit…" He advanced, still moving slow, and set one hand on her right shoulder. "Genevieve and you were so close. I'm not sure I could have made myself do that, even if I had clear evidence she was plotting against us. You have to believe me when I say you are the only thing that truly matters. I quit C-Branch once I learned you were in the apartment when the strike went down. I thought…"

She gave up trying to stop the tears, and let them stream down in silence. It took her a moment to find a voice that didn't quiver. "You cared that much about someone else's daughter?"

Garrison sighed. "You weren't part of the plan. She wasn't supposed to have had a child with him. I only found out you existed after everything was in motion. I… I signed off on an operation that I'd believed resulted in the death of an eight-year-old innocent. That was it for me. I couldn't do it anymore."

Risa didn't need the somatic system's indicator to believe him. A crash of nausea and elation hit her at the same time. Claws retracted with faint *snaps,* and she raised her arms up to hug him. *If he breaks my neck right now, I won't even care.* He seemed to relax.

"You weren't sure I couldn't do it." She sniffled.

He patted her back. "I know how you get when you have an idea stuck in your head. I'd hoped… but, I didn't want to let you do something you'd regret."

She cringed. "I wish you'd thought that way before I got wired up. You know they call me the Black Phantom in Germany?"

"It's kind of catchy. *Schwarzgeist?*" He held her out to arm's length, a hand on each shoulder. "I think that winds up being closer to black ghost, but it's nothing like you."

Risa covered her mouth and nose, breathing into her hands for a moment to calm down. "Please tell me this isn't another brain fuck. You really didn't try to kill Gen?"

"No." He blinked and gave his head a light shake. "You're saying she's alive?"

"Yeah. She's been hiding in Araphel for years, not knowing who tried to kill her." Risa shuddered. "It's horrible there. Like prison. No wonder they leave it alone." She rubbed her hands up and down her arms, offering a wistful smile. "Chaia said I'd find someone I thought was dead for a long time."

He made no attempt to hide a cringe. "Psionics give me the creeps. Not sayin' they should be hurt or anything. Just sayin' I don't want to be around 'em."

"You should have told me." Risa made a fist, but did nothing with it. "You let me go off the deep end. If you'd told me there was no one out there to find and kill…" She squinted at him as a chill of suspicion ran down her back. "Or would that have denied the MLF its 'most dangerous' weapon?"

He smacked his lips; his expression seemed to say 'I deserved that.' "No. I was worried you'd hate me. I worried you'd run away and get yourself killed or worse. Even if I had to lie to do it, I wanted you to feel safe *somewhere*. Guess I didn't do a good job."

Risa tried to doubt him, but couldn't. "Sorry. My head can't take any more surprises. If that woman shows up out of nowhere now, I think my brain will leak out of my ears."

Garrison walked backwards to his desk, and sat. His terminals flickered back to life sensing proximity. "Which woman?"

"Umm." Risa pulled out her NetMini, and projected an image showing a much younger Garrison in military camo getting cute with a woman also in uniform. "This one. That file had a bunch of pictures of you with her when you were active Delta."

He stared at the image. All the life drained out of his expression and a tear streaked down his face. A whisper audible only to augmented ears left his mouth. "Serena."

"Sorry… I didn't know she was dead." Risa went to close the image, but he reached for it.

Garrison cradled the small device in his hands, staring into the washed-out image. Monochromatic blue-green gave it a look of night vision. He tried to reach into the hologram and touch the twelve-inch-tall figure. After a second of fingertips piercing the veil of light, he drew his hand back over his mouth.

"Sorry." Risa looked down.

"This was about eighteen miles southeast from Bucaramanga, Columbia. Probably 2388 or '89. My third operational assignment under SOG-D. Her first. I… I'd like a copy of these images if you don't mind."

"Yeah, sure." *Why do I feel like such a bitch?* "What happened to her?"

Garrison handed her back the NetMini. "She was killed in the line of duty. But you knew that."

Risa closed the image display, the holo-panel becoming a sea of icons. Inhuman dexterity turned her hand into a blur as she selected all the images with Garrison and Serena, brushed them into the mail client, and tossed them onto his contact tile. "By who?"

Garrison's eyebrows crept together. "Andriy Voronin."

3

A PROPHECY CLEAR

Silence hung over Garrison's office as heavy as a wake. For a full two minutes, the only disruption in the perfect stillness came from one of Risa's old plasfilm posters scraping the wall whenever the fan rotated all the way to the right. He looked at her as though she'd said something mind numbing in its stupidity.

"Uhh, sorry. I'm... I get it now. Why you killed him. I mean, he killed someone you love, right?" She shifted her weight. "Guess we have that in common. He killed my mother too." She shuffled over to the desk, half sitting on the edge. "I wasn't sure how to feel about him at first when I learned that. I'd always assumed my mother left us."

"Risa..." Garrison, for the first time she could remember, seemed at a loss for words.

She took his hand.

"She'd really fallen for him. It was supposed to be an assignment. She was too good at her job. All she had to do was keep tabs on him, warn us if he was planning something big." He slouched, looking defeated. "I don't know what she saw in him. She thought their love would overpower whatever hold the ACC had on him, but..."

"Yeah. I read the file." Risa looked down and fidgeted with a small piece of 'desk kitsch,' a silver eagle on a pedestal. After a few minutes of tense silence, she stopped touching it. "How long ago did he kill Serena?"

Garrison's chair groaned in rusty torment as he leaned forward. "Risa... Do you know who Marisa Donnelly was?"

"Of course." She draped her arms in her lap. "My mother. They named me 'Risa' as a shortened form of Marisa."

"You don't remember what she looked like, do you?" Garrison rubbed his chin. "Of course not, you were barely two years old when he killed her."

She stared at him. "You're hesitating now." *Why does that name sound like I've heard it somewhere before? Serena Var...* Tightness gripped her heart as the face of General Everett came back to her, pointing a handgun at her in a dim hotel room.

Her name was Serena Var. She worked for C-Branch, posing as Marisa Donnelly.

"Oh, shit!" Risa covered her mouth. "You were dating my mother."

She ripped the NetMini out and opened the picture again, unable to stop sniffling and crying at the image of her mother. She looked to be about the same age Risa was now. Even in low-res night vision, a resemblance emerged—once she thought to look for it.

"We were married less than three months when she drew that assignment. Command had tapped six female operatives, but he didn't show the least bit of interest in any of them. They'd been worried he would figure it strange if women kept coming out of nowhere seeming interested in him. By number five, we all thought he'd get spooked and burn the identity, flee back to the Corporates... I guess my luck was really that bad."

Her hands trembled. "S-Shiro... He said my dad should've dragged me around by the wrist more. He thought you should've forbade me from getting cyberware." She bit her forearm in an effort to keep from throwing up. When the nausea subsided, she stared through tear blur at him. Chaia's words came back to her, along with the flavor of shrimp Caesar salad. *Someone you thought dead for a long time is not.* She gawked at Garrison. He'd been married to her mother. *I've thought my father dead for a long time.* "No... she had to mean Gen."

"Genevieve had nothing to do with your mother's death... or Andriy. She would've been six or seven years old when Serena died."

Risa lifted her gaze to meet his. Her entire body trembled. "A-are you *really* my father?"

Garrison drew in a breath to answer while denial swam over his face. He hesitated, closing his mouth without making a noise. The effort of thinking twisted his eyebrows. "I... The only way that would even be possible is if she'd become pregnant within two weeks of taking that assignment, and never told me. I... They did a physical on her two weeks before she started. They would've pulled the plug on the operation if they found her pregnant. I... admit to perhaps being unprofessionally angry with Andriy over having a child with my wife." Garrison exhaled. "And stealing her from me."

She wiped her face. "Yeah. You're right. I guess that doesn't make a lot of sense. She'd have told you. How much sex could the two of you have had in two weeks?"

Garrison's cheeks went a bright shade of maroon. "Some questions should not be asked."

Risa laughed despite herself. "Consider that un-asked. Silly to think about."

He leaned to the side and braced his hands on the desk, head down. "At the time she accepted the assignment, we were as in love as two people can be—or so I thought. There's no reason I can think of she would've held something like that back. I'm sorry, Bit. I don't need genetics to *feel* like your father."

I was so close to killing him. She pressed a hand to her neck as another wave of bile danced in the back of her throat. "I, umm. Sorry."

"It's all right. You don't need to apologize to me. Someone else has been worried about you."

"I'm sorry I didn't come back sooner... We got held up at the outpost, and by the time we landed, I could barely walk."

Garrison smirked. "Sounds like Pavo missed you."

Her face burned. "You did not just say that."

"Had to retaliate for your question." He winked.

"I was exhausted. Nerves fried. Emotions hanging on a thread. Body said 'enough, sleep now.'"

"Been there." He idly flicked at his terminal, checking off approvals for basic budgetary requests like food, water, and clothing. "Glad to hear he's okay. Your text message wasn't very detailed. Understandable given your location."

Risa recounted her infiltration, locating Pavo's cell, and walking straight into General Everett on the way out. Garrison didn't look as surprised as she thought he would. "You knew he was PVM?"

"Suspected. I'm more alarmed about Shiro. None of our usual sources picked up anything out of the ordinary. They went the extra mile creating his existence. Go take care of your daughter. I'm going to rattle some trees."

Risa squirmed. "Kree's not my daughter... She's a kid I almost killed with a fucking bomb you people sent me to plant."

Garrison shot her an accusing glare. It lasted a moment before softening. "You don't really mean that. It's not all on us. The target was good, even if it was one of our own. You'd always been so meticulous about ops before that."

Risa slid off the desk, standing. "I rushed it. I had the revenge I'd spent so long wanting right in my hands and I... didn't want them to get away."

"That little girl needs you. And, even if you don't want to admit it, you need her. You keep saying you're tired of all the lies." Garrison reached over and squeezed her hand. "Does that include the ones you tell yourself?"

Eyes downcast, Risa trudged to the door. While crossing the large room, she stared at her childhood bed. Once, it felt like the safest place in the universe. All she had to do to get away from bad things was curl up under a blanket. *Kree doesn't deserve to grow up like I did.*

She hurried out into the hall and raced across the command floor. A few heads popped up as she speed-walked to the base of a long curving ramp, which led up to the third level. Technically the second, as the command area and officers' quarters were one level beneath the 'ground' floor.

The stained metal plate marked 'Death Row' swayed back and forth over the mouth of the corridor by where her private room waited. Any Liberation Front operative involved with demolition work got their own private bedroom. More than most, they knew every mission they accepted could easily be their last. The short waiting list surprised no one. Bunk beds and group showers seemed a better alternative to a sudden, painless death.

Risa stopped at her door, hesitated for a moment, and crept in. Kree sat amid the floordrobe, sideways to the entrance, wearing her oversized purple 'moon boots,' underpants, and an electronic helmet with a black visor over her eyes. It didn't look like a Sens-helmet, which meant her consciousness remained in the real world—though the video game sucked up her attention.

Without lifting the visor, the girl grabbed a small plastic box and hurled it in the general direction of the door. "Go away! I'm not hungry."

That wasn't aimed at me. She hasn't looked. Risa pushed the door closed behind her. Kree screamed "Go away!" three more times before jumping to her feet and tearing the helmet off, holding it over head in both hands as if to hurl it at the person intruding on her space.

As soon as the child looked up, the tiny rage-filled face relaxed to a momentary expression of bewilderment. Three seconds later, Kree dropped the helmet in the pile of clothes. Two seconds after that, she burst into tears, wailing and crying in place.

Risa blinked. *That's not the reaction I was expecting.* "Hey..." She walked over and sat as close as she could on the bed, arms wide. "What's wrong?"

"I'm mad at you!" Kree sniveled. "You went away, an' I tol' you not to go, but you went away. I tol' the angel I wanted you to be my mommy, so you'd die 'cause I was mad at you..." Venom left the little girl's voice, reducing it from a shriek to a soft mewl. "An' then you didn't come back..." Silent tears gushed down the child's face.

Kree thought she *killed me.*

Risa bit her lip. She lowered her arms as the six-year-old made no move to come to her. For a moment, she glanced at the door and pondered leaving, unsure how to deal with the little tornado of emotion in front of her. The girl's chest heaved from great, gasping sobs. Prominent ribs made her worry about Kree's health. *How many days has she been 'not hungry?'*

"I'm sorry." Risa gazed down at the floor. "I thought Pavo was going to die if I didn't help him. He was in a bad place, and I needed to help him."

Sniveling gave way to irregular sniffles punctuated by short bursts of crying.

"Do you still want me to go away?" Risa regretted the question as soon as it took flight. *What if she says yes? Do I brush it off?*

"No!" Kree yelled, stomped, and flung herself into Risa's lap, again lost to sobs.

She cradled the girl, holding and rocking her for a few minutes.

Osebi poked his head in. "Every 'ting all right?"

Risa sniffled, and nodded. "She's..."

"Happy ta see ya." He winked, and backed out.

With a little person clinging tight to her, Risa's doubt grew into a tsunami. How many orphans had her bombs created? Saris, the synthetic millipede driver, had a point. No matter what humans did, there would always be a government. Even if the MLF had been genuine, and succeeded in burning the Earth-loving UCF and ACC to the ground, they had no guarantee the political creature reborn from the ashes would be better. It might very well be much, much worse.

I'm saying you should endeavor to be happy, said Saris in her memory.

"Yeah, right," she muttered.

Kree gave up trying to grab a hold on her ballistic stealth armor, and gathered her hands at her chin. Risa plucked a blue shirt from the rug and pulled it over the girl's head to improvise a dress.

"When was the last time you ate?"

"See-bee made me eat a egg." She wiped at her eyes.

"You need to have lunch. Come on."

Kree didn't move, so Risa carried her down the hall to the nearest common area. Her cybereyes' chronometer indicated the time as 13:22. Ralek lay on the ground half under one set of bunk beds, pounding metal on metal. His muttered tirade of obscenities switched to nonsense words after Kree giggled.

"I don't think even your angel's gonna be able to fix this pad. It's gotta be replaced, and this frame is so damn old we can't get one with a compatible socket. Every five years, they change the design so you gotta buy a new one." Ralek grumbled a few unintelligible words and pummeled something under the bed.

Risa shifted the girl onto her hip, holding her with one arm while dialing up a small bowl of OmniSoy mac and cheese. After carrying both child and food to the round steel table, she set Kree on the edge of the table and put the bowl in the chair.

"Hmm. That doesn't seem right."

Kree laughed.

She rearranged them, and nodded. "Much better."

Risa took the next seat, and handed Kree a plastic spoon. The girl dug in without hesitation. Lancaster passed by the opening at the front of the common area, sparing a wave.

"Good to hear about Pavo." He smiled.

This is supposed to be a shadow force of military intelligence, yet no one can keep their damn mouth shut. She braced her cheek on one hand and chuckled. Kree's smile threatened to collapse back to tears.

"It's okay." Risa pulled the girl's hair off her face, attempting to tame the wild mane with a few brushing passes of her fingers. "I'm sorry I scared you."

"Are you gonna go away again?" Kree froze.

Risa continued fussing with the girl's hair. "Not if I can help it."

Kree seemed satisfied, smiled, and resumed her assault on the faux pasta. The more Risa watched her eat, the more profound the sense of being responsible for the little person's life became. She pictured the bomb timer stalled at two seconds. All the political strife between two planets paled in importance to the innocent child in front of her. *If Kree deserved anything, it wasn't having her mother murdered by thugs, living on the street for a few weeks, and getting killed in a terrorist bombing.*

She cringed at the voice in her head. *Yeah. Terrorist. What else do you call someone who uses bombs on civilians?* The other kids from the mine all thought her 'weird' for talking to angels, or scary. None of them ran away from her out of fear, but they didn't want to hang out with her all the time. Each had found someone within the Front to latch on to. *Survival mechanism.* Risa sighed. They didn't belong here, but she couldn't say they'd be better off on the street than with the MLF. Garrison saved her from who-knows-what. Drugs, the Syndicate, gangs… young girls didn't last long on their own in the deep tunnels of Primus. Even the worst of gangs would generally protect *little* kids, but once a girl got past a certain age…

"Finished." Kree sat up, smiling.

Risa spent a moment washing out the plastic dish before tossing it in the bin next to the reassembler. Ralek was gone; she hadn't even noticed him leave. Kree followed her back to their room, where she asked Risa to put on a cartoon. Risa set up a datapad to serve as a holo-bar, projecting a meager twenty-four-inch panel. They sat on the bed, and Kree became engrossed in the laughter of a bunch of animated mushrooms of various pastel colors.

Her thoughts drifted back to the picture of Garrison and Serena. A knot clenched and unwound in her stomach. Killing Andriy had been more than an assignment, more than national security—it had been personal. The man stole his wife. Serena's undercover assignment turned into a legitimate affair. Garrison had to be heartbroken as well as furious to watch her fall in love and have a kid with another man. Risa ran a hand over Kree's head. The girl smiled and snuggled closer.

With the little video game mushroom villagers' journey occupying Kree's attention, Risa slid the NetMini from her belt and called up the picture on the physical display so the holographic light didn't cause a distraction. The two-by-four-inch screen left the image too tiny to see well, so she zoomed in on their faces, staring at them for almost fifteen minutes while feeling heartsick at the turn all their lives had taken.

Serena, Garrison, Kree… and her own. She looked up from the screen at the pink doll perched on her desk. The one she'd relentlessly begged her father for at eight.

Who would I have become?

She unconsciously tightened her arm around Kree and glanced down at the NetMini. Two little dots of violet light drew her attention to the reflection of her face on the touchscreen surface. Lifeless silver eyes and stark, luminous pupils. Risa tried to remember what her real eyes looked like. Raziel had given them to her, frozen in medical gel. Gruesome as it was, she pictured the two orbs suspended in peach-hued slime. Jade green.

Like Garrison's.

The NetMini slipped from her fingers. She grabbed for it, and stretched the image so his eyes filled the small screen. Her breath caught in her throat.

I gotta know.

Risa sat up and set Kree on the Comforgel pad. "I'll be right back."

Kree gave her a look as though she'd announced suicide.

"I'm not leaving the safe house." Risa gripped Kree's shoulders. "I promise I am not going outside. I need to talk to Garrison. Only a couple of minutes."

A lingering suspicious squint remained on the child's face, but she calmed. "'Kay. 'Member, you promised."

Risa kissed her on the forehead, then darted out the door.

4

SOMEONE THOUGHT DEAD

The slam of the door against the wall startled Garrison's attention off his terminal. His pistol fell inches short of aiming at Risa as she darted across the room. At the sight of her, he dropped it and jumped to his feet, rushing around the corner of the desk to catch her in mid sprint.

"What happened?" he asked.

Risa stared into his eyes. "I… Your eyes are green. Jade green."

"That's… not exactly a secret. What's got you riled up? The look on your face, I thought something'd happened to Kree."

"I have to know." She looked down.

"Know?"

"If you're really my father. What's her name…? Maybe-Hannah, the medic. She can check." Risa pulled on his arm. "Please?"

He stiffened. His expression flickered to fear, then pity. "What if this test doesn't give you the answer you want?"

Risa took a deep breath, held it for a few seconds, and let it slide out her nostrils. "Then I'll have to figure out how angry I am with you for ordering my father's death."

Garrison looked to his side and down.

"You're afraid of knowing…"

He pivoted a quarter-turn to the right, took one step, and stopped, hands on his hips. "If it's true, and the odds are damn remote, that'd mean she lied to my face and *wanted* to be with that Corp son of a bitch, knowing."

She grasped his arm, above the elbow. "Maybe she didn't even know. It's not like our tits light up the instant we become pregnant."

He wiped away a chuckle and smiled for a moment before the somber expression resurfaced. "I suppose, given the short time frame, it's possible she might not have realized. I'd like to think she'd have changed her mind about the assignment if she knew." He raised a hand. "But this is mental jumping jacks. The odds of me being your genetic father are about as good as—"

"Five minutes. Please."

Garrison pinched the bridge of his nose. "I don't know."

"You're scared you'll feel different about her death, like the way my feelings about Andriy changed when I learned he killed my mother."

"Yeah." He hardened his gaze on her. "All right. Fine. You never were able to back down once you got an idea in your head. Are you sure you want to know?"

"I'm sure." She risked a smile.

He leaned over his desk long enough to lock the terminals and re-holster his sidearm. "The medtech's name *is* Hannah, by the way. She works with Eva and Neal."

"We have three medics?" Risa followed him to the door.

He shook his head as he walked. His expression revealed he didn't much want to go, but his pace said he'd rather get it over with. "Neal and Hannah came in with the Benton Mining Company people you evacuated. Both agreed to stay on with us at least for a little while."

Risa nodded, not that he saw her, and kept at his heels until they crossed the command room, headed up to the first floor, and down a hallway deeper into the compound that led to the garage as well as the infirmary. As luck would have it, Hannah happened to be on rotation when they walked in. The blue-eyed blonde looked up with a half-awake smile.

"Sir." She jumped up. "Am I supposed to salute you, or—?"

"Not important to me, but Maris will lose his mind if you don't." Garrison chuckled.

"Hi, Risa." Hannah grinned at her. "What's up?"

"Do you have the equipment to do a paternity test?" asked Risa.

Hannah covered her mouth and glanced at Garrison. "He wants to know who to kill?"

Risa blushed. "Uhh, no." She dropped her voice to a whisper. "I want to know if Garrison is my father."

"Ohhhh." Hannah fidgeted until he nodded. "Yeah, it's a pretty simple process, really. Most med scanners can do a rudimentary cross-check on nuclear DNA. It'll take a couple of minutes and a drop of blood."

Risa grabbed the edge of the desk to keep her hands still. "Okay."

"Do it," said Garrison.

Hannah ran to a table past a row of eight cots, mercifully empty of wounded, and scooped up a handheld device about the size of a brick. She grabbed something out of a large plastic cylinder, nabbed blue sanitary gloves, and hurried across to the right side of the room. After setting the items down on a white table, she beckoned them over with a wave. The objects from the cylinder appeared to be disposable lancets. Beeps and chimes came from the device as Hannah navigated a software menu, then snapped a lancet onto the end of the brick.

"Okay, who's first? Need a hand." The blonde smiled and held up the device.

Risa held her arm out.

Hannah pressed the tip to her wrist until it clicked. A mild nip signaled a hair-thin needle extracting a drop or two of blood. She swapped the lancet for a sterile one and repeated the process on Garrison's forearm. After tossing the second tip into a trashcan, she typed with her thumbs on a touchscreen. A pair of empty helix patterns appeared in a counter-rotating spin. Bit by bit, colored blocks filled in.

"About two minutes." Hannah smiled.

"What, no juice and cookies after taking so much blood?" asked Garrison.

His deadpan left the woman speechless for a few seconds until he smiled.

Risa held her stomach to keep the butterflies from rioting. She glanced up at him, trying to plan her reaction to the results in either direction. Garrison remained as blasé as if he waited at a noodle counter for his lunch. She threaded her arm around his and held his hand, taking his calm as a sign the answer wouldn't affect his opinion of their relationship. *He already thinks of me as his... Nothing would change when the machine says negative.* She swallowed. *He's convinced it will.*

Hannah looked up at a *beep* from the device. She swiped it from the desk and regarded the screen for a moment. "Uhh, wow. I honestly wasn't expecting that."

"Expecting what?" Garrison's grip on her hand tensed.

"Umm..." Hannah glanced back and forth between them for a moment. "The creepy eyes kinda threw me, but yeah... I can see it." She held the device up so they can read the text superimposed over the now-stationary DNA helixes: 'Probability of parental relation 99.015%.'

Garrison fell into a chair at the end of the table, likely for a patient to use while receiving shots or having blood drawn. He stared into space. Risa held his hand, covering her mouth with the other.

"I... no idea you were in that apartment. They could've killed you." His unfocused gaze found her. "I never knew."

Risa attempted a casual shrug. "Hey, I almost killed Kree with a bomb. Guess nearly killing our daughters runs in the family." Three seconds of giggling melted into crying.

He pulled her into his lap. Hannah gave them space, returning to the desk by the infirmary entrance. Risa thought back to the look he'd given her the first night she felt safe enough to sleep on the cot he'd gotten for her rather than crawl into the vents to hide. It hadn't registered much with her then, but now, it made her feel like clinging to him and hoping Daddy made the bad things stop.

A few minutes later, she calmed down enough to risk speaking. "I'm sorry, Dad."

Garrison reached up and pulled her head against his chest. "I don't know what to say."

"Dad? I... I can't do this anymore."

"Do what?" He let his hand slide from her head to her shoulder so she could look at him.

"*This.*" She waved an arm at the wall. "I want out. This damn war ate my childhood. It ate my body... and my soul. Every time I set off a device, I'm a wreck for days. I can't do it anymore."

"Done."

She blinked. "That easy? Not going to try and talk the superweapon into staying?"

"It never really did sit well with me, watching you go out there." He chuckled. "I kept seeing you as that little girl I found in the square, thinking that's who they'd sent into danger. You won't get an argument from me if it keeps you safe."

I can't tell him about Bliss. He'd kill me. "I know I never saw eye to eye with General Maris, but he's right. He's the reason Shiro's team is after us."

"What?" Garrison glanced around, and repeated his question in a whisper. "What are you talking about? Maris is involved?"

"Not directly." She stared down at her hands. "Guess he's not as much of an asshole as I used to think. Maris kept refusing orders to run false flag operations on UCF targets. Someone high up the food chain said the MLF 'grew legs,' and wants it back under complete control. Maris knows it's foolish to try fighting two wars when both sides are a thousand times bigger than you. We can't take on the UCF *and* the ACC at the same time. Technically, we're part of the UCF military intelligence command, right? Maris didn't want to strike our own citizens."

Garrison sighed. "I'll reach out to some old contacts. In the meantime, it's no longer your problem to worry about. Take Kree topside and try to find that life we all took away from you."

Risa picked at her belt, staring down. "I don't know… Kree deserves a real mom, not some Cat-6 wired-up terrorist."

"No!" yelled a tiny voice. Kree zoomed in from a shadowed teal curtain by the infirmary entrance, tears already in full bloom. "You said you wouldn't go away!" She glared at Risa, bottom lip shaking. "I thought you wanted me."

"Oh, Kree." Heaviness settled over Risa's heart. She slid from Garrison's lap to her knees, and wrapped her arms around the girl. "I do." *It's probably stupid, but I do.* "I'm just scared something's going to happen to me. I've made a lot of people very angry. I don't want you to get hurt."

"But… but…" Kree looked at her, wide-eyed. "You have speeware! No one can hurt you."

Risa squeezed her, and peered up at Garrison.

He ruffled the child's hair. "You care more about that kid than all of Mars and her people."

"Garrison—Dad…" *That's going to take some getting used to.* "Not fair."

Garrison smiled. "That's not what I mean. I wasn't criticizing you. A *mother* should put her child first."

Risa cringed, arms clamped around Kree, bracing for a shouted declaration of non-mommy-dom, but the child remained quiet. After another minute of no protest, Risa looked up at Garrison. He seemed pale, perhaps even older than she'd thought him to look minutes ago. She tried to force the idea of what her bomb might have done out of her mind.

"Dad… I know exactly how you feel."

5

DEATH ROW PARDON

F lat on her old bed, Risa stared up at the wall full of plasfilm posters at her right.

Roughly one-third depicted the six preteen members of a boy-band named 'Fifteen Minutes,' which despite the name being intentionally ironic, turned out to be an apt description of how long their fame lasted. Her twelve-year-old self couldn't get their music out of her head. *I bet it was all computer generated.* The centerpiece of her display, an eleven-by-fourteen-inch sheet of plasfilm, bore the likeness of Alexis Santiago, tanned, blonde, and strutting around in nothing but a few patches of yellow fabric clinging to her skin in a creative interpretation of a bikini. When the image was taken, the woman had been twenty-one.

Risa smiled at the memory of Garrison's face when she'd asked for that swimsuit. She'd figured he'd give her a hard time over the two-thousand-credit cost of a 'garment' consisting of three scraps of cloth smaller than napkins that used nanofilament hooks to cling in place, but hadn't been prepared for his reaction. *Now* it made sense, though he hadn't known for sure. *Did he suspect?* Then again, even an adoptive father would've nearly passed out at a tween wanting a bathing suit like that.

The mere act of lying in her old bed made her feel sixteen again. Risa closed her eyes and tried to dream about her life before she'd ever killed anyone, before so much metal wound up seared into her bones. Quiet chirps emanated from a holographic jigsaw puzzle on the floor beyond the end of her bed. Kree had fallen in love with the puffy cartoon rabbit and become absorbed in seconds. Tiny hands shimmered wherever she 'grasped' the floating pieces and twisted them into place in midair.

Garrison gave her that puzzle less than a month after finding her. Nine-year-old Risa hadn't much bothered with it. She'd only wanted to hide. *I probably hurt his feelings.*

"This is hard." Kree whined.

Risa sat up. Thin bands of static appeared at the edges of the holographic pieces, making the swarm of them dizzying to look at. A patch about the size of a dinner plate floated a few inches away from Kree's face; though their shapes fit, the images didn't belong together.

"You should start with the corners." Risa scooted to the foot end of the bed and sat on the edge.

Kree, kneeling by the emitter, looked back and up at Risa for a few seconds before frowning at the huge cloud of pieces. "I can't find them."

There's another reason I gave up on this one. Risa slid to the floor behind her. "You check that side, I'll check this side. Find the corners or any pieces with a flat edge."

"Okay." Kree slapped at the assembled patch, 'breaking' the virtual puzzle pieces apart. They flew like fireflies back into the cluster.

Minutes later, Risa had a collection of nine edge pieces.

Kree leapt to her feet, 'holding' a two-inch slice of hologram dark blue on one side and grassy on the other. "Got a corner!"

Risa smiled. "You found one before I could."

"You gotta find one now." Kree reached up and 'put' the piece into play. The orientation of the illustrated grass meant it had to be the lower left corner.

Over the next twenty or so minutes, the swarm surrendered the remaining three corner pieces. Risa claimed the second, and spotted the other two—but let Kree find them 'first.' Another fifteen minutes later, Garrison walked in wearing a weary countenance.

He glanced in her direction, and a smile brightened his features. After standing there watching them for a little while, he crept to his desk without a word. Kree had a run on the right vertical border, placing twenty-two pieces in a blitz. She stood on tiptoe, reaching for the last piece but still falling short. A moment later, she looked about ready to burst into tears until she honed in on a battered chair across the room.

Risa stalled her with a hand on the shoulder. "It's not a physical board. It's light." She winked, 'grabbed' the entire puzzle, and pulled it down.

Fourteen inches of holographic cartoon rabbit went into the floor. "You can move it around."

Kree tried to repeat the gesture of dragging the whole puzzle around. It took her a moment, but she eventually found the proper hand shape to trigger the computer in the projector. More amused by the ability to reorient the puzzle than continue working on it, she proceeded to swing it back and forth and spin it.

Garrison chuckled under his breath.

Risa leaned to her left to peer around the end of the hospital barrier that separated her 'bedroom' from the office. "Thanks."

He raised an eyebrow.

"For giving me that," she whispered.

"Risa... I got that for you almost sixteen years ago."

She looked down. Shadows whirled around small fragments of rock as the puzzle continued spinning. "I know. I never did really say thanks. I'm sorry if it made you feel—"

"It's fine." He smiled. "You'd been through hell. I didn't take it personally."

They spent a few minutes in silence, save for the whirring desk fan, watching Kree amuse herself moving the hologram around.

"Bad news?" asked Risa.

Kree appeared to tire of playing 'spin the puzzle,' and resumed her hunt for border pieces.

He rocked back in his chair. "I wouldn't call it *bad*, but Maris isn't exactly thrilled by your change of status to inactive."

"I can't say I'm surprised." Risa patted Kree on the head, whispering, "Need a minute to talk adult stuff."

Risa stood and walked to the desk. Kree's fear faded when she realized Risa wasn't leaving the room, and she resumed sifting among floating jigsaw tiles. Garrison hadn't bothered unlocking his terminals, and peered over a password prompt at her as she crossed in front of him.

"Of course, you know there's going to be some repercussions." He tapped his fingers on chair arms.

Risa leaned on the corner at his left, one ass cheek on the desk, one boot on the ground. "Figured I'd have to give up my spot on the Row."

"Probably." He chuckled. "Maris wanted you to train up your replacement, but I put the brakes on it. I'll deal with that. I've got a feeling it'll be a little while before we need another device planted."

"There's a political shitstorm brewing. Everett didn't say much about it, only that he thinks the director of military intelligence is going to be an issue." Risa traced a clean squiggle in the dust on the desk. "If he wants me off the Row right away as some kind of middle-finger gesture, mind if I crash here when I'm 'in for the night?'"

He nodded. "It's still your bed. And now you've stopped listening to that atrocious electronic garbage, you're welcome to stay as long as you want."

She stared down. "It's going to be awkward enough being here and off the roster. I have no idea how much longer the Front is even going to be around. Something bad is coming, and I don't want Kree to have a front row seat like I did."

Garrison leaned his elbows on the desk and cradled his head. "They assured me you would be extracted from the site prior to engagement. They were *not* supposed to initiate unless you were confirmed clear. I had no idea you were still in there when I gave the go-ahead."

"Raziel." She sighed. "He took out the 'kidnapper' with a PubTran. Da —Andriy came straight to my bedroom and stuffed me in the vents, like he'd been given instructions."

Garrison rubbed his temples. "Why? Why would he do that?"

"He's an AI, Dad. It's like playing chess against a computer that's forty moves ahead of you, with a thousand variations of each game played to the end, depending on how you react. Best guess, he wanted me to grow up pissed off at the UCF military so I'd be willing to fight both sides."

"You're saying"—Garrison looked up—"Raziel is part of this dirty op too?"

She shook her head. "No. He really wants both sides driven from Mars. Most of our people are either born UCF and have a natural loyalty to the government they've known their entire life, or they're defected ACC who view the UCF as paradise by comparison. He wanted me pissed off and ready to lash out at either side. But I'm only guessing he told Andriy to stuff me in the vent. Not like the guy would randomly do whatever a supposed angel told him to out of the blue."

"Target of opportunity." Garrison ran one hand over his head and groaned.

"Yeah, something like that." Risa folded her hands in her lap. "I used to believe he was a real angel from Heaven, who chose *me* to do his work on Mars. Now that I think back, it does sound crazy. He tricked me out of my innocence. I am *not* going to let this war do the same to Kree. I'm not going to do the same to someone else's kid."

"As long as humankind has war, people who fight in it will die."

She swished her dangling foot back and forth. "I'm not a soldier. I was an angry kid with an immortality complex and too much augmentation. I can't even say how many of the people my bombs killed were soldiers."

"Those scientists were weaponizing nanobots for use against civilian targets." Garrison's expression hardened. "They're worse than soldiers. You didn't kill people, you stepped on roaches."

"I guess." She picked at her fingers.

"If you learned the ACC was planning an attack that would kill innocents, would you stop it? Would you feel guilt over anyone you had to kill to prevent someone from hurting Kree?"

"Two free shots on goal, Dad. Cheapshot penalty."

Garrison smirked. "This isn't Gee-ball, Risa."

She lifted her head to make eye contact. "You said you were okay with me getting out. Now you sound like you're trying to change my mind."

He took her hand. "No. I am completely at ease with you staying safe. What I'm trying to do is make sure you understand why we asked you to do those things. I'd kill as many enemy troops as it took to keep you or any innocent citizen safe. I'd do whatever it took, and I wouldn't lose four seconds of sleep over it."

"You're a soldier." She smiled. "Deep down inside, I'm a plays-with-dolls sorta girl. In another world, I'd probably scream at the sight of bugs."

Garrison laughed. "Now that, I can't even picture."

"I want to give Kree the life I never got. School, a real apartment… not living like rats in a catacomb. Maybe you can get out too, *Gran'pa*."

He grumbled, glanced away, and keyed in his password to unlock the terminal screens. "There's no 'out' for me, Risa. I can't give up on it yet. I'm in way too deep. If this business with Everett goes south, I'll do everything I can to shield you, but there's no pulling my ass out of the fire by my own bootstraps. Besides, I'm still more than a little pissed off at Command for what happened to Serena."

She pushed off the desk and stood at his side, hands on his shoulder. "I'm sorry. Maybe she was tired of pretending to love Andriy and rushed things along? What if she lied to him to make her move to turn him too soon because she wanted to get back to you? Everyone's assuming she did it because she fell in love with him. It's possible she might've been trying to play him."

He let off a sad chuckle. "Wishful thinking, but thanks. What do you think Andriy would've done if he agreed to defect, and as soon as he's in our hands, she forgets he exists? If he doesn't have an immediate meltdown, his loyalties shift back home and we think he's ours. It's dangerous and foolish, and the Serena I know wouldn't have taken a risk like that."

Risa leaned to the right. "You knew the Front was—"

"A cover story for C-Branch? Yeah. I wasn't about to start a coup over it; I needed *this*." He gestured with both hands at everything.

"This?" She stretched up to check on Kree, who continued to paw at the maelstrom of flying puzzle pieces.

"A degree of separation from the sons of bitches who think sitting behind a desk with stars on their shoulders makes them heroes. The solitude, the dark, and being 'in the shit' again. At my age, straight-up field work was off the table. This is at least close."

"You still want the UCF off Mars?" She smiled at Kree and sank down from her toes to stand flat.

He grinned. "They've proved to be somewhat poor policymakers. Arden was a damned mess. However, when you've got a monster on one side and an idiot on the other, only a fool worries about anything but killing the monster first."

"I caught a ride on a millipede driven by a synthetic; he had some interesting opinions on that." She fussed with his olive-drab shirt, plucking lint clusters. "He said it didn't matter what we did, because humans would always organize into some manner of government. If we did manage to win our ideal victory, something new would form, and it might be worse."

"Sounds like one o' them 'free-thinker' types."

Risa smiled at his overdone 'unintelligent person' voice. "He had a point. He also mentioned how few people there really are on Mars. We should be worried more about surviving as a species than who's pulling the strings."

He threw his hands up in a mock gesture of frustration. "Wanting to go on the inactive list, talkin' all kinds of politics… Next thing I know, you'll be lookin' to go to university or something."

She offered a 'who knows' shrug. "Maybe. I'll need to have some skills beyond killing people to get by."

Garrison swiveled the chair to face her, brushing a finger over his lips in contemplation. "What happened to all that 'the UCF is a fascist police state that needs to be burned out like the malignant tumor it is' rhetoric?"

Did I really say that? She cringed. *Yeah. I probably did.* "I thought the military killed my father... killed one of their own men for objecting to political ideals. I didn't know..."

He stood, placed his hands on her shoulders, and pulled her close until their foreheads touched. "I don't have words for how relieved I am that my hot-headed little girl didn't get herself killed."

Risa considered pointing out how he'd had every chance to stop her from accepting General Maris's offer of cyberware, but decided against it and managed a weak smile. "Me too, but the storm's still overhead."

"So, what now?" He sighed.

"Now..." Risa walked back to Kree. "I have a puzzle to solve."

A SMALL HAND ON RISA'S SHOULDER NUDGED HER AWAKE. THE WEIGHT OF A child pressed into her chest. She opened her eyes to find Kree nose to nose, laying on top of her. She suppressed a yawn, blinked, and noted the time display floating in her vision: 08:18.

"I'm hungry," said Kree.

Risa grinned. "When did you become a cat?"

Kree scrunched her nose. "Huh? I'm not a cat."

"Never mind." She threaded a hand up out from under the blankets and brushed the hair from Kree's face. *She needs to eat. I shouldn't make her wait.* "Food. Right."

The partition in Garrison's office provided a little privacy, but she'd still gone back to the private room on Death Row to claim a long shirt to sleep in. Of everyone in the safehouse, she'd only ever felt uncomfortable undressing around Garrison. He'd never been her commander as much as Dad, even when she felt like an adopted stray. Knowing the truth made the awkwardness more acute.

Kree leapt from the cot as Risa sat up. The girl stepped into her boots and tromped for the hall in her underpants. Risa swung her legs over the side and sat for a moment holding her face, trying to force consciousness into her brain after only five hours of sleep. A *squeak* from the door startled her upright; the clock had jumped six minutes forward.

Garrison entered, Kree over his left shoulder like a sack of potatoes. "She's hungry."

"Yeah." Risa stood, ignoring the frigid floor underfoot, and collected the girl as he passed on the way to his desk. "Thanks for intercepting."

She ducked behind the partition and changed into her armor, pulled

Kree into her clingy long-sleeved shirt and fluffy purple skirt, then led her by the hand to the dining area. If she inhaled deep enough, she picked up the scent of vindaloo lurking in the background. Kree waited patiently at the table while Risa dialed up two plates of the machine's interpretation of pancakes, plus one milk and one coffee.

The child disregarded the plastic fork and attacked her food with her fingers. Risa propped her cheek up in one hand, alternating between eating and slurping coffee with the other. *I've got to get her out of here.*

"Do you remember Pavo?" Risa smiled.

Kree nodded.

"You liked him?"

"He's okay." Kree made an appraising face. "Smells funny."

Risa leaned close to the table, and lowered her voice. "How would you like for us to live with him? Like a family?"

Kree shrugged. "Okay."

That was too easy.

The girl used a scrap of pancake like a rag to mop up syrup from the plastic plate, and packed it into her mouth. Risa couldn't help but grin at the puffy hamster cheeks. They ate without another word for a few more minutes. After clearing her plate, the child drained her milk in one long chug, and gasped for breath.

"Is Pavo gonna be like a daddy?" Kree set the glass down.

Risa bit her lip. "Something like that. If you want to think of him that way."

Kree squinted. "If he hits you, are you gonna shoot him?"

"Uhh." *Shit. I guess I know what happened to her father...* "Pavo's not like that. He wouldn't hit me."

"She said that too." Kree stared at her plate. "But she lied."

Risa waved at Kree to come closer. The girl ducked under the table and climbed into her lap. "Most men don't do that. Some do. And it's not right." *I can't believe I'm talking about this with a six-year-old.* "Pavo is not the type of guy that would ever hurt me... or you."

Kree fidgeted, looking nervous.

"I don't want you to think he's capable of anything like that, but if he ever did, it would be the last day we stayed with him."

"Okay." Kree smiled, seeming calmer.

"Let's grab some stuff and we'll go see his apartment."

Kree went rigid. "O-outside?"

"Of course." Risa kissed her atop the head. "He's got a big apartment.

You can have your very own room, and you won't have to deal with Osebi's gas."

"I don't wanna go outside!" Kree yelled, clamped on, and trembled. "Please don't make me go outside."

The sudden change in the girl's demeanor shocked Risa mute. She held her for a few minutes until the wailing faded to soft sobs. When Risa tried to stand, Kree struggled to get away, erupting in a new barrage, shrieking "no" repeatedly.

Risa held her firm. "Okay, okay. I'm only going to Garrison's room."

Kree ceased thrashing, but continued shaking.

"Shh. It's all right. Nothing's going to hurt you."

Risa patted her on the back while carrying her down the hall and the curved stairway to the third level. Everyone in the safehouse seemed to be looking at her as if wondering what awful thing she'd done to the child. Risa couldn't get into the hallway past the command room fast enough, away from accusing stares. Once inside her new sanctuary, she shot Garrison a helpless look and carried Kree to the cot. As soon as she put her down, the child dove to the floor and crawled under the bed, curling up against the wall as far back out of reach as she could get. Risa stood straight and pressed the heel of her right hand into the headache forming over her eye.

"Ugh."

Garrison hurried over. "What happened?"

Risa took his arm and walked him to the back of the room, hopefully far enough for Kree not to hear a controlled mumble. "I asked her about going to live with Pavo. She seemed okay at first, but panicked when I told her he lived in the city."

He offered a comforting expression. "She's a lot like you were at first. It's going to take time."

"Yeah…" She glanced back at the partition. "Can you watch her for a little while? I need to deal with something."

"Deal with something? Who's the target?" He chuckled.

She punched him in the side, a bit harder than playful. "I'm not an assassin, and I'm not going on a 'mission.' I want to see Pavo, and… I have something I need to do. No bombs, no guns, and no blood involved." Risa shivered. "Okay, maybe a little blood."

"That's got me curious."

"Don't worry about me." She smiled for a second before leaning up to give him a quick peck on the cheek. "I'll be okay, Dad."

Risa crept over to the cot. "Sweetie?"

"I don' wanna go," whined Kree.

"I'm not going to make you. I need to go do some things, okay?" Risa peered under the blanket. The girl looked like a terrified porcelain doll with fluffed-out black hair, huddled in the corner. "I'm not going *away*. It's not a mission."

Kree sniffled. "No bombs."

"Promise. I'm only going to talk to Pavo. I love him too and I'd like to see him. You can come if you want."

"No." Kree shook her head hard, and pressed herself against the wall.

Risa sighed. "Okay. I'll be back soon. If you get scared, you find Garrison and he'll call me."

Kree stared at her.

"Back soon." Risa stood. *It's not supposed to be this difficult. I can't choose between them... I can't leave a child in this place. Too dangerous... and if they ever decide to disavow the MLF, they're gonna close it down.* She gazed up at the dingy ceiling of dented plastisteel tiles and dangling wires. *So, Raziel turned out to be software. Guess I'm a fool for hoping there's something up there.*

She moped on the way out past the command room, eyes downcast. Plain grey floor, interrupted every few feet by a ribbed cable sheath or an unidentifiable bit of metal junk, passed in silence. Risa counted her steps, taking a left at the top of the stairs and a right sixty-four steps later into the corridor that would lead her to the safehouse main entrance.

"Risa." General Maris blocked her path. "A minute."

She stopped and looked up at him with a weary expression.

Confusion lingered in his eyes; evidently, he'd expected her usual acerbic response to his presence. "I have to ask. Is there anything I can do to change your mind about going inactive? We've got two-hundred-and-forty-nine operations personnel, only eight of whom possess any skill with demolitions. And precisely one operative with enough augmentation to do what you can do."

Risa looked down and to the right, tapped her foot, and brought her stare back up to meet his. "If C-Branch is willing to pay for me to visit Reinventions every few years to keep me in my early twenties, I'll consider going active again once Kree's eighteen and on her own."

Maris set his hands on his hips and shook his head. "Doubtful. That would cost more than a new set of implants, even with your neuralware upgrade... and the Japanese don't sell that part you've got."

She cocked an eyebrow. "You're telling me they've got better tech than

C-Branch? If this operation becomes official, there'll be no need to pull the barely-hanging-on ragtag group of fugitives thing. Fully trained official operators are more than capable of handling anything I can. I've had the ass-kicking to prove it."

"We've got similar tech, but the Japanese version you're using is a little smaller. Uses a little less juice, and lasts longer before wire burn sets in. We're talking a couple of seconds here, but what you're asking for... millions of credits for a maybe."

She winked, and brushed past him. "I know."

Maris's subdued laughter echoed off the walls behind her. "A simple 'no' would've worked."

"Nothing here is ever simple." She paused and glanced back at him. "I've got someone to live for now. Two someones. And I'm not so sure we're doing the right thing anymore. Can't even say we'er trying to wage war on two fronts... *We* aren't waging war at all. We're a tool for political deniability."

"I know." He rubbed a hand over his mouth. "I'm well aware of the tactical idiocy of that. It's coming down from on high. I suppose they got tired of me telling them to stuff it." Maris approached. "You've got a reputation. *They* might think you're either too dangerous to let go or too valuable to lose."

Risa stared at her boots. "If anything happens to my family, I will rip the guts out of whoever is responsible... or die trying. There is no forcing me back into 'the life' by killing them. That starts the nuclear option."

General Maris raised his hands. "Whatever you may think of me, that's not how I operate. Don't think I'm unaware that message was for me."

She exhaled. "Sorry. I've had a rough week."

"Be careful."

"Thanks." She started to walk away.

"Oh, Risa?"

She froze, but didn't look back. "What?"

General Maris raised both eyebrows. "I have to ask you to give up the private room if you're not going to be doing demo work."

Risa threw her head back and laughed.

6

THE LAST DAY ON MARS

The line of passengers waiting to board the Elysium-bound shuttle queued at a gleaming white door set in a recessed alcove carved of Mars rock. To the right, a fifteen-meter-long 'window' offered a digital recreation of the surface tarmac two stories up. Wisps of fog drifted among the landing gear of four large RedLink shuttles, lined up like massive piglets suckling from the building.

Risa kept her head down, feeling trapped in a wall of bodies with too many people behind her for comfort. She counted the alternating dark-grey and navy threads in the coat of the woman in front of her up to four-hundred-and-sixty-two before a chime sounded overhead and made her lose track. A sleepy-looking man emerged from a curtain on the right side of the window.

His bright-crimson jumpsuit bore the logo of RedLink Corporation on a patch over his left breast. Wild white hair in a short bob gave him the look of an electrocuted dandelion. He put on an expression of happiness and flashed a plastic grin as he trotted over to a podium by the large door. A holo-terminal appeared over it, and after a few taps, the boarding tunnel opened. He continued to smile while an automated female voice took over.

"Good morning. Shuttle 907C departing for Elysium City is ready for boarding at terminal R. The gate is now open. Please form a single-file line and await confirmation of your boarding scan before proceeding."

One by one, people ahead of her walked into the opening, each person accompanied by a *beep* from the wall as a sensor scanned their NetMini to verify their ticket. A man close behind her and to the left made faces at thin air and wobbled his head, likely having an agitated conversation with someone via an implanted link. As the line thinned, he shouldered Risa out of his way and cut ahead. His daughter, perhaps three or four, looked up at her with an apologetic expression.

Once the girl made eye contact, she screamed and pointed. "Daddy!"

Risa cringed, hiding her face and staring down. *That* was the reaction she'd expected from Kree, or any child for that matter. For two months after the surgery, she avoided mirrors.

The man glanced at the girl, at Risa, then back to the child. "What's wrong?"

"She's scary!" The little one hid behind her father.

"Uhh, sorry." He offered a weak smile, picked the kid up, and hurried down the tube.

Violet light from her artificial eyes reflected on a thin metal strip where the boarding tunnel door sealed into the wall when closed. She cringed at the distancing sound of the little girl sniffling and crying. The people behind her managed to wait six whole seconds before the throat clearing started. By ten, a woman yelled, "Get on or get outta the way."

Risa hurried forward; a vibration and *beep* from her left hip startled a yelp out of her as her NetMini linked to the RedLink service. At the end of an air-conditioned tunnel with silvery paneled walls, a mechanical stairway offered an easy passage up a spiral into a round-walled surface building. Glowing blue hologram arrows with black text bearing her flight number pointed the way across the huge space to the correct docking tube.

A pair of circular bots zipped about cleaning the floor, like a game of air hockey playing itself with pucks the size of dinner plates. They came close enough to spook passengers into flinching, but never made contact. Risa trudged over the polished white tiles to a plastic-walled flexible tunnel, lit brown-orange from sunlight beating on it. Reddish dust caked the few inches of shuttle hull visible inside the air seal on the far end. Eventually, she emerged from the press of bodies and slipped into a window seat in the third row from the back. All the while, she hid her face behind her hair, not wanting anyone to see her demonic eyes.

Twenty-seven minutes after landing at the Elysium shuttleport, Risa approached the door to Pavo's apartment. It chirped and slid into the wall as soon as she got close enough for the reader to pick up her NetMini signal. The reminder Pavo had added her to the security settings teased a smile out of the oubliette into which her mood had fallen. She sucked in a breath, which lifted her spirits further, and strode inside.

Aurelia and Genevieve jumped, disentangling themselves with as much speed as possible without falling off Pavo's couch. One look at their mussed hair and near-lack of clothes told Risa all she needed to know. She winked at Genevieve, made a 'carry on' gesture, and headed for the inner hallway leading to the master bedroom. She approached the bedroom door, but slowed at the sound of Pavo emitting repetitive grunting sounds.

Eyebrows raised, she pushed the frosted plastic door aside and peeked in, dreading the sight awaiting her. "Got started without me?"

Pavo, head engulfed in a Senshelmet, punched, kicked, and grappled at thin air. Relieved she had misinterpreted the nature of the grunting, Risa leaned on the doorjamb, admiring his body. Clingy black boxers didn't leave much to the imagination. Muscles swelled in his shoulders and upper chest when he moved, as if catching someone leaping at him and hurling them to the floor. He dropped to a knee, delivering a rapid downward punch, his fist stopping short of the carpet by less than an inch.

"You know a plug-in would be safer. Or at least get a non-cheap helmet so you don't move around. You almost broke your hand."

He didn't react, likely unable to hear her over the soundtrack of whatever game he'd plunged into. Not wanting to catch an accidental foot to the nose, she stayed at the door. Pavo twisted right before grabbing and pulling in a gesture that let her imagine a wrist lock. He drove his knee up into the phantom's gut, and finished the attacker off with a downward elbow—likely to the back.

Risa ached to touch him. Behind her, the sounds of Aurelia and Gen's kissing grew fervent, bringing heat to her cheeks, and elsewhere. She tugged open the MolWeave fastener on her armor to let in some air. *Gen needed that. I hope they work out and stay happy together.* Over the next ten minutes, Risa's eyes drank in Pavo's figure. He was quite a few synthetic hormone shots away from the physique of a Gee-ball player, but then again, those guys looked like inflatable caricatures of humanity. Pavo had an athletic build, to the point every muscle showed clear definition beneath his skin. Besides, she didn't feel attracted to anyone so bulky he couldn't reach to scratch his own chest.

When she couldn't take the wait anymore, she kicked on her speedware long enough to blur into the room and hit the power switch on his helmet. He flailed about in a startled windmill; she caught his arm to keep him from falling over.

"Dammit." Pavo pulled the helmet off and looked at the controls on the right side. "I just charged this damn thing."

"Intense game?"

He whirled, raising his arms in a defensive posture for two seconds before recognition set in. "Fuck's sake…" He relaxed, and sighed. "Don't sneak up on me. Please. Not after…"

She stopped smiling. "I'm sorry. I didn't even think. Watching you was… distracting."

Pavo crossed to his desk, where he placed the helmet on a charging stand. A spray of blue light lit the wall behind it. He returned and wrapped his arms around her.

She stood in silence for a few minutes. The knowledge he'd been 'kept safe' by a supposedly friendly faction of the military didn't make her feel less guilty. *What did they do to him? Is he going to have flashbacks? PTSD?* She clung to him and sniffled.

"Hey, stop it," said Pavo. "I'm not upset. It's okay."

"Is it?" She took a meditative breath, and calmed herself. "What they did to you…"

He leaned back enough to look at her, and smiled. "I'm more pissed at myself than anything."

"You were running a combat sim, weren't you? Not a game."

"Little of both." He chuckled. "There's a story and objectives, but the combat is realistic enough to serve as practice. I used to think I can handle myself."

"You can." She shrugged out of her weapons harness and set the laser pistols on the desk by the helmet. "It's not like you were jumped by thugs. There aren't many people alive who could fight off a seasoned special ops team alone. At least, not without augments."

Pavo shivered; a reaction nigh imperceptible, though she caught it. Rather than return to his embrace, she leaned on the desk and stared at the rug. He fanned himself.

"Gonna grab a shower."

"Okay." Risa didn't look up.

He walked into the attached bathroom, not bothering to close the door. *He cringes every time I mention implants. He won't even look at Hanover.* An image of the MLF's other aug came to mind. Risa, even as a grown woman, only stood as tall as his pectorals. Both arms, from fingertip to shoulder, were plastisteel: UCF Marine Corps assault models. The story of how he got them varied from one telling to the next, with the common thread of losing them in action. Acid, bomb, missile, Cydonian crab, vibro-sword… did it really matter? *I wonder what happened to him… he used to be Garrison's shadow. Haven't seen him in a while.*

The autoshower whirr started. She glanced up at the open door, half tempted to watch. Her eyes felt like weights in her head, their inhumanity pulling her down a slippery passage of self-loathing. She dragged herself to the bed, sat on the edge, and freed her feet from her boots. After wriggling out of the ballistic suit, she lay back, laziness battling with the potential awkwardness of Aurelia walking in while she reclined in the nude.

She's busy with other things.

Rattling vibration from the bathroom faded to quiet. Pavo walked in with a towel around his waist, which he dropped as soon as he saw her. He swung by the door long enough to flip the lock, and crawled up beside her.

"Couldn't wait, eh?" He flashed a Devil's smile.

Pine-infusion from the autoshower soap made her cough a second after she rolled on her side to face him. "More like I wanted out of the armor. I think I'm getting sick of it, and everyone keeps telling me it's unhealthy because it doesn't breathe." With Pavo stretched out naked in front of her, she found it difficult to stay gloomy.

"Well, you do kind of live in the thing." He reached up and played with her hair. "I'm not going to complain if you'd rather not wear it."

She grinned.

"What's wrong? Why aren't you looking at me?" He caressed her cheek.

Risa protested his lifting her chin with one finger for a few seconds, but relented and let him force eye contact. "You're horrified at my eyes."

He brushed a thumb across her cheek, below her right eye. "You're beautiful with or without them."

She scooted closer, face to his chest. "When my headware fried, I couldn't see. I haven't been that terrified since the night my... I mean Andriy died."

He slid a hand over her shoulder onto her back, pulling her snug. "Thousands of people have prosthetic eyes."

"Yeah, but they *look* normal. I look like a damn killer robot." A sour frown twisted her lips. "It wouldn't bother me so much if I'd gone blind somehow and needed these things, but I gave my real eyes away... over dustblow."

His breath puffed warm into her hair as he kissed the top of her head. She looked up at him, and he repeated the kiss on her lips. She crept a hand up his side as the kiss deepened. His growing erection brushed her thigh. *I don't want to lose him again.* Risa moaned into his mouth, wanting him, needing him, unwilling to let him go. She tilted her head to the other side, sneaking breaths as their tongues entwined. He squeezed her ass, and she pulled her fingernails across the small of his back.

"I want my real eyes back." The words came in a breathless whisper.

He pushed her onto her back. "Do you even know where they are?"

The last time they'd made love before he'd 'been killed,' he'd surprised her from behind. Being taken had been scary as well as thrilling, but she lacked the desire to be passive at the moment.

"My turn." Risa caught him off guard with a shove, rolling him flat before climbing up on top of him. "And yeah. Raziel had them."

Pavo grinned, resting his hands on her hips. He spent a few minutes licking and teasing at her nipples, sending wave after wave of energy cascading down her spine. She grasped his head in both arms, holding his face tight to the space between her breasts. Three-day beard scratched her skin as he kissed his way up from her sternum to the front of her neck.

Risa shivered, paralyzed until their lips met again. He stared long into her gaze; she thought—no, *knew*—there would never be another like him. "Promise me you won't go away. I want you forever."

"You are all I thought about in that tiny little room." He kissed the side of her neck with a gossamer touch. "You kept me going."

"When I thought I'd lost you, I gave up."

He rolled her right nipple between his fingers, eliciting a faint squeal. "I want you to promise me, right here, right now. If anything should ever happen to me... I do *not* want you hurting yourself."

"Okay."

"That includes not stopping someone else from hurting you." He grasped the back of her neck, forcing her to look him in the eye. "I mean it."

"I promise." Risa's gaze fell onto his chest.

"Hey. I'm not planning on checking out." He winked. "Stop looking like that."

She smiled, despite tears welling up. "I don't want you to be disgusted by what's in my head."

"I'm not." He grasped her face in both hands, palms to cheeks, and pulled her forehead to forehead. "You are perfect."

Pavo... She swallowed hard. "I love you."

"I never thought I'd find a woman who makes me feel like time stands still."

She bit her lip. "That's just the speedware."

He chuckled. "I mean it. Whenever I see you, it's like the world stops and you're the only thing that matters. I love you, Risa Black."

They held each other for a while in adoring silence before he resumed playing with her nipples. A shudder ran from head to toe; need burst within, a force she could no longer hold back. She pushed upright again and reached between her legs to guide him inside her. After easing herself down, she adjusted her balance and got into a rhythmic motion. She caught hold of his hands as he reached for her, pushing them up, pinning them over his head as her mouth found his. Their fingers laced together. She leaned back, leveraging her position and twisting her hips until he hit the right spot with every thrust.

She gasped, breathless as she rode faster. The Comforgel pad undulated beneath them, the fluid inside it amplifying their motions. All thought melted away, all worries gone. For what seemed like the first time in a decade, she felt truly happy.

Pleasure bloomed at her core, spreading over her like the ethereal light of a *real* angel. Pavo filled her soul in a way Raziel never could. She trembled with ecstasy, clinging to him until neither of them could move. When the blinding light in her everything faded and her body relaxed, she collapsed on top of him.

"There is nothing more important to me than you." He stroked her hair.

She smiled, not that he could see with her cheek to his chest. "I have to tell you something."

"I know you want to adopt that girl. Sounds good to me."

"More than that." Risa gripped his shoulder. "I'm out. No more bombs.

I told Garrison to take me off the roster. Oh yeah, I also found out he's my father."

"He basically raised you."

"I mean my *actual* father. He married my mother a few months before she got the assignment to monitor Andriy."

Pavo exhaled. "Shit... Did he know?"

"He had no idea... I think learning that hit him harder than it did me."

"So you're a civilian now? You're welcome to move in here whenever you want."

"Uhh." She sighed. "I want to. Kree's still messed up by what happened to her mother. She's afraid of leaving the safehouse. As soon as I figure out a way to get her out of there..."

"Easy. Feed her a sleeping pill. She wakes up here and she'll feel safe. This is still 'inside.'"

She poked him in the ribs. "I am *not* drugging a child. She was okay in the mine and on the walk to the safehouse. I need to figure out what's got her so spooked. I gotta get her out of there before something happens."

Pavo rubbed a hand up and down her back. "You think something is going to go down? Depending on what Everett manages to pull off on Earth, maybe they won't do anything drastic up here. Of course, if loverboy goes off the deep end..."

Risa narrowed her eyes. "If Everett doesn't deal with him, I will."

"You really want to tangle with Shiro? If he's a C-Branch operator..."

She scowled. "He might not know I know. I can play dumb. Get close. He'd never see it coming." Her heart grew leaden at the thought. *I'm not an assassin. He saved my life... took me to the hospital when I was blind.* A faint growl rumbled in her throat. *He tried to kill Pavo. He doesn't love me; he wants to own me.*

"I'm scared." She clamped on to him. "I'm worried something is going to happen. Maris might be lying. Everett might be lying. Someone might be watching us right now. What if they learn about Kree? What if they decide I'm too dangerous to let walk away? Are they going to shoot me or remind the authorities about all the crap I did for the Front?" Thoughts of being back in a prison transport on the way to execution made her tremble.

Pavo held her until she calmed. "I won't let anything happen to you. I've got friends among the PVM. They already know about the Front's true origin."

"You told them?" Risa squirmed around to look at him.

"Yep. As you said, we don't know whose dicks are in whose asses."

"How... eloquent. I did *not* say that." She let her head fall against his chest. "Why do men always use sex metaphors?"

He shrugged. "Dunno. Probably because nine out of every ten thoughts in a male brain is about—or at least related to—sex."

"What's the tenth?" She smiled with her mouth half-open.

Pavo winked. "A coin flip between killing something or eating bacon."

Risa chuckled for a second, then fell somber. "Do you think I'm stupid for wanting my eyes back?"

"You're perfect either way. It's your body, Risa. The only opinion that matters is yours."

She sighed. "Tactically speaking."

"I thought you quit?"

"I did. But I don't trust anyone... except you." She reached up and laced her fingers behind his neck. "And if I shouldn't... If you're playing me too, I don't care if it kills me."

"What you see is what you get." He patted her butt. "I'm no spy. Honestly? Your eyes are three generations removed from current. Modern military prosthetic models look like normal eyes. All of the visual interface capability passes through your NIU, anyway. The same tactical feeds work fine without electronic eyes. They can be fed into the brain directly rather than using electronic retinas like tiny display screens."

I want to be human again. "What about sensors? The Wraith? Night vision?"

"Wearable gear. Armored visors or ear-clips can do the same thing."

"And they won't blind me if they overload."

Pavo rolled over, putting her on her back as he straddled her. "Sounds like you've made up your mind already. You know what you want, you're only afraid of doing it."

"I should get my eyes back?"

He leaned down and kissed her until she had to push him off to breathe. "It's your body. Only you can make that choice. You're perfect to me either way."

Risa glanced down past her chest at him. "Ready again?"

"Your choice." He winked.

She traced her hands down his sides and back up. "Aren't you going to be late?"

He shook his head. "I'm off all week. Evaluations and such."

"I like the sound of that." Risa embraced him.

A few minutes into round two, the feeling of *too perfect* washed over her. Her boosted ears didn't detect any sign of Aurelia and Genevieve having fun anymore; perhaps they cuddled. Unable to shake the nagging worry she'd lose him again, she made love to him like this would be their last day on Mars.

7

SO SHINY

D ark sunglasses covered the violet glow emanating from Risa's eyes. The periwinkle blue babydoll top with attached pleated skirt reminded her of Chaia, and made her wonder what the girl was doing at that moment. The cute-but-oh-so-creepy tween had sent a Vidmail a few days ago from a colony named Alumiera, still in the Milky Way, but far enough to require a jump.

Chaia admitted freaking out at the breathable gel tanks, but wound up more afraid of what extreme g-forces would do to her inside bits without the protection. The few photos she sent depicted a pleasant apartment, courtesy of the biopharma company sponsoring the colony, the one Caiden's mother now worked for as a mechanical repair technician. Chaia spent the last five minutes of the recorded message whining about having to physically attend school rather than sitting at home with a helmet.

A gloss-black purse sat in Risa's lap, secure under her arms. Hugging it and keeping her head down made her feel like a scared tourist. Bland-scented air fell on her from vents in the shuttle roof; the tethered datapad attached to the seatback in the next row cycled among a preview menu of pay-per-view movies. Even if she could bring herself to pry her arms open, the flight from Primus City to Arcadia wouldn't give her enough time for a full-length entertainment holo.

Risa squeezed her bag tighter to her chest, clutching the brick-shaped object inside. She stared at the thin black fabric clinging to her legs, hating it for not being armor. *I'd feel less naked... well,* naked, *than walking around in plain clothes.* She risked a hesitant peek up at the people across the aisle. No one paid much attention to her, at least no one she could see. Being out of armor, carrying something so precious—her natural eyes frozen in gel—kept her hands shaking.

Beep.

The sound, a solitary digitized tone, one she'd heard tens of thousands of times, struck her as confounding as the sight of a blue elephant with six human arms. The second time it beeped, she remembered her NetMini. An instinctive grasp at her left hip found only cloth. It took her two more beeps to realize the device sat at the bottom of her purse.

Like a normal person.

She fished it out and stared at the screen: 史郎 (Shiro).

An image of Pavo, the bedraggled, manic face she'd seen at the remote installation, rushed into her mind. With it came a torrent of anger. She managed to hold her rage back enough not to hurl the NetMini down the aisle, and let it drop into her bag. Twenty seconds later, it beeped again. Risa seethed in place, but made no move to grab the device. The words 'missed call' appeared in midair courtesy of her headware, lingered for three seconds, and faded away. Six seconds after that, 'New Vidmail: 1' appeared.

With a thought, Risa swiped the notification off the left side of her vision.

Anticipation built over the next forty-odd minutes until deceleration made her lean forward. She raised her head, peering through an ebon curtain of hair at the window. Arcadia City sat like a glimmering water bubble set in brick-red sand, still miles away. The newest, and most advanced, city within the UCF territory, it had only a meager underground presence. Enough for maintenance conduits, sewers, and infrastructure, but no one lived or worked underground here.

What it lacked in depth, it made up in footprint. The city covered an area over four times the total surface area of all of Primus's 'civilized' tiers. Enormous towering buildings at the northwestern corner marked the heart of the UCF military complex, accompanying starport, and associated structures. So much greenery littered the place, it resembled a city scooped away from Earth and transplanted. She clenched her fists, surprised at herself for feeling like a traitor. *I guess humans want to recreate their home.* A sigh slid past her teeth. *This is my home.*

The pale blue glimmer of atmospheric retention fields grew nearer as the shuttle circled to the southeast, putting the city to her side of the ship. Before long, individual hovercars became noticeable in the air and, minutes after that, much smaller advert bots appeared as fast-moving specks. Unlike Elysium, Arcadia did not possess a physical dome; the entire shield consisted of projected energy, intangible to solid objects, but impervious to loose gases.

Risa remained in her seat, head down, hoping no one noticed her inhuman eyes. The NewsNet had run a 'wanted' ad campaign for the MLF's most notorious terrorist, though the woman they'd shown looked closer to forty, and far more sinister. Though, any Marsborn woman with Generation 3 Nishihama Oracle cybereyes could find themselves a target for overeager bounty hunters or bored Defense Force officers.

One more reason. She hugged her purse.

Her NetMini beeped again.

Leave me alone. The thought of being within claw reach of him made her shake. Shiro technically commanded the team that hit Arden when General Maris refused. Had he been there? If he was half as skilled as the C-Branch operator who nearly killed her, she'd be in trouble. Even with Tamashi's help providing a hand-to-hand training sim, she didn't feel confident. A couple of virtual weeks being thrown around by a virtual old man wouldn't make up for years of actual combat experience.

The want to kill him clashed with a feeling she couldn't remember having before: fear. Worry that she'd die. *Kree, Pavo... Garrison.* She cringed. No matter which way she ordered the names in her head, she felt wrong about it.

The disturbance of people moving startled her out of her debate. She looked up at an aisle crammed full. Men and women jostled each other, vying for space to access overhead bins or force their way past the congestion. Two RedLink employees offered pacifying comments in a tone too calm to be heard over the clamor. Risa waited in her seat. Nine minutes later, the crowd had dispersed, so she slipped out of her seat and walked the empty aisle to the boarding tube. A couple of Earth tourists diverted to the luggage pick up, evidently about to embark on the ride home after a Mars vacation. Their son, a boy about Kree's age, lay draped over a wheeled suitcase, sleeping while his mother pulled him along.

Risa clung to her bag, a covetous squirrel clutching the last acorn in the world, and kept up a brisk stride to the street. Outside, the air smelled... strange. Perhaps all the living plants here made the air more Earthlike and less filtered-stale. Ion engines whirred overhead from streams of hovercars fifty stories up. Risa hustled down a forty-meter-long flight of shallow white steps trimmed in silver—the irritating kind only half the height of a normal stairway and too broad to take two at a time.

When she paused at the bottom to look for the shortest line at a PubTran kiosk, a body pressed up against her with a grip on her shoulder and a hard object poking into her spine.

"Don't scream or move. That's a gun." A man's voice rode a foul wind of cheap SynVod.

Thin cloth did little to mask the boxy plastisteel weapon touching her. The idea of what a bullet would do to her without her beloved armor dragged her voice down to a squeak as pitiful as she must've looked.

"What do you want?"

He chuckled. "If you gotta ask, you're as zoned as you look. Walk to the right, slow. Don't try to signal anyone, or I'll kill them, then you."

The man let his hand slip off her shoulder. He groped her breast through her shirt for a few seconds before nudging her forward with a body bump. Risa pivoted to her right, obliging his command. Terror and rage played rock paper scissors as she walked, but they kept picking the same thing, ending in a draw. She kept her head pointed down, and closed her eyes. Her Wraith implant sensed motion, allowing her to see in total darkness by rendering nearby objects as grey ghosts floating in void. Anything or anyone up to about forty feet away appeared in a surprising amount of detail thanks to recent upgrades to her headware. The man behind her looked unshaven, gaunt, and either drunk or high. His weapon hovered about ten inches away, too far to chance a sudden twist.

"Sweet little pretty thing. Be a shame to hurt ya. You be a good little girl and I won't kill you. Be extra good and I won't even have to hit ya. See that green ball? Turn right." He inhaled deep. "I love those leggings you got on. So tight. Don't work with those heavy ol' boots though."

Okay. I take back saying that I'm sick of my armor. Eating a bullet in the back with the stealth suit would hurt, but a pistol slug couldn't pierce. *I'd take two just to shut this piece of shit up.*

She looked up enough to spot a two-foot hologram of a green disc bearing a white outline of a coffee cup, complete with three squiggles of steam. The corner café abutted a shadowed alley on the far side of a restaurant that had tourist-pit practically written on the walls by virtue of overdone 'Mars Aliens' kitsch.

"You wanna do it here? In an alley?" Risa stepped into the dark. "Why don't we get a room or something? This is my first rape. I'd prefer if it was a little more high class."

"Shut up," he yelled.

The instant he raised his weapon hand to hit her, she activated her speedware, plunging the world into slow motion. Eight-inch Nano claws erupted from her fingertips as she whirled, bashing her left forearm into the man's right wrist, forcing the gun to the side while she swiped her other hand at his throat. He squeezed the trigger a nanosecond before she felt the telltale hesitation of claws on spine, not that the monomolecular edges stalled much on mere bone.

Her claws passed through his entire neck before his facial expression showed any sign of having noticed her move. In her accelerated reality, a bloom of bright azure fire flickered from the barrel of the weapon; filters in her boosted ears blocked off the deafening report. An 8mm slug, warped hexagonal by the barrel, emerged from the tip of the flames, corkscrewing into the air a safe distance to her side. As the man's mouth opened, the first traces of pain showing on his face, she raked her hand back, severing his forearm.

The gun, his hand, and three flesh discs as wide as the spaces between her claws, tumbled downward as if in syrup. Her rapid spin launched the sunglasses away from her face. She glared into his eyes and shut down her speedware.

"I got nothin' to say to you."

Risa kicked him in the groin, causing his head to fall off his body. A geyser of blood spurted up from the carotid artery; she leapt back. Slabs of tissue with glass-smooth edges toppled from the stump as he went over. She stooped long enough to wipe the blood from her claws on his pants before retracting. After recovering her glasses, she strolled onto the street.

As the idea 'call PubTran' formed in her mind, a virtual panel opened in space. It bore a cartoon taxi with large sorrowful eyes and an apologetic frown.

"We're sorry, you are currently within the Arcadia City Starport transportation zone. Due to licensing agreements between RedLink and PubTran, we can only service requests from approved PubTran podiums. Please—"

Miserable bastards.

She jogged the two blocks back to the starport and got on line again where people formed up by a row of teal and grey obelisks. Adrenaline lent a tremble to her limbs. *Okay, I was asking for that. Walking around with my head down looking like a tourist. I had 'easy prey' written all over me.* Risa straightened, keeping her head high and striking a pose one might expect from a soldier on perimeter guard. While waiting for a car, she examined her dress for traces of blood, happy to find none.

An advert bot, a fourteen-inch orb gussied up like a coffee pot, made the rounds by those waiting. As much as she wanted it, and as much as the artificial smell it exuded beckoned to her, she politely declined. Hopefully, the sick feeling in her gut and the paranoia that came with it would subside by the time she reached the hospital. Adding caffeine to her stress wouldn't be wise.

After an annoying sixteen minutes, she found herself on the curb, staring at a waist-high podium about a foot square, with rounded corners. The angled top held an edge-to-edge touchscreen, showing the estimated wait for a car at four minutes, twenty-eight seconds.

When the little grey and teal car whirred up to park in front of her, she almost cheered. The side hatch opened. She glanced to her right while climbing in; the alley where she'd killed a man remained quiet, devoid of interest or alarm.

"Thank you for choosing PubTran Corporation for your transportation needs. Please state your destination," said a placid male voice from a metal panel on the left wall.

"Arcadia City Medical Complex, please."

"Destination found. Trip distance five-point-one-nine miles. Trip cost C93. If you are injured, expedited arrival is available for an additional fee of—"

"Regular ride." Risa waved her NetMini by the console, earning a pleasant *beep* from the car. The side hatch closed. Pitiful acceleration eased her into the seat. She eyed the dark alley as they bounced past it. Whenever she completed an operation for the Front that involved bombs, she'd wind up crippled with guilt hours later, questioning herself. She squinted. All she felt about that man was the urge to kill him again.

A few seconds shy of fourteen minutes later, the self-driving vehicle swerved to the left across four lanes of oncoming traffic in the way that only an AI could pull off, and slowed as it climbed a curved approach ramp to an enormous white façade.

After Bliss, the risky maneuver only caused her to raise an eyebrow.

"I didn't pay for expediting."

A cartoon car appeared in hologram over the dashboard, smiling at her. "Based on an analysis of approaching traffic, the next window of opportunity to enter would have occurred in three minutes nineteen seconds. PubTran Corporation regrets any unwanted stress you may have experienced. We offer a 'serenity' option if desired, otherwise trip efficiency is maximized."

Two fountains flanked a patch of grass in the shape of a D, with the flat side facing the road. At its center, a silvery stone with a mirror-polished face bore the engraved text: Arcadia City Medical Complex. At the apex of the curve, a long awning kept the main entrance in shade in front of three octagonal-walled skyscrapers, the shortest of which had to be over a hundred stories.

The PubTran whirred to a halt by the curb. Risa hopped out and hurried into the lobby. Proximity to her goal simmered in her stomach, exacerbating the lack of anything else in it. Five people in all-white outfits, three women and two men, sat behind a chrome-finished desk in the middle of the lobby. Minute flecks of metal in the grey floor sparkled in a shimmering cascade that seemed to sweep across the room as she walked. A confusing mess of signs hung over three large hallways that led deeper into the complex, on either side of a bank of elevators.

She stopped at the desk.

"Good morning, miss," asked a slender man. "Do you require assistance?"

"I have an appointment, but I'm not sure where to go."

He gestured at a NetMini reader. "Please."

Risa hesitated for a second, extracted the device from her purse, and held it out. A chime emanated from his holo-terminal. A moment later, he looked up with a smile.

"Ah, yes. Miss Aum. It seems you're a few minutes early, but that's not a problem. Your appointment with Doctor Haltemeyer is scheduled for ten."

The numbers floating in the corner of her sight read 9:44.

"Little nervous." She forced a smile.

"What healthcare"—the clerk raised both eyebrows—"never mind. I see you've prepaid." He tapped a few holographic buttons, causing his terminal to emit a staccato series of *tweeps*. A four-inch white orb-bot levitated out of a round hatch in the desk and glided over to her. "The orb will lead you to where you need to be."

"Thanks." She looked at the spherical floater. "Lead on."

"This way, miss," said a voice that sounded like it belonged to a little girl. As it spoke, pink light pulsed within the seams of its plating.

Risa followed the fist-sized robot across the lobby to the middle hallway. The combination of intense light, white walls, and an oval shape to the passage made her feel as though she navigated the interior of a starship. Fifty meters later, they entered an octagonal space with access to a cafeteria and gift shop on the right, and 'outpatient care' on the left. The orb headed for the center of the room, where a round column held six capsule-shaped elevators. It glided into one without hesitation, so Risa followed. The orb hovered by the console, selecting the forty-second floor after the doors closed. When they arrived, it zipped down another white corridor, square and antiseptic. After two left turns and a right, it glided to a halt by a silver panel bearing the words: Procedure Room 09FC.

"Doctor Haltemeyer will be with you in a few minutes. Please go inside and have a seat in the blue chair."

The door opened on its own, revealing a room with a standard floor-to-ceiling medical tank, an exam table, several shelves of what appeared to be tiny cybernetic parts shrink-wrapped in silvery translucent plastic, and a common workstation with holo-terminal. A blue chair of the type one might expect to see in a medical waiting room faced it, far less fancy than the black imitation-leather one intended for the doctor.

She sat in the indicated spot, clutching her purse in her lap.

Less than two minutes later, a middle-aged man with light brown skin entered. A close-trimmed afro had long ago lost the war to grey, and a scattering of darker spots lined both cheeks. She wondered if he'd been exposed to unfiltered sunlight too often.

He approached with a broad smile, offering a hand. "Miss Aum. I'm Doctor Haltemeyer. May I call you Raina?"

Risa stood, accepting the handshake. "Of course."

He sat in the expensive chair, which tilted back and raised the armrests a few centimeters to fit his ergonomic profile. The whirring of tiny actuators set off her augmented hearing and caused a tremor to travel down her spine.

"You seem on edge, Raina. I can understand that. The procedure you have arranged is not a minor one, though you have come to the right place. There is no more advanced medical care available anywhere on Mars."

"That's, uhh, reassuring." She smiled and pulled the silver bar from her purse. Cradling it in two hands like a sacred relic, she offered it. "I'm more afraid you'll tell me they're no good."

The doctor took the case and slid the protective plastisteel shroud off, exposing the glass. Two eyeballs, each with a short scrap of attached optic nerve, sat in frozen peach-hued gel. He studied them. Every twitch of his brow or shift in the posture of his lips made her heart flutter. After a cursory visual examination, he plugged a wire from his terminal into the inch-thick metal base on one end of the bar, and set it on end atop the desk.

Risa averted her gaze, thinking it looked too much like a gruesome office achievement award.

"They appear to be in excellent condition. From what I can tell here, this is the original surgical storage unit these eyes were placed in after removal. According to the file, the donor was eighteen at the time?" He sighed. "We live in a strange world, don't we? Young people selling themselves... and not in the way one would expect from the term."

She removed the sunglasses, waited a tick, and looked up. "They're actually mine, Doctor."

He blinked. "Oh, my."

"Doctor-patient confidentiality?"

"Of course." He smiled.

Especially when I'm prepaid, right? Risa held back the grumble. "My former employer required me to get some mods for the job. My contract is over, and I want them back."

"Ah, I see. Well, that certainly does simplify any issues of tissue rejection." He disconnected the wire from the obelisk of eyes, and offered it to her. "Would you be so kind as to connect that to your M3?"

Risa took the wire, tossed her hair over her shoulder with a head motion, and stuck the asterisk-shaped prong into the socket behind her ear. Aside from the *click* resonating in her skull, nothing noticeable happened.

A few seconds later, the right side of the Doctor's face lit up green as text and diagnostic information unfurled in full holographic glory. He studied it for a few minutes, making a series of appraising nods and hums.

"You have some interesting augmentations, Miss Aum. While much of the utilitarian functions you've grown used to from your electronic eyes can be replicated by direct-to-brain transmission via your Neural Interface Unit, your Oracles have several visual enhancement modes that require hardware to support. Namely, night vision, thermal, metallurgical scanning, and of course the ultrasonic sensors for the Wraith."

Risa fidgeted with the pleats of her attached skirt. "I know. I'm not planning on needing them much, but if I do, there's always a ViewPane, right?"

Doctor Haltemeyer chuckled. "Sure, if you want to go back in time a few years. I have several clients involved with dangerous work. The old 'slab of metal' over the face can come in handy to stop the occasional bullet, but newer tech replicates the effect in slim wearables. Or, if you've got the budget, there's a Prismacor Beholder."

His terminal created several holographic images. The first piece of headgear consisted of a thin, clear band across both eyes, the next a headband with six visible lenses on spiderlike mechanical arms, followed by another device, which appeared to perch over one ear on the side of the head, projecting holograms in front of the eyes. Last, he brought up an image of a generic man's head, with hair-thin fiberoptics embedded in the skin. Nine cameras, each half a millimeter in width, arranged for full 360 vision—a mere ℂ800,000.

Risa smiled. "Thanks. It's something to think about for later."

Doctor Haltemeyer nodded. "Understood. Since we'll be working deep in your brain today, I only mentioned the Beholder as it wouldn't incur any additional surgical fees."

I wonder how much Prismacor pays him. "I understand." She traced her fingers over the back of her left hand. "I'm trying to get back some humanity, not stuff more tech under my skin."

"I see." The doctor leaned forward. "Tell me, Miss Aum, are you experiencing any feelings of disassociation from society? At any time, do you feel like you're above 'mere humans,' sense a desire to 'transcend the flesh' to a higher state of being?"

She exhaled. *Time to watch what I say.* "I had a little kid panic when she saw my eyes. I don't feel superhuman if that's what you're mining for. I'm... I regret getting perfectly good eyes replaced, and I don't want to turn into a machine."

He smiled. "Very well. You received the pre-procedure notifications and whatnot. Can I trust you haven't had any food or drink for the past twelve hours?"

Risa's stomach churned. "I haven't."

"Alright. Please disrobe and step into the tank. There are buttons on the floor to wrap a privacy curtain around it once you're inside. I'll give you a few minutes to get situated." He stood and gestured at a small metal door embedded in the wall. "You can leave your things in that storage locker."

"It's okay, Doctor. I'm not shy." *Get it over with before I chicken out.*

She reached down to unclasp the row of five fasteners on the outside of each boot, stood, and stepped out of them. *Why does every hospital have such icy floors?* The doctor seemed to focus his attention on his terminal while she removed her clothes, put everything in the locker, and stepped onto the tank's base, a metal disc about a foot raised from the floor. At the point where the beveled edge became flat, a ring of two-inch-thick clear material circled her. The tube had retracted downward, flush with the pedestal. She clasped her stomach, trying to tamp down the butterflies while avoiding stepping on the grille via which the gel would flood the tank. Soon, her skull would be open, skin peeled away, brain exposed.

For two minutes that felt like twenty, Risa waited on the metal disc, shivering, trying to force that thought out of her mind. Eventually, the squeak of a chair made her look up. Doctor Haltemeyer rounded the edge of his desk and walked over. After a few routine questions about known allergies—none of which she had—he tapped a button which caused the cylinder to rise until it sealed against a matching disc on the ceiling.

"Miss Aum. Before we continue, I am required to ask that you acknowledge this is an elective procedure not necessary for the preservation of life. While we strive for perfection, there is always the outside chance a patient's body may react in unpredictable ways. Are you certain beyond a shadow of a doubt that you wish to continue?"

There's something about being stuck naked in a clear cage that's intimidating in a way even hanging off a tiny combat aircraft can't match. She continued to shiver, unsure if from the freezing air or her nerves. A moment's concentration on the memory of the little girl having a freakout at the sight of her, plus so many hours of regret, steeled her nerves. "I'm sure. Please go ahead."

The doctor nodded and hit another switch. Risa jumped as a heavy *clank* shook the platform, and mechanical whirring vibrated the chamber. Within seconds, viscous peach-hued slime welled up out of the vent slats on either side of her feet. Compared to the air and metal floor, the warm ooze felt like a welcome blanket wrapping around her.

"Miss Aum, since you did not ask any questions about the gel, I assume you know how it works."

She gave a thumbs-up as the substance climbed past her thighs and over her hips. Breathing slime didn't rank high on her list of fun things to do, but eight years of activity with the Front necessitated a certain amount of tube time. Wonderful warmth passed her breasts and reached her neck, buoyancy taking her weight off the ground. She exhaled as much as she could, the last second or two bubbling as the liquid climbed past her chin. Once she floated free and submerged, she stopped trying to hold her breath and let the substance fill her lungs.

Mild pain lingered in her chest for the first minute as her system adjusted. It took all her concentration to resist the primal terror of drowning; she repeated 'I can breathe' over and over in her mind until she reached a state of calm. Her waist-long hair hovered around her like an inky phantasm, spreading outward.

She glanced up at a mechanical noise. A fist-sized hatch in the upper platform opened, and her biological eyeballs dropped into the tank with her. Revulsion and curiosity stalemated; she neither cringed away nor studied them.

Three more figures in white entered: a dark-skinned and bone-thin woman about Risa's age, a heavyset red-haired woman creeping up on forty, and a blond man who looked like a ten-year-old boy stretched to an adult's height. The male medtech seemed startled at the privacy curtain being open, and gawked at her until Doctor Haltemeyer sent everyone to various workstations near the tube.

One of the floating spheres seemed to swim like a malformed sperm, guided by invisible nanobots. When it glided up to her face, she locked eyes with herself.

"Priya is going to administer and monitor the anesthetic now." The doctor's voice thrummed in the gel. "Relax, and I'll see you in a few hours... though to you, it will feel like only a moment." He twisted away from his terminal to look back at her, smiled, and spoke into the mic again. "Last chance to change your mind."

Risa thought about giving a thumbs-up, but the next thing she knew, it felt as though someone had smashed her in the head with a metal pipe. Instinctively, her hand moved to her face, finding a soft, padded blindfold. It next occurred to her that air streamed in and out of her nose and the warm squishiness of a Comforgel pad embraced her. She returned her arm to her side. Aside from a sheet, she remained nude. Blindness made the woozy feeling worse, creating a sense of falling backward through the bed into an endless spiral. The glowing cyan time display at the lower left corner of her vision that she'd grown so accustomed to stood out as glaring by its absence. Without its light, a hollow void consumed her world.

She clutched the bedding, a feeble effort to fight the vertigo.

When she tried to move her eyes around, the tremendous headache intensified. She gritted her teeth and moaned. Minutes passed in dark silence. At a trace of autoshower soap in the air, she wondered who bathed her to clear the residue of the medical gel. She reached both hands up and examined the thing on her head: padded, cloth, probably black. It *felt* black. Her fingers teased at the mask. Fear of being so helpless clashed with worry she'd hurt herself if she took it off.

Throbbing eyeballs made it difficult to think about anything. Time seemed meaningless. Again, she glanced low and left for the spot where her time display had always been. She couldn't remember being without it, even though it had only been seven years. Her jaw clenched. *The entire time Kree has been alive, I've had metal eyes.* She fidgeted, unable to tell if she'd been awake for minutes or hours. Eventually, the constant pain in her skull started a swirl of regret.

A soft hiss suggested a pneumatic door sliding open. Scuffing shoes and a rush of cooler air confirmed it. Someone approached the side of the bed. Seconds later, electric chirps emanated a few inches away from her head.

"Welcome back to the land of the conscious," said Doctor Haltemeyer. "I'm pleased to report that everything seems to have worked out fine. You may be experiencing some discomfort around the eyes. This is due to the reattachment of your extraocular muscles. You've had metal eyes for some years now, so we had to regenerate quite a bit of tissue in there."

"*Some* discomfort? It feels like my eyeballs are six times bigger than the sockets."

Another few beeps happened, followed by a spot of cold on her right shoulder and a soft *hiss.*

"That should help with the pain. You can remove the padding if you feel up to it."

An onrush of dizziness accompanied the drug, though it did dull the sense of eyes swollen to the point of bursting. Risa lifted the mask, expecting to cringe at painful light, but discovered her blindfold to be white and the room tolerable in brightness. She pulled it off the rest of the way, and squinted at the doctor. He hovered close, holding a small handheld device over her left eye for a few seconds, then the other. The noises it made sounded reassuring. A moment later, he backed off, and she sat up, cradling her face in her hands.

Her head felt like an inert twenty-pound orb bot balanced on a stick. Every surface around her appeared glistening and smooth.

"Why does everything look weird and shiny, like it's all wrapped in plastic?"

The doctor tucked the device into his medical coat pocket. "You'd been using electronic eyes for a long time, rather old ones at that. Do you remember when you first got them? Did you perceive a screen effect, as if you were looking at the world through a tiny mesh?"

She tried to rub her nose, but it hurt too much. "Ow. Yeah… kind of."

"That was your brain perceiving the individual pixels generated by the image sensors in the eyes. Eventually you became used to it, and no longer perceived the grid; however, that grid would've imparted a drabness to your vision, desaturating all color. Natural eyes don't pixilate. The world is going to appear a little strange to you until your brain rewires itself."

"Oh." Risa stumbled out of the bed on jellied legs. "Great. I should go home." *I'm too vulnerable here.*

She took three steps toward the door before the doctor cleared his throat.

"Forgetting something, Miss Aum?"

Risa kept going until she reached the exit, then leaned one hand on the doorjamb and glanced back at him. "Huh?"

"You aren't wearing anything." He pursed his lips.

She blinked down at herself. *Oh wow. I must be high. Didn't even feel naked.* "Ngh. It hurts so much I'm not sure I care."

He guided her back to the bed. "The headache should subside in a few hours. Please rest. I'll need to send one of the medtechs in in a little while to make sure everything is working before we can release you."

The floor raced up to meet her, but the doctor caught her. He helped her get back in the bed before covering her with the sheet again.

"Maybe I should rest. I seem to be a little high."

He smiled.

"MISS AUM?" ASKED A WHISPERY FEMALE VOICE.

Risa startled out of a half-awake state. Mercifully, the headache had almost faded, but her muscles remained 'gooey' and unresponsive. Her clothes sat folded on the table next to the bed, but she couldn't remember anyone bringing them in. She yawned and sat up.

The dark-skinned woman who'd monitored her anesthetic walked over to the bed and smiled. "Good afternoon. I'm Priya. Are you feeling up for a few tests to make sure everything is working?"

"Headache's almost gone." Risa yawned again. "Sure. Why not?"

Priya took a datapad from the large pocket on the left side of her coat. "Can you try to activate your virtual interface and let me know if you see anything unusual?"

Risa thought about accessing her NetMini over the wireless link. The virtual screens she'd grown so accustomed to appeared as before, but seemed more *real* somehow... as if rather than a digital display, she witnessed a hole in reality looking into another world.

"Is something wrong?" asked Priya. "You look confused."

She stared at Pavo's face in her contacts list, and unconsciously tried to touch him. "It's so different. They look like they're right in front of me, not like I'm staring at a virtual holo-panel."

Priya smiled. "That's your new cortical interface unit. The resolution is much sharper. Plus, it is feeding data directly to the vision-processing centers in your brain, rather than using the image sensors of artificial eyes as an intermediary. There is zero pixilation. Is everything working as it should, aside from being more vivid?"

She navigated several floating menus; the system seemed a little faster, another side effect of the hardware upgrade. After testing video playback, and sending an 'I'm okay' message to Pavo, she glanced at Priya and activated her combat tactical processor. Glowing dotted lines appeared, indicating motion paths for the four most efficient ways to kill the woman. She deactivated it, closed her eyes, and tried the Wraith. Amid the blackness, the words 'No ultrasonic system detected' floated as if carved of ruby.

"Everything but the Wraith seems good."

Priya tapped the datapad, typing in notes. "Any dizziness, nausea, blurriness, or headache?"

She rubbed her temple. "Only the headache I woke up with."

"Good." The medtech smiled, and switched off the datapad. "You'll be better off using the interface as little as possible within the first forty-eight hours. The spatial relativity processor requires input from ultrasonic emitters and detectors, which your artificial eyes had. I assume that's why your employer opted for the Oracle series." She sighed. "They're rather startling in appearance."

"Yeah, so I'll need a wearable sensor for the Wraith, got it." She bit her lip. "C-can I see a mirror?"

Priya stepped back and turned ninety degrees, like a human door opening out of her way as she gestured to her right. "In the bathroom."

She felt fine until she attempted to put weight on her legs—and collapsed. Her knees hit the floor with a loud *crack*, but she didn't feel it. "That should've hurt, shouldn't it?"

Priya helped her up. "You've had a rather large dose of pain medication. Perhaps you should rest a little longer."

I need to get back before Kree has a meltdown. "I—"

Motion at the door stalled her voice in her throat as Pavo walked in wearing a rogue's grin. Two steps past the door, he froze, staring. Priya edged backward without a word as he approached the bed, one arm extended. His fingertips brushed her cheek and lifted her chin. The adoring look on his face caused tears to gather in her eyes.

She offered a weak smile. "Surprise…"

"Beautiful…" He stared at her for another minute in silence.

Risa looked down at her lap. "I'm an idiot. I never should've let them—"

He pressed his thumb into her lips. "Regret is a futile burden; to worry about that which you cannot change is to cast your heart into a bottomless pit."

She pulled his arm down, smiling despite having the sniffles. "Okay, fortune cookie. How do they look?"

"Perfect."

Every unshaven whisker on his face seemed to wave at her, the overhead lights gleaming on his forehead.

Risa squinted at him, stroking her fingers over his cheek. "You're so shiny and smooth."

"I see someone's found the narcoderms again." Pavo scooped her up in his arms.

"Not now." She leaned her head against his shoulder. "I've got a headache."

He chuckled, and set her on the edge of the Comforgel pad. "Seems you had a problem walking."

"Pain meds." She grabbed her clothes and glanced at Priya. "Am I okay to leave?"

"For the next four to six hours, you're legally impaired. Careful what you attempt to do." Priya seemed hesitant. "I suppose since you have someone to help you, there's no need to insist you stay here. Let me get Doctor Haltemeyer to sign off on your release."

Pavo presented his MDF badge. "I'll make sure she doesn't try to drive, operate any heavy equipment, or incite a rebellion in a small unaffiliated colony."

Risa laughed into a bundle of periwinkle blue cloth. The room spun when she tried to stand to get her leggings on.

"Whoa." Pavo caught her before she fell again. "Why don't we get a room nearby? You're in no condition for a shuttle ride for at least a few hours, and it's a tenth the cost of a hospital bunk."

"Sounds... fine." She again stared at him, tilting her head and marveling at the bright spot on his forehead. "You're... so... shiny."

He kissed the tip of her nose. "And you are quite high."

"I am high, but you're shiny because of pixels." She sat on the edge of the bed, limp and laughing at her rubbery arms while he dressed her like a toddler. "Or, no pixels. Something like that." She got a bad case of irresistible giggles.

Pavo put her boots on for her, then picked her up. Her chemically relaxed body curled against his warm chest without conscious thought.

"I'm glad you found me," she whispered.

For the first time in seven years, Risa Black closed *her* eyes.

8

THREAT NEUTRALIZED

R isa looked up and pulled her hair off her face. Stark naked, she sat in the aisle seat on what appeared to be a Maglev monorail, rushing along without a sound. Around her, morning commuters went about their business, not one giving her so much as a second glance. Blood rushed to her face while she covered herself with her hands as best she could. Murmurs of indistinct conversations surrounded her, single words leapt out clear every so often: meeting, finance, budget, coffee, sales quotas... nothing about a nude woman. Risa cringed in on herself, paralyzed with dread as though the slightest motion would cause everyone to notice her all at once.

She kept her head down until the tram stopped an agonizing few minutes later. Bodies shuffled in and out via five pairs of doors. Risa shivered in her seat, mortified, unable to will herself to break and run for the safety of the terminal platform. She stared helpless as the doors closed and the tram resumed travel. A pudgy man in a dark-brown coat approached her, gesturing at the window seat two spaces away.

"Excuse me, Miss."

Risa gawked up at him. Without a word, she shifted her legs to the right so he could move past. He smiled, seeming oblivious to her lack of clothing. As soon as he sat and settled in, he took out his NetMini and lost himself in the screen. She looked at him for a few minutes, waiting for the subtle tilt of the wrist that gave away him taking a picture of her, but he didn't.

She pondered the bizarre non-reaction of everyone around her until the next stop, where she summoned the nerve to get up. No one in the crowd pressing in from all sides so much as gave her a second glance. As soon as her foot touched the terminal floor, the tram doors snapped closed behind her, blasting her with a gust of warm air that pushed her forward a step and blew her hair over her shoulders. Before she could turn to look back, the tram blurred off into a tube.

I've got to be dreaming. I can't remember how I got on the train.

Risa continued trying to cover herself, but no one on the platform seemed to care. Perhaps they'd all become numb to it because of the 'neko' cyber fad—people who took the cat cyberware thing too far. Some didn't bother with clothes. Even if full blown nudity had become an avant garde fashion trend society begrudgingly tolerated, there should have been at least *one* pervert checking her out. Unease bubbled in her gut as she walked across the PubTran station, pulled by an inexplicable urge. Aside from the occasional grumble of annoyance as someone darted around her, she may as well have been invisible.

The beckoning feeling led her to an escalator bank, and up to a twenty-meter-long flat space before another set of escalators continued. To the left against the wall, a group of street urchins played electronic music while begging for handouts. She watched them for a moment, finding them *too* familiar.

Kree and Kyle both operated flashing devices part keyboard part computer while singing into little microphone booms. Behind them, Sam and Brett coaxed haunting music out of elaborate rigs far too expensive to be theirs. A pair of six-year-olds and a pair of ten-year-olds, the youngest four children from the mine she'd almost destroyed. Risa wiped her eyes. *I'm dreaming.* When she looked at them again, a slim woman in ballistic stealth armor and waist-length black hair strolled up to them, approaching an upturned box labeled 'food please,' as if to drop in a tip. Not-Risa withdrew a compact bomb from her coat, armed it, and tossed it in. All four children smiled at the false version of her. The evil woman peered over her shoulder at Risa, tiny dots of bright violet at the center of shiny steel eyes. She winked, and sauntered off into the crowd.

No! screamed Risa in her head. She wanted to run and save them, but the air had become dense syrup she could barely move in. All the people on the platform behind her stopped walking and stared at her. Their eyeballs leapt out of their skulls, flying toward her with little wiggling strands of optic nerve behind them.

She screamed and fought her way through the bizarre thick air to the box, sliding to a halt on her knees. As soon as she grabbed the bomb, it melted into a wad of sticky, black goo. Risa pulled her hands apart, but the tarlike mass stuck to her skin. It crept up her arms, swimming over her shoulders and down her body, solidifying into a sinister version of her stealth suit that tried to squeeze the air out of her. Unable to breathe, Risa rolled over backward and stared up at the ceiling. False Kree kept on singing, oblivious to her.

"Risa?" yelled Chaia. The too-cute-to-be-real tween with the piercing blue eyes and platinum blonde bob appeared at the top of the second escalator, waving. "This way."

The armored suit ceased crushing her. Air flowed into her lungs and she tumbled to her feet. A mass of disembodied hovering eyeballs hung like a curtain behind her, every one of them watching, every one of them judging.

Despite knowing she dreamed, Risa couldn't walk away and leave the grimy not-Kree busking for food. After Chaia called for her again, she forced herself to walk away. The curtain of eyes pivoted to follow her, radiating scorn that she'd dare think of taking Kree. Those people thought themselves better than her, thought Kree should die on the street rather than be with Risa. Their toxic derision made something snap inside her.

"No!" shouted Risa at the eyes, sprouting claws. "She's *mine!*"

The eyes scattered, swarming around each other in their haste to get away and fly down the first escalator. Relieved, Risa spun toward the children, but only empty instruments remained.

"Come on, Risa!" shouted Chaia from the top of the second escalator.

Bewildered, she turned in place for a few seconds before stepping onto the moving steps. Chaia waved to her from the top of the stairs before giggling and running out of sight. Risa stood still, riding the escalator up to a plain steel cube of a room. It had no furniture, doors, or windows. The only way out appeared to be a small square opening centered on the far wall at ground level. She glanced over her shoulder, but the escalator to the tram terminal had vanished, replaced by a solid wall. With nowhere else to go, she crept across toward the hole.

A sudden breeze over bare skin startled her. Her armor had vanished. She gazed down at her nine-year-old body clad in only a set of child's underpants—the same pair she'd worn to bed the night Andriy Voronin died, and for months after. As if on autopilot, she padded across the room and squatted to peer into the vent opening.

"No. This isn't right." Her childish voice echoed in the metal chamber. She placed a hand over her flat chest. "I don't want this anymore. There's no going home." Risa stared at her reflection, a blurry smear of white on the burnished plastisteel over the vent tunnel. "I know what's waiting at the other end…"

Fire.

She shivered at the remembered smell of a man's flesh burning, and curled in a ball.

"That one will do," said Raziel.

Risa's head snapped up. The robe-clad figure of her pseudo-angel appeared near the middle of the room, white-feathered wings resplendent in an otherworldly glow. General Maris stood at his side, a manic look in his eyes. He raised a three-pronged pincer attached to a pistol grip.

"Hello, sweetie," said Maris. "You have such beautiful eyes."

Risa leapt to her feet and tried to run, but black snake-like tendrils shot out of the walls and wrapped about her arms and legs. General Maris loomed over her as the cords tightened about her little body, holding her immobile against the freezing metal wall. He placed a hand on the top of her head, thumbed her left eyelid open, and held the evil pistol-shaped machine up to her face. The blade-tipped prongs edged closer and closer to her eyeball. She struggled, but couldn't escape the black cords tying her down.

"Trust me, child. You'll thank us for this."

"No!" Risa screamed as she snapped awake.

Covered in sweat, she curled on her side in bed, her arms crossed defensively over her face. It took her brain a few seconds to accept that a giant General Maris wasn't towering over her with eye-gouging claws. Shaking, she gasped for air.

One thing the dream had gotten correct: naked. She clasped her hands to her chest and tried to rein in her breathing. Her surroundings appeared to be a middle-of-the-road hotel suite. A short distance to her right, tall vertical blinds blocked off what she assumed to be an outdoor patio. A long, low cabinet beyond the foot of the bed held a holo-bar, food reassembler, and her neatly folded clothes wrapped in plastic.

The large Comforgel pad had enough room for two, and the other side looked slept in.

"Pavo?" She glanced left, at the short hallway leading to the exit door. Halfway between the room and the exit, a bathroom sat dark and empty. "Pavo?"

She listened to silence for a little while before sliding her legs out from under the blankets. At her motion, a palm-sized, round black device on the night table chirped and projected a holographic version of Pavo's face. Next to it, two-inch holographic numbers floated over a tiny silver bar: 10:08 a.m.

She'd slept thirteen hours

"Hey, beautiful," said the recorded message. "I'm really sorry I'm not there. Captain Vasquez didn't give me much choice. I had to report in to the Defense Force office in Elysium. I... didn't want to cause any uncomfortable questions for you, so I figured it would be best if I not put up a fight. I sent your clothes out to ReadyKleen. Call me when you wake up. Don't panic if I can't answer. We have to shut off our personal devices while on duty." Holo-Pavo winked. "I love you, Risa."

The message playback stopped with Pavo's holographic face frozen on a permanent smile. Flecks of dust in the air shimmered as they glided through his face. She set her elbows on her knees and braced her head in her hands. The headache had faded to a painful memory, though whenever she moved her eyes, a trace of soreness in the muscles remained.

She stood, stretched, and walked around the bed to the cabinet. As soon as she stopped looking at the emitter, Holo-Pavo disappeared with a flicker. Her NetMini sat next to the wrapped clothes, boots on the floor nearby. Two taps of a finger unlocked it, and she selected Pavo's contact information.

Connecting...

"Hi, this is Pavo Aram. I'm unable to answer at the moment. Please leave a message. If this is an emergency, tap this link"—a holographic finger entered the frame, pointing at a spot where a bright red button appeared—"to contact the MDF."

Beep.

"Hey, it's me. I'm awake. Gonna grab a shower. I'll try again in a few minutes."

Risa set the NetMini down and wandered into the dark bathroom. The lights came on automatically, the room flashing blinding white in an instant. Risa caught a glimpse of herself in the mirror and froze, hands over her mouth to stifle the gasp. Deep jade-green eyes stared back at her. She'd gone from some terrifying steel-eyed specter to a vision of near-innocence. Faint bruising circled both eyes in a raccoon mask.

She leaned close, the tip of her nose an inch from the glass, and stared into her reflection. Any hesitance or regret she'd had at having them put back in evaporated. *I did it. I'm really free...* Once the magic waned, the sticky sweat from an awful dream pulled her into the shower tube.

As the water started, pop-ups on the in-tube console offered additional perfume or hair conditioning options (at an extra fee, billable to the room). She surrendered to a bit of whimsy, and opted for a honeysuckle and coconut body wash for Ȼ35.

Fifteen minutes later, a dry and relaxed Risa stretched out on the bed, NetMini in hand. She dialed Pavo again. This time he answered, even though he probably shouldn't have by regulations. His bust appeared hovering over the device in hologram, red MDF armor on his shoulders.

"You look amazing." He winked. "I was in the middle of a medical evaluation when you called last time."

"Guess you passed if you're in uniform." She smiled, and tilted the NetMini enough so he could tell she didn't have anything on. "Is everything okay?"

The background scenery blurred as he twisted in a rapid turn. "I'm out in public. They've got us on a 'low-impact' security detail for a little while. Aurelia insisted on returning to active duty. Says she's fine despite what happened to her. With both of us being targeted, captain's being cautious for the time being."

"You didn't tell me if you're okay or not." Risa found the look on his face amusing. "I haven't unwrapped my clothes yet."

He gave her a longing stare. "I'll be off by 16:00. Another perk of the readjustment period—normal hours. Where can I find you?"

She stretched. "I'm going to try and pick Kree up and bring her to your place if that's okay."

"That's not okay." He shook his head.

Risa blinked. "What?"

"Calling it *my* place. Consider it ours." He grinned for a second before glancing to his left. "Crap. Shoplifter. Gotta go."

"Ass." She muttered, after he ended the call.

She let her arm flop on the pillow over her head, NetMini still in hand. *Bringing her outside the safehouse is going to be a project.* Eyes closed, Risa idly scratched at her stomach as the last traces of shower dampness faded into the air. *The longer I cave in and let her stay there, the harder it's going to be to get her out.*

The door hissed open. Risa suppressed the urge to yelp and scrambled under the blankets as a figure in a long, white coat walked in. Shiro halted at where the short corridor ended, and glanced to the side until she'd covered herself. He approached the edge of the bed, eyes hidden behind dark glasses, a trace of a smile on his lips. She couldn't help but notice the distortion in the lay of his coat that gave away the presence of a katana.

"I was not expecting you to be so... comfortable."

Her cheeks warmed. "Do you always just walk into random hotel rooms, or should I feel special?"

"You weren't answering. I wasn't sure where they'd sent you off to. I've been worried."

She pressed herself into the Comforgel pad, hands together, holding the blanket at her chin. *Everett was going to deal with him... Worried my ass. Shit, he's evaded them and come to kill me.* An attempt to call Pavo with her implanted comm ended with his 'busy at work' message. *He'd never make it here in time.* She stared down at her blanket-covered hands, wondering when she'd become so small and terrified, wanting Pavo to come rescue her. Pavo, the same man only months before she could've killed without a second thought. Indignation stirred deep down, but if Shiro possessed anywhere near the same skills as the operator from Arden settlement, even her old self wouldn't be able to take him without ambushing him unaware.

She felt naked in every sense of the word.

"I... uhh... It was a rescue op. UCF Military holding facility. Sneak in and out. Pretty easy really... almost like they wanted us to get away."

Shiro chuckled and clasped his hands behind his back. "I'd heard you'd gone to Bliss. Garrison didn't seem to think you planned on coming back. You can understand my concern."

"A-at the time, I... guess I didn't." Random images of the man from Arden came and went, along with remembered bruises. When she'd been armed and armored, he'd made her feel defenseless, as well as inept at hand to hand combat. A sour malaise settled in her stomach. *I've gotta get him off his guard.* She forced herself to lower her arms and sat up, hoping he didn't notice the stiffness of her motions. "It's been hard coping with everything."

Shiro glanced at the carpet for a few seconds before reaching up to remove his glasses. He folded them with one hand and slipped them into a breast pocket on his faux-leather coat. "What have you done to yourself?"

Risa drew her legs underneath her, keeping her body hidden from the waist down by the blanket. *That's it. Stare at my tits. Get closer.* "What do you mean?"

"You upgraded your eyes?" He smiled, and reached across the bed to caress her cheek. "They're so close to the same color you were born with. Stunning."

His touch sent a tingle across her jawline and down her spine, but not the same warm tingle she got from Pavo. She suppressed the need to squirm. "I found them." *Shit, he knows. Play his ego.* "You were right, Shiro. Raziel is a load of dustblow... he's not an angel; he's a synthetic. I feel so stupid for listening to him. He found my real eyes, and took them off the market."

"You look so innocent. You could pass for eighteen again. Such a pity." He let his arm fall.

She thought of Pavo, bored at work and desperate for his shift to end so they could be together. Picturing what this room would look like when Pavo found her body, she clutched her fingers into the bedding. Every muscle locked with fear. *He's toying with me.* Air rushed in and out of her lungs, breasts heaving. She had Pavo back... she had Kree... she had a father again. *No! Not now.* The urge to end him where he stood battled with the hope he might not have shown up to start a fight she couldn't win. If she made a move, and failed, she'd be killing herself. *They made this sound so easy... show some skin, get in bed, kill. Why isn't it working?* She couldn't suppress a tremble. "I'm out, Shiro. I quit. I can't do it anymore."

"You look so innocent." He caressed her face again, slid his hand under her chin, and traced the back of his knuckles up the other cheek.

She lifted her head, trying to act interested in having him touch her.

"Risa..." Shiro sighed. "Innocent girls don't lie."

Her heart almost stopped, feeling like a lead weight in her chest. She couldn't tell if he had armor on under the coat, not that it would matter... her Nano claws would tear through almost anything shy of hardened plastisteel, and that would stop them only due to her lack of physical strength. His stance gave away his tension; he expected a strike. As soon as she moved, it would be a duel of speedware.

"The worst part about having someone to care for…" Shiro lowered his arm and took a half step back. "…is being afraid to die."

She flattened her fingers—a gesture he took note of. The sides of his coat opened, powered MolWeave strips splitting to reveal the grips of a pair of handguns on his belt, though he made no attempt to grab for them.

"I know what your mission was." She locked stares with him. Her tactical computer presented only two paths for attack. All the gleaming golden graphics appeared like glass threads, mesmerizing and beautiful. With each inch further away he edged, her odds of survival dropped by eight or nine percent. Risa worked her right foot into the bedding, trying to find a solid brace she could use to kick off into a leap.

Shiro rendered a slight bow, the kind a superior gives an underling. "It seems we both have our secrets. If you wish to dress, I will not stop you."

Risa tensed. "I've got a thirty-one-percent chance of survival right now. If I walk across the room to my clothes, that drops to nothing. I'm more comfortable naked. Hope you don't mind."

He smiled. "Not at all."

She narrowed her eyes. "Ral Narim… the man Walsh sent me to kill. You did it."

"Yes. I am aware of how you feel about assassinations. When I saw an opportunity to resolve your obligation to the Syndicate and spare you guilt, I took it." He sighed out his nose. "You may not believe this, but I do care for you."

Risa kept eye contact and pulled the blanket away. *Last thing I need is this thing tangling me up.* He showed no outward reaction as she extended her left leg forward, hooked her heel on the edge of the Comforgel pad, and pulled herself over. She faced him, left foot on the bed, knee beside her head. A solid foundation to spring from. Shiro's blasé demeanor softened; the full-frontal view must have worked.

"Got an 'elf' a few years ago." Risa winked, hoping her calling attention to permanent nanosurgery to remove all body hair below the waist would cause a fatal distraction. She shifted, lowering her right leg while leaving it wide enough to give him a good look. "Life's too short to waste time shaving, especially in my line of work."

"Risa. Do you want to kill me?" His gaze seemed to take her in entirely, not zeroed on any one part.

His question stalled her. The breath she'd taken and held in preparation to leap at him leaked between her teeth. At a hint he might not be there to give her 'two to the head,' she thought back to his bringing her blind ass to the hospital. It had felt different from when Pavo carried her. Shiro thought her a delicate flower in need of protection. Everything he did hinged on *obtaining* her. It didn't feel like love. Or at least, not the way Pavo loved her, a companion and equal.

"You tried to kill the man I love." Her tone came out sad, rather than angry. "I've wasted so much of my life on revenge. So many years, all that drove me was the need to find the person who'd killed my father. Then I discovered he wasn't who I thought him to be. The UCF hadn't killed one of their own. As soon as I came to terms with that, as soon as I hoped this world might allow me to be happy, I thought Pavo dead. And I started right back down that road." She stared at the wall for a few seconds. "Maybe it's twisted of me or maybe I'm afraid, but I don't really feel like killing you."

Shiro drifted to the left, turning his back as he approached her clothing. He gathered the packets, and threw them one by one, like Frisbees, onto the bed. Thinking them a distraction for a bullet in the head if she broke eye contact, she ignored them.

He held the last packet, staring down at it, flicking at the corner of the plastic. "Your body language says you want to."

"What I want right now is not to die."

He tossed the packet onto the bed next to her, still with his back to her.

Maybe he can't do it if I'm looking at him. "I guess I'm not feeling suicidal. The operator at Arden would have killed me if not for Raziel. You got what you came for. I'm out of the MLF. A non-threat. You tried to have Pavo killed. I don't want revenge; I want the life I never got to have." She glanced at the square of periwinkle-blue fabric beneath a transparent plastic veil. A frosted watermark of a smiling delivery bot with a ReadyKleen logo adorned the center of the package. "If anything happens to Kree, there—"

He raised a hand. "Only a weak man harms a child."

Relief came on with a slight slouch.

"Old men, on the other hand." He shook his head.

She leapt to her feet, tears gathering in her eyes. "Why? You're all working for the same bosses. This is completely insane."

Shiro moved his hands nearer to his pistols, spinning to face her.

"Garrison is going to run out of usefulness, eventually. Sooner if he cannot follow orders. Once Maris has been removed, it will be on him."

Risa advanced two steps, pointing at him. "Orders to blow up our own citizens aren't legitimate. Your bosses are as bad as the Corporates. What the fuck are you doing? Fighting for greed? What happened to defending our nation? Command knows you deviated from your mission parameters on a personal project." She moved closer. "You wanted me broken. You thought you could glue the pieces back together and have me."

His arm blurred, pointing a gun at her heart. "My mission parameters were to assess your intentions, and if necessary, remove you as a threat. I didn't want to kill you. I didn't want to fall in love with you either, but I did."

She kept walking closer until the cold tip of his pistol pressed into the skin between her breasts. Risa leaned up on her toes, pressing herself against the weapon. "I'm no threat to you, or your bottom-feeding masters back on Earth. Your mission is over. Go home, Shiro... or whatever your real name is."

His deep chocolate-brown eyes seemed to vibrate in his skull. The venom in her last few words reduced his determined glare to a defeated expression. He pushed her back a half step with the gun, and lowered it. She settled flat on her feet, still leaning at him. A red mark remained on her skin, molded in the shape of the barrel.

Risa trembled, more from adrenaline than fear, and raised her arms out and wide. "This is me. Naked in front of you in every sense of the word. I know the MLF is a load of dustblow set up by C-Branch for plausible deniability. I'm tired of the killing. I love Pavo. There's a child who thinks I'm her own personal superhero. I wanted to set the people of Mars free from a corrupt government that murders its own citizens. Not one of the people gave a shit. The NewsNet made them see us as the enemy. We were doomed from the start, weren't we? As soon as they didn't need us any more, all the protection we got from the law would go away. Another feel-good moment to fool the masses. Once the ACC fell, we'd be 'caught,' sit through a mockery of a trial, and probably executed as traitors live on pay-per-view video. That girl's the only person who's ever made me feel like I made a difference. I can't be part of this crazy world of backstabbing and shadows and bombs and lies anymore."

Shiro slipped his sidearm back into the gap in the coat. "You think you can have a normal life? Kids, nice apartment, maybe an office job... the whole nine?"

"If things had been different. If I'd never met Pavo..."

"You two could be over each other in a year." He showed a little hope with a half-smile.

"I suppose it's possible, but doubtful." Risa relaxed, backing up until she bumped into the bed. She fumbled behind her for the plastic, and tore open the package containing her top.

"It's a nice dream, but you'll never enjoy it."

She held her breath, risking the loss of eye contact long enough to pull the garment on. The attached skirt covered about a third of her thighs. It wasn't armor, but it felt like it. "I think I will."

He trudged to the hallway leading to the door, and paused. "Every time you take that little girl out somewhere, you'll always be looking over your shoulder, wondering who might be following you, wondering if she's going to watch you eat a bullet. Every time Pavo goes to work, you'll wonder if today's the day he doesn't come home." Shiro tilted his head. "Well, I suppose that would be true for any MDF officer."

"Is that a threat?" She straightened her fingers, claws a synapse-spark away from erupting.

He lifted his head, a look of sorrow on his face. "No. It's the skeleton The Life leaves sitting in your closet that you can never be rid of. The ACC, Benton Mining Corporation, extremist 'patriot groups' who view the MLF as terrorists... you've made a lot of enemies. How many of them do you think will let you traipse off into the sunset?"

Shiro stared down at his boots for a long few seconds, then drifted out, silent as a ghost.

The squeak of the automatic door closing seemed as loud as a thunderstorm. Could Shiro be right? Should she grab Kree and Pavo and run off to some far-away place on Mars no one could ever find them? She lowered herself to sit on the edge of the bed, staring at her porcelain-white feet against the dark-blue carpet. After a few minutes, she rolled to her left and crawled onto the bed in a fetal position. Adrenaline faded, leaving her shaking and struggling to swallow bile.

Once she gathered her composure, she shoved herself upright and pulled on her leggings. *What if he couldn't do it? His team might be coming. I have to get out of here!* She threw the NetMini into her purse, grabbed her boots, and ran barefoot to the elevator, putting them on only after she started the descent to the main floor.

The elevator chimed, doors opened to a calm lobby with a handful of Earth tourists—and no sign of Shiro. *He's playing with my head.* She strode across the cavernous room of maroon tiles and marble-inlay columns, into the simulated summer warmth of Arcadia City's outdoors. Tall buildings surrounded her; six or seven blocks to the right, a spread of green trees broke up the silver and glass with a sizable park. Any of ten thousand possible hiding places for snipers.

Risa pressed a hand to her face, chilled by the horrible thought he'd been right.

9

QUALITY TIME

A squeak emanated from the door as Risa pushed it aside, revealing her soon-to-be-former room on Death Row. She expected Maris or Lieutenant Kendrick would've given her lip about not clearing it out yet, but it's not as if the MLF had people lined up waiting for a spot on demolition detail. Perhaps news of her change of status hadn't been made open knowledge yet. Her vacating the room would invariably trigger questions Maris might not want to answer.

She stepped in, finding Kree sprawled on the floor, scissoring her legs while drawing on a large white 'paper' projected on the floor by a device sitting on the edge of the desk. The girl's hardened glare evaporated with a gasp. She sprang to her feet, tears streaming from her eyes, and ran into a hug. Risa knelt, her arms wrapped around the trembling child. *Every time I go 'outside,' she worries I won't come back.* Risa swallowed hard.

"Hey, kiddo. Sorry for taking so long. What are you drawing?"

"Speeware," mumbled Kree. She led her by the hand to the middle of the room and flopped back on her stomach by the drawing.

The child traced a silver stylus around a crude human figure she no doubt meant to be Risa: boxy legs and body filled in with zigzags of black, a circle for a head with long hair in wavy squiggles and two purple spots for eyes. Massive blue lines streamed from the figure's circle-hands, Nano claws taller than the stick figure wielding them.

Bodies, cut clear in half, littered the area. The child drew in a smaller version of Risa, also with claws, standing behind her.

Kree glanced back and up at her, and pointed at the drawing. "That's you."

Risa eased the door closed behind her, dimming the light from the corridor outside. Her ballistic suit rattled on a hanger as she brushed past it to sit behind the girl. Kree held the stylus up and said, "colors," which caused a palette to scroll open in midair. She poked the tip into a square of deep red, and resumed drawing—adding blood to the dismembered figures, coloring with such energy her body shook from the side-to-side motion of her arm. Flecks of black glitter in the girl's gauzy skirt glinted in the light from the projector.

Lines around the scene, meaningless before, changed in Risa's perception into the basic suggestion of a subterranean corridor. A phallic shape sticking out of the ground near the left edge became a PubTran podium. *Is this what she thinks would've happened if those thugs attacked me instead of her mother?* Risa put a hand on Kree's head. *What am I supposed to say to this?*

"You're pretty good at drawing. What's happening?" She tried to sound cheerful and interested.

Kree's arm moved faster, grinding the red into the picture as her lips curled in an angry sneer. "The bad people tried to hurt you."

Risa lowered herself onto her stomach, lying next to her. "You've got claws too. Did you help?"

Her rage faltered. Kree sat still for a little while in silence, then shrugged. "No. I wanted to be scary so they didn't try an' hurt me."

Risa leaned on her elbows, watching as Kree switched to a dull grey-blue, and filled in the walls, outlining what appeared to be the entryway of a store. She switched to black again, adding crude figures in the window. *It happened near a clothing store. Maybe it got caught on cameras. Pavo might— Oh, what am I doing? I'm not going to hunt down random gang thugs.* "I won't let anyone hurt you."

"I know," said Kree.

Risa stared at the childish rendition of such a gory scene, unsure if she should try to distract the child from that memory or talk about it more. *She's opening up in her own way.* "I have bad dreams too."

Kree looked up, mouth open as if to speak. For ten seconds, she stared, gaping, and emitted a startled shriek. "Your eyes!"

When the crying started, Risa pulled her close, rocking and whispering reassuring things until the wailing subsided. "What's wrong?"

"You broke it," whined Kree. "You broke your speeware."

"I've still got my speeware." Risa grinned, activated her neural wiring and tickled her all over.

Kree quieted. After a few stuttering post-cry breaths, she giggled and squirmed. "Why did you get green?"

"These are the eyes I was born with. Raziel had them." She pushed herself up to sit on the floor. "They're real, not electronic."

Kree crawled into her lap, staring close. "Can you still see in the dark?"

"If I have a headset on, yes."

"I guess they're okay. The purple was prettier."

Risa laughed, and ruffled her hair. "I have to ask you something important."

"I wanna stay with you." Kree pouted. "The boys all think you're creepy and weird, but I don't. Garson said you're scared you won't be good as a mom, but... but..." She broke into sniffles.

The projector's light cast harsh shadows on the little face staring up at her; Kree seemed to be fighting hard not to lapse into uncontrolled bawling.

"He's right, but my real fear is that I'd go out there one day and get hurt... and I didn't want you to go through that again."

"But you can't get hurt!" Kree leapt into a hug. "You're a speeware." She sniveled. "I mean, you got speeware."

Risa patted her on the back. *I'm not the only one. C-Branch operator with ten years of combat experience + speedware = Risa in a box.* "I'm not gonna do that anymore, okay? I would rather look after you."

Kree smiled for a moment, before crying more.

Risa rocked her. "I don't want you to stay down here. These people are like my family, but it's too dangerous here for a little girl."

"I don't wanna go outside." Kree's eyes glazed over. She curled fetal and stuck her thumb in her mouth, trembling. "Don' wanna."

Shit. Uhh, now what? "Okay... okay... not yet." *Dammit, I can't keep caving in.* "Shh. You're safe, kiddo. No one is going to hurt you."

"I don' wanna go outside. The bad people are outside." She cuddled tighter against Risa's chest. "Please don't make me."

How much would it cost to fly Chaia back here to make her forget? Risa leaned forward, touching heads. *Don't be silly. Be a parent.*

Kree whined.

Okay, it won't hurt to wait another day or two. Maybe Gen has an idea how to deal with this. "Okay. Wanna play *Space Rabbitz?*"

"No." Kree sat up, frowning. Aside from the tears still running down her cheeks, she looked irritated rather than scared. "*Colony Commando. Space Rabbitz* is too cute."

"But the rabbits have giant missile launchers and grenades and swords."

Kree folded her arms. "They're cartoons. It's a stupid game 'cause you can't die. It's made for little-little kids."

"*Colony Commando* it is."

Risa shut off the art projector and pulled her Yume Koujou game console out from under the floordrobe. Kree put on her visor helmet while Risa used the screen of a fifty-inch holo-bar. She would've plugged in direct, but didn't want to abandon her awareness of the world. Even here, she couldn't let her guard down.

Soon, two overbearing caricatures of the 'grizzled space commando' descended on an alien-infested colony world and set to the task of committing gratuitous animated violence on bug-like enemies.

She scooted over to use the bed as a seat back, and Kree tucked in against her right side. Despite the game's complexity (power and ammo management, as well as each soldier having to constantly adjust command settings for a support bot), Kree held her own. *This kid's going to be a techie from hell.* She blinked. *Shit. I never even thought about school.*

A beep in her head preceded the words 'Inbound Call' rendering in midair. Without the pixilation of cybereyes, the feed directed into her visual cortex made the letters appear as if they'd been carved from solid amber.

The system didn't give her the chance to decline; after one beep, the face of General Everett appeared. Super high resolution made him eerie, as if his real floating head and shoulders had appeared in the room with her.

<General...> Risa spoke to him with a thought, but kept her attention focused on the screen so her space commando didn't die.

<Apologies for the sudden break in. I know this is an unlisted head.> He grinned. <I wanted to give you an update.>

"Grenades!" yelled Kree. "Got a bad guy behind that rover."

<Go ahead, General.> Risa had never been big on video games, and using a handheld controller made her reaction time even slower. She managed to get a grenade over the top of a flipped six-wheeler, but took

three hits doing it. Kree guided her soldier over and administered 'first aid,' which added quite a bit of green back to her life bar.

"You're not very good at this," said Kree. "Gotta keep behind cover."

General Everett cleared his throat. <I've been working from the back end to stall the DMI. That's the Director of Military Intelligence, General Deirdre Murray.>

<Damn Earther.> Risa scowled. "Cover me, kiddo." Her commando sprinted from cover and jumped over a cluster of broken tires. Energy 'bullets' from the alien soldiers too stupid to duck Kree's suppressive fire whistled by. Controlling a character who didn't have speedware sucked. The child killed three of four before her ammo ran out.

<Yes, yes. General Murray is originally from Earth. There's too much paranoia about Martian Independence to let anyone born there rise high up the ranks yet. Anyway, I've managed to get some good news at least. General Murray is not the cause of our problems, it's a Senator.>

Risa cringed. <You said good news. That sounds like a shitstorm of interplanetary proportions.>

<Well, it is, but it's also good in a way.> Everett smiled. <I don't have to ask you to assassinate a standing military officer.>

<Oh, and sending me off to kill a Senator is better? I already told you. I am *not* an assassin.>

Everett chuckled. The amount of grey in his short afro seemed to have tripled since their last meeting. <I'm not going to split the semantics with you. Silenced weapon at close range or a bomb from a safe distance. Six of one... Anyway, in the meantime, I am suppressing requests from filtering down channel to your unit for strikes.>

"My turn!" yelled Kree. "Cover me. Imma run to the trench and blow up the glowy thing."

Risa hit the button to make her soldier stand, and fired her plasma rifle in the general direction of enemy troops. The AI was good enough to duck behind nearby objects, making suppressive fire a useful tactic. Kree's blue-armored space commando vaulted a portable barricade and landed in a metal-walled trench. As soon as Kree's avatar was safe, Risa followed.

<I told Garrison I'm not interested in planting bombs for the Front anymore. I want off the roster. Civilian. Even if the strings are pulled from Earth, the UCF isn't so bad... plus, human settlement on Mars isn't developed enough to survive total war.>

Another six-wheeled rover came speeding around the corner of a distant building, coming to bear on them with a pair of lasers that fired long-duration beams. Risa swapped weapons to a rocket launcher as big as her character, wishing this 'inventory' thing worked in the real world. Her missile went short, but detonated in the ground close enough to flip the vehicle up so its nose pointed skyward. She fired a second missile into the undercarriage, destroying it in one shot.

"Cool!" yelled Kree. "You know the secret. Takes four missiles to kill 'em if you don't do that."

"Good thing I got lucky." She winked, though Kree couldn't see her with the visor on.

Everett's lips turned downward in a grim frown. <I'd like to be able to assure you that walking away from it all will be possible. Technically, you and your people aren't on the roster as active duty, with the exception of General Maris and Colonel Tanais.>

<Garrison's still active duty?>

<Yes,> said Everett, chuckling. <I understand where you're coming from, but you have to accept that you—as well as everyone else associated with the Front—are in a precarious position, both legally and politically. If the wrong side wins the argument behind closed doors, you're terrorists. All that protection you've enjoyed goes away.>

RISA'S GRIP ON THE CONTROLLER TIGHTENED. NAVIGATING A NARROW metal trench where turret guns popped out of the walls at random intervals didn't help her nerves. She yelped in surprise when a second gun sprang out and nailed her. Out of health points, her commando crumpled to the ground. Kree blasted the turret, walked over, and crouched. Her avatar waved a white rectangle with a green plus on it back and forth over Risa's 'dead' character.

"You're gonna need to get better at this game," said Kree.

"Yeah." Risa glanced at Everett. "I guess I am." <Can I trust Maris... or Garrison?>

Everett wiped a hand over his mouth, then tapped a finger on his chin for a moment. <Maris is a good man. He has refused any order to strike a friendly civilian target. He's also ducked a few requests to hit so-called 'low-value' military targets command was willing to sacrifice for 'the greater good.'>

<You mean propaganda. Or scaring the Senate into approving more money for military operations on Mars. What about Garrison?>

<Colonel Tanais is a former APSE intelligence commander, ex-Delta

soldier... He retired, but Maris handpicked him and brought him back. That's all I know. I haven't seen anything to cast doubt on him.> Everett raised his greying eyebrows. <Are you wondering because he killed your father?>

Risa smiled. <No, General. Colonel Tanais *is* my father. He didn't even know.>

Everett coughed, near to choking. <What?>

<Serena Var was my mother. Garrison met her while doing black ops on Earth, Central America. They got married only three months before she caught the assignment to watch Voronin. I must've been conceived a week or so before she started.>

<That's...> General Everett scowled. <You were going to carve me up like a turkey because you thought I ordered the death of a man who wasn't even your father.>

Risa flashed a cheesy smile. <Sorry. I've been known to act before thinking sometimes.>

His seriousness shattered to laughter. <Suppose I got you back for that.>

<By making me think I was being carted off to my execution, or by not telling me you had Pavo alive?> She tapped her fingers on the controller while Kree's character hovered by an enormous machine of unknown type, 'planting a bomb.'

<Somewhere between the two, I suspect. Look. I'm not about to force you to carry out clandestine operations on enemy territory, *but*... if you want any chance at all of walking away from this in one piece, I am going to need your assistance with a *very* delicate matter.>

Risa sank in on herself. Could she bring herself to conduct a targeted killing? Ever since she'd gotten enough hardware to have people call her a *tí-zhèn*, everyone assumed her to be an assassin. The mere word made her blood boil. Of course, Everett did have a point. Her bombs had likely killed far more people than most 'assassins' ever murdered over their entire career. If it took one more death to buy peace and security for the people she loved... how could she say no to a single drop added to an ocean?

<I understand, sir. I'll await further orders.>

General Everett smiled. <Good to hear, Lieutenant. Keep your head down for the time being. I'll be in touch as soon as I can.>

His apparition faded, tricking her brain into seeing that part of the room darker for it. If only she knew who she could trust. Maybe a shuttle ticket for Chaia wouldn't be a bad idea after all. Having a mind reader along would make everything so much simpler. She wobbled her head side to side to match the rhythm of their virtual commandos tromping with heavy boots down a metal corridor inside the alien base. The repetitious *clank, clank, clank* of digital boots felt as though it tapped on her brain.

Damn. She sighed. *No. I can't drag another child into this mess. This fight is all mine.*

10

THE EYE OF THE STORM

At 6:10 a.m., Risa dragged herself up to the apartment door. Half an hour ago, her "I'm going to see Pavo, do you want to come?" elicited a calm "no" from Kree, but also a frightened stare. The child backed into the corner, as if expecting to be hauled bodily out of the safety of their room. Risa tried something new. She sighed, said "okay," and trudged out with an expression like her dog died.

Kree seemed caught off guard, but didn't follow.

Risa let herself in, not surprised, but also not comfortable with the sight of Genevieve and Aurelia entwined on the sofa bed in the living room. It felt too much like an invasion of their privacy. She shied away, hurrying past them to the hallway beyond. Being around Genevieve in the MLF shower room didn't bother her, but seeing her 'big sister' in a romantic context was an entirely different matter.

She crept up to the bedroom door and peeked in. Pavo lay at a diagonal across the king-sized Comforgel pad, arms splayed to the sides like a crime victim. Forest green satin covered him to the middle of the stomach. Light snoring escaped his open mouth.

After setting her coffee on the bureau, she shrugged out of her weapons harness and boots, then slipped off her ballistic suit. Nude, she crawled onto the bed and climbed over him, draping herself low enough to graze the tip of his morning erection. When she reached his face, she lowered her lips to his. He awoke in a few seconds, and smiled.

"I'm not supposed to be up 'til six thirty." He slid a hand over her cheek and gripped the back of her neck. "You look ready to pass out."

"Stayed up too late. I'm a horrible parent. We didn't crash until almost two."

He pulled her into another kiss, and rolled her to his left so they lay on their sides facing each other. "I want to wake up to this every morning for the rest of my life."

Risa's heart raced. She hated the phrase 'rest of his life,' as it could mean only minutes on a bad enough day. The idea brought immediate tears, but also a wide smile. "Can we stop making bets on your lifespan?"

He stroked her hair. "I can't get over how different you look."

"You lied." She smirked. "You wanted me to get them back."

"Guilty. I'm glad you made the choice on your own."

Risa flattened her palms on his chest and slid them up and over his shoulders. "I know. My body and everything." She narrowed her eyes. "Speaking of implants. There's something else I'm hoping to have put inside me."

"Bigger claws?" He cocked an eyebrow.

"You're either not awake yet or messing with me." She swatted at his head.

Pavo chuckled for a second before kissing her again. A moan escaped her as his lips pecked at her skin, tracing a path down over her neck to her sternum. Writhing, she arched her back as he circled a tongue around her nipple while sliding a hand up between her legs. Risa closed her eyes, surrendering to waves of ecstasy coursing through her. A good while later, when her breaths became short and rapid, he grasped her shoulder and pushed her onto her back. She cooed, expecting him to move on top, but shot him a mischievous glance as his arm slid under her. He drew her close against him, the coarse hair on his pectorals teased at her shoulder blades. With one arm across her chest, and their legs entwined, he entered her.

Risa gasped, floundered at the bedding for a few seconds before grabbing the forearm that held her tight to him. Her eyes clamped shut. Her toes curled. She let out a low, deep groan and shuddered. For a handful of perfect minutes, she flew free of all care, until a rush of pleasure locked every muscle in her body. She bit her lip, trying to stifle the moans so Gen didn't hear too much.

Once his gyrations slowed to a halt, he kissed the nape of her neck and dragged his beard stubble over her shoulder. She twisted around and kissed him again.

"Is this real?" Warmth spread over her face and chest. Worry pushed tears to the corners of her eyes. "Am I really here? Did I die on The Strand? Is... this all happening in the three-tenths of a second my brain has left?"

He made a contemplative face for a second, and pinched her nipple.

"Ow!" She curled up, covering her 'wounded' breast with both hands. Laughing and angry, she tried to jam a finger into his groin. "What the hell was that?"

Pavo caught her hand. "You're not dreaming."

She rubbed her breast, scowled at him a second longer, and snuggled against him. "I'm going to seek retribution for that at some point."

"Are you ever going to tell me what happened there?"

Risa stared at the black forest of hair spread over an arctic white chest an inch in front of her face. "You don't want me to."

"Almost got yourself killed?" He squeezed her.

"Yeah." She traced circles around the sheet with her finger. "I thought you were dead. Maris got orders from on high. They wanted someone to kick the Corporates in the balls where they'd never expect it. I'd been trying to hold on to the hope you might not really be dead, but everyone kept saying..." The lump in her throat grew too large to speak past.

He leaned up and put an arm around her. "Promise me you won't give up again, no matter what happens."

Her hand on the front of her neck, she nodded.

"I need to get ready for work." He rubbed her back for a minute or four before moving to get out of bed.

She grabbed his hand, doing her best attempt at a child's 'please don't go' stare. "I won't. Give up, I mean. The Front isn't going to last much longer."

Pavo pulled her into an embrace. "I got that feeling. The PVM isn't going anywhere, and I'm still loyal to them."

"You're..." She coughed. "Even after what they did to you?"

He cradled her face in both hands, smiling. "What did they do? They saved my life. Okay, being stuck in a tiny room for a few weeks, I could've done without, but I get why they did it."

She let her forehead thump into his shoulder. "I don't know who to trust anymore."

"Trust your instincts. You knew I wasn't dead." He patted her on the head. "I'm willing to see if their 'political change' methodology works... but we've got an actual foreign enemy to deal with before we try to change things internally."

A chill tickled at Risa's heart. She snapped her head up. "What if they don't really want to? What if the Corporates and the Senators are working together? Endless war for profit."

He blinked. "Whoa. You *have* been doing this too long. You're starting to spin conspiracies out of thin air. Some of the stuff I've heard makes that sound impossible."

She pushed him toward the bathroom. "You're going to be late."

"I'm going, I'm going." He jogged over to the autoshower.

They shared a wash, after which she plodded back to bed while he shaved.

Risa closed her eyes and listened to the sound of the e-razor humming. In what felt like a split second, his hand touching the side of her head woke her. He had his MDF duty armor on and smelled like cheap spray soap.

"Enjoy spending all day in bed." He winked.

She rolled her eyes. "I'm not. I'm going to spend the day trying to talk Kree into letting me bring her here."

"Okay." He stood and leaned back to stretch while glancing around. "I'm going to need a bigger place."

Pavo pulled the blanket up, tucked her in, and backed up to the door.

Three and change hours of sleep made her limbs feel leaden—and the pillow feel amazing.

11

GENEVIEVE

R isa's eyes peeled open, breaking a thick glue of crumbles. She forced herself from the bed to the shower at 9:28 a.m. Since she'd brought only her armor to wear, she ran the dry cycle twice to ensure no trace of moisture remained, and stepped out into a room cold enough to make her squeal. Compared to the bathroom, the air in the bedroom was arctic. She cringed, and slid a leg into the smooth, freezing suit. At the instant the crotch made contact, she sucked a breath between her teeth. Once the paralytic effect faded, she slid her arms in and sealed the MolWeave fastener up to her jawline.

Boots could wait a few minutes.

Risa padded to the kitchen, where Genevieve appeared to be well into a staring contest with the food reassembler, scratching her left calf with her right foot while drumming her fingers on the countertop.

"Hey," said Risa, heading for a chair at the table. "Dial me up some eggs?"

Genevieve straightened. "Why don't you do it? You know I have shitty luck with these things."

"They're still talking about the vindaloo incident." Risa changed course for the counter. "What did you want?"

"French toast." Genevieve took a seat at the squarish white table.

Pavo went economy. Everything in the place had been styled in 'postmodern bachelor' with a touch of Epoxilboard, the kind of furniture people had to put together themselves. She felt certain he had a drawer somewhere overflowing from all the leftover screws, grommets, and pegs. One chair still had its reference stickers, the ones they put on each piece in case someone bothered to look at the instructions.

The 'sem beeped as Risa selected French toast and inserted an empty plate. When she hit the 'start' button, a half-dozen metal spider legs inside whirred to life, 'printing' the breakfast out of molecularly reassembled OmniSoy protein strands. Before long, the smell of cinnamon filled the kitchen. While the machine worked, Risa used her implanted comm to order coffee from the nearest Morning Bean. 'Semmed food was one thing, but doing that to coffee constituted a crime against humanity.

Risa carried the plate of pseudo-French-toast to the table and set it in front of Genevieve. She raised an eyebrow at red lines around her friend's wrists. "What happened to your arm?"

"Perks of dating a cop. You should ask Pavo to try it sometime."

Risa shivered. The last time she'd made love to him before thinking he'd been killed, he'd held her down and taken her from behind. *That was scary enough... binders? No thanks.* "Uhh, I'll take your word for it. I'm really happy for you. The two of you make a great couple."

Genevieve blushed and smiled, sectioning off a piece of toast with her fork. "Thanks. She's been lonely for a long time."

"So have you." Risa returned to the 'sem and dialed up an omelet.

"What's bothering you?" Genevieve stabbed her fork into the little square of egg-saturated bread slathered in syrup, and raised a hunk of it to her mouth.

"I'm that transparent?" Risa contemplated if all that sugar would have the same effect being it had all been rearranged from OmniSoy, or if it would retain the same nutritional value as the beige slime from whence it had come.

"Please..." Genevieve smirked. "I'm practically your mother."

"Sure, if you had me when you were like eight." Risa took her breakfast from the machine and sat catty-corner at the kitchen table. "That works both ways, you know. Something's bothering you too."

"You first." Genevieve excised another bite of her meal with surgical precision.

Risa muddled through an explanation of Kree being terrified to leave the MLF safehouse, and her indecision regarding how to handle it. "I tried guilt this morning, but it didn't work."

"You could slip her something to knock her out? You know,

sometimes it's easier to ask for forgiveness than permission." Genevieve sopped up stray syrup around the edges of the plate with a square of French toast impaled on a fork. "From what you've been saying, a storm's coming. You need to get her out of there before something goes down."

"Pavo said the same thing." Risa shook her head. "I'm not doing that. She trusts me... not an easy thing for a kid in her situation. I'm not going to betray it."

"But it's in her best interest. You need to be her mom first, friend second. She might not see it that way now, but later on, when she's older—"

The doorbell rang. What little color existed in Genevieve's face evaporated.

"I ordered coffee. It's okay." Risa stood.

"Bring a weapon." Genevieve seemed ready to crawl under the table.

Risa held her hand up and waved her fingers as she walked out. "I *am* a weapon."

A cube-shaped delivery bot hovered outside, bearing the logo of Morning Bean: a cartoony man with glasses and 'electrocuted-Einstein' hair holding two enormous mugs. She retrieved her order without incident, and returned to the kitchen.

The redhead sniffed at the cup Risa put in front of her.

"Cinnamon spice latte."

"You remembered!" Genevieve seized it in both hands.

Risa finished off her omelet before it could melt back into goo. Her two-extra-shot cappuccino made the perfect ender. Maybe it'd give her enough energy to deal with Kree. "So, what's yours?"

"What are you gonna do about the kid?" Genevieve slurped her coffee. "Oh, wow this is... Damn."

"Forty credits a cup." Risa winked. "It's worth it. I'll figure something out. I'll give her another day and if she doesn't come around, I'll carry her out screaming. I won't trick her, though. Your turn."

"Nothing's really wrong with me. I'm worrying to worry." She kept her gaze on the coffee cup.

"It's about Aurelia, isn't it? Expecting problems?"

"No." Genevieve looked up... too fast. "Not really."

"Remember that 'been around you long enough to know when something's not right' thing?"

"Yeah." Genevieve picked at the cup. "Aura offered to let me move in with her. Wants me to go out to eat and she keeps talking about this live theater company. Can you believe there are really still people out there who act? Like, *not* computer generated?"

"You're afraid to go outside."

She blushed. "I'm... Yeah."

"Gen... Garrison didn't try to kill you. Neither did Maris."

"So who did?" She cringed.

"I don't know."

Genevieve shivered. "What if they're still out there? What if I get seen?" A nervous laugh leapt out of her mouth. "I guess I'm just like your kid now. I'm terrified of leaving this apartment in case whoever tried to kill me sees me." She whined. "I should've stayed in Araphel. At least I could sleep there."

"You were pretty zonked when I got here. I got the full view on my way in."

"Uhh, sorry. I feel safe with her..."

Risa reached across the table and held her hand. "Not safe enough to go outside." *There's one way to find out. Heitzenroeder is still out there. If the detonator was already rigged when he sold it to us, we need to have a chat.* She thought about her eyes, about the nonfunctional Wraith, her lack of night vision or targeting optics. *Unless he's hiding in the tunnels, I'll be fine.*

"Something's different about you." Genevieve looked up. "Holy crap! Your eyes!" She sprang from her seat and grabbed Risa's head in both hands. "Bit! You got your eyes back."

Risa grinned. "Took you long enough to notice."

"Lot on my mind." Genevieve hugged the breath out of her. "Oh... No wonder you seem so much happier. You look like you're seventeen again."

"I'm not, but thanks." Her eyebrows drew together. "You're the first person not to assume I'd gotten realistic artificials the same color as my original eyes."

Genevieve tapped a finger on Risa's cheek, below her left eye. "There's a tiny little spot of yellow-gold under the pupil."

"Wow." Risa laughed.

"I'm observant. Guess it makes up for my awful luck. Comes in handy when playing with bombs." Genevieve held her hand up. "Which I am *never* doing again. I want to take an e-learn course and get a degree or certification. Some kind of electronics work. Net school I can do from anywhere... if I can find a way to pay for it."

"Gen." Risa grabbed her 'sister's' hand. "I'm going to track down whoever tried to kill you and deal with it. I can't stand seeing you like this."

"Like what? Not ready to run off and blow up Corporates?"

"Afraid to set foot outside. You used to be so fearless. Larger than life." Risa looked down. "Always laughing… like no matter what happened around us you were in on some happy secret."

Genevieve shrank in on herself. "Guess I got old or something. Grew up. One too many close calls."

"I can't handle having two girls in my life scared of their own shadows." Risa took a long sip of coffee. "Not when I know I can help at least one of them. Might as well get *some* use out of all this hardware."

"Don't do anything stupid for me." Genevieve hugged her before returning to her seat and grasping the cinnamon latte. "I can probably handle a move to Aurelia's apartment, but—"

"You'll shut yourself inside there too." Risa stood. "Not happening. Give me a couple hours."

"Be careful."

Risa walked out of the kitchen. "You know me."

"I do. That's why I'm worried."

She made it to within three steps of the door before remembering she lacked boots or laser pistols. After a quick jog to retrieve her footwear and weapons harness, Risa drained the last of her cappuccino and went outside.

Via her headware, she sent a text-only message to Garrison, ‹Running an errand for a friend. Please keep an eye on Kree. Don't worry, no fireworks involved.›

FOOLS AND SHADOWS

R isa walked among the people of Primus City, her confidence restored thanks to having her ballistic stealth armor. Fabric clothing might be comfortable in a physical sense, but it would be a while before she could truly enjoy it.

Cramped subterranean streets packed with small merchant stalls, prostitutes, chem-merchants, and an uncountable number of people were not for the skittish. Her gloss-black suit attracted an unusual amount of attention. About a third of the people who afforded her more than the customary one-second 'oh, there's someone there' glance seemed worried at what she was up to. Even without glowing purple eyes, some still saw a *tí-zhèn*. The rest admired every curve.

Maybe I should use this stuff like it was designed for and wear clothes over it. She picked up her pace, not wanting a repeat of the shuttleport attack. *Normal people hope to get through a day without a headache. I'd be happy not having to kill anyone.* According to Pavo's grumbling about his light duty assignment, he and Aurelia had been put on patrol around the Tier 2 Mall. The worst issues they had to deal with so close to the surface usually involved gangers with a credit skimmer sniffing for NetMinis, or a shoplifting teenager who 'did it for the lols' even though they could afford to buy whatever they stole.

The major downside to Primus, of course, was the utter lack of PubTran cars. A handful of people operated manual-drive taxis, but most of them clustered in the Tier 2 Mall waiting to ambush tourists... and in some cases, 'ambush' went well past metaphor.

Thirty-nine minutes after leaving Pavo's apartment on Tier 4, Risa emerged from an inter-tier stairwell at the southernmost point of the mall area, into a 'street' wide enough for cars, though no one bothered. Farther south, the level became a residential district for the well off, despite no one truly considered wealthy remaining in Primus. The few executives required to show a physical presence in the surrounding offices commuted. Despite that, the rent within easy walking distance of the mall remained out of reach of most citizens, leaving the surrounding streets largely empty—except for private armed security.

She headed north past rows of shops, taken by whim at the sight of a Cyberwave outlet, the only 'chain' cyberware store on Mars. Most were sole proprietorships, small quasi-legal operations that kept their heads down. Deep enough into the lower tunnels, one would eventually find a cyber-doc willing to sell or do almost anything. Cyberwave didn't deal in any parts deemed too risky, nor did it run showrooms as large as official Intera emporiums on Earth. She couldn't help but think of white orchid cyberlimbs on the heels of the word Intera. Celebrities with replacement limbs all opted for one of those... at two-million apiece, they offered as much status as function.

Still, Cyberwave happened to be right in front of her, and they might have something basic she needed. Risa ducked under the glowing holographic letters forming the store's name, into a puke-green room with four rows of various demonstration model parts set up inside bullet-resistant cases. Pressed for time, she headed right for the clerk.

A teen with an erratic explosion of medium-long pink hair, and a dull green tunic top lifted his head to get a better look at her. He maintained perfect eye-to-tit contact when she reached the checkout terminal. According to a thin strip of grey plastic on the left breast of his shirt, she had the joy of being ogled by Sanjay.

"Welcome to Cyberwave. Can I help you find anything?"

"I'm up here, Sanjay."

He made eye contact. "Uhh, sorry. Is that what I think it is?"

Hands on her hips, she raised an eyebrow. "Consider carefully your next words."

"The armor." He gestured at her chest. "That's armor right? Kinetic-hardening anti-ballistic suit?"

She relaxed—a little. "Maybe. What do you have in wearable units with support for magnification optics, targeting, night vision, metallurgical scan, thermal, and maybe ultrasonic?"

"Shit, you know where you are, right?" Sanjay gestured at the backwards letters of the outdoor sign. "This is the Cyberburger of tech. If you can afford that suit, what the heck are you doing here?"

Risa smiled. "Opportunistic hope."

He sighed. "*If* this place had all of that in one unit, it would be as big as a Senshelmet, and"—he lowered his voice—"overpriced. I have a technical skate though..." He tapped on the terminal. A few seconds later, a disc-shaped hoverbot glided over with a box on top of it. "This was made for gaming." He took the box, set it on the glass counter, and opened it. "But, it just so happens it works perfectly fine for real guns too."

A silver device approximating the shape of an ultra-thin headband sat in white foam within the square box. A row of four one-millimeter metallic green squares lined the front—holo projectors.

Risa smirked. "Why the sidestep? Firearms are legal."

Sanjay lifted the headset out of the box and held it up to her. "Liability issue. Corporate doesn't want to get sued. This way, they can say the 'product was being used in a manner inconsistent with its intended purpose,' which puts the liability on the person."

"Riiight." She examined it for a second before finding the power button. When she put it on, it let her see an 'initial configuration menu' in a floating amber panel. Despite the actual display being less than an inch across, from her point of view, it looked like a full-sized holo-panel. She navigated the menu with eye flicks, flying through the setup process to create the wireless link to her headware. The device's optics offered a four-x zoom as well as the most rudimentary of targeting support. "Ugh, this thing is IPv12 4.1. Is there an upgrade? They hacked that wireless last year. Everyone within a hundred meters will know what I'm looking at."

"Uhh, one sec. Let me check." Sanjay poked at his holo-terminal.

"I'm testing. Don't panic." Risa pulled one of her Hotaru-6 laser pistols from her harness and hit the little button above the trigger guard to open it for sync mode. *Sorry little buddy. Not quite the military grade stuff you're used to...* The pistol beeped, as did the headset. Five seconds later, whenever she pointed the pistol at anything in her field of vision, she got two crosshairs—one from her headware, fed right into her visual cortex, the other as a hologram in front of her eye. *Oh, that's only a little annoying.*

"There's an upgrade to the firmware available for download via the manufacturer's virtual office," said Sanjay. "Teradyne. Can't miss it."

Her muscles locked when a younger teen boy somewhere behind her screamed and ran out the door. She sighed, re-holstered her weapon, and pulled the headset off. "This thing is pretty much a toy, but my options are limited. How much?"

"Sorry, it's not part of our Cyberwave Surf Special… C630."

I'll regret not having it. Not like it's expensive. "Okay." She put it back on and pulled her NetMini. Once Sanjay processed the order, she waved it over the reader. "Thanks."

He bagged the box containing the packing foam and charging cradle, and handed her a dark-blue bag with a paler blue Cyberwave logo. "Thanks for shopping at Cyberwave."

Sanjay sounded about as enthused as Risa felt.

She took the bag and headed for the exit. The double sliding door parted at her approach. A split second after her foot hit the ground outside, a shadow to her left moved in. Instinct triggered her speedware. The sense of a leaping body dragged to a ponderous mass gliding toward her. Virtual hours spent in Tamashi's martial arts simulation paid off. Risa spun into her attacker, seizing his arm as she curled under it and pulled. Her back to him, she twisted around in a maneuver that flung him onto his chest before pinioning his arm to the side and pressing her knee at the back of his neck; the hold could break it if she applied enough pressure.

Another shadow moved from the other side. Risa twisted in that direction, reflexively thrusting her arm out like a spear at the attacker's face. The instant the tips of her Nano claws touched solid material, her brain processed the design and shape of a Mars Defense Force helmet. Eyes wide, Risa pulled her attack before her Nano claws pierced into the wearer's skull. She stared past five transparent blue blades at blood droplets splattered from her deploying claws, trickling down the featureless slab of crimson composite armor. Little camera dots at the top corners glowed. Risa shifted her gaze to the woman's chest, and the nametag: Imari, A.

"Ugh," said Pavo from the ground.

"Oh, hi!" Risa smiled, and lowered her arm. "I was looking for you guys."

"Holy shit! She killed two cops!" yelled the boy who'd run screaming from the store.

Risa lowered her arm and retracted her claws before helping Pavo up. "Sorry about that… I just saw someone jumping at me… not who."

"Fuck," said Aurelia. Her helmet opened, faceplate retracting up over the top, exposing cheeks almost as white as Risa's. "I think I just pissed myself."

Pavo rolled his shoulder, rubbing it. His helmet opened as well. "That kid said someone was robbing the Cyberwave."

Risa pointed at the headset. "I was calibrating the Hotaru... and what happened to 'MDF, don't move?'"

Aurelia closed her eyes. "That usually gets us shot at by anyone stupid enough to try and rob a store on Tier 2."

"Not the smartest of people." Pavo chuckled. "Damn you're fast."

"Are you gonna arrest that bitch?" yelled the boy.

Pavo took in a breath, held it, and let it out through a placid smile. "I got this."

While he walked over to the 'good Samaritan,' Aurelia leaned on the wall and removed her helmet, brushing a finger over the four tiny gouges on the faceplate.

"Damn. You okay?" Risa offered a hand. "Really, I didn't realize who was trying to jump me."

"All I saw was a fuckin' black blur. If you wanted to kill me, that would've been that. My head would've been off before I even knew you had claws."

Risa looked down. "I wouldn't have killed you. Even if you were a pair of idiots looking for an easy mark."

"*You* wouldn't... but what if it was some psycho aug?" She breathed into her hands. "Crap, maybe I *do* have some mental damage."

Risa clasped her hands together, bag and box bouncing off her knees. "Most people who get tortured for a few hours with a knife can't even function. You're tough."

Aurelia smiled at her, and took a few breaths. "Thanks."

Pavo sauntered over, thumbs hooked on his belt. "Well, that's taken care of. Poor kid thought he was gonna get a reward." He shook his head. "So, felt the urge to shop?"

"Actually, I was coming here to find you guys. Store was random opportunity. Coffee?" She gestured across the mall at a Morning Bean.

"I don't want caffeine right now, but I'll go for one of their chocolate things." Aurelia pushed off the wall. She took three steps before spinning around and pointing at Risa. "Holy shit! What did you do?"

Risa smiled and tilted her head up to show off her eyes. "What do you think?"

"Are they Interas? AC9s?" Aurelia leaned in close. "Wow, they look *so* real."

"That's because they *are* real," said Pavo.

The three fell in step, headed to the coffee place. Risa related the story of meeting Raziel in Araphel, how he'd kept the eyes she'd foolishly given up at eighteen after intercepting them from the 'parts market,' and about how the 'angel' she thought she'd been hearing turned out to be the AI godfather of all cyberspace cowboys. By the time she finished, they'd taken a table in the café. The barista comped Pavo and Aurelia's orders since they were on duty, though Risa had to pay for hers.

"Okay, so what happened?" Aurelia stirred her drink; she'd changed her mind and gotten a dark chocolate mocha. "Something happened if you're out here looking for us."

Risa slid a vanilla chai back and forth across the table between her hands. "I need to find someone who doesn't like being found. It's about Genevieve."

Aurelia's expression hardened. "What happened to her?"

"Nothing new... can I talk off the record?"

Both Pavo and Aurelia fiddled with their helmets.

"Almost seven years ago, someone arranged for a sabotaged detonator to fall into her hands. They rigged it to go off instantly when the countdown was triggered."

Aurelia glared at nothing in particular. "You found out who did it?"

"No. Gen got a hold of a data tile she thought contained sensitive information about someone high up on the food chain in the Front. Before she could decrypt it, boom. I... we all thought she was dead. I found her in Araphel, hiding. She's got horrible luck, so she always triple checks everything. She found the sabotage when she tested the detonator. She faked her own death thinking our commander was trying to kill her."

"Maris?" asked Pavo. "Didn't Tamashī say Garrison was the one who'd met... Oh shit. You're looking for Heitzenroeder, aren't you?"

Risa sipped her coffee. "Yeah. It wasn't Maris, and it wasn't Garrison. The trail's cold. He's all I got left."

"*That* son of a bitch tried to kill Genny?" Aurelia fumed.

"Genny?" asked Risa and Pavo at the same time.

"Shut up." Aurelia grumbled.

Pavo swung his left arm up in front of himself and typed on his forearm guard. In a few seconds, the holographic head of a thin man in his early thirties appeared with short blond-tipped hair that darkened toward the roots, and piercing ice-blue eyes. Between the glint in his stare and cocky, smirking grin, he practically dared the planet to get in his way. A shading of black tattoos crept out of the neckline of his shirt. A second Defense Force booking image showed him shirtless, a tattoo of raven's wings across his shoulders.

"He's off the grid. No official record or legal name," said Pavo. "Heitzenroeder, as he is known among certain circles, is believed to be a native of Earth who emigrated to Mars at an unknown age. Defense Force intel is fairly limited on him up until he emerged as the figurehead of a gang known as the Jesters."

Risa blinked. "The Jesters?"

"Yep." Two taps of Pavo's finger dispelled the image of the man, replacing it with text too small for her to read backwards. "His crew blurs the line between street gang and criminal enterprise. They're nowhere near as widespread as the Syndicate, and they're a lot more organized and armed than your run-of-the-mill gang. Still, they're closer to thugs than anything."

"Sounds like I need to pay this guy a short visit." Risa took another sip. "As soon as I finish this. It's too good to rush. So where is he?"

"I didn't know you liked chai," said Aurelia, raising an eyebrow.

Risa shrugged. "Never had it before, but I've had three cups of coffee already today."

"From what our investigative people have found, he's made his home in HB-17 on Tier 7. It's a residential-zoned district built years ago but never occupied by paying tenants. By the time Primus had enough people to populate that far down, the area had... devolved." Pavo lowered his arm, causing the display to flicker off. "You should wait until we're off light duty. I don't want you going down there alone, and I can tell Imari wants a piece of him."

Aurelia snarled.

Risa lifted her cup to her lips, savoring the scent of vanilla. "Why do cops and soldiers always call each other by last name?"

They both shrugged.

"How long?" asked Risa.

"Couple weeks," said Aurelia, sounding defeated. "As much as I want to punch that shit-eating grin off that son of a bitch's face, I know what she's talking about. Genny is terrified. I've been trying to get her to go out and do things, but she always comes up with some excuse. I'm concerned she's going to expect me to feel like *I'm* the problem." She shook her head. "I'm gonna tell her tonight. You should go put her fears to rest."

"Wait," said Pavo, struggling not to grin. "You're going to send my girlfriend down to Tier 7 so your girlfriend can sleep better at night?"

"You're lucky you're smiling or I would've seriously hit you." Aurelia grumbled. "But yes, basically."

"I'll be fine." Risa wanted to make the final few sips of chai last longer, but it had already become perilously close to not being hot anymore. "They're nothing more than a street gang, right? No training?"

Pavo hemmed and hawed for a moment, but wound up nodding. "Yeah. No training, but they've got better weapons than you'd expect from a gang of punks. With your augs, you should be fine if you don't do anything dumb."

Risa smiled.

"Go back to Earth, darkie!" yelled a maybe-eighteen-year-old Marsborn. He, with two of his friends cheering him on, pointed at Aurelia.

"The hell's an Earther doing wearing cop armor?" yelled a chubbier young man.

"Yeah," yelled the first guy as he hurled a pastry at her.

Speedware slowed the flying cupcake down to an easy grab. As time snapped back to normal, Risa held it up, perched like a big diamond on her thumb and two fingers. "Black forest? You should be ashamed of yourself for wasting this."

"Aww, shit," said the shortest kid. He looked about fourteen, and scared shitless. "That chick is a *tí-zhèn!*"

"Ahh, the entertainment's arrived." Pavo put on his helmet and pulled a stunrod off his belt before offering his hand as if inviting his partner to dance. "Shall we?"

Aurelia's response came as a growl. Risa swirled the last inch of tea around her cup as her two friends chased the punks. She helped herself to the intact confection, making a startled "mmm!" when a burst of cherry compote filled her mouth. About forty yards from the coffee place, Aurelia caught up to the heavyset teen and body-checked him into the stone wall of a clothing store. Pavo tackled the cupcake thrower, sat on top of him, and wrestled him into binders. Considering they appeared to be little more than shithead teens, Risa figured Pavo and Aurelia would only give them a bit of a scare. Only a real prick would charge someone for assault over a thrown cupcake.

Takes a real genius to antagonize the Defense Force. Stimpaks hide a lot of sin.

The teens did a total 180, shouting apologies as Pavo pretended to start filling out an inquest record. She could tell by his tone of voice he wasn't serious—but the boys couldn't.

Risa shook her head and hurried to the stairway at the south end of the mall. At least one out of four people she passed checked her out. Far more than usual. For most, interest ranged from a two-second glance, the instinctual reaction to an approaching person, to unabashed leering. No one, at least not on Tier 2, gave her the sense they'd do anything more than stare.

Okay, maybe having metal eyes did have one *upside.* She hardened her glare and kept her attention sharp. *I really hope I don't have to kill anyone other than Heitzenroeder.* Risa entered the square-walled stairwell, wide enough for six people to walk abreast. It coiled in a switchback arrangement in half-story segments separated by landings full of beggars, hawkers, prostitutes and dosers. With each tier down, they got thinner, dirtier, angrier, and more dangerous.

A woman, over six foot tall with a large frame and bulging arms, locked eyes with her on Tier 6. She wore a thin red one-piece dress short enough to reveal the truth of her feminine sex. *Damn... is it still considered prostitution if the client doesn't want it?*

"Well, look at this sweet little upsec," said the muscular prostitute. "You best keep on walking, honey. I own this tier."

"The only tears you own fall from the eyes of any man dumb enough to actually think about fuckin' you." The raspy voice emanated on a cloud of luminous blue vapor from a doser in the corner. Notes of tinkling glass rattled in his subsequent chuckle, and a trace of peppermint wafted by.

Risa cringed away, afraid even smelling it would be enough to get her high on Icewhisper.

Two thinner, younger prostitutes hid their faces against the wall, trying to suppress the urge to laugh. The big woman stormed across the landing and set to repeatedly kicking the frail man in the head. Risa hurried past. On the way down the last set of stairs to Tier 7, she secured her NetMini in its belt pocket with the strap she'd never before bothered using.

13

THE MERCHANT OF DEATH

HB-17 occupied the southeast corner of Tier 7. Sixty-two years ago, workers carved the housing block district out of Mars rock. An entire complex of fully furnished homes waited for the ideal middle-class families that never came.

Primus, the first true city the UCF set up on Mars—aboveground pod colonies notwithstanding—had been the product of exuberant idealism that caused the developers to dig chasing rosy predictions. Alas, before the population could grow down to Tier 7, other cities sprang up, attracting those who had already stigmatized depth with social standing. The eventual lure of Elysium's surface living, of not being trapped underground for the rest of one's life, drained away the builder's last hopes for the future. The deep tunnels became homes for the poor and unwanted.

Risa halted in a dim octagonal chamber seven stories plus twenty meters below the surface of Mars. Metallic-blue tiles glinted on the floor and walls around empty booths and vendor stalls that had never seen a single credit pass over their counters. Trash gathered in clusters the way tumbleweeds might have in Earth's Old West. A large collection of spent instant-warming meal packets piled up against the face of an information desk in the middle of the open space. The look of the furniture, the benches and stools around the food court, and the clothing style of people on nearby adverts made her feel as though she'd gone back in time. A plasfilm poster on the wall showed a smiling family: man, woman, son, and daughter. Each held a neat little suitcase, too small to carry anything useful.

"Find your perfect life on Mars! Emigrate to Primus City," said a scratchy electronic voice as she walked close to it.

On another poster, a military man in an armored space suit proclaimed Primus 'The future of humanity!'

She shook her head at the decades-old idealized fantasy of Mars life and headed down an offshoot east toward where her floating virtual map placed HB-17. Her position indicator inched along in the upper-right corner of her vision. Elements of the display reacted to light in the real world; the amber map grid, sapphire dot, and dotted green line gleamed like glossy gems whenever she walked under a struggling LED. It would take a few weeks to get used to not having a mesh 'pixel screen' overlaying her vision.

Empty storefronts lined both sides of the street, filled with shadows and dashed optimism. She instinctively tried to turn on night vision, but got an 'unsupported vision mode' error in unfriendly red letters.

You wanted this. Risa steeled herself with a deep breath. *Yes. I did. Why does it feel so strange to have my living eyes back? I can buy a night vision mod. I can't buy my way out of going blind if the NIU fries. Not like Shiro's going to help me out again. Who am I kidding? That was government money, not his. Money he probably hadn't been authorized to even spend on me, considering they sent him here to take me out.* She concentrated more on her augmented hearing. Even if she couldn't see what lurked in the dark, nothing short of an actual ghost would be able to get close enough to be a threat without making a noise she could detect. Her ears hadn't changed.

The cry of a raven, as loud as if she were inches away from it, made her jump. She whirled to the side, locking stares with a massive black bird on the other side of an intersection. It perched on the backrest of a bench wrapped around a tree planter filled with cups and plastic cartons rather than soil. Alarming sentience dwelled in the animal's onyx gaze.

What the hell is that? It's huge.

It snapped its head to the left, peering at her with its other eye. A second later, it let off a low *caw*, and leapt into the air. Risa jumped back, but it headed to the right, flying in the same direction she wanted to go, vanishing in seconds amid the dark. She remained motionless until the whispery flutter of feathers faded to silence. Chances are, the Jesters wouldn't be happy to have guests. Risa advanced, staying close to the wall in the shadows to avoid the open street. This necessitated climbing through four empty planter boxes as well as a dry fountain.

About fifty meters later, a barricade made of Epoxil slabs—likely doors removed from the various housing units—blocked off the street. Two patches of auto-spray graffiti depicted a grinning white face with an exaggerated pointy chin and belled jester's hat. It would've been creepy even if the eyes weren't drawn hollow.

Her quick glance gave no indication of a way in aside from going over it, as the bird had. *Yeah, and as soon as I pop up, I get shot.* She backed up to a doorway on the right labeled 'Leasing Office,' and froze. The façade, as well as the bench to the right matched the image of Garrison meeting with Heitzenroeder. Four seconds of meditation helped convince her he hadn't lied when he said he had no idea he'd obtained a rigged detonator.

He didn't know he was my father then. Risa trudged into the leasing office. *Okay, he acted like it anyway. I was the angry one who always ignored him.* She climbed over a waist-high wall dividing the customer area from the employee area, and headed to a vent on the left wall. *Put that crap in a box. Don't get emotional now.* Deep breath. *Stow it for later, like when you planted bombs. Ice time.*

Risa reached up and clawed at the vent cover, slicing metal until it opened. She closed her eyes and cringed away from a dustfall, but managed to catch the slats before they made noise. Pulling herself up and into a narrow shaft rumbling with the noise of distant fans felt like old familiar routine. Since Habitation Block 17 was officially 'not in use,' none of the local air pushers should be on. The weak breeze on her face had to be coming from the primary distribution fan for the entire tier, easily a half-mile from here.

The low ceiling prevented her from getting fully upright on all fours, so she crawed on her elbows. Her headware estimated she traveled one-point-three meters forward before she could turn right, and then nine-point-six meters later, she hit a T-junction. She went left, which pointed her back towards the Jesters' home, and crawled for another thirty-seven meters before the shaft offered a new option: up.

Risa stopped, stretching her arms out over her head and lying flat to give her muscles a break. While she relaxed, she compared her approximate position with a map overlay. The schematic of HB-17 resembled a grid of nine large squares with the main access street protruding out of the left side. The central space appeared open, while the others all contained four smaller squares along each inner line. Based on the notes in the City Records Archive, each grid square held sixteen residences, while the middle area was designated as a 'park,' where genuine plant life would assist with air quality.

Going up would lead her into the rock slab between Tier 6 and 7, and likely give her free access to everything inside. Renewed, she squirmed around to sit and worked her way up the narrow channel. She ascended by bracing herself between opposing walls, and slithered over the top into a mercifully larger conduit where she could crawl normally.

Minutes later, her map dot glided into the area of the southwest section of HB-17, putting her about forty meters south from the entry street. *I'm inside someone's house. Well, it would've been someone's house if anyone legitimately lived here.* She crept ahead, peering into each vent grille on the way. Occasionally, she'd spy people sleeping, lounging about, or screwing. The Jesters all had a fondness for black clothes and wild hair colors—lime green, powder blue, and fuchsia among the favorites. Most appeared to range in age from late teens to late twenties, and all of them looked reasonably content.

Heitz is going to either showboat in the center of the park, or be as deep inside as he can to put the maximum number of thugs between him and danger... or between someone he wants to kill and the way out. Risa thought about that cocky grin on his mugshot and opted to try the park first. Ten feet from where the ductwork met the edge of the central space, narrow pipes entered from overhead and ran along the lower-right corner of the airway. *Guess the plants would've needed water.*

The first grille she found let her peer down on a nightmare of dead things. Bushes, flowers, and even a handful of trees sat amid a field of brown grass littered with more plastic garbage. Shot-up lamps, artificial sun pumps, dangled on loose cables. Scratching sounds in the largest tree attracted her attention to the enormous raven. It flicked its head about, stared at her for an instant, and flew off to the east, heading for the connecting passage to the middle space in the easternmost row, the deepest section. HB-17 was a dead end with one way in, making that the easiest to defend.

Risa took the first opportunity to go right, and crawled as fast as she could without making too much banging and clattering. Voices echoed in the duct, all male, discussing particulars of a deal to sell a handful of pulse laser rifles to a mercenary squad. According to her map, her dot entered Courtyard 6, the middle box in the farthest right column. She rushed up to a grating in the bottom of the vent that offered a view into the central courtyard between the apartments. A bad angle didn't allow her to see faces—only a couple pairs of legs and long, dark coats to the left.

"I'm all for depriving fools of their money, but your interests would be served more readily by ballistic weapons. Perhaps a 60mm rocket. FMMC security uses energy-resistant armor." The silky, cocky voice with a trace of grit reminded her of one of those 'elves' from a Monwyn holovid. "Everyone on Mars uses lasers, friend. A wise man does the unexpected."

That's gotta be Heitzenroeder. If not for his attempt to kill her adopted sister, Risa might've allowed herself a little space-pirate fantasy. He sounded quite the rogue.

The raven cawed. A deeper-pitched man yelped at the sudden fluttering of feathers.

"Oh, don't mind, Muninn," said Heitzenroeder. "He's merely a raven."

Men murmured amongst themselves.

"Damn ravens ain't that big," said a wheezy man.

"We don't wanna be luggin' ninety pounds of ammo across the middle of nowhere. I want some energy weapons involved. Gimme two of the Matsushita rifles, two of the DTF assault rifles, and throw in the missile tube."

"Deutsche Technik Firma… an excellent choice," said Heitzenroeder. "Twenty-eight three for the lasers, 9,750 apiece for the ballistics, and an even forty for the sixty-millimeter. 116,100. Are you sure you don't need any demo charges?"

"Nah, that tube will do the job."

Electronic chirps broke the subsequent silence.

"A pleasure." Heitzenroeder chuckled.

Risa waited for the footfalls of men carrying heavy things to get quieter. She extended the claw from her right index finger, sliced out the vent slats, and lifted the assembly into the shaft. Her NetMini served as an improvised fiber-optic cam. After linking the optical sensor to her headware, she held it down only enough for the lens to get a view of the chamber below.

A man with an appearance matching Pavo's picture of Heitzenroeder stood with his left side to her, the enormous raven perched on his shoulder, more than twice as tall as his head. Most of him hid beneath a heavy, black coat. A long folding table beside him held an array of weapons ranging from pistols to rifles, at least three broadswords, and two other blades that resembled elongated katanas.

He reached up and stroked a finger under the bird's chin. "What whispers do you bring from the fickle muse of fate, Muninn?"

It didn't bother her that he seemed to be talking to the raven in whispers, but it did catch her off guard when the animal spoke back.

"A woman cloaked in shadow has infiltrated the court."

Risa almost dropped the NetMini. Expecting general alarm, a massive gunfight, and a missed opportunity, she shoved the device back in its pouch and jumped down. Boosted agility and a quick tuck and roll took much of the noise out of her landing. Still, to her tweaked ears, she sounded like a drunken janitor doll. She took cover behind a decorative partition, perhaps intended to separate each resident's 'front yard,' and looked among dead grass, withered trees, and the skeletons of decades-dead bushes for anything that would provide cover.

The bird stared at where she hid.

"To what do I owe the pleasure of your visit?" Heitzenroeder turned ninety degrees, presenting a sideways silhouette, and speaking in a rapid cadence as if reciting some ancient play. "Only a fool sneaks *into* the house of Death, yet perhaps we fools are drawn together. Dost some poor deluded fool approach, seeking the king of fools? Who can say then if you are as such? I certainly cannot, in the absence of first sight." He laughed. "Why have you come?"

If the words themselves didn't, intonation and pace of his speech made her question his grip on sanity. Nothing in the MDF files indicated he had any sort of augments. Risa drew both pistols and stood, for the moment leaving them pointed down. "Information."

Muninn flared his wings, a span of almost seven feet, and balanced on Heitzenroeder's shoulder as the man rotated to face her. His 'I won before you even knew what the game was' smile irritated her as much as it nudged her off balance. Her second instinct, metallurgical scan to check for implants—from the cybereyes she no longer had—generated an 'unsupported vision mode' error in annoying red letters along the bottom of her view.

"So you have not come to steal the king's crown from his head?" He held his arms up, a gesture part shrug, part invitation to hug.

"If by that you mean kill you, I haven't made up my mind yet." She stopped walking a few steps from the narrow end of the table of weapons.

As she neared, the indistinct dark spot on the front of his neck became apparent as a tattoo of the same smiling jester face plastered all over the area. Dark around his eyes could have been either cosmetics or another tattoo. Muninn's wings folded; the animal's unflinching glare seemed to bore into her soul. Fragments of conversation echoed everywhere, loudest from the four narrow streets leading out of the 'park' behind her to the west. She glanced at detonators and small limpet mines stacked among various weapons, the kind of things she once sought to buy from men like him. When she cringed away from the explosives, her gaze settled on a skull, two black candles, and a deck of large, ornate cards.

"Ask whatever is on your mind." He brought his hands together, fingertips touching.

She couldn't help but stare at the skull, wondering if it was real. "Jesters is an odd name for a gang that sells this kind of hardware."

Heitzenroeder walked to the edge of the table and set his hand upon the tarot deck. Never taking his eyes off her, he lifted it, shuffled, and set it back upon the table. His rogue's grin deepened as he slid the top card away and turned it up to examine with a furtive flick of the eyes. A sinister chuckle broke the silence. He threw his head back, laughing in a dark tone before tossing the card at her. The tarot twirled through the air in a fluttering arc. Risa ignored it, watching him, but he made no move to attack as the card landed with an audible *pat* in front of her. She risked a two-second glance down at an illustration of a medieval figure in a black cloak and jester's cap clutching a scythe while seated upon a throne.

"The last laugh is reserved for Death." He covered his mouth with his thumb pressed to his index finger. A quiet chuckle grew to a laugh. "Do you find my tricks amusing?"

"She is *tí-zhèn*," rasped Muninn. "The errand girl of Colonel Tanais. Be wary."

"Ahh, grand." Heitzenroeder gestured at the demolition electronics. "Death's daughter shopping for toys?"

Risa scowled. "One of your *toys* killed someone close to me. It malfunctioned—on purpose."

He leaned back, causing the raven to flare its wings, and pressed his fingers to his chest. "Poor naïve girl. The fool tells the joke; who the truth offends he cannot control"—he pointed at her, but didn't so much as slow down for a breath—"I sell the party favors but how they're served is not up to me." Heitzenroeder made a gesture of wiping his hands. "Not my concern."

Risa growled in her throat. "The NTC-11 multi-channel you sold us was rigged to disregard the timer and trigger the charges as soon as the countdown started. If *you* didn't try to kill her, someone wanted us to think you did."

Heitzenroeder flashed a pacifying smile. "Only a boor mixes business with pleasure. When someone gets on my bad side, I don't make the poor sot pay for the instrument of my satisfaction."

The pleasantness in his expression faded to a glint of malice. His gaze flicked past her.

Muninn emitted a weak croak of a caw.

When he stepped to his left, Risa kicked on her speedware. *Sniper behind me.* She flung herself to her right in a dive for the ground while spinning to the rear. Azure muzzle flare bloomed in the dark of the passage connecting the courtyard to the central square. The spiraling projectile glided toward her, perceptibly moving at the speed of a brisk walk. Risa fired both Hotaru-6 pistols while falling, walking seven hits of ten shots up the man's chest. The last beam she fired before her back struck the plastisteel floor nailed him in the throat. The incoming bullet glided two feet over her and struck the ground where it splattered as if made of liquid.

She tapped her momentum, rolling out of her landing into a reverse somersault. When she came upright again, a fist-sized black orb wobbled toward her; Heitzenroeder hung near-frozen in time, his right arm outstretched from lobbing the grenade. Muninn's wings beat in slow motion, lifting the great raven from his master's shoulder. Risa threw her weight backward, swinging her right leg up to catch the grenade in a bicycle kick that launched it off to the side. She flipped over with the maneuver and oozed flat on her front like a liquid cat, landing a half-second before the explosive careened into the bay window of a facing residence.

Cobweb cracks raced across the glass amid the delicate *clinking* of fragments as the black orb punched a hole and fell out of sight inside. Distorted screams lasted another second before a dull *whump* preceded a flash of light, and pulverized window snowed outward in a haze of glimmering frost crystals.

Risa aimed at Heitzenroeder, hesitating only because he had information she still needed. He swung his arm to the side, a gesture to add speed to his leap for cover. Two men and a young woman came running in from the north chamber. The white-haired man had a rifle, the other two raised smaller submachine guns. Risa shoved her arms down, catapulting herself up on her feet. She darted to her left, not confident any of the lawn partitions could stop bullets better than her armor.

The speed at which she moved caused the lavender-haired woman and the Jester with the rifle to lose their killing zeal, which melted to panic. The other man standing between them fired his sub-machine gun at the spot of ground where she'd been five seconds before to her perception, a quarter-second to them. She triggered twice from her main hand, putting two emerald streaks into the thug's chest before any sign of realization that she'd moved appeared on his face.

With the other two skidding on their heels and starting to twist away, Risa felt no need to murder. Dread fear of *tí-zhèn* showed on their faces; they wouldn't return. She surged ahead, vaulting over the table. Muninn came out of nowhere behind her, sinking his talons into her back. The claws failed to pierce her suit, though the beast did secure a grip on her weapons harness that arrested her leap before her boots touched down. Shock at the raven being strong enough to carry her aloft triggered a two-second fit of kicking and flailing. Her flight curved around, heading for the tunnel that led to the southeast corner of HB-17, and a large collection of angry voices.

Risa pointed her laser pistol back over her shoulder and fired blind. Talons released her to free fall. She landed in a forward roll and scurried behind one of the partitions; Muninn, right wing smoking, careened downward and crashed through the window of another residence.

After three seconds of silence, a weak rasp emanated from the darkness inside. "Bitch."

She blinked.

Another woman, more than a head taller than Risa but scrawny, came charging out of the southern passage with a broadsword clutched in two hands. She looked high, a touch insane, and wore no armor. Jester symbols adorned her black shirt and long coat, but none of it would stop a laser. If Risa learned one thing in her years of infiltration work for the MLF, it was never to take a bizarre sight at face value. Anyone willing to charge into a gunfight with a sword probably had some reason to believe they could survive it—a reason she had no interest in discovering.

Three shots put the charging gladiator down; the large woman rolled to a halt on her back, stifling an agonized scream with a clenched jaw. Risa kept aiming until the wounded Jester dragged herself back the way she came, coughing up blood. The abandoned broadsword glinted in the weak glow of a few LED work lights dangling loose from open ceiling panels.

Huh. No rage? No 'ware? Maybe some people really are *that stupid—or high.* She sprang upright, aiming around as she yelled, "Heitz! Tell your people to back off. They're not tall enough to ride this ride."

Muninn dragged himself to the doorway; milk-white fluid leaked from a three-inch hole in the leading edge of his left wing, rimmed by charred feathers.

Of course. The bird's synthetic. She pointed a gun at the raven, and he scooted backward out of sight.

She stomped closer to the building she believed Heitzenroeder had gone into. Augmented ears picked up the word *'ti-zhèn'* whispered from all three tunnels out of the section. Most seemed to think the Jesters had pissed off someone with deep pockets and hired her. A slight majority wanted no part of dealing with a 'pro.' For once, being thought of as an expensive assassin didn't strike her as repugnant. In a paradoxical way, it prevented her from having to kill more people. These thugs feared her the way she dreaded a rematch with a C-branch operator, perhaps even more so. After all, if she had to fight an operator again, she'd have at least a small chance of surviving.

Risa leaned back and rammed her boot into the door, knocking a brown Epoxil slab off its rails. The residence, a pre-furnished affair, employed a style several decades old, lending the place the feel of a holo-vid set rather than someone's actual house. A green wingback chair sat in the far-right corner, farthest from the front, opposite a powder-blue couch. Besides a coffee table made of two superimposed triangles, like a pair of arrowheads flying in opposite directions, the living room held nothing else. She crept inside, right hand pistol pointed forward at an archway leading to a kitchen, while her left hand covered a passage to another room.

Muninn offered a dry *caw* from outside. Risa didn't pay him much attention; the bird couldn't fly much indoors, and if he had an implanted laser, he would've used it already.

The back of the green chair exploded in a cloud of white stuffing. Two gunshots preceded two slugs slapping her in the chest. Winded, she stumbled against the wall. Hands appeared on either side of the chair an instant before the person hiding there hurled it at her, fouling her attempt to shoot back. She managed one ill-aimed laser blast, scoring the chair's side and lighting it on fire, before crossing her arms defensively to block most of the impact. By the time she shoved the chair aside, Heitzenroeder had made it three-quarters of the way across the room toward her. She raised her pistols, but aborted the shot to duck a swing from two twelve-inch plastisteel claws protruding from his clenched fist.

She braced for the ear-splitting screech of vibroblades, but much to her shock, none came. *He's got normal claws?* His blades shredded drywall at the level her head used to be. Risa leapt back, shooting him twice in the chest. Emerald lasers melted holes in his coat and filled the air with the awful stench of melting plastic. One side effect of laser weapons on armor —no impact force. A slug could knock the wind out of an armored target, but focused light did nothing if it didn't pierce.

Heitzenroeder laughed, though the sound turned demonic by her accelerated perception of time. She considered a headshot, simple given range and speedware, but that would guarantee she never found out who wanted to kill Genevieve. She took a deep breath, the motion of which dislodged the two bullets stuck to her chest. They rolled away from the dense, rubbery material and fell into the debris all over the floor.

She put a streak of laser past his left ear, and corrected her aim. "Who?"

He grinned. "Oh, you wouldn't shoot me in the face, would you? I'm too handsome. Only a barbarian destroys art."

"It'll make a small hole. They can patch it for the wake." Risa squinted. "Besides, your bird called me a bitch."

"Well, he is a good judge of—"

A *crunch* came from behind.

Speedware surged, seeming to freeze time. Risa swiveled to her left and fired at a man lining up a rifle shot on her from the window. Both laser blasts caught him in the cheeks, launching an explosion of steaming bloody gore out the back of his head as well as his eye sockets. The distraction allowed Heitzenroeder to lunge in, slashing at her; Risa crossed her arms to catch his downward strike at the wrist. She recovered her balance from the force of his attack and flung her weight forward while hooking her leg behind his, tripping him backwards.

He flowed from falling into a capoeira-like spin, kicking her legs out from under her. Speedware ramped to the limit, she seemed to hang in midair. Already, he thrust his blades at the spot he expected her head to be when she landed. Without her augments, she'd have been dead before realizing he'd taken her legs out. She twisted her body and kicked out to change the angle of her fall. Rather than stab her in the skull, his blades gouged the floor. She landed flat on top of him, but leapt to her feet before he could perceive the motion.

A kick slapped her boot across his face before he seemed to notice she wasn't where he expected her to be, though he didn't move much from the hit. He sat up in a motion that would've been inhumanly fast to someone without speedware, and tried to wrap his arms around her legs. She leapt away, leaving him sitting on the floor hugging himself.

"Oh, fuck this. You're not gonna give me anything useful." She aimed both guns at his head. "Is Death still laughing?"

"Wait." He raised his left hand as if trying to stop traffic. The 'ahh, ya got me grin' he flashed would've been appropriate for her walking in on him cheating… and might've smoothed things over. "Perhaps I have underestimated your capabilities."

Muninn let off a low *caw*. "Perhaps."

Heitzenroeder gave the bird the bird.

"I'm listening." She scowled over the pistols' iron sights at his striking blue eyes.

"A trade. Information for my hide remaining free of unwanted holes." He flashed the same roguish grin that made her feel like she owed Pavo an apology.

"Dismissing me proved harder than you thought, so now you're trying a trick?"

He retracted the blades protruding from his right fist, and chuckled with a shake of his head. "No tricks. I've got a certain degree of pride, but you're a bit more than what I'm used to dealing with. I've got Death's PID, but I'm not all that keen on meeting him yet."

"So, I caught you unaware. You feed me some dustblow, gear up, and I wind up having to do this whole dance all over again. The Front doesn't like being fucked. Did you screw them over or did the guy who picked up the hardware arrange for it to be hacked?"

"Absolute sincerity." He coughed. "It was a guy named Staanek."

"Lars?" Risa narrowed her eyes. "That's not possible. Lars is after *me*, and I wasn't doing demo work back then. When you gave us the rigged detonator, I was still a kid."

In the doorway, Muninn pecked at his wing; the laser hole already seemed smaller.

Heitzenroeder shrugged, stood, and dusted himself off. "That's the name they used. You got one of those somatic things?"

Risa activated it with a thought. Lines and graphs appeared around his head. "Yeah."

"Lars Staanek offered us a buttload of credits to shortfuse the MLF. Not only did he pay for the hardware, he added a healthy discretion payoff. He wanted us to do damage to the MLF, so it would've been stupid to tell the guy who picked the device up it was rigged."

Despite whining about the headband's low-res camera with an exclamation point in a yellow triangle, the somatic system detected no stress flags to indicate a lie. Risa lowered her arms. "It doesn't make any sense."

Muninn stretched his hurt wing, a few streaks of white synthetic blood the only trace of a prior wound.

Risa glanced at the dead guy lying on the ground twenty or so feet from the window. *Do I believe his life matters less than Gen's?* She scowled at Heitzenroeder. *He went lethal first; the body count's on him.* "I've heard about you."

"Pleasant comments, I hope." He smiled, clasping the lapels of his trench coat.

She considered holstering her guns, but decided against it. "Not exactly. Words like capricious, vengeful, arrogant, and mildly insane were used. I'm not sure I trust this is over."

He put a hand over his chest as if shot. "Miss... you wound me." His sapphire eyes glimmered with mischief. "Though, I can't say you've been misled. My opinion relies in large part on who learns the source of your information. I am not an unreasonable man."

"I'm so deep in secrets, I can't even tell what truth is anymore." Risa drifted to the door.

Muninn whispered, "Death doth cloak herself with innocence."

Heitzenroeder chuckled. "He has a point. I've got a feeling ol' Lars isn't long for this world." His mirth faded to an icy stare. "Don't tell him I sent you."

She stopped. "Are you afraid of ghosts?"

"No." He flicked the safety on his handgun and tucked it under his coat. "Microphones."

Risa smiled. "You see through the bird."

Heitzenroeder laughed.

She eyed the green chair. "Nice shot. I didn't see that coming."

He bowed with a flourish. "I noticed you didn't ask me for a guarantee of safe passage out."

"That would imply I'm at all worried. If your Jesters want to commit suicide, who am I to stop them?"

The best dustblow has a foundation of truth.

Outside, the courtyard hung in fatal silence. A dead sniper slumped in the west-leading tunnel, and a few bodies littered the immediate area. Moans came from the house where the grenade went off. She felt a little better at the proof it was a stun bomb and not a fragmentation charge. Her boosted hearing caught Heitzenroeder advising the Jesters not to attack her. As a sign of truce, she put her guns back in the harness, but kept her senses wide open.

Claws first, questions later.

She walked past the sniper, holding her breath to avoid the smell of laser-charred meat. Pavo's assessment of the Jesters proved true; almost no training, but the man had a fifteen-thousand-credit Metkiy rifle, top of the line ACC military gear, the kind of thing their soldiers had to buy with their own money since their military issued cheap crap. Three dozen glaring faces lurked in the shadowy periphery of the park square, men and women all seeming a pin drop away from violence. The giant raven glided in to land on the thickest branch of the largest tree. Perhaps the presence of the bird kept them at bay. *Or he's waiting for me to be vulnerable. Men like him don't surrender.* Fear he'd come back for revenge at a bad time made her think of Kree. *Should I have killed him anyway?* When she continued east down the next corridor to the westernmost grid square, Muninn glided on ebon wings to a landing atop the wall made of doors. From the inside, the way to open it was as obvious as a glowing control panel in a dark room.

Risa glanced at the raven. "He can hear and see me."

It tilted its head in a manner one might expect from a bird.

"Don't give me that. I know you're intelligent."

Muninn emitted a scratchy *caw.* "You didn't ask anything. There was nothing to say."

"Fine." She stared at the wall. "There are people I care about that I do not want getting involved in any bad blood. I have doubts a man like you is willing to let me walk away after being so close to killing him that I'm tempted to turn around and do just that."

"He says you are welcome to try, but he won't go so easy on you this time." Black feathers ruffled. "Of course, he suggests another deal if you are that concerned. Owe him a small favor."

"I'm not an assassin." She closed her eyes and seethed.

"Oh, but of course you aren't." Muninn made a noise startlingly close to a chuckle. "He agrees; no hits."

Do I want to sign a deal with the Devil? She again pictured Kree's face. If it kept her from getting caught in the middle of revenge, what choice was there? "Alright. I'll owe him a small favor that does not involve a targeted or indiscriminate killing."

The raven mimicked his master's bow.

Risa pushed the blue button and waited for a door to rattle out of her way on a pair of motorized chains. Up until now, she'd regarded Staanek as little more than annoying. Some idiot trying to trick local gang punks into collecting the bounty the UCF put on the head of an 'MLF terrorist,' a problem she thought would go away when General Everett was finished. Risa sighed.

I keep sliding deeper. Am I ever getting out of this hole?

14

STREET CRED

No one bothered Risa on her journey from the bowels of Primus City to Tier 1. The last time Lars Staanek had interfered with her day, by virtue of a pack of thugs using a strange little girl named Chaia as bait, it had been in Elysium. Picturing that eerie too-pretty blonde kid got her thinking about Kree.

The idea of her... daughter in the MLF safehouse unsettled her. Whatever General Everett had planned wouldn't be good. *I don't even know if I can trust him either.* She hovered at the glittery silver doors to the shuttleport, debating between flying or going back down to drag Kree out of there. No matter how much the child screamed, it had to be done sooner or later.

Preferably sooner, before all hell broke loose.

A soft *hiss* came as the starport doors parted for a group of four men and a woman, all in designer black suits with cobalt blue trim at the cuffs and collar, and in the woman's case, skirt. Aside from one man focusing on an in-head Vidphone call, they shot her annoyed looks. She could fly to Elysium, which had the added benefit of being near Pavo's apartment, and rattle the proverbial timbers of street thugs in an effort to track down Lars. *That'll take days... and who knows how many people will get shot before someone talks.*

Risa entered the starport atrium, squinting at a blast of super-cooled air conditioning and the smell of sweet coffee. About ten paces in from the door, a pair of young girls in crimson Mars Cadet uniforms smiled from behind a table full of cupcakes. The confections all looked the same, but a quarter of the table was sectioned off with a sign 'C10 each.' The majority sat behind a sign reading 'C35.'

"Hey lady," yelled one of the tweens. She had Marsborn white skin, but her hair was lemon-blonde. "Wanna buy a cupcake? We're trying to raise money for the One-Winged Angels."

Risa felt like a fish on a hook, but walked over. "Never heard of it. What's with the price difference?"

"One-Winged Angels is a charity set up to help take care of wounded war veterans." The taller girl grinned. Like Risa, she had ebon hair and green eyes. She clasped her hands behind her back and swayed slightly from side to side. "Did you know that there are three-hundred-and-ninety-seven-thousand military personnel medically retired from duty due to injuries sustained in the conflict with the Allied Corporate Council? Over half of them are considered homeless."

The blonde girl sighed. "Our government sends them off to protect us, but too often, they refuse to cover the cost of cybernetic prosthetics if the person is mentally unfit to continue fighting."

"All the cupcakes we made are tiramisu. The more expensive ones have a cream filling with espresso liqueur. Those"—the black-haired girl pointed at the ten-credit ones—"don't have alcohol."

"Are you two alone?" Risa bought one of the 'good' ones.

"Our moms went downstairs to the Tier 2 Mall. We're okay here. It's only Tier 1 and…" The blonde pulled up her thigh-length crimson skirt enough to reveal a small pistol strapped to her leg.

"Right…" Risa offered an uneasy smile. "Don't be too quick to use that thing. Regret is a crappy roommate."

She wandered off into the giant shuttleport facility, tuned out to the ambient din of a hundred conversations and intermittent announcements in a too-placid electronic voice. Every so often, *beeps* and *bongs* from waiting passengers' NetMinis announced boarding times. Risa approached a solid brick-shaped bench, silver paneled with a red cushion, and sat.

Raziel, are you still out there?

She rested her elbows on her knees, holding the cupcake in both hands. After a moment of silence, she picked at the thin plastic, peeling it off the confection. The scent of alcoholic coffee wafted to her nose.

Guess that's a no. I was going to ask for your help again. Genevieve is afraid to go outside.

After emptying her lungs with a sigh, Risa bit into the cupcake, and cringed at the overwhelming sweetness. The wave of sugar passed, replaced by a tidal wave of *coffee*. She opened a call with her headware to RedLink, and threw C240 at a ticket to Elysium. The tiny tiramisu survived two more bites. Despite the strong flavor of alcohol, she didn't feel much.

Thank you for keeping my eyes. I had them put back in.

She hung her head, and waited two minutes. When no response came, she called Garrison.

His virtual head and shoulders appeared as if hovering in front of her; given her current posture, it made him appear to be lying on the floor. <Hey Bit. Where are you?>

Risa sat up, more to not feel like she spoke to a man lying down than because her mood improved. <Shuttleport. I'm heading to Elysium. How's the situation at, uhh, home?>

<Quiet. No word from any direction yet.> The uneasiness in her gut intensified. <That's good. Heitzenroeder gave up the name of the person who arranged the broken clock. Lars Staanek. I think he's in Elysium… or at least someone there knows where he is.>

Garrison rubbed his chin. She gritted her teeth at the sound of his beard bristles scratching. <That name sounds familiar.> Soft beeping from holographic keypresses emanated from the other end of the call. <Oh, that's right. A few of our people have heard rumors a man by that name is throwing around a 'bounty' on you. Uhh, last count a hundred grand alive, ten-k dead. We don't have much solid, but I'll get the 'net team looking.>

No wonder Staanek is only sending idiots after me. Anyone who thinks they have a reasonable chance taking out a ti-zhèn isn't going to work for so little. <I guess I didn't piss him off enough. Thanks. Can you put Kree on?>

He nodded. A second later, a basketball-sized planet Mars with 'MVCC' stamped into its surface replaced his holographic figure. Glowing green words 'call on hold' orbited it. A voice-only ad from Mars Video Communication Corporation flooded her ears with a rapid-talking woman offering cheap unlimited calls to Earth for C625 a month. 'Unlimited,' of course, had an asterisk next to it, connected to fine print at the bottom of the image too tiny to read.

Kree appeared after a short wait. At her size, the hologram showed her from the waist up instead of a bust. One of Garrison's olive-drab T-shirts covered her like a dress, though it hung far off her right shoulder to the point where the wisp of a girl was a bounce away from slipping entirely out the neck opening. <Hi.>

<Hey kiddo. I'm still helping my friend. I've got to take a trip to Elysium.>

Kree's dark-blue eyes widened.

<I can't bring you with me this time. It's not safe for a kid.>

The child slouched in relief as she gave a heavy exhale. <Okay. When are you coming back?>

<I don't know for sure, but I'll definitely be back for dinner. Hopefully sooner.>

Kree nodded. She shifted and walked to her right, though the hologram remained static in front of Risa. The child flopped on the floor, allowing a corner of the cot in Garrison's office into the image. <Can you stay on the call?>

The loneliness in the girl's voice pulled at Risa's chest. *Kicking and screaming, she's out of there as soon as I get back.* <Okay.>

For twelve minutes, Kree explained how her new video game worked. She'd found it free on an abandonware site. The space-exploration game came out in 2407, making it five years older than the child playing it. About twenty percent of it consisted of piloting a space ship, the rest wandering around 'alien ruins' around mazes of underground tunnels. Her description of blown-apart aliens made Risa worry the graphics were too gory for a six-year-old.

Kree pointed at some of the planets on the star map and matter-of-factly said, <Those are too scary, so I don't go there.>

Risa jumped when her NetMini buzzed to announce her shuttle boarding. She hurried along to the indicated terminal, following virtual navigation arrows all the way to her designated row inside the craft. The illusion created by her headware call reoriented itself to appear as though Kree knelt in the empty seat next to her. The eighteen-minute flight passed in a flash while listening to Kree ramble about the game.

<I'm landing now, kiddo. Gotta go. See you in a few hours.>

Kree pouted. <'Kay.>

Risa felt like a monster. This, of course, leaked into her attitude toward Lars, making her hate him even more. She jogged down the boarding tunnel into the Elysium terminal and air tinted with the scent of honeysuckle. Immense white pots throughout the arrival terminals bloomed with all manner of living plants.

Since Raziel's either ignoring me or offline... A few seconds later, the visage of a teenage Japanese girl appeared by virtue of her headware placing another call. Tamashī gawked at her and spoke in rapid Japanese. White text scrolled along, translating: <Heavenly feces! What did you do green to your eyes?>

Risa laughed, both in her head and aloud. No one reacted; random laughter or shows of emotion had long ceased startling people used to cyberware. <Slow down. The translator is butchering you.>

Tamashī leaned closer, until her face took up the entire virtual projection, making her eyes the size of grapefruits. <Wow. Wow. Wow. They're *so* pretty. Intera?>

Risa explained.

<Oh... you meat-graded. I guess that's nice.> The woman's enthusiasm leaked away on a deflating sigh. <What's up? You coming to hang out?> She held up a chocolate-covered cookie stick. <I got more pocky.>

Risa hurried down a long, curved corridor past small shops and cafés, heading for the exit. <I'd love to, but I don't have time right now. I need your help.>

<Maybe...> Tamashī pointed the pocky at her. <But you owe me a sleepover. Bring that kid you keep talking about.>

<You've been spending too much time in the body of a thirteen-year-old. It's affecting your brain.> Risa grinned. <Fine. I need to find a prong named Lars Staanek.>

<Fourteen, and no problem. You got any images or video of this guy?>

<No.> Risa slowed for a security scan tunnel. A ten-foot slab of onyx-hued glass behind her depicted a blue-line skeleton, with all her cybernetics, and her laser pistols, rendered in white. A younger man in MDF armor did a double take and stood from behind the monitoring station. <Oh, shit. I gotta go. I've been 'randomly selected.'>

<Right. I'll call you when I find him.> Tamashī winked, and ended the call.

Risa put on a pleasant smile and approached a plain plastisteel table with a number of brown plastic bins. "Morning, officer."

"That's some fancy hardware you got, miss..."

"Thanks. They're natural."

The man coughed, and shot a nervous glance at the two other MDF officers working the security scanner. "I... uhh, that was not intended as an inappropriate remark. What's the purpose of your visit to Elysium? Which corporation do you work for?"

She thought back to stories that used to float around the safehouse when she was younger about how police were once prohibited from asking such questions without 'probable cause.' *Suppose nine-million credits of cyberware is probable cause?* "I'm looking for a man who may or may not exist. I believe he paid off a black market arms dealer to murder a close friend of mine. Once I find him, I'm going to do your job for you." Risa smiled.

The man blinked.

"Seriously though, I'm only going home. Unit 144C on Tier 4, in the Colossus Apartment block. It's registered to Sergeant Pavo Aram, MDF. He's my boyfriend."

"Uhh." The man stared at her for a moment. "That came out awful smooth for being a load of dustblow. You sure you're not doing a hit? What corporation do you work for?"

"None." She smiled, clasped her hands behind her back, and leaned close enough to whisper. "I'm probably putting you at risk by saying this, but I'm undercover with C-Branch."

"Riiight."

"Don't believe me?" She straightened. "Call it in. Have your boss verify me with Major General Donald Everett."

A warbling voice, too muted to make out words but loud enough to recognize as Pavo, mumbled in the man's open-faced helmet. His military bearing relaxed. "Oh, never mind. Pav says you're good."

"Is he giving you too much information?" She shifted her weight onto her right leg, which accentuated her hip, and raised one eyebrow.

Again, the man stammered, and waved to the side. "N-no. Just go before I get written up."

Risa waved at the officers and strolled into the terminal proper. *This place is built on so much deceit they don't recognize truth when it flashes its tits in their face.* The Elysium starport sat on the surface, one facility used by both intercity shuttles as well as larger, interplanetary ships. A multifaceted dome of thousands of hexagonal windows covered the main area, laced with flower-bearing vines. Whenever something big came in to land, the cyan-white glow of ion thrusters lit up the atrium, and the ground rumbled.

A pack of grade-school children made soft 'oohs' as an enormous civilian starship glided overhead, gleaming silver against the sky. The ship had such length, it took a full two minutes to pass by. Cruise liners didn't often come in to land like that, so she figured it for a maiden launch fresh from the shipyard. Risa looked away as the plastisteel hull caught the sun and glinted. *Son of a bitch.* She rubbed her face, having forgotten how painful glare could be. Nishihama Oracle cybereyes automatically filtered flashes like that out. Once she recovered the ability to see, she made her way to the nearest Morning Bean, got an orange creamsicle tea latte, and took a seat in a narrow two-person table by the window looking out into the concourse. *Already had enough caffeine today.*

Tamashī buzzed back in ten minutes later. <Bad news. I can't find a damn thing on this guy. He's completely off the grid. I pinged a couple people I know who don't spend *all* their time in the virtual world. Only two recognized the name, but they only heard he'd been throwing credits around for some bounty. Sorry.>

<Dammit.> Risa clenched her hand into a fist on the table.

Tamashī frowned. <You don't have to come to a sleepover since I didn't find anything.>

<Oh, it's fine. Hanging out with a friend isn't 'payment.' I'll stop by as soon as I can. Things aren't exactly stable right now. I'm sure Kree would love to co-op *Colony Commando* with you. Maybe you'll be able to keep up with her.>

A tall dark-skinned man passed outside with dreadlocks down to his ass. He looked like a corporate type, but the sight of him gave her an idea. <I'll call soon. Thanks for trying.>

Tamashī held up two fingers, smiled so hard her eyes closed, and cried out in a chirpy voice. <*Dōitashimashite!*>

White text translated to 'you're welcome.'

Hard to believe that woman is old enough to be my mother.

Risa slugged down the last bit of tepid tea, tossed the cup at a floating trash bot, and raced out into the street. A short jog brought her to a stairway leading to Elysium's underground portion. The Tier 1 mall looked much cleaner than its equivalent at Primus, and had about half the people. *I guess humans don't want to go underground when the sky won't kill them.* She frowned. *More evidence I'm messed up. I prefer the dark.* She touched her cheek under her eye. *Maybe not so much.* Her protector—complete darkness—was no longer a friend. Without the ultrasonic sensors in her metal eyes, her Wraith couldn't work. The dark would blind her as sure as anyone who wanted to hurt her, but she had spent many years in vents as a child before getting them.

Screw it; I'm retiring.

She threaded her way among the sparse crowd, giving a wide berth to a trio of wingnuts looking for gullible fools to join their cult worshiping some artificial intelligence, and hustled down a subterranean street tinted blue by newer plastisteel. Somewhere along the line, she'd learned that the tint indicated a higher content of indirium, a metal so far found only in asteroids, much tougher than normal plastisteel. Of course, the downside was weight. Plastisteel weighed about the same as plastic. Indirium weighed somewhat more than ancient stainless steel.

A mental nudge initiated another call. Forty seconds later, a midnight-dark face framed by a cascade of snow-white dreadlocks appeared. Luminous amber eyes mesmerized her; she'd never seen him without a ViewPane covering most of his head. The apparition created by her headware stood like a ghost among pedestrians unaware of his presence.

<Lady Black,> said the man.

<Aon.> Risa offered a head-bow. <Nice hair.>

<Change be good, girl. An' see I not d' only one ta think that way. Dem eyes look good.> He flashed a blinding smile. <What'cha need? Ay got some new Usagi-6; ay 'member ye be fond o' it.>

Risa drifted over to the left wall. <Information.>

His eyebrows rose. <Again? Always wit da' information. P'raps ay ought'a be chargin' for it dis time.>

<Lunch on me? Wasabi Dragon?>

<Alright. Twenty minutes?>

Risa hurried across a packed intersection where two streets met; the corners had been mined out to make room for two ramen bars, a porn shop, and a sandwich place. <On my way.>

Aon's virtual body dissipated. She plotted a route to the sushi place, which appeared in her vision like a trail of glimmering gold pixie dust. On the stairs down to Tier 2, she found herself stuck behind four twentysomethings with nowhere to be and all day to get there. Of the two girls, one looked like a neko: cybernetic cat ears, long furry tail the same shade of iridescent purple as her hair, and not a scrap of clothing. Her friends, as well as people walking the other way, paid little notice to her exhibitionism. The tail swished in a lazy side-to-side gesture while the group meandered down a step at a time, seeming to go even slower the more Risa wanted to hurry up.

Miss Kitty and a short man on the far left giggled at something the other woman muttered. The other girl disappeared in a sea of black: long shirt, combat boots, lacy skirt over black leggings, and dark hair.

Risa stuck her arm between the catgirl and the doom princess. "Excuse me; gotta be somewhere."

When they glanced at her, the innocence in the purple-haired woman's face shifted in an instant to venom. A second after Risa forced her way past the group, the neko held her hands up and sprouted thin metal claws from her fingertips, the cheap version of Risa's. A pink gemstone heart dangled from a blue choker made to look like a cat's collar.

"You got a problem, bitch?" asked the neko girl.

Risa glanced back, raised an eyebrow, and turned to face her. "Oh, how cute. Kitty's got claws." She raised her hands, and popped hers. Transparent Nano caught the overhead lighting, and glowed pale blue. At the slightest sign of motion from the woman, she'd kick on her speedware.

"Whoa…" The white haired guy on the far left took a step back. "Uhh, Tam…"

"Bring it!" Miss Kitty snarled, baring fangs; her tail fur fluffed.

The other guy, a Marsborn with straight black hair down to his butt, put a hand on the neko girl's shoulder. Narrow silver lettering on his black shirt read: 'Mars Academy of Engineering - Arcadia.' "Tam, don't… them shits are Nano."

"This takes 'cat fight' to a whole new level," said the doom princess, in a dry tone. She fumbled with a tiny skull-shaped purse. "Hang on you two. I need to get this on video. Can I interview you after you kill my roommate?"

Risa glanced at the young woman. *Friends like these…*

Tam's tail thrashed back and forth. She glanced at the synthetic diamond claws, a good inch and a half longer than her plain plastisteel ones, and shrank back. "Sorry."

"Oh, darn. I was hoping for some uberviolence." Doom Princess sighed and put her NetMini back in her purse.

The short man gave her a 'please don't kill us' stare.

Risa retracted her claws, shook her head, and dashed down the steps to the second tier. Wasabi Dragon, according to her navigation app, was eight-tenths of a mile away. *After sprinting across The Strand, this is easy.* She ran in the most direct path, dodging pedestrians, vendors, beggars, pickpockets, two street vendors selling cheap shit for tourists, and one man in a bright yellow robe offering the 'word' of the Church of New Mars.

Her final left turn put her on a street wide enough to have an island down the center with benches and plastic trees. Five buildings away on the left, she spotted the familiar round door painted to look like gold and carved with giant Kanji her headware translated to 'Wasabi Dragon.' Asian dragons, holographic ghosts as big around as a man's arm, swam about in the adjacent bay window making it look like an aquarium out of the Monwyn franchise. Despite her intention to take Staanek out making her stomach knot up, the sight of the place got her hungry.

As soon as she walked up to it, the portal emitted a subdued gong noise and rolled aside, into the wall away from the window. Aon, already in the waiting area, got up from his chair and smiled. In the dark room, his eyes shone like flashlights set into a powerful face that grew broader toward the jaw. He met her by a podium, behind which waited a young woman in a pink T-shirt bearing a cartoon kitten wielding two katanas.

"Sorry. Got stuck in traffic. Slow tourists." Risa blinked. "I don't think I've ever seen you without your visor before."

He patted his coat pocket. "Oh, I still got da ting. Seem rude ta' wear it in 'ere."

They followed the woman to a booth table, and sat facing each other.

"So," asked Aon. "What sort o' 'information' ye be needin' this time?"

"I need to find Lars Staanek."

Aon brushed his fingertips over his chin a few times. "I 'ave 'eard the name. Most ay talk wit' t'ink he be a fixer with a vendetta, but 'e been 'round 'ere a long time. Dis is new business."

"Yeah." Risa grumbled, waving her hand to flick the pages of a holographic menu. She poked her finger at it, selecting a basic 'sashimi lunch.' "I need to find him."

"Bad blood?" Aon ordered something, evidenced by his menu chirping.

"The worst. You remember Genevieve?"

"Aye. You tell me 'bout her couple o' times. Damn shame."

Anything I tell him will be all over the Martian underworld in an hour. "I traced it back to this guy."

Aon pursed his lips with a scolding headshake. "Now, I t'ought ye say you no assassin."

They both fell silent and leaned back from the table as a waiter set a teapot, two cups, and heated towels in front of them.

Risa wiped her hands, then dropped the steaming cloth near the edge of the table. "Assassins get paid. This is a personal vendetta. He killed someone I considered my sister."

"Fair point. De man is a shadow. De people I associate wit' aren't de kind to trust a man goin' about tings de way he's going about dem. Ay know he been trowin' money 'round, lookin' for t'ugs to take a pass at you. 'E ain't serious. Not wit' dat kind o' money, an' not offerin' it ta dat kind o' muscle."

The waiter returned with two bowls of miso soup, set them on the table, and left.

"You're right. He has been around awhile. Long enough to arrange for a bad detonator. That's what this is about. Do you know where he is?"

"I maybe can find out, but I do not know." For a big man, he handled the spoon with the delicacy of a debutante.

Risa called Tamashī again, while sipping soup. <Another quick favor. Can you get into the Elysium municipal archives? I need citycams from about three months ago.> She sent a nav pin of the approximate area where gangers trying to collect Lars's bounty had tried to abduct her by threatening to kill Chaia.

<Looking...> Tamashī leaned her head far to the right, held it there for a second, and bobbed it all the way left. <Looking.> She repeated the side-to-side gesture like a living progress bar.

"You plannin' a short meetin' with this man if you find him, yes?" Aon smiled.

"As short as I can make it." Risa slid the empty bowl over by the used towel.

The waiter returned and set a long rectangular plate in front of her with six sushi pieces and a sliced-up maki roll. In front of Aon, he placed a bowl of soup almost large enough for Kree to take a bath in, and added a tiny plate with two fried tempura shrimp.

Aon stirred it, lifted udon noodles from the broth, and let them back down. "I should let dis sit a moment. Too hot."

<Got something,> said virtual Tamashī.

Risa glanced at the false hologram floating in front of her. <You're looking for a gang bitch holding a gun on Chaia.>

<Who?> asked Tamashī.

<The creepy kid who got upset when you thought she was a doll.> Risa swiped her chopstick at the wasabi without looking and dipped a piece of tuna sushi in soy sauce. She stuffed it in her mouth, but only

chewed twice before a fiery flare blasted out her nostrils, watering her eyes and making her cough. *Damn, too much!*

Aon chuckled. "Ay t'ought ya come 'ere alla time?"

"I do." She covered her mouth long enough to finish chewing and wiped her face. "Too much wasabi."

He shrugged. "When they name the place after it, you gotta expect it."

<Score,> yelled Tamashī. Three ten-inch boxes appeared with images. Her friend found a perfect shot of them a little while before Risa got there, while they forced the girl to walk to the ambush point. <How's this? >

<Great... Dammit, how does no one notice three thugs abducting a girl with her hands tied behind her back? They walked right across the damn mall and no one got in their way.>

"You seem distracted," said Aon. "What be on ya mind?"

"Call." Risa tapped her head. "Got a friend trying to help me find this guy, too."

He nodded.

Tamashī shrugged. <No idea. Maybe because she looks so calm.>

<Any chance you can identify that woman? Don't bother running the guys. They're both dead.>

<Already tried. She's really far off the grid. Sent you a bunch of images.>

<Crap. Thanks.> Risa took another bite of sushi. <I'll try to get over soon.> She thought about smiling at Tamashī; her NIU animated it on the far end.

The hacker waved and hung up.

Risa slid her NetMini off her belt, pulled up the best image cap of the female gang thug, and shifted from 'onscreen' to 'hologram.' "How about her? Any idea who this is?"

"Hmm." He reached across the table, cradled her hand in his, and pulled it closer. Steam from his soup shimmered in the hologram and coalesced as fog on the NetMini's black screen. "Think I've seen that one 'round. She buy Sylph sometimes, smileys too. Far as I know, she goes by Alys. I believe she run wit' da Nines. Smart girl, avoid de Nightcandy an' Zoom."

"She's not *too* smart to take a job hunting a *tí-zhèn* for what Staanek is paying. Know where I can find her?"

He flashed his blinding grin. "Of course." The steady amber glow in his eyes fluctuated for a fraction of a second, and her NetMini vibrated. "At night, anywhere on the surface lookin' for a scrap wit' SecSpiders or Titans. Right about now? Follow de nav pin. She loiters on Tier 5. De Nines got de name from chems or booze. Dey're always 'to de nines.'"

"Great. Bottom feeders living on the bottom." Risa sighed. "That's going to be a great place to visit after eating raw fish."

"You could order it to go." Aon winked.

Risa clamped her chopsticks around a piece of spicy tuna maki, brought it to her mouth, and paused. "I'll hold my breath. I hear this stuff doesn't keep well."

THE NAV PIN AON PROVIDED LED RISA FIVE STORIES BELOW THE SURFACE. Expansion downward from Elysium initially started as a failsafe. When the city had been planned out, faith in the technology for a dome that large had been weak. For years, all citizens had been forced to drill and practice a rapid evacuation underground in the event of catastrophe. As luck would have it, the dome held. These days, terraforming made the odds of a serious incident minimal. Air in this region of Mars was close enough to Earth to allow a person to last a few hours outside without breathing apparatus. Plenty of time to head down in the event the dome failed. Tunnels existed deeper than Tier 5, though they'd never been finished off. Perhaps if the SPEE (Secundus, Primus, Elysium Express) tunnel made it all the way south, they would have.

Risa's nerves vibrated with anxiety as she moved among tiny dwellings lining the sides of a cramped passage. Tarnished plastisteel panels, quite stark in contrast to the hospital sterility of Tier 1, hid behind piles of shipping cartons, old furniture, and scorch marks.

Someone's got missiles down here? She walked faster. In the middle of the day, most of the unfortunates who lived this deep worked on the surface at menial jobs or slept off the aftereffects of the night before. A shadow moved, watching her. The turn of her head that so often sent threats scurrying away in the other direction had no effect. No glowing purple eyes, no outward clue she was more trouble than she'd be worth. Pavo said she could pass for eighteen again. She didn't consider herself abnormally short, but she *did* have an almost 'elven' physique. Being so thin made life in the tunnels easy, but without her metal eyes, it also made her look like an easy target.

At least people won't assume I'm an assassin. The nav pin led her to this neighborhood, a tight interconnecting grid of pitiful tunnels. Residents paid paltry rent, a mere thousand credits or so per month compared to eight or nine times that for a surface apartment. The poorest ones squatted wherever they could, often shooting at anyone who tried to kick them out. For most of them, prison would be an upgrade.

The figure emerged from shadow, a man somewhere in his twenties with indigo hair and dull-crimson eyeshadow. She stopped walking and met his hungry gaze. Based on the look in his eye, he thought her an easy mark despite the laser pistols. She grinned. *Bet he's expecting me to run.*

Risa swiveled to face him, and rushed forward. In a blur of speedware, she closed the distance to him, jumping into a knee strike to his chest that shoved him against the wall he'd been leaning on. Before his facial expression had changed in reaction to her motion, she had one hand worth of Nano claws teasing at the side of his neck and jaw.

Speedware off.

Two of the slender points drew blood.

He yelped. "Gah! Shit!"

She spoke in a low tone, as menacing as she could make herself sound. "I'm in a hurry. You're in my way, and no one will miss another wannabe rapist. Where's Alys?" Risa narrowed her eyes.

"I ain't no rapist." He tried to sound tough, but a trace of a whimper threaded under his words. The man attempted a weak smile. "Just lookin' for creds. I ain't know no Alys."

Risa frowned. "Too bad. That means you're not useful."

"Wait." He stood on tiptoe in an effort to distance his neck from her claws. "Street E5-11, Apartment 18."

"Thanks." She took a step back and retracted the claws, curling her fingers to smear the blood from the tips. "I'm going to walk away like we never met. Don't give me a reason to remember you."

He scooted to his right and slipped into the door of an apartment. She walked fast, trying to project as threatening a visage as possible while hiding her worry. Without the Wraith online, her speedware wouldn't auto-activate if it sensed an incoming projectile. Granted, it never worked on energy weapons—they had no substance to detect.

Three streets ahead, she turned left, went down four more, and followed the numbers on the left until she found Apartment 18. A corroded plastisteel slab hung in the doorway, not quite on its sliding rails. She pushed it aside and stepped into a living room flooded with boxes, both full and empty... mostly stolen consumer electronics, shoes, clothes, and a few cases of OmniSoy packets for a 'Vari-Quik' meal reassembler. One company's experiment in proprietary serving-sized packets for the base protein slime wasn't the runaway success they'd hoped for; rather than capture the interest of busy families, their one-meal pouches had become a staple for college students and druggies.

Snoring led her down a short connecting hall. She peered into a side room where a jumble of small limbs occupied a Comforgel pad. At least six underwear-clad preteen boys slept in a mass, like wild wolf pups clustering together for warmth. The room smelled like wet dog and stale soda. Risa backed away cringing, and kept going down the hall past a dark bathroom where a nude, scrawny woman—not Alys—about her age sprawled on her back between the toilet and the autoshower. A collection of autoinjectors of various colors—yellow, green, orange, red—lay scattered around her arms and legs. Risa stared for a moment at the woman's concave stomach until she could perceive movement.

The money Lars offered had to seem like a fortune... maybe a lifeline. I was wrong. Her coming after me wasn't stupidity... it was desperation.

In the back bedroom, the object of her search—the woman who'd put a gun to Chaia's head—occupied a queen-sized Comforgel pad, draped half off the side, face over the carpet. With only skin-hugging underpants on, she looked far less threatening than Risa remembered, despite her muscular build. She didn't trust the woman's apparent vulnerability. No one who lived in this part of the city in a perpetual high had the time (or willpower) to work out. Alys didn't have the physique of a pro lifter, but appeared far too jacked to be a run-of-the-mill doser.

Risa tensed as she reached the door. *Just want info. Don't make me kill you.* Augmented hearing picked up breathing right inside the door to the left, and the creak of tendons.

She activated her speedware as she rushed in. A slow-moving man, clothed only in dirt lunged at her with a punch wrapped in a set of spiked indirium knuckles. Risa leaned to her left, flowing around the incoming fist, and grabbed his wrist with her right hand. Twisting the limb away from her, she pushed his punch to the side and drove her left forearm into the back of his elbow, breaking the joint. A quick yank on the arm changed his charge to a stumble.

Her motion continued in a fluid spin; she delivered a reverse roundhouse kick to the back of his head, which flung him face-first into a wall-mounted storage bin on the opposite side of the bedroom door. Dust erupted from two drawers slammed closed by his impact. The metal knuckles slipped off his fingers and struck the floor with a heavy *clunk.* He wobbled around to face her, blood running out of his nose. She spun the other way, kicking him across the jaw.

His face warped and flapped like a layer of thick rubber stretched around a Gee-ball orb. Both eyes rolled up into his head as he fell to his knees and went over sideways, unconscious.

Risa shut down her speedware.

"Stop makin' so much fuckin' noise." Alys moaned. "Tryin' ta sleep."

A three-second glance around the bedroom found nine pistols, three knives, and one shotgun leaning on the wall by the headboard. She grabbed a length of cord from the floor, pounced on Alys, and bound her wrists behind her back before the woman regained coherence.

"What the fuck are you doing?" Alys squirmed.

Risa put a hand on the woman's shoulder and pushed her down onto the rug. "It was faster than safing all the guns you've got stashed here." She held her right hand in front of the woman and sprouted claws.

Alys trembled.

"I see you remember me."

The woman strained to look around, panic clear in her eyes.

"Relax. The psionic kid isn't here. She's not even on Mars anymore."

"W-what do you want?" Alys struggled to free her hands, muscles bulging in her arms. "I didn't tell him shit. I said you were fuckin' crazy and I ran away. Son of a bitch never said nothin' 'bout you bein' no *ti-zhèn.*"

Risa flicked her index finger, shaving thin slices from an empty instant ramen bowl on the carpet by the bed. "My interest in Lars changed. Where is he?"

The woman ceased struggling when she noticed the unconscious man. "You said you wouldn't kill me..."

"How can someone with six—or is it seven, kinda hard to tell from that pile up—sons threaten to kill a child?"

A nervous laugh escaped Alys. "If you had any, you'd understand how you'd be tempted to shoot one."

"Guess we're wired different." Risa shredded the remainder of the bowl in one swipe. "Or maybe girls are easier."

"Hey!" Alys tried to squirm away. "Only one of the little buggers is mine. The rest'r his friends 'at never leave. Me an' Zane don't beat on 'em like their people, so they stay here. Doz might be an orphan."

Risa sighed. "You don't have to flog the sympathy bit. I didn't come here to kill you. All I want to know is where you found Lars."

"S'not dustblow." Alys grumbled. "There's all kinds of security systems and sensors and shit. Lars will see your tweaked ass coming."

"Don't be so sure." *Tamashī should be able to deal with that.*

"He's gonna kill me if I tell you anything."

Risa got off the woman's back and stood. "I sincerely doubt Lars will be doing anything after I'm done with him."

Alys rolled on her side to look up at her. "You're going to kill him."

"Yeah." She turned her hands palms up, and curled her fingers. "That's probably the best way to deal with this."

After a long stare, Alys broke eye contact. "You seem different somehow. Look, I know you can kill me before I can say 'holy shit.' Cut me loose, and I'll tell you whatever I know."

Risa leaned over and severed the binding with her pinky claw.

Alys pulled her arms around front and rubbed her wrists. "Mind if I put on a shirt?"

"Do it slow." Risa glanced at the door. *Hmm. Raziel's not a real angel. Who do I pray to and ask that the kids stay asleep? It's well past noon. What are they doing in bed now, anyway?*

After pulling on a ratty Mars-camo T-shirt, Alys got up from the floor and sat on the edge of the Comforgel pad. "He haunts this nightclub on the surface—Iniquity. It's mostly full of emancipated."

"Sounds lovely." Risa frowned.

"I heard some rumors that he paid off the owner to let him like live there and stuff. Guy lurks in the back of the place like some kind of crime lord. I heard about that bounty he put out on you. Couldn't resist. Got pointed at a chem dealer who sent me to a pimp, who—after I messed him up—sent me to some fixer name'a Hayato. He's the one who told me to go to Iniquity and order a 'purple fairy' from the bartender."

Risa rubbed her face. "Who the hell is this guy?"

"He looked like any other prong in a suit. He ain't no Marsborn, that's for sure."

"If you're giving me a dead end, we'll meet again." Risa backed to the door.

Alys gazed down at the glowing red Comforgel pad and reached across her chest to scratch her arm. "It's as much as I know. If he left…"

"Who's that, Mom?" asked a small voice.

Risa glanced back at a thin black-haired boy somewhere between nine and twelve with shoulder-length jet hair mushed all to one side from how he'd been sleeping. His dark-blue eyes reminded her of Kree. The boy blinked at the man face down on the floor, right arm bent back at an unnatural angle.

"She had a couple questions for me." Alys pulled her hair out of her eyes. "Go back to bed for a few minutes."

The boy stared at the man, looked at Risa, and laughed. He ran out, still laughing, and slammed a distant door. A muted "Zane got his ass kicked by this skinny chick" came through the wall.

Risa cracked a smile.

Alys looked away from an expression that had to come off as psychotic, given normal ears couldn't have heard what the boy said. She kneaded her hands in her lap, eyeing the shotgun by the wall.

"Kid said something funny." Risa faced the door out. "That all you got about Lars?"

"Yeah," said Alys.

Something's not right. Risa narrowed her eyes at the woman. "So why'd you grab Chaia?"

"Uhh. This is gonna sound like I'm feeding you dustblow, but…" Alys closed her eyes and leaned forward, face in her palm. "Lars said you had a thing about kids. You aborted some mission because some were in the way. He suggested I use that somehow." She scowled. "I wish he'd warned me you were augged."

Pressure weighed down on Risa's heart. *How the hell could he know that?* "If he told you that, you wouldn't have taken the job."

Alys sucked in a breath in her nose. "I found some muscle at Iniquity willing to split it three ways. We had no real idea where to find you. All we had was a cam-grab of you. We threw some creds at this fringer deck jockey one of 'em knew. Dude got into the cams. Couple days later, he buzzes me, says he got a ping. So we haul ass out there. Goin' through this merch quad by the Silver Palm, and we see this kid alone, hiding in the corner."

"Random opportunity?" Risa wasn't sure what to make of the disoriented expression on Alys's face.

"I… She looked right at me with those creepy eyes. Smiled, like I was her long-lost mother or something come to save her from the street. She walked right up to us, no fear at all, and asked if we were looking for 'the purple-eyed lady.' Next thing I know, it seemed like a great idea to grab this kid and drag her along as a hostage." Alys hid her face in her hands and shivered. "Damn psios. One minute I think she's adorable, the next I wanted to hurt her."

"Damn..." Risa sighed. "Well, the three of you *were* planning on jumping me."

"Maybe... but I was pretty close to chickening out," said Alys. "The whole thing didn't feel right. Then when that kid... all the worry evaporated. Creepy little thing even handed me the cord we tied her with."

Risa pictured the wide grin on the girl with the too-blue eyes, unsure what to think of her now. "Chaia sees the future. She had to know I wasn't going to kill you." *She told me to go for the men.*

Alys stared into nowhere. "The kid led us to that alley. It went from not feeling right to being totally fucked. I don't remember everything clear. Vak and Piston kept talking about having a little fun with you before we handed you over to Lars. Vak wanted to kill the kid too, you know... no witnesses. I felt like two different people. One screaming *run the fuck away* and the other all pissed off and fearless."

"Maybe I don't feel so guilty over killing those two." Risa edged to the door.

After a minute of vacancy in her expression, Alys looked up. "That's what's different. You got new eyes."

"Sorry about your boyfriend's arm."

"It's hard to find a guy that ain't an asshole down here." Alys glanced at him. "Did you kill him?"

"No. Probably gave him a concussion."

"We cool?"

"Yeah." Risa walked out. "We cool."

15

ONE LESS MONKEY

A clean, cool breeze blasted Risa's hair off her shoulders when she emerged from the last leg of the stairwell leading to the surface. She never realized how stagnant and metallic the air in the underground was until having her first taste of surface fresh.

After agreeing to help, Tamashī ran off somewhere in cyberspace doing the 'ninja cat' thing around the virtual recreation of Iniquity. She'd also hacked an order of OmniSoy and kids' clothes into the TMC online store for Alys. Hopefully, the bottle of headache pills would tell the woman who sent it.

'Part 1: cut the balls off Lars's surveillance system' was underway. Time for 'Part 2: look inconspicuous'.

She checked the local MarsNet in a large, curved wraparound 'screen' her headware pumped into her brain. It took less than a minute for her to find the nearest walk-in shop selling the sort of clothing that wouldn't stand out in a crowd of mixed gangers. She summoned a PubTran car to her location, and hopped in. The store, 'Nothing Matters,' sat six miles away on the opposite side of the city.

The term 'emancipated' had once referred to a specific gang, which disappeared long before she'd been born. They'd been the first gang large enough to attract the attention of the Defense Force, though their only real agenda had been anarchy. They considered themselves apart from society, beholden to no laws but their own. *They were sort of like the MLF, if the MLF was real.* Of course, the Emancipated didn't try to liberate anyone but themselves.

These days, the word meant anyone affiliated with a street gang, from the ones who wanted nothing more than to sit around and get high all day, to the vigilantes, to the criminals, to the psychotic murder machines. Risa sighed. *I'm walking into a mess.*

She hopped out as soon as the self-driving taxi opened. A silvery-grey building covered in 'artistic' swaths of barbed wire, bullet gouges, and graffiti looked open but deserted. *Guess they're still asleep. Lucky for me.*

Dark cobalt-blue letters faded in and out over the door, a holographic rendition of the store's name. Two mirrored panels opened at her approach, clearing the way for a wall of sound to smash into her. She cringed. The boosts in her ears dampened themselves, reducing the music to a tolerable level. Less than twenty seconds after she walked inside, her headware identified the net stream from whence the music originated, patched it into her auditory controller, and blanked it out of her awareness. As far as Risa was concerned, the only noise in the room came from her boots squeaking on the polished black tiles.

Ah, much better.

Shelves and stands packed the place full of gang couture. She spent only a few minutes hunting, not being picky, and grabbed a gauzy black skirt similar to Kree's, which also happened to be flecked with black glitter. *She's going to lose her mind.* Risa grinned. She snagged a hot-pink, midriff-baring, mesh tank top as well as a mini-jacket baggy enough to hide her laser pistols.

"Hey, what the hell are you doin'?" Across the store, a man shouted over the electro-slam she could no longer hear. "There's a goddamned customer over there. Go help her."

"Fuck off," yelled a young-sounding female.

"You wanna get fired?"

After a short pause, the girl laughed. "Go ahead. This job sucks anyway. If you fire me, you lose access to this pussy."

"Tia, your father isn't paying me to be a babysitter. I'm paying *you* to supposedly work here. What's he going to say when I tell him all you do is stand around?"

She scoffed. "What happened to 'Nothing Matters?' What do *you* think my dad will say when I tell him I've got your baby in me and I'm moving out?"

The man emitted a strange gargling noise.

Risa emerged from the tight-packed shelves. A thirty-something guy, tall, with deep-blue hair in a spherical poof stood near a girl that could've been anywhere from fourteen to nineteen. He had one fist pressed to his mouth, eyes closed as if meditating.

The black-lipsticked girl rested her elbows on a shelf behind the register area, her body draped in a casual backward lean, a dark 'I win' smile on her face. Another half-inch, and the entire store would see under a skirt so tight it made her hips look like polished volcanic glass. Half her hair was black, the other dark purple, and two shirts engulfed her insubstantial body: a baggy lime-green rag hanging off her right shoulder with a white half tee under it.

The man smiled at Risa and leaned closer to the girl. "At least ring her up. Do *something* to justify being here."

"*Fine.*" Tia muttered and pushed off the shelf, sulking as she dragged herself up to the terminal. "Hey. Welcome to Nothing Matters and shit." She grabbed the skirt, mumbling at a volume she thought the music would eat. "Oh, this is cute… if you're six." She scanned it and stuffed it in a thin plastic bag.

Risa ignored the jab, studying the black eyeliner on the girl's face. The thought of using CamNano usually came with the unpleasant feelings associated with going out in public naked. Today, the nanobot-powered chameleon implant would be free of anxiety. Only invisibility required a lack of clothes as it wouldn't be effective if people saw hollow garments moving around. Risa changed her skin tone from Marsborn to pale-Caucasian, and darkened the area around her eyes in a complex fade from black through indigo to violet, inside the shape of painted stars.

"Whoa," said the store manager, mesmerized by the change.

Tia grabbed the jacket, fluffed it out, and scanned it while yelling, "Okay, this is cute. Plenty of room for extra e-mags too."

Blinding hot pink spread along the length of Risa's hair, welling up out of the roots and racing down to where the tips hung a few inches from her belt. The skin tone effect reached her hands, as if color oozed out of her sleeves and wrapped over her fingers. She felt like a stranger in her own skin.

Tia looked up with a forced smile; her expression faded to shock for an instant, and she screamed. "Holy shit! Don't do that!"

Risa plucked two Hello Kitty hair ties, hard plastic cat faces about an inch across, off a small rack by the terminal and added them to the pile. "Sorry. I'm in a hurry. Mind if I put this stuff on now?"

"I'd go into the back. You might wind up with a dick in a place you don't want it to be." Tia nodded at the guy to her left.

Risa looked at the man, who raised his hands in a 'this chick is crazy' gesture, and shook his head to the negative. *This stuff is made to hide under clothing... I'm not going in there unarmored.* She stepped into the skirt, pulling it up over the ballistic suit. The pink shirt came next, followed by the jacket. Between the gauzy skirt, top, and boots, her armor looked like leggings. Last, she put her hair up in pigtails.

"Ugh," said the clerk. "Where'd you learn how to do pigtails... you, uhh, are trying to do pigtails right? You kinda suck at it."

Risa raised an eyebrow. "That bad?"

"One's almost on the top of your head, the other looks like it's sticking out of your ear. They're not even the same length or thickness." Tia let off a noise part sigh and part exasperated yell, and darted out from behind the counter. Risa tensed at someone moving up behind her so fast, but kept herself still as the teen redid her hair into two neat pigtails. She even tied bows in the red-black ribbons on the hair ties. After securing the second one, she grabbed Risa's arms and spun her around. "Oh, that's so *surface*! Is that makeup or a tat job around your eyes? Like... *all* the colors."

"Makeup." Risa glanced at the manager. Her soma read high levels of frustration and embarrassment. *Nah... she's just busting his balls.*

———

From the relative safety of a dark maintenance passage between two residential towers, Risa observed the front of Iniquity. Strong spotlights bathed the place in an otherworldly crimson glow. Both bouncers by the entrance had cosmetic cyberware comprising devil horns, yellow eyes, and black teeth. The larger of the two musclebound oafs even opted for a skin color shift to demon-red. At a touch past two in the afternoon, a crowd of forty-odd disaffected youths lurked in a mass out front. Most openly partook of various chems: inhalers, derm patches, pills, or synthetic alcohol.

A cough from behind startled her, though she held back any outward reaction other than a casual glance to the rear. Not quite thirty meters away, a teen girl sat up out of the trash. Naked, save for a thick, black choker, she gazed around as if confused by the presence of narrow pipes running along both walls in the narrow alley. A strip of fluorescent green over the center top of her head hung midway down her back, the sides shaved.

"Ugh, not again." She rolled onto her hands and knees, grabbed one of the wire conduits, and pulled herself upright. The aftereffects of sex dribbled down her leg, and she spent a few seconds wiping with a scrap of trash before rummaging around the pile in search of her clothing. "I can't believe those assholes just left me here again."

Risa turned her attention back to the club. *Too many people in the front.* She watched for a few minutes, paying little attention to the echo of rustling. Somewhere within the red building, she hoped to find Lars Staanek. *You've been a flea on my ass for months. I don't get why you're only trying to be annoying. Are you teasing me or sincerely incompetent? Whatever. Don't care anymore. You crossed a goddamn line trying to kill Gen.* She sighed. Another alley, wider than this maintenance conduit, on the left side of Iniquity offered the possibility of either a back door or a better way in.

"Fuck!" yelled the girl. "They swiped my shit too." She growled.

Again, Risa looked to the rear. The teen had either recovered or scavenged clothes: a dark-blue bra, shiny leggings the same color, a black miniskirt, and heavy-duty combat boots similar to Risa's. She shook a tiny purse as if the only reason drugs hadn't fallen out of the empty bag was that she hadn't thrashed it hard enough.

The girl made a sour face. "He's a piece of shit."

Risa walked out into the open, adopting the erratic sway of someone high on Zoom. She widened her eyes and stared into space, pretending to see hallucinations. Every so often, she waved her arms about as if for balance or tried to grab things that weren't there. A Zoom high would have one of two effects on the average gang thug: either they'd stay well away from her, due to the tendency users had to swing in an instant from placid to violent, or they'd try to take advantage of a helpless girl.

She hoped for option one. The less of a scene she caused on the way in, the better.

Tamashī called in to her headware, which created a life-sized bust floating in space. Her avatar resembled a ten-year-old girl in a ninja costume, with cat ears, claws, and a tail. *Well, that should help with my act.* <Hey. I'm in.>

<That's adorable,> said Risa.

<You like it?> Tamashī's voice rose to a near-squeak, and throbbing cartoon hearts replaced her eyes for a second.

<Please tell me you don't kill people like that.>

<No way.> Tamashī shook her head. <I'm strictly a sneaky kitty. Looking like a kid makes people hesitate. Sometimes when I get caught where I don't belong, I can just say I got lost. Anyway, I'm in. Your boy's got some serious stuff set up in there, but nothing I can't get past. I'm a little confused. The hardware feels like it's mil-spec, but the processing power and memory are limited.>

<Military?> Risa blinked. <If Lars is C-Branch too, I'm going to move to a colony.>

Tamashī made a whiny, pondering noise. <Meh, I don't think so. C-Branch has better tech. This is probably a few-generations-old black market or recycled unit. I made their network my bitch.>

<So they're not scanning?> Risa peered out from the maintenance passage, looking left and right.

<They are. I'm standing behind a monitoring construct now that runs all the eyes and ears on the place. This stuff would've picked up your speedware and claws from about two hundred feet. It's all mine now, so don't worry. You're safe to go in.>

<Thanks. I owe ya.>

Tamashī's head quadrupled in size, went cartoony, and flashed a wavy grin. <Yep! You do.> She resumed normal proportion with a sound like a bubble popping. <Go on. I'll keep them blind. By the way, you're a psychotic dark faerie. It's a good look for you.>

<All I need are wings.>

<They can do that, you know.> Tamashī smiled. <I mean, you can't fly with them, but you can get faerie wings. Holograms or even physical ones.>

<No thanks. I'm trying to get closer to human, not go off the deep end.>

Tamashī giggled, and hung up.

Risa loped among the emancipated, holding her breath whenever she walked into someone's vapor cloud. Though she had a Tox Filter installed in her trachea, she didn't trust it to capture all traces of narcotic immediately. With some of those chems, like Lace, all it would take is a couple of molecules getting in and she could wake up an addict. Fortunately, Lace had to be injected, not inhaled. No chance of catching it on someone's breath.

About fifteen paces from the alley she aimed for, two guys wearing the logo of the Karnal gang took notice of her.

"Hey, check out the zoomie." The one on the left elbowed his friend and pointed at Risa. "Think she'd go for a three-way?"

His friend shrugged. "Maybe. Easy to find out."

She scowled, entertaining a momentary daydream of luring them into the alley and killing them, even if they intended to ask rather than take. Who knew what a person on Zoom would see in the middle of sex. They might mistake the dick heading toward their mouth for food, or a serpent that wanted to swim down their throat and eat their heart... or maybe it would sprout eyes and start talking.

As much as their assumption she'd freely open her legs for them bothered her, Lars took precedence. She didn't want to waste time even trying to tell them to piss off. A brief tweak of speedware allowed her to snag a knife from a nearby belt so fast no one noticed the motion. She moved as though pulling the knife out of her coat, hissed, and tried to stab thin air. Risa activated her Fangz, a faint whirr vibrating her skull as cybernetic canines extended, and changed her affect from dazed to wild-eyed mania.

The emancipated took more notice of her, but those who did all backed away. A few hands settled on weapons, but no one drew.

"I won't let them get me," said Risa in a raspy whisper. "Damn clowns are everywhere." She sliced at nothing, directing her wobble to the alley. "Mommy, where are you? I keep killing the clowns, but I can't find you."

The Karnal thugs halted. They seemed to weigh the odds of being mistaken for a clown against their being able to sneak up on her. She acted as though she ducked a punch, and charged into the alley with the knife raised to stab something.

As soon as she left the glare of the crimson light, she pressed herself against the wall and waited, letting her weaponized teeth retract to normal. After a minute with no sign of the thugs following, she darted across the alley to the other side and studied the outside of the club. It felt strange being *outside* and looking at a building with an actual roof, not walls that connected to rock overhead. The exterior offered no way in, only plastisteel panels and grating-covered windows painted black. Whatever went on inside wasn't meant to be seen from out here.

At least this isn't a Syndicate place. Everyone screwing here is at least willing.

Using square outcroppings of panels, wire guides, and window cages, Risa scaled the wall to the roof with ease. A rattling air handler, plus creative use of Nano claws, provided entry to the building's ventilation system. She slipped in and lowered herself along a vertical shaft. The fan blade whirring below her feet slowed to a stop.

<Thanks again.>

Tamashi's voice giggled in her head. <You're welcome.>

Risa climbed down past the fan mechanism, which started up again as soon as she cleared. A cartoon black cat popped into existence in front of her, waved, and trotted off. *Okay, that is the strangest waypoint software I've ever seen.* She followed the cat along a length of conduit, turned left, and entered another fan chamber. The cat leapt onto the spinning machine, becoming a blur of black. The device powered off, the smear of ink resolving once more into a cat as the fan slowed. When the blades stopped, the animal perched on the tip of one, licking its paw. It jumped off and led Risa around another series of tunnels before diving down a vertical conduit.

This has to be the ground floor ceiling now. She squatted, leaving a hand on the corner for balance, and looked both ways. The cat trotted off behind her. On all fours, she crawled after it to the first opportunity allowing her a right turn about thirty meters later. A cone of light radiated from the ground a short distance from the corner, painting the top of the shaft with lines from a grille.

Risa crept closer and peered down at a stage area made to look like a ziggurat carved from obsidian, bedecked with demonic statues and imagery. Two bored-looking guys tinkered with electronics inside an opened hatch, propped up on pneumatic struts like the hood of a car. Open ground surrounded it to at least sixty feet in all directions. Stains, some alcohol and some blood, spattered here and there. Small bots raced about collecting trash, mostly cups, as well as dead inhalers, spent derm patches, or boot-crushed plastic autoinjectors.

The place isn't even open yet. Perfect.

<Meow.> The cartoon cat cleared his throat with the voice of an English butler. <This way, ma'am.>

On two legs, the cat walked off, forepaws clasped behind his back.

She followed until it made an abrupt stop, holding up a paw. Three seconds after she thought to yell 'what' at it, she spotted the telltale glow of a laser grid. Night vision mode used to make those bright and obvious. <I almost crawled right into that.> She clenched a fist, but resisted the urge to punch the ductwork. <I need to get a better visor.>

<Got it,> said Tamashi's disembodied voice. <And yeah, you do. Even if you're only gaming, the one you're using now is cheap trash.>

She frowned. <Needed something and it was right there in front of me.>

<Not judging, merely advising.>

The cat brought her down another sixty meters of thin metal ductwork, a hands-and-knees crawl the entire time. At long last, it stopped by another grille and pointed at it like a game show hostess indicating the prize up for grabs. After a bow, the feline dissipated in a swirl of pixels.

From inside, a male voice muttered in Russian, sounding angry.

Risa crept up to the vent. A pale man in his early forties with tight curly hair burnished with silver over his ears sat behind an ornate desk that appeared to be carved from real wood. Two tall electronic paintings of nude crimson women with draconic wings and long spaded tails flanked the door connecting the inner office to the rest of the club. The succubi writhed and danced, an endless cycle of the same alluring gestures. Another digital painting, covering the entire wall opposite her vent, depicted a massive throng of demons rampaging over a medieval village, copulating, killing, and devouring everything from goats to elderly villagers.

Risa blinked. *Okay, there's messed in the head and then there's whatever these people are.* A few mental urges activated the Russian language chip still in her head, and started an audio/visual recording.

"... failure to produce any actionable intelligence on the MLF. We already know their command center is in Primus. You haven't given us anything to legitimize your continued operations budget. While you're dicking around with thugs, the target is out there."

The man's eyes swelled with exasperation. "Sir, I—"

"Interrupt me again, and I'll have your testicles in a jar on my desk while you're digging rat shit out of ventilation ducts on a remote mining station. The Senior Vice President of Tactical Operations himself has asked me what the fuck you're doing up there. You are going to capture this operative, kill this operative, or get your pathetic ass back to Munich for a new assignment."

The man she assumed was Lars Staanek bristled. The urge to scream and lash out brimmed in his eyes; the way he glared at the holo-terminal made her think him a psionic about to crush it with his mind.

"Do you understand, Staanek? You've been on Mars long enough to have completely dismantled this group, yet for everything you've attempted, they are still there. They are *still* causing catastrophic damage to our interests, and you are *still* living like a king in exile. Did you even bother to read the incident report of that fiasco in Bliss last month? Forty-nine-billion credits in damage"—the voice coming from the terminal rose to a near-shrieking rage—"and you're balls-deep in sixteen-year-olds without a care in the world! This stops now, Staanek."

Lars scowled. "Sir, I am trying to present the appearance of plausible random acts of violence. If I were to employ our usual tactics in dealing with this woman, their intelligence operatives would become aware of my presence. The MLF does not possess the financial resources to replace her. I have information that proves she's recently upgraded her capabilities. Our friends in Japan would take a rather keen interest in learning the make and model of her neuralware. It was only the small hope that we may turn her to our interests that has kept me from contacting them."

"Hope? Are you a fool, Staanek? Those 'worthless rebels' managed to send a *single* agent into Bliss of all places, where she proceeded to eradicate forty-seven percent of our military infrastructure on Mars."

"All due respect, sir." Lars spoke in a cold, snide tone. "I'm not the one who decided to run a Cryomil line over a canyon or fail to install a firebreak between pipe and reservoir tank because it cost too much. Perhaps you should be asking other questions of other people. Or, better yet, perhaps you should look into why the security at Bliss was lax enough that an untrained civilian with a couple of augments could stroll right in *and out*."

The voice emanating from the terminal growled. "You've had years to track this bitch down, and still nothing. I wouldn't be surprised if she's on her knees under your desk right now."

Lars leaned his weight on two fists, knuckles whitening, as he loomed over the immaterial screen. "You're fishing for a scapegoat. Do you honestly think the Board is going to look at me as being responsible for Bliss or the six-thousand people in the Combat Operations division who were *supposed* to be paying attention to their surroundings instead of each other's dicks?" He straightened and lowered his voice. "You are the director, are you not? I'd say Bliss security is your responsibility, but there *is* no Bliss to defend anymore. It's not my ass in the fire, Nikolas. It's yours."

A jab at a holographic button cut off the call before the other man's incoherent scream morphed into words. Lars, hands clasped behind his back, paced.

Risa's jaw hung open. *Son of a bitch. He's ACC Intelligence. Right here in Elysium. He wasn't after Gen personally, he was throwing shit at the MLF in general.* Her intent to call Everett resulted in a small 'signal unavailable' message floating in space. *Shit. Jammer.* A cold sweat crept down the back of her neck at the worry some of his equipment might've picked up the attempt. She eyed the distance from the vent to the desk where Lars continued pacing, muttering in German.

Too far. I have to assume he's got speedware. Both Hotaru-6 pistols felt like lead weights under her arms. *They'll go through the walls and all hell will break loose. I gotta do this silent.*

Risa backed up to the junction and rapid-crawled back the way she came. *I'm not an assassin.* She continued for fifteen meters and turned left. *I can't leave him. What if he disappears?* She scooted up to a ventilation grille overlooking an L-shaped corridor outside the inner office. Left led to the double doors behind which Lars likely still paced. Shadows moved to the right, the sign of at least one bodyguard. Risa huddled against the cold plastisteel. *How tweaked is this? I'm part of a false C-Branch operation and I'm doing actual C-Branch work.* She wiped sweat off her palms. *Beats planting bombs in civilian areas.*

She sprouted one Nano claw from her right index finger and all five on her left hand. After spearing the five into the vent grille, she sliced around the outside with the single claw and drew the loose metal slab into the duct. Claws retracted, she rolled onto her belly and slid out, hung from the edge for a second, and dropped the last few inches to the floor.

Get close. Take him out. Leave the way I came in. Easy. She stepped up to the double doors feeling like a twelve-year-old sent to the principal's office. *Wait a minute. I'm not an assassin, dammit. What if...* She grinned. Deep breath. Dazed expression. Acting scared was easy; she merely stopped hiding her feelings from the world. Risa opened the double doors and stumbled inside as if shoved from behind.

Lars stopped pacing and glanced at her.

She clasped her hands in front, kept her gaze down, and trembled. "Blackstar sent me as an apology for not doin' that job yet."

He frowned, speaking English with a perfect regional accent. "Remind me which organization you belong to?"

"SecSpiders. I'm just a prospect tryin' ta get in." She crept up to the desk, kneading her skirt in her hands. Only the thought she had no intention of *doing* anything let her continue talking. "They said I had ta let you do whatever you wanted to me."

Lars unclasped his hands and sauntered around the desk. He lifted her chin with a finger and regarded her face.

Shit. She added trembles and tried to shy away. CamNano augmented her blush.

"You're about sixteen or seventeen?" He raised an eyebrow.

Risa's adrenaline had cranked up too far to permit fake tears. She wobbled as if light-headed, and added a trace of daze to her voice. "Sixteen… two weeks ago." *Now's my chance.* She leaned in to kiss him.

Lars's light grip on her chin shoved her to the side with enough force to leave her half-sprawled over the desk. "I'm not interested in children. If this 'Blackstar' is so keen on apologizing, tell him to send me Risa Black… or at least an adult whore."

He turned away, paused a second, and took three steps to a wet bar along the back wall, where he un-stoppered a tall, rectangular bottle a quarter full of a reddish liquid while grumbling under his breath in English about wanting to cut the testicles off whoever started the rumors about his being attracted to underage girls.

Risa pushed herself off the desk and stood. *Did a Corporate just refuse sex with a sixteen-year-old? Now I really think I'm losing my grip.* She spun to face him. "Mister Staanek, if I go right back outside they're gonna think I chickened out and beat the shit outta me."

He poured two fingers into a tumbler glass.

She walked up behind him. "It's cool you don't wanna make me do anything. I didn't expect you'd be like so… honorable or whatever."

"Mmm." He took a sip and loosened a silvery-black cravat. "There's probably quite a bit about me you don't know." Lars grinned at his own joke.

She hugged him from behind. He tensed, but seemed to have bought her scared teenager act. "Can I tell you a secret?"

He flashed a half-amused smile, took another sip of his drink, and let out a heavy breath. "So hard to find decent cognac here. Okay, I'll bite. What's your secret?"

She loosened her hug as he turned to look at her. "I'm Risa Black."

Speedware stopped the world. She leapt into a kiss, firing jets of tranquilizer from her Fangz implant down his throat. In her accelerated state, the lip lock seemed to take a full minute as the chem flowed. At half a dose, Lars screamed into her mouth, filling it with the taste of harsh, burning liquor. When the streams spraying from her metal fangs stopped, she pushed him away. He bumped against the bar counter and slid to sit on the floor, already showing signs of paralysis, his expression frozen in a mask of total disbelief. A few drops lingering in her mouth numbed the tip of her tongue.

"You…" He twitched as if having a stroke.

Risa let the Caucasian color fade from her skin, and the pink melt out of her hair. His eyes widened as if staring up at the Schwarzgeist that rumor made her out to be, come to take his soul. His leg twitched, his arm lifted, stiff as a board.

"I came here planning to kill you, Lars. But… I changed my mind. I think you've been taking your sweet time, hiring incompetent morons, because you like it here and don't really want to go back." She backed up two steps and fell seated in his desk chair. "Mind if I borrow your Vidphone?"

Lars slumped over to the side, unconscious. Risa swiveled around in the seat, and connected her NetMini to the M3 jack on his terminal with the spare wire she carried in her weapons harness.

<Tamashī, are you still there? Can you go all bad kitty on this terminal? Go in through my 'mini.>

<On it,> said Tamashī.

While she waited, she resumed her pink-haired ganger girl coloration. Fourteen seconds later, the login prompt became a holographic desktop. Risa poked General Everett's PID in her contact list, and the desk terminal—which bypassed the jammer—initiated an outbound video call. The echoes of footfalls came from beyond the double doors, someone approaching in the corridor.

She leapt out of the chair, pulled the skirt off, and threw it over the terminal in plain sight. After dragging Lars behind the desk where he wouldn't be visible, she straddled him and moved up and down as if riding cowgirl. If the bodyguard walked too far into the room, he'd see her still completely covered by her armor… and know she lied. If that happened, she'd have to move fast.

When the doors clicked open, she added moans and squeaks.

"Mr. Staanek, I heard a loud bang, like a body hitting the floor. Is everything okay?"

Virtual holo-panels popped into being in front of her. She mentally dragged the icon of the recording of Lars's conversation with his superior into the control interface for her vox unit. She moaned louder.

General Everett's face appeared on the desk terminal. Fortunately, the sight of a pink-haired woman bouncing up and down and emitting sex-type squeals stunned him mute.

"Mr. Staanek?" asked the man in the doorway.

Risa's heart stopped for the three seconds it took for a 'ready' to appear. She activated the mod with a thought, and spoke in her electronics' best recreation of Lars's voice. "I'm busy."

The guard tilted his head.

'Lars' gave an annoyed grunt. "Other way, bitch."

"Okay," said Risa in a demure whimper using her normal voice.

She spun around, to face the room, grabbing the desk, surreptitiously eyeing the bodyguard through a drape of her hair. His right arm was an obvious cybernetic augmentation, sporting an implanted ballistic gun. He also carried a laser carbine in his left hand. Risa faked an expression as if Lars was too big for her, and it hurt. Everett recognized her right away; his look of displeasure, likely at being pranked, became one of confusion. She hid her face behind the terminal so the bodyguard couldn't see her, then mouthed 'need a minute' without lending voice to it.

"Sorry, Boss." The guard backed out and closed the double doors.

She made a dismissive grunt in Lars's voice, and squealed in hers afterward.

Click.

Risa stopped bouncing and whispered, "Sorry."

"I'm sure there's a very interesting story behind what I'm watching." General Everett smiled.

"There is. Would you believe me if I told you the Corporates had a spy in the middle of Elysium City?"

"I'd find that highly improbable."

Risa pulled Lars up into the view of the terminal's camera. "Meet Lars Staanek... or whoever he is." She reached up to the NetMini and flicked her recording of his earlier conversation at the terminal. "Have a look at that. I'm sure you've got lab rats who can run a voice print analysis on it and figure out who the other guy is. I've got about twenty minutes of tranq in this guy. I was hoping you'd prefer to take him alive rather than scrape a body off the rug. Also get the feeling he likes it here, so he might be willing to change sides if given the right offer."

Everett's dark complexion went a little grey. "Risa... That's Nikolas Zheleznov on the other end of that vid. Are you able to secure the area? I can have a team there within ten minutes."

She eyed the vent. "I'm not sure I want to be here when they show up."

He raised a hand. "Nothing to worry about. You've been on the payroll for years, even if you didn't know it. The team lead will be informed you are an undercover asset."

"Fine. Whatever. Hurry up if you want him alive. He's gonna wake up soon." She slipped off the chair and crawled over Lars to hunt for weapons. "Who the hell is Zheleznov?"

"Senior Vice President of Military Operations Mars Division. An executive. Probably the number three or four man they've got up here." Everett looked as worried as he did hungry. "Lars sounds unhappy."

She shivered. "Yeah. I don't think he appreciated my visit."

Everett chuckled. "They're on the way."

Heaviness coalesced in her gut as the terminal went dark. She removed one full-sized handgun from under Lars's suit jacket, and small holdout pistols from the back of his belt and left ankle. Nothing in the room looked useful for binding him. After putting her skirt back on, she planted herself in the corner forty feet away, seated on the floor, and kept one of her Hotaru-6 pistols trained on his head.

Eight minutes of idle trigger flicking later, screaming filtered in from the vents as the emancipated dispersed in a panic. Forty seconds after the first shout of "cops!," a brief exchange of gunfire erupted close to the double doors. An explosion of Epoxil dust trailed a bullet into the room near the ceiling. The door opened at the push of a nondescript Marsborn man with short hair wearing a sand-brown coat over a familiar bodysuit, only dark grey instead of black. Two figures in MDF armor behind him raised laser pistols toward her, but the lead man waved them off.

A woman and two more men wearing the same semi-rigid bodysuits she'd seen on Everett's people at the remote base brought up the rear. The woman dragged the dead bodyguard by his arms in from the bar area.

"Agent," said the man in the raincoat as he approached. "We'll take it from here."

Risa let her pistol droop, stood, and tucked it back under her jacket. "Fine with me."

He walked up beside her, staring at Lars. "Nice catch... at least if this guy turns out to be the genuine article. You have an out? Need a fake arrest to exfiltrate the scene?"

She looked at the vent. "Nah, I'm allergic to binders."

An androgynous-looking operator, fully covered in armor whistled, then spoke in a woman's voice. "Wow, did you go all out with Reinventions for this cover assignment? You legit look sixteen."

Risa chuckled. "Had some work done on my eyes."

"Climbing down from the roof looks suspicious. No need for cuffs." He waved one of the MDF guys over. "Just an innocent misguided teen being 'escorted out of the area.'"

It would *be less work than climbing through all those vents again.* She sighed. "Okay, fine."

The armored man waved for her to follow and walked out. When they neared the door to the bar room, he grabbed a fistful of her jacket and began pushing her along.

She ran with the act and struggled. "I didn't even do anything. Damn cops, what the fuck?"

He remained silent as he dragged her out the front doors to the street in front where two plain black cars and a handful of marked MDF vehicles parked, red roof lights popping in staccato camera flashes.

"Get your fuckin' hand off me! Damn police state!" Risa twisted back and forth in a more than a halfhearted attempt to pull free.

He hauled her to the perimeter of the cars and gave her a toss hard enough to cause a stumble; if not for boosted agility, she would've flown into a chin-plant. She controlled the wipeout, falling anyway, but without injury. A MDF officer stomped over and descended on her as if about to continue with a beating. She rolled onto her back, grabbing his forearm as he took a fistful of her jacket in a strangling-tight grip, and pulled her close.

"Everett got the neural memory dump from your friend. Nice work." He flung her to the ground. "This one's underage. Damn kids. Go back to school so you can get a real job."

Risa curled up in mock fear, raising her arms to guard her face. *That's not a bad idea.*

Someone skidded to a halt behind her. "Hey, girl. You okay?"

She looked up at the face of a teenage boy with aqua hair. His black mesh top showed off a glowing NanoLED tattoo of a flying dragon on his left shoulder. "Yeah... I think so."

He helped her up. "I thought that prong was gonna light your fine ass up. I just scored some Proteus. Wanna go evolve?"

"I gotta go. Runnin' shit. Three more drop offs. It's my ass if I'm late."

The boy nodded, holding up a strange hand sign. "Righteous."

Risa jogged down the street. A few blocks later, she collapsed against a wall, face in her hands, and hyperventilated. For all she knew, Lars could be as deadly as the operator from Arden. Then again, the ACC *was* cheap.

He might've been all charisma with minimal combat boosts. She head-dialed a PubTran car and sank into a ball with her arms wrapped around her knees. A strange mixture of relief and worry enveloped her.

At least Gen's not in the crosshairs. We all are. Perhaps me more than most after Bliss.

16

AUTONOMOUS

Death Row already felt different.

She never truly thought of it as home, or even a safe place. Her chamber in the ventilation system had more emotional attachment. Now, she felt as if she lugged an empty plastisteel cargo box down the corridor of someone else's home. Despite being two inches longer than a standard footlocker the container weighed two-ish pounds. At one point, it had held medical supplies, stimpaks mostly, which the MLF had 'liberated' from a military shipment. In retrospect, she wondered if that cargo had left the base with the intention for it to wind up here.

Probably.

She butt-bumped the door open and set the box on the floor near the bed. Within seconds, Kree stood inside it, gawking at Risa's matching glittery skirt.

"It's like mine!" squealed the girl.

Risa grinned. "When I was your age, I liked girly stuff."

Kree folded her arms, eyes narrowed in doubt.

She twisted side to side, modeling it. "I had to get dressed up to meet someone."

"Pavo?" Kree tilted her head.

"No." She laughed, picturing his reaction to her 'gang teen' outfit. At least disabling the CamNano let her into the safehouse without being teased. "Just someone I had to talk to."

Kree nodded and sat in the box.

"What are you, a cat?" Risa picked her up and set her on the bed. "All these clothes have to go in there."

"All of them?" asked Kree.

"Yep. The entire floordrobe." Risa grumbled in her head. As long as she crashed on her old cot in Garrison's office, she'd have nowhere to put them. Not like she could 'explode' all over that room. "We can't stay in this room anymore."

Kree flopped on her side. "Why?"

"Because I am not going to hurt people with bombs." Risa sat on the floor, grabbed the nearest bit of clothing, and folded it. "Down here, you have to do bad things to have your own bedroom."

"I don't like bombs." Kree stared down at her chest.

Risa burst into tears before her thinking mind processed all the guilt she felt at those words. *Two seconds more and I'd have killed her. I knew there'd always be casualties, but kids? And that was one bomb... how many innocent people did I catch in the blast zones of all the others? Street rats? Citizens? Workers? The cleaning people weren't part of the war effort.* Kree climbed out of the box and put a hand on her shoulder. *How did I ever justify this?*

"I'm so sorry, Kree..." Risa wrapped the girl in a hug, clinging to her as if she were a giant doll. "I didn't know you and your friends were in that tunnel. I didn't know..."

Kree waited for her sobbing to quiet. "I believe you."

Risa leaned back and looked her in the eye.

"If you wanted to hurt us, you wouldn't have gone back to turn it off." Kree squirmed into a hug, resting her cheek against Risa's neck. "It was a accident."

"I'll never let anyone hurt you." Risa squeezed her.

"I know." Kree stepped back and smiled.

Sniffling, Risa wiped her face on the back of her arms, before resuming packing. A little over an hour later, the box approached full. Two small hands stuck a gauzy black skirt in. Risa smiled at a rather naked Kree, save for her favorite moon boots.

"What are you doing?" Risa laughed.

"You said *all* the clothes." Kree looked up with an expression of complete innocence.

"Not the ones you're wearing, goof." Risa plucked a small plum dress from the box and pulled it over the child's head. "We need to do some shopping. You've only got two outfits."

Kree shrugged.

Risa dug around the box. "Where's your underpants?"

"I burned them."

"What?" Risa blinked. The answer came too fast for it not to be true.

"See-bee said I had them on so long I should burn them before they walk by themselves." She shook her head. "I didn't wan' them to walk. Underpants aren't s'posed ta be alive."

She buried her face in her hand. "It's a figure of speech... he didn't mean for you to light them on actual fire."

"Oh." Kree looked down. "I'm sorry."

Risa dug out the girl's leggings, and handed them over. "Put those on. Next time I go to civilization, I'll get you some new things to wear."

"'Kay." Kree sat on the floor and kicked off her boots.

For a minute, Risa looked around at the small, private room. Considering how long it had been assigned to her, she hadn't spent much time here. Certainly, it never felt like home, or safe, or even a place she'd *wanted* to be. She'd only taken it out of a weak sense of tradition, or maybe some feeble tribute to Genevieve.

She smiled. On the way back to the safehouse, she'd called her friend to relay the news the rigged detonator had never been meant for her personally. An enemy operative had been trying to strike at the MLF, regardless of who they killed. Genevieve let off such a scream of relief it hurt her ears even though they had nothing to do with hearing the audio of a headware call. By now, she and Aurelia were probably out somewhere for a romantic evening.

That got her thinking about Pavo.

"Kree, honey... it's not safe for us to stay here. Do you want to come with me outside?"

"No." Kree shook her head. "I don't wanna go outside. I'm scared."

"I can—"

"No!" shrieked Kree, before diving under the bed and wailing.

Maybe Gen was right about knocking her out. "Okay... Okay... not now. Dinner time."

Sniffling.

"Come out from under there. We're only going down the hall."

Kree crawled out, stood, and stared at her with red-rimmed eyes. The look would've been appropriate if Risa had killed a cute furry animal in front of her. A lump grew in her throat. She picked up the box and carried it out into the hall. Kree followed her to the end of the corridor, down the curved ramp, across the command center, and down another passage to Garrison's office. He wasn't there, which meant a likely meeting with General Maris. Given Everett's moratorium on operations, they hadn't been doing much but sitting on their thumbs.

Wonder what they're discussing?

She took Kree by the hand and walked her back to the common area where Genevieve set off the 'vindaloo incident.' Osebi, Ralek, Donovan, and Huang sat at the round steel table. All picked at various forms of food. Osebi and Donovan played cards, while Ralek engaged Huang in a holographic versus match that seemed to combine chess with a fighting game. Whenever a 'capture' took place, the holograms grew to nine inches tall and played like a standard over-the-top punch up type game.

Kree shadowed her to the 'sem, remaining silent as Risa dialed up two plates full of 'chicken nuggets,' and glided like a mini ghost back to the table. As soon as Risa sat, Kree crawled into her lap.

"What's dis I 'ear 'bout you goin' inactive?" asked Osebi. He glanced at Donovan. "Two cards."

The other three men froze, hanging on her reply.

"There's no point feeding you dustblow. I'm done." She tossed a nugget into her mouth.

Kree bit two nuggets in half and pushed the remaining bits together in an attempt to re-form a whole one.

"Done?" asked Donovan. He gave Osebi his cards, keeping his hand tucked against his chest while Risa got the eyebrow lift. "How can you just be 'done' like that?"

Risa let out a silent sigh. "It's complicated."

"Found out that angel of yours ain't real, so you don't feel 'protected' now? That it?" Donovan raised an eyebrow. "Don't think we're all not scared."

She nibbled the tip off a nugget. "That would be an easy explanation, but if I wanted to lie to you, I would've said that."

Osebi gave her a concerned look. "Ya still believin' in dat ting?"

Risa shook her head. "That's not the part of it that would be the lie. Raziel really does exist, but he's a synth, not a literal angel."

"How come Donnyvan doesn't talk funny?" Kree leaned her head back, staring up at her. "He looks like See-bee."

Both men chuckled.

"Osebi talks like that because English isn't the language he learned as a kid. He's from... uhh, Earth. Donovan grew up on Mars."

"Nigeria," said Osebi. "Tis nice most days, but I be allergic to bullets. Always be someone wantin' ta take ovah. War all da time."

Ralek grinned. "So you joined the Front to get away from constant war. Great plan." He moved a game piece onto one of Huang's. A scantily clad woman with nunchaku squared off against Huang's power-armor-encased Valkyrie.

Donovan offered an almost apologetic shrug before patting Kree on the head. "I grew up in Secundus. No great stories here. Shit, I didn't see a green plant until I was twenty-four."

Kree pointed at Huang's character. "Her armor's weak in back. If you get behind her, she takes double damage."

Huang glared at the child. "Don't help him... he's already winning."

"So... what'cha mean done?" asked Osebi.

"I mean I'm done. No more bombs. That last mission was... too close." She pushed nuggets around her plate.

Osebi patted her shoulder. "We all told ya not ta go. Glad ye be in one piece."

She held back tears as she smiled; trying to talk would break her outward calm.

"Eat my nuts," yelled Huang.

The Valkyrie lay 'dead.' After a two-second fanfare, she floated up off the table in a dazzling array of shimmering light and resumed her fighting stance. A tinny voice said, "Round 2. Fight!"

Kree grabbed the controller away from Huang, leaving a nugget stuffed in her mouth. Ralek's grin evaporated in eight seconds. Kree anticipated his attempt to jump behind her, and caught his nunchuck-bimbo with a rearward strike and cornerized her against the arena wall, beating his toon to the ground before he could so much as move it again.

"That's cheating!" yelled Ralek.

"I didn't cheat!" shouted Kree.

"Not you." He pointed at Huang. "Giving the controller to a little kid. Unfair advantage."

Risa laughed. "I'm... not sure what we're doing is right anymore. Our ops never have the desired effect. The NewsNet always makes us out to look like terrorists. The war is no closer to being over than it was ten years ago. Even the people we're trying to liberate think we're criminals and killers."

The men murmured varying degrees of agreement.

Ralek didn't try to jump over the Valkyrie on round three. After twenty seconds of nickel-and-diming each other, Kree grabbed and judo-flipped his avatar whenever he blocked. The fourth time, Ralek snarled. He moved in to grab Kree's character when she blocked, but she was faster and staggered him with a series of light pommel strikes from the power armor's vibro-sword. Ralek managed to get a block going by the fifth tap, only to have Kree grab and throw him again. His scream of rage overpowered the game playing nunchuck-bimbo's 'fight lost' wail.

Kree cowered behind Risa's arm at the look he gave her.

Risa glared at him. "Maybe you should cool off."

"Maybe Huang should play his own damn game instead of hidin' behind a little girl."

Kree stuck her tongue out at Ralek.

Huang picked up the controller. "Fine, fine…"

"He only likes that character on account of her boobs hanging out." Donovan laughed. A few seconds later, his expression became serious. "You mean assassinations? You think it wrong?"

Risa nodded. "Yeah."

"If you had the chance to sneak into an enemy location and take out one or two key personnel to prevent a lot of other people from dying, would you do it?" Huang moved a tiny four-legged robot into an unoccupied space.

Risa gnawed on a hardening nugget. Already, it had lost any chicken-like flavor. "I'm not an assassin."

"Would you though?" Osebi folded, revealing a hand with nothing good. "Plant a bomb and take out an entire facility, or sneak in and kill the commander. Kill one or kill dozens to stop them from doing the same to us."

She sighed. "If I *had* to pick one, of course I'd kill the one person over the many. I…" *Can't tell them this is all C-Branch bullshit.* "There's got to be some other way. Besides, I've exceeded my limit for near-death experiences in one lifetime. I've got Kree to think about now." *Fuck it.* "Look, the MLF is…" *Damn.* Risa lifted Kree off her lap and placed her in Osebi's. "Watch her please. I need to see Maris."

"You got it." Osebi winked.

Risa stood, shot Ralek a warning glare, and walked out. She headed back downstairs, crossed the command and control center, and jogged down the corridor past Garrison's room to the office at the end. Much to her surprise, Garrison wasn't there.

General Maris looked up from his terminal as she strode in. "Risa."

She stopped in front of his desk. "Why are we lying to them?"

He raised both eyebrows. "That's a little vague."

"Our people. About what the Front is. The only reason to keep them in the dark is so they won't hesitate if they are ordered to attack a UCF target."

Rusty springs creaked as he leaned back in his chair. "Your assumption is only partially correct. If the enemy captures any personnel, their not knowing is proof against interrogation. If they genuinely believe they are part of a resistance movement, even a hostile telepath cannot know."

She exhaled, tapping her foot and thinking. "Someone high up is PVM. They agree with you about not wanting to strike friendly targets. Shiro and his team were sent here to kill you because you're not playing their game."

"So who is it you think is on our side?" He tilted his head to the right.

Risa studied his neutral expression for a moment. "Don't take this the wrong way, but I'm not inclined to say. After everything that's happened, I don't trust anyone."

General Maris chuckled. "You never did like me."

Her lips curled in a wistful smile. "I used to think you were so full of yourself. Some revolutionary leader with a bunch of pissed off teenagers who decided to call himself a general." She lowered her voice to a whisper. "I didn't know you really were one. No wonder you got so pissed whenever I made fun of your rank. I guess it was hard to resist choke-slamming me like some shithead private."

For the first time since she'd known him, General Maris leaned back and laughed with apparent genuine amusement. "Don't think I hadn't thought about it... Though, the idea became less appealing after you got wired up." He shook his head, mirth fading to a look of somber regret. "I felt bad for you, girl. I was worried your misdirected anger would cause mistakes. Then I started to question your sanity. Eventually, I learned about Raziel and wondered about your loyalties. This Raziel is an enigma. It may be chance that his and our goals align now, but I always questioned what kind of pawn you had become."

Risa chuckled. "I don't think he's talking to me anymore. No idea what he's doing. Probably looking for someone else to use."

Maris exhaled. "Great."

She gazed into his eyes for a few minutes in silence. "Are you who you say you are? Are you really a general in the military intelligence division? Tell me you're not an ACC spy."

"I'm not Corporate." A trace of anger flashed in his glare, though she got the feeling it wasn't aimed at her. "I am who I claim to be."

Risa sank into a rickety chair facing the desk, and recounted her tracking down Lars. "… and I walked off like some gang punk."

At the revelation of his affiliation with the ACC, Maris scowled. "You should've gotten angry at him sooner."

She shrugged. "He barely rated as mildly annoying before. Then I found out he's the one who almost killed Gen."

He grumbled. "How did they miss him?"

"You're PVM, aren't you?" She smiled at her lap.

Maris remained quiet for a moment; his slow laugh broke the silence. "I was not expecting it to take you that long to connect those particular dots."

"General Everett." Risa's gaze crawled over the junk on his desk: inert hand grenade mounted to a wooden pedestal, ammo magazines for a ballistic pistol, two combat knives, and a melted e-mag. "He's either going to pull the Front back in as official, or disband it. Either way, it won't be the same."

Maris studied the ceiling. "Perhaps it is not a bad thing. It would be nice to see the sky again."

"Yeah." Risa stood, took four steps to the door, and paused. "Sorry."

"It's not your fault." He tapped a finger on the desk. "It was only a matter of time before an operation like this spiraled out of control."

She let her head sag forward. "No, I mean for being shitty to you for so long." She chuckled. "Heh. Listen to me… You're the last person in this place I ever thought I'd respect."

"No one stays an angry young thing forever. And for the record, I didn't send you to Bliss to get rid of you. I'd hoped you could pull it off." He sighed. "I suppose we both suffer from the curse of hindsight. Someone was trying to take you out of the equation. I should've told them it was a suicide mission."

"It was, and I still agreed to go. You didn't force me." She stood straight. "Call it even?"

"Done."

She glanced back at a bright smile spread over his dark face. "Take care of yourself, General."

"You too, kid. You too."

Butterflies swarmed in her gut as she walked out. Whatever Everett had in mind for the Front was going to be big. Maybe Maris could keep everyone from getting buried up to their eyeballs in a shitstorm.

Maybe the crap will only come up to our necks.

MARIONETTES

Thick silence hung over the control center as Risa emerged from the hall leading to the command offices. Thirteen men and women, a handful not even eighteen yet, peered at her from behind a wall of dim-glowing holographic panels. She made eye contact with one after the next; expressions shifted among curiosity, fear, and confusion. A subtle thrum of active electronics vibrated the air, the loudest sound in the room, save for the occasional sharp intake of breath when someone noticed jade green in place of glowing violet light. The youngest looked at her with expectation, waiting for instructions.

Risa stared down at the floor, thinking about how Maris always called her 'lieutenant.' She'd never taken it as anything but 'boys playing soldier,' but he'd probably been serious.

Her leap from the disintegrating Strand onto the hull of a tiny fighter aircraft flashed in a daydream. She clenched her hands in fists and managed with a moderate degree of success to hide the tremble. The harder she tried not to think about how close she'd been to death, the more she couldn't put it out of her mind.

Some people lose their nerve. I crumpled mine up and threw it. She walked to the base of the curved ramp, scanning the group of faces tracking her every motion. *They all believe we're fighting for a 'free Mars.'* She looked down, unwilling to shatter that many dreams. *I went back there and no screaming happened; they know something's not right.*

A second after her boot hit the ramp, the whispering started. Some wondered if she resigned or finally got sidelined due to 'mental issues.' One woman asked the guy seated next to her if Maris forced her to give back the 'expensive military cybereyes.' Several commented on her 'defeated' look.

Primus Safehouse, the largest, held the 'brain' of the MLF. Only Maris, and possibly Garrison knew how many others existed for sure. Risa guessed at least seven. Most consisted of ten to twelve people embedded in small settlements. It made sense to her now why they didn't have anything set up in any of the other major cities in the UCF. *Why bother. We aren't at war with ourselves.*

She backed away from the ramp and walked up to the cluster of desks; murmurs and whispers quieted at her approach. *What'll happen to everyone?* These people tapped into a wide array of networks. Some infiltrated via cyberspace, some maintained contact with Front personnel hidden within resistance cells located in ACC-controlled territories. Their best feedback on what happened in Bliss had come from operatives inside. She wondered if they'd gotten out in time. No one, not her, not the MLF, and certainly not the ACC expected the Cryomil explosion that wiped most of the complex. Her sources indicated the explosion only torched military facilities, confirming all the civilians lived on the ground in the Melas Chasma. The ACC claimed tens of thousands of civilian losses. Risa mostly believed Maris's numbers, but the specter of doubt whispered across the back of her neck.

All eyes focused on her. Four or five people looked about ready to run for cover at her approach.

"Some of you have been with me out there." She glanced at one of the younger teens. "A couple of you just arrived, but you've all gotten involved with something bigger than any one person. We all want the same thing: to live on a Mars not controlled by people from another planet, where decisions are made to benefit *everyone* and not only the powerful. We want control of our own destiny." Murmurs of agreement rumbled among the group. "Many of you have spent the past few years whispering about me when you thought these boosted ears of mine couldn't hear you."

Someone whispered, "Shit."

Two men leaned back as if to run away.

She smirked at them. "I'm not Cat-6. I was gullible and I was angry. It's true that I'm going inactive, but it's my choice. I don't believe in angels anymore." Motion high and left drew her attention to Kree at the railing one story up. "At least not ones with wings."

"You get hit with a psio?" asked Caerys, a woman with cobalt blue hair in a pixie cut. The voice had been on her comm so many times, yet she wouldn't have recognized her. "You seem so different."

"Worse. I got hit with truth." Risa leaned on the nearest workstation. A panel to her right showed an image of a street that could've been lifted from a post-nuclear-war entertainment holo. A stream of Cyrillic characters scrolled along below. "There's no point keeping you all in the dark anymore. This"—she waved around—"isn't what you think it is."

Little footsteps tapped down the ramp, then scuffed over dirt behind her. Kree clung to her side. Osebi waved from overhead. She smiled at him, and he walked off.

"What are you saying?" asked Gevan, perhaps the oldest of the command center staff. "Is that why you're flying a desk?"

Risa put a hand over Kree's, against her stomach. "Have any of you ever wondered why we rarely strike UCF interests, and when we do, it's always a decommissioned base or a target with unusually low propensity for fatality?" She inhaled, held it a moment, and let the air out. "Two words: plausible deniability. I didn't get the green light to spill, so if you want it straight, ask Maris. What I thought was an angel was an AI who hacked my headware. What I thought was a revolution wasn't. What I thought happened to my father didn't. I don't know what the future's got waiting for us, but I do know I'm not prepared to blow people up based on an endless firehose of dustblow."

"Wait, you're saying this is… we're sanctioned?" Caerys gasped.

Risa smiled. "I didn't say that. You inferred it. I can neither confirm nor deny. The Corporates treat their citizens like expendable inventory. There *is* a worthwhile fight on Mars, but it's not going to be won by dividing our efforts."

She took Kree by the hand and walked upstairs. Discussion filled the air behind her, people trying to make sense of what she'd said. Sam and Brett, two other kids she'd almost blown up in that shaft, zoomed by, eager to get to the armory and Kendrick's supervision while they learned how to shoot. Risa gave the boys a sour look once they'd passed. *Why are we training ten-year-olds to fight? This is wrong.* Kyle rounded the corner about ten seconds later, yelling 'wait up.'

Kree seemed to shy away from them.

"What's wrong?" Risa looked down at her. "You haven't been playing with them lately."

The child's sad face turned angry. "They think you're scary. They think I'm weird because I'm not scared of you."

Risa's heart felt heavier. The shadow of rumor that kept the adults at arm's length from her had spread over Kree, and had the same effect on the other kids. *Did I make a mistake bringing them here?* She heaved a mental sigh. *I couldn't leave them out there begging and stealing.* "Come on. Their loss."

Kree grinned.

They wandered the corridors for some time. Memories of a childhood spent in these tunnels came back piece by piece. Hide and seek with Genevieve, the terror she'd felt the first time someone asked her to bring something across the facility to Osebi. Not until the man freaked out had she realized she'd been holding live hand grenades. Talo, the guy who'd asked eleven-year-old Risa to carry them, died three years ago during an operation. Osebi had beaten him bloody for giving explosives to a child, after which Garrison read Talo the riot act. Risa choked up at the memory. Of course, Garrison didn't know the truth back then, but his fatherly anger made so much sense under the lens of hindsight. Maybe some part of him always suspected?

Is that why he was reluctant about the test? He didn't want anyone telling him he wasn't my dad.

She choked up. Her mood worsened each time she passed someone in the hallway and thought about the first time she'd seen them. Some were ex-military, though now she wondered if maybe they'd been assigned here on purpose, and weren't as 'ex' as they claimed. Others, like half the people she'd rescued from Benton Mining Company's prison camp, had criminal records. Violent offenders and murderers—at least the ones able to focus their proclivities on an approved enemy—were handy for a 'terrorist organization.' Not so much for military intelligence.

What'll happen to them all if Everett shuts this down?

The more she roamed, the more she remembered—and the more it seemed her father tried to keep her separated from the violent part of his life. *What parent wants their kid to grow up as an insurgent? People here die so often.*

"Ow," said Kree. "You're smashing my hand."

"Wanna go for a ride on a Foxbat?" Risa smiled and relaxed her grip somewhat.

Kree narrowed her eyes. "Is that outside?"

Risa nodded. "Yes, but it's *outside*. Wide open space. No one can sneak up on us."

The child shivered in her boots for a moment, bit her lip, and looked up. Tears gathered at the corners of her eyes, but didn't fall. "O-okay."

Filled with hope, Risa led her to the motor pool chamber. Kree amused herself by jumping over hoses and cables strewn about the floor as thick as her thighs. When they reached the garage, Risa headed to a row of four Foxbat quads, two of which had side-mounted pulse lasers. She approached the nearer of the two unarmed ones and walked around, conducting a brief inspection. Content it had no significant damage, she threw a leg over and sat. Kree approached the side of the four-wheeler and leaned up to look at the console.

"Do we need helmets?"

Risa grinned. "We should... but kids aren't supposed to be here, so they don't have any small enough for you. The air is fine outside Primus, and I'll drive slow."

Pria, a sylph of an almost-eighteen-year-old, slid out of a prowler's underbelly and climbed down the nine-foot tire to the ground. She gave Risa a quasi-hostile look and approached. Kree glanced between them for a moment before tilting her head.

"Why doesn't that lady have boobies?" Kree blinked.

Risa clapped a hand over her mouth to keep from laughing. "People come in different shapes."

"Heard you're chickening out," said Pria, arms folded. "That true?"

"It's complicated." Risa pulled Kree up into the seat in front of her. "I've got more than me to think about now."

Pria set her hands on her hips. Dark lubricant smeared almost every inch of her mostly bare chest. A scrap of cloth across her breasts, a shredded remnant of an old T-shirt, soaked black in the same substance. Crimson fatigue pants hung low on her hips, burdened by six pockets full of spare fuses, bolts, nuts, small batteries, and other tools. "That kid's exactly what you should be thinking about. Thinking about giving her the Mars we all deserve."

Risa pulled her NetMini from her belt and swiped at the file system until she found the recording of her 'work' at Bliss, the file she couldn't bring herself to watch. Living through it once was plenty. She wagged the device at Pria, transferring the file to the 'mini in the girl's back pocket. "Watch that and tell me again how much of a chicken I am." Her expression hardened. "Takes some nerve to sit here tweaking wrenches all day and call me a coward."

"Uhh." Pria's Marsborn-white face tinted with blush. "Not what I meant. I mean... You're walking away. How can you give up like that? We've gotta kick them off our planet."

She threaded her arms around Kree, holding the girl close to her chest, and rested her chin atop her head. "You're still young, Pria. You're in the same pissed-off idealist mindset I had when I was seventeen. Don't be so ready to give your life away to the war like I did." Risa sighed. "At least, if you do... make sure you know what you're fighting for. I've gotten into dozens of places, planted at least thirty charges... I can't count how many people I've killed." Tears ran down her cheeks.

"Stop crying in my hair," said Kree, squirming.

Pria thrust her arm at the garage door. "But you killed the enemy! That's how war works. One close call, one kid, and you forget all about the people of Mars?"

"You don't know who I killed. I'm not even sure I do." Risa closed her eyes. "You don't see, do you? The people think we're the bad guys. The NewsNet twists everything we do. It's all dustblow, anyway. The Martian Liberation Front is fake."

"Fake?" Pria's conviction seemed to waver with her voice. "What the fuck do you mean, fake?"

"We're part of a military intelligence operation designed to allow the UCF to strike deep in ACC territory at questionable targets, targets they make look like civilian installations but are, in actuality, military. An overt combat action would trigger a media backlash on Earth, and they'd blame the UCF for murdering civilians. C-Branch invented the MLF to do what the government couldn't."

Pria froze as if she'd been slapped across the face.

"*That's* why I'm getting out. I'm not angry anymore. I don't know what to believe."

"But..." Pria grabbed Risa's shoulder. "If it's all dustblow, what the fuck was up with the prison camp thing? Those sons of bitches kept me locked up for months! They treated us like total shit. Was that all 'keeping up the illusion?' Was leaving me in a freezing cell for two days with only chains on fake too?" She lifted her pant leg to show off a line around a stick-thin ankle. "I *still* have fucking scars from those shackles. You're damn right I wanna blow some people to hell for that."

"I don't know. Nothing makes sense." She relaxed her grip on Kree.

"The people at the top, over Maris, are pulling strings in different directions. Maybe they rationalized it as survival training... trying to prepare you for what the ACC would do to you if you were captured. That whole team was too young... Maybe they wanted to scare you off."

Pria growled. "I can't believe this." She pressed the heel of her hand to her eyebrow, as if trying to hold back a migraine. "Even if what you're saying is true... that's your answer? Run off an' hide?"

"Yeah." Risa powered up the Foxbat. "Hiding's what I'm good at."

"Don't you care anymore?" Pria's face went from pink to red.

"Someone who cares thinks about what they're doing. They don't act blindly. I can't trust anything about this anymore. Look. You've got real skill with these machines. You don't have to waste your life on being pissed off. I don't know you. I don't know where you came from or what's lit the fire under your ass, but I *do* know you can get out before all of this collapses on top of us."

"I grew up in T-84. Ever hear of it?" Pria walked over to lean against the Foxbat parked next to the one Risa sat on.

"Can't say I have."

"It was a small settlement in Tharsis, maybe twenty families."

Risa cringed. "Near the southern edge of UCF territory."

"Yeah." Pria looked away and folded her arms again. "Too close to the front lines. ACC hit us; guess they mistook us for military or didn't care. We saw it coming, tried to call for help, but the UCF never bothered. Guess our town wasn't 'significant' enough. Whoever survived the attack, mostly kids, got rounded up and locked in the generator building. Once the ACC realized T-84 was a shitty little settlement with no strategic value, the commander told them to kill us and pack it up."

Risa scowled.

"We got lucky." Pria covered her mouth for a moment, fighting tears. "The two men waited for the commander to walk out and shouted over the screaming and begging. They told us to be quiet like we were dead or they'd shoot us for real... and then they shot up the other side of the room. Couple hours later, we got out. I found my parents' bodies. That was six years ago."

"I'm sorry." Risa guided Kree's grip to the handlebars. "I won't tell you what to do. I understand how you feel, really... I do. Before you sell your body to revenge, make damn sure it's what you want. Once you get to where I am—if you even live that long—there's no going back."

Pria stared at the floor with an unreadable expression somewhere between sorrow and anger.

After a quiet moment, Risa squeezed the handlebars and drove forward, past the open doors and down a quarter-mile of tunnel to the Martian surface. Kree's scream of fright became a squeal of delight as the wind and sun hit them. She drove around in lazy circles up and down hills, scrunching up her face whenever Kree's hair blew into it. The sound of a little girl giggling took her far, far away from who she'd been.

For a little while, the war ceased to exist.

18

GHOST ON THE WIRE

Martian dirt sprayed to either side as Risa steered into a tight, decelerating turn. Much to her surprise, Kree reacted to the outdoors with wide, eager eyes. Like a cat stuck in a moving car, she leaned from side to side, staring at everything. Her theory proved correct. The child wasn't afraid of 'outside' as much as she dreaded the tunnels of the subterranean city.

A handful of dingy metal buildings covered in silt clustered in the distance by the 'official' entrance of Primus, lurking in the shadow of shuttle huge landing pad next to a terminal building full of elevators. When the city had been the main presence of human habitation on Mars, interplanetary shuttles landed on the dirt. No one had built an actual starport until Elysium. Primus got one about ten years after, and from here, it looked like a glorified camping stove, a raised metal surface you could put a thermogel can under and a pot on top of.

Of course, it *was* four miles away. Kree held on to the handlebars, shrieking with glee as they bounced over a run of head-sized rocks. Twenty-odd miles per hour felt scary fast without helmets. Risa always wondered how the UCF managed not to find them when the safehouse connected to a manmade cave tunnel straight to the surface. Roughly two centuries ago, the shaft had been used for carting away the dirt and rock that once took up the interior of Primus. She used to think they ignored it because it would've been too obvious a place to look, so they didn't bother. Funny how so much started to make sense now.

They've known where we are the whole time. Risa glanced down at Kree. *Fuck it. I'm driving to Elysium right now. I'll deal with the panic attack later.*

The child giggled as they crested a small hill with enough speed to make it feel like a jump, though the wheels never left the surface. She plotted a route in her headware so Kree wouldn't see the screen. At current speed, their estimated arrival showed as seven hours. *Shit. What am I doing? I promised myself I wouldn't trick her.*

She steered down an incline, feathering the brakes to keep from going too fast. Kree held her hands up, reveling in the breeze.

"This is fun," yelled Kree.

Not so fun when you're stuck on one of these things for three days. "I'm happy to see you smiling."

"What's that?" Kree pointed at the sun.

Risa tried to explain as best she could. Kree asked about the gradient shades of blue and indigo in the sky, and got a basic overview of terraforming: wind-driven bands of different atmospheric compositions, a blending process that would take decades before an Earthlike atmosphere covered the entirety of Mars. Primus sat under one of the major downdrafts from the North Polar Region where most of the terraforming machines were. A few miles south, and the wind diffused into the ambient atmosphere too much to breathe. Being here amounted to being in a room of unbreathable air while holding your face in a blast of breathable air blowing out of a hole in the wall.

Beep. An incoming call flashed in the top-left of her vision, an icon with Tamashī's face.

<Hey.>

Risa smiled at the apparition of her friend. The smile faded in seconds under the weight of a pleading stare. Despite knowing she looked at a forty-something woman inside a body subjected to enough nanosurgery to make her look thirteen, her friend's expression triggered motherly protective instincts. <What's wrong?>

<I need your help, or I'm gonna die.>

Risa stopped the Foxbat, set her feet on the dirt, and stared at Tamashī. <Whoa, slow down. Is that teenager 'I'm going to die,' or are you being serious?>

<Serious die.>

<Okay. What do you need?>

Kree twisted around to look up. "Why'd you stop?"

"Tamashī called. One minute, kiddo." Risa pointed up at an incoming inter-city shuttle.

"Wow!" Kree stared.

Tamashī shivered. <I have two ways out of getting my head cut off. One of them is wiping out the entire executive board of a corporation. I'm pretty sure you're not going to want to do one of them. I need a second brain for a net job. Either that, or could you do me a huge favor and kill off the entire executive team of Míngtiān Corporation? You'd umm, have to go to China, but I'd hack your ticket.>

Risa blinked.

<Didn't think so.> Tamashī smiled for a nanosecond. <I cost them a couple billion credits a few years ago and they finally found me. They offered to buy me from the Syndicate, or pay them to kill me slow. Walsh said he agreed to protect me, and doesn't want to go back on his word, but that means I gotta do this job for him... and I can't do it alone.>

<Tamashī... I'm not a deck jockey. I dabble. It would be like me taking Kree on a job for the MLF and expecting her to help. I'm willing to try, but I don't know what you're expecting me to do.>

A whirlwind of dust and tiny stones pelted them as the shuttle passed a few hundred yards overhead. Kree held her ears, guarding against the roar of ion engines. Risa closed her eyes; only Tamashī remained against a field of endless black.

<It's not that bad. This network has a particular type of construct that's impossible for one person to get past. All I need you for is killing enemy programs. Need another body in there with me so I don't get overrun. I'll do all the heavy lifting; you just kill stuff.>

<You want me to kill programs?>

<Yeah. Not people.>

<Okay. I'll be there as soon as I can.>

Once Tamashī's digital apparition faded, she leaned down over Kree. "I have to go help a friend. It's like playing video games. She's in Elysium. Do you want to go with me?"

"Do I have to?" Kree shivered.

Risa debated saying yes, but caved in to the power of wide blue eyes. "Only if you want to."

The child sniveled and looked down.

"Okay. It's all right." Risa kissed her on top of the head. *I'm not bringing her to a Syndicate hotel.* "You can stay with Garrison."

Kree nodded.

She turned the Foxbat and drove back to the cave, cursing in her head over and over about caving in, Tamashī's bad timing, and still being no closer to getting her child out of the safehouse. Kree hid her face in her hands once no trace of daylight remained behind them. The child trembled against Risa's chest until they pulled in to the motor pool garage, at which point she seemed comfortable again.

Pria hadn't moved from her sidesaddle perch on the other ATV. Clean streaks in the grease on her face betrayed dried tears. Risa parked the quad, picked Kree up, and looked at the teen.

"Hey," muttered Pria. "Thanks for bringing the 'bat back."

"You okay?" asked Risa.

Pria shrugged. "If you had a wish, would you go back to seventeen and do shit different?"

Risa shook her head. "No."

The girl blinked, confused.

"I'd go back to *seven* and stay the hell away from this war." She shifted Kree to a better grip. "But my life isn't yours. What do you think would make your parents happiest?"

Pria laughed out a few more tears. "Not getting myself killed."

"Sounds like a plan." Risa winked at Pria, took Kree's hand, and headed off to Garrison's room.

ONE HOUR AND SIX MINUTES LATER, RISA WAVED AT THE BLACK METAL skeleton lurking in the corridor outside Tamashī's room at the Orbital Hotel, and went in. Her friend sat under a pile of blankets and pillows as if hiding from the 'closet monster.'

"Risa!" Tamashī leapt from the bed in a spray of pillows, almost climbing out of her knee-length white T-shirt in the process, and tackle-hugged her. "I'm so scared. Walsh is gonna hand me over to Míngtiān if I don't get this done." A few trembling seconds later, she sat on the edge of the Comforgel pad, shaking. "Do you think Walsh will keep his word? I mean, what's to stop them from handing me over even if I do this?"

"For some of the things they do, I want to kill every last one of them... but, they do have an odd sense of honor. I know it sounds completely messed up, but I'd trust what they say more than the government."

Tamashī scrunched up her nose. "They sell orphans into prostitution, do contract murders, trade in drugs, extort money from corporations."

"That's different from government how?" Risa sighed. "There is *one* difference. The Syndicate doesn't try to hide what they are."

"The government doesn't grab kids off the street and make them whores." Tamashī scooted onto her bed and uncovered two net decks from the pile of pink blankets.

"No, not in so many words. But lack of infrastructure and support plus so many war orphans basically forces them into it, anyway. Does it really matter if the bedroom door is literally locked or they're trapped there out of fear of starvation?" Risa examined the silver slab in front of her. "I hope you know what you're doing here. I'm going to feel like dead weight."

Tamashī smiled. "It'll be easy. That's a Nishihama Netspider. It's optimized for data combat and ghosting. All you have to do is attack something like you're used to doing in the real world. I set up all the combat routines to feel like using claws with Kung Fu and a bit of Aikido. Everything should feel natural. Oh, if you wanna borrow a shirt, go ahead. You probably don't want to wear that suit while we're in. It doesn't breathe."

"Right." Steeping in her own sweat didn't seem like an awesome idea. After a quick run to the bathroom, Risa stripped out of her ballistic stealth suit and slipped into a red knee-length tee with a psychotic cartoon bunny rabbit holding giant rocket-pistols. "The sleepover from hell."

She lay sideways across the foot of the bed, pulled her hair away from her neck, and plugged the asterisk-shaped prong into the M3 port behind her left ear. An instant later, she felt as though the bed expanded to become a bottomless void, into which she plummeted headfirst.

Several seconds of falling/flying later, the darkness in front of her exploded in a kaleidoscope of vibrant color. A loud sonic boom came with a white flash, and she wound up lying flat on a surface that looked like a Comforgel pad stretched to the horizons. She looked down at herself: a black and violet lace corset made her smallish bust seem a cup size larger. Risa sighed to herself, slightly embarrassed. Around her waist, she had a gauzy skirt like the one she'd worn to sneak into Iniquity. It bared most of her thighs, only this one had glowing purple sparkles instead of black glitter.

"What on Mars?" The tiny, squeaky voice coming out of her made her grab her throat. "What the fuck?"

A reverberating bellow came from the left—a slowed down, twisted version of Tamashī laughing. Risa looked to her right at a knee the size of a small house. Tamashī, in the guise of a nine-year-old ninja girl with cat ears, towered over her like a ten-story building.

"Okay, what gives?" Risa thought about standing, and found herself hovering on indigo faerie wings. "Oh, great. I'm three inches tall. Wonderful."

Tamashī apparently couldn't handle the squeaky voice and doubled over laughing.

Risa folded her arms and tapped her bare foot on nothing. "I can deal with Goth Faerie, but can I at least be normal sized?"

A minute or two later, Tamashī recovered her composure and sat up. "Okay." Her expression shifted to contemplative.

"Eep." Risa squeaked as the room shrank around her, fast enough to make her cringe. When she risked a peek, everything appeared normal in terms of size, including Tamashī, who looked only a touch bigger than Kree. "You're adorable."

Tamashī hopped off the bed. "Thanks, but cute isn't going to work for this job." The child-sized ninja expanded to a seven-foot-tall cloud of diaphanous black vapor with two silver glimmers in the approximate shape of eyes near the top. Her voice changed from that of a little girl to a glassy, scratchy whisper that sent icy shivers down Risa's spine. "Gonna go back to my original avatar. Tamashī means 'spirit' or 'soul.'" A wispy shadow-finger traced '魂' in midair. "Saw some drawings of this thing when I was sneaking around the Division Zero database on Earth. It's supposed to be a 'harbinger' or something like that. Sounded scary as hell."

"So what are we doing?" Risa thought about popping claws, and sure enough, her fingers sprouted blades. Only in cyberspace, instead of transparent synthetic diamond, glowing purple plasma stretched out to searing edges two-feet long. "Damn."

She waved them around, mesmerized by the luminous trails they left behind in the air.

"We are breaking in to RedEx's network to insert shipping documentation for stuff the Syndicate needs to transport. Hiding it as legitimate cargo."

Risa retracted the laser claws. She felt fine until she glanced at

Tamashī. Her mind blanked from the visage of infinite darkness creeping toward her. Flickering mercury eyes pierced her soul; dread clutched her heart in an icy hand, crushing, freezing the blood in her veins. For two seconds, she forgot how to breathe—then let off a scream of terror.

"Oh, shit. Sorry." The billowy wraith cringed. "I gotta set up an exception for you. I'm running a program that causes other avatars' decks to tweak a fear response by stimulating the amygdala. It's a super rare technique. Not many people know how to do it. Feeling like supernatural terror in cyberspace is so freaky it gets a lot of people to run away and leave me alone."

The strange fear vanished as fast as it had manifested.

"Whoa. That's... *so* twisted." Risa concentrated on stopping the involuntary trembles in her legs. "Look. If you're hiding human trafficking, just book me a flight to China and tell me who needs to die."

"Wow." The shadow-apparition's silver eyespots doubled in size. "Really? You'd do that?"

"I'm not going to help them sell people. I'd rather kill corporate slime." Being hugged by a semisolid mass of cold phantasmal goo was perhaps the single strangest feeling Risa had experienced up to that point in her life. "Eek."

"You're an awesome friend. Don't worry. It's not people. They're shipping chemicals, weapon parts, and stolen high-end cybernetics for re-sale on Earth."

"Oh, that's better." Risa rolled her eyes. *Lesser of several evils, I guess.*

Tamashī flowed to the door. "This way."

"We're walking?"

"Flying technically, but... well super-technically we're not moving at all, but... Teleporting in the net is tricky. For whatever reason, they made it illegal. It's like way hard."

"I thought you were good?" Risa winked.

"Teleportation is still a bit iffy for me. It also stands out like a beacon if anyone tries to backtrace the infiltration. Trust me; it's easier to hide playing by the rules."

After walking out of a virtual recreation of the Orbital Hotel, Tamashī the wraith glided into the sky. Risa growled under her breath for a moment until she remembered she had the body of a giant faerie, and at a thought, flew after her. The wraith's shadowy grip encircled her right wrist, and pulled her along at a speed more akin to a military fighter craft than an anachronistic pixie. Fortunately, the wind-in-the-face effect created by cyberspace ignored real physics, so her skin didn't peel off or burn at such speeds.

Tamashī led the way to Arcadia across a long expanse of simulated open Mars. Twenty-three virtual minutes after leaving Elysium, they plunged down past the jewel-like dome of the 'prettiest' city in the UCF, and flew among silvery skyscrapers, parks, and advert bots.

"You're kidding me," said Risa. "They've got advert bots in Cyberspace too?"

"Oh yeah." Tamashī skimmed along the ground. "About thirteen times more since they're free here, only program code."

Other living users were easy to spot: anyone who screamed and ran away from the wraith had to be an avatar of a real person. Anyone who showed zero reaction to the black apparition did not have a biological brain to tweak. A few minutes after arrival, Tamashī stopped in front of a glowing black archway covered in bright-blue circuit lines. Beyond it lay a courtyard where a RedEx shuttle perched on a pedestal amid an impossible fountain. Serpents of water raced around in an elaborate midair ballet, in full defiance of gravity.

"One sec," said Tamashī. "I'm messing with their border router so it doesn't log our entrance."

Thirty seconds later, the wraith drifted into the arch, pulling Risa along. They went around the fountain and past the front door into a lobby decorated in red and white. Considering the size of RedEx, the décor seemed plain. Even in a place where extravagance cost only a net developer's time, the company kept with its basic aesthetic.

Tamashī headed across a hundred-meter-long room full of bench seats facing a row of window stations where forty live avatars dealt with customer service issues. A throng of other avatars waited their turn, ranging from ordinary looking people to powered armor, wizards, dragons, aliens, and bizarre creatures Risa had no name for. Her cute-creepy faerie persona seemed tame by comparison. No one reacted to their presence, allowing them to approach a door marked 'employees only' at the far end of the room.

"Why aren't they running?" asked Risa

"We're ghosting." Tamashī's 'scraping glass' voice made her shiver again. "None of them can see us."

Risa waited nearby while the wraith stuck her ethereal fingers into the wall by the access panel. Despite her corset being pixels, she found it difficult to breathe. In a few seconds, the door exploded into a cloud of silver dust, which promptly began to coalesce back together as soon as it burst. Before it became solid again, Risa darted after Tamashī.

The space beyond it resembled an ordinary hallway in a corporate building. Grey carpet bore a repeating pattern in red: the company's name. Contrast made the word 'RedEx' seem to vibrate and float away from the floor. Looking at it for more than a few seconds at a time proved dizzying. Her shadowy friend glided off past rows of empty cubicles. When they reached a ninety-degree turn in the corridor, a man with the build of an assault infantry soldier appeared out of thin air in front of them. White shirt, silver badge, black pants, and a stunrod gave him away as a security officer.

"Kill it!" yelled Tamashī. "It's not a real guy."

"Unauthorized entry detected." The man stepped out of himself, becoming two exact copies of the same person. Both converged on Tamashī, who had been closer.

"Riiiisa!" yelled the wraith. "If it surrounds me, I'm dead."

Tamashī leapt at the left one, sending tendrils of wispy smoke around the guard's throat. Risa extended her laser claws as she rushed to attack the other copy. *This isn't complicated. Think of it like a video game.* Her instinctual desire to activate speedware didn't do anything, leaving her yelping as the second security construct swung a stunrod at her. She managed a clumsy but effective block that kept the glowing blue weapon away from her, but sent her flying into the wall.

The first security construct writhed in place as smoky tendrils invaded its eyes, nose and mouth, while others held it still. Risa's opponent swiveled to ambush Tamashī from behind. Risa lunged again, taking advantage of the ridiculous length of her virtual claws to attack in a wild series of haphazard slashes.

Two of nine swipes connected, leaving smoking gouges across the perfect white shirt. The construct spun and thrust its baton at her. She resisted the urge to use speedware that didn't exist here and reacted with a spinning block, forcing the program's weapon to the side while maneuvering in closer. She swiped at the thing's head, but the false man fell flat to the floor in the blink of an eye—an impossible move too fast for any human.

Before she could recover from her swing, the fake man reappeared on its feet behind her and jabbed the stunrod into her back. For three-quarters of a second that felt closer to twenty minutes, Risa screamed as though her blood had been drained and replaced with boiling battery acid.

Pain receded before the construct could smash her over the head, and she more fell out of the way than dodged, whimpering. The guard loomed over her, baton raised, and disappeared. Risa flipped over on to all fours. Tamashī's tendrils crushed the first construct, wispy fingers leaving behind a suspension of shattered pieces, as though a painted glass statue of a man exploded in their grasp. Fragments rained to the ground amid delicate twinkling.

"Perfect," said Tamashī. "This is going to be easy now."

Risa hugged herself, shaking from the memory of that agony. A good piece of her wanted to whimper and cry for Daddy.

"Hey, you okay?" Tamashī glided closer. "Oh, it got you with a Mindwank soft."

Teeth chattering, Risa lifted her head to look at her friend. "What? That doesn't sound good."

"It's like being hit with a stun gun. Makes the deck shock you in the brain. Non-lethal, but it hurts a bit."

"Y-y-ya think?"

"The deck should've intercepted the signal. Hang on." Tamashī put a spectral hand on Risa's shoulder. "Yeah, your deck killed the stun a few microseconds after it started."

That was a microsecond? "Ow."

"Those constructs are nasty. There's no way for a single person to fight one alone." Tamashī pulled her upright. "Come on. We have to hurry. Every second we spend in here is another chance of being spotted or another one of those spawning in on us."

Risa decided to run instead of rely on the unfamiliar feeling of having wings. They hurried down the corridor to a four-way intersection, where Tamashī went left, heading for a red elevator door. When it opened, another security man stepped out.

"Dammit, we already killed him."

"It's another copy of the same software." Tamashī's fingers grew out to tendrils again. "They all look the same."

Risa, anticipating the split this time, charged. The guard slid sideways, another impossible maneuver; her laser claws ripped up the wall. She recovered in time to duck when it swung its stun baton at her like a sword. Risa leapt at the program again, this time expecting the floor drop. She feigned high with her left hand while striking at the ground with her right. The construct flopped using the same maneuver the previous one had, but this time, she impaled it through the chest with five scintillating energy blades.

It tried to sit up, roaring. White light streamed from its eyes, and a second later welled up within its mouth. Crimson glowed beneath the surface of its face, making the skin appear more like plastic. A second later, the body exploded in a cloud of iridescent particles that hung in the air like slow motion snow.

Tamashī's copy disappeared in a quiet instant.

The wraith twisted to face her. "Nice move."

"Kill one they both die?" Risa stood. The melt holes her claws left in the floor sealed. "Figured if it's a program, it was going to run the same routine as the last one."

"See? You're not a noob after all." The wraith winked. "And it's not really *both*. It's still one program. That defense proggie is multithreading."

The elevator changed floors in an instant. Two minutes, and another security construct later, Tamashī defeated the lock on what appeared to be an armored vault door leading to a room that stretched too far into the distance to see the opposing wall. Virtual storage cabinets, ten-foot-tall monoliths of shiny silicon lined with horizontal bands of glowing cyan, stood in eight rows. Thousands of data nodes.

Risa whistled.

"Hey, you two," yelled a woman's voice. Another white-shirted security officer entered the virtual representation of a massive neural memory cluster, though instead of a stunrod, she carried a boxy assault rifle. "You will submit to a traceback and arrest, or I will end you right here and now."

Tamashī whirled around, raised her spectral hands, and let out a keening, polyphonic wail from the bowels of Hell. The wraith form grew and darkened, tatters billowing.

The security woman leapt back, screamed, and lapsed into a brief series of convulsions before she transformed into a crude blue wireframe human shape, and disappeared.

"Did you kill her?"

A childlike giggle came from the spirit. "No, but I probably killed her pants."

Tamashī brought her hands in front of herself, sinking wraithlike talons into her insubstantial chest and pulling it open like a cloak. From within an even blacker void inside her, round, head-sized ghosts spat out.

In stark contrast to their mistress, they looked cartoony and cute. After the twentieth bubble went flying, she closed her chest. White orbs zigzagged everywhere, flying in and out of data cabinets.

By the time two pronounced clusters had formed, identifying the memory locations containing the records Tamashī needed to alter, six more security constructs had attacked. Fortunately, every last one of them evaded with the same preprogrammed floor drop, making them easy to kill by repeating the same feint. Risa draped herself against one of the nodes while Tamashī stuck her hands into the nearer of the two the seeker sprites had selected.

"Why am I out of breath? This isn't real." Risa wheezed.

"Your body can't tell the difference. It's reacting like you are really getting into fights. Be glad you took off your armor. We're both working up a sweat in meatspace."

"Ugh. Are you almost done? I'm worn out."

"Yep. Just a little longer here and one more set of files." Tamashī focused on the cabinet in front of her for another six seconds and withdrew her shadowy hands. After gliding two rows to the left and about twenty cabinets down, she thrust her claws into another. "Almost done. The good news is we don't have to walk back. We can just log out."

The spirit withdrew from the second data construct twelve seconds later, and headed for another.

"I thought you said you were done?" Risa grumbled.

Tamashī giggled. The sight of such a creature covering its 'mouth' with a shadow-taloned hand unsettled her almost as much as the fear program. "We are. Since we got noticed, I'm making a few clumsy changes in other files so they don't figure out why we really came in. If they think they found my 'poor attempt' to insert some free shipping records, they'll think they cleaned everything up, and might not look deep enough to find the real change."

"Oh." Risa searched for more energy, having the strangest feeling they weren't done fighting yet.

A squeak came from the entry door, followed by a seemingly endless onrush of security men.

"Oh, fuck." Risa slapped Tamashī on the shoulder and pointed. "We got incoming."

"How many?"

"Couple hundred."

The wraiths' head twisted to the left. Mirrored eyespots tripled in size to dinner plates. "Wow. Guess we pissed them off. Hosting that many simultaneous constructs is taking cycles away from their order processing CPU. They want our asses bad enough to lose money."

"They think we're stealing?" Risa extended her claws.

"No. They just have this whole pride thing. They think they're the Silver or something."

"What does that mean?" Risa glanced at her for a second.

"I'll explain later."

A crashing wave of men in white shirts washed over the near end of the room, so many they seemed a contiguous mass of white and black.

"This is gonna hurt." Risa raised her claws, backing up. "Like, a lot."

"Log out!" yelled Tamashī. "We're good."

The wraith vanished.

Risa sent the mental command for log out, but nothing happened. As the thought to scream some foul word formed at the tip of her brain, a hand closed around hers and pulled her into a rectangle of searing white light opening like a door behind her.

She threw an arm over her eyes and cried out. Cold smoothness met her bare feet. She lowered her arm, risking a hesitant peek. The data room had become a pure white floor with a high gloss finish, empty to the horizon in all directions, where snow-capped mountains and blue sky glowed. Her dark faerie outfit was gone, replaced by a garment composed of a wide strip of white cloth wound around her body, making her feel like some ancient goddess from an old painting. She still had wings, though they had become white and feathery.

Raziel stepped out of a cloud of silvery fog in front of her, his face hidden by a voluminous hood. He kept his hands tucked inside opposing sleeves of a heavy white robe with gold trim marked with ancient runic symbols. A trace of cobalt light reflected on the inside of his hood and his chin from the three wing-shaped bars adorning his face below each eye.

Risa pressed a hand over her chest, trying to calm her heart. The security constructs got way too close for comfort. The sudden shift from chaos to perfect silence left her speechless.

"Hello, Risa."

She bowed her head in greeting. "Raziel."

"I have been somewhat busy as of late, focusing on Earth."

Risa examined the outfit, grateful for the corset's absence. "At least I can breathe in this."

"The open back frees your wings." He took a step closer. "I would like you to reconsider your role in the liberation of Mars."

"You know what happened in Bliss." She turned away, head down. Her wings shrouded tighter around her. The oddity of it happening on its own in response to her frightened mood stalled her thoughts.

"I do. If it did not affect you, you would not be human. I do not have the ability to empathize with how a biological mind copes with stressful situations. I can understand on a theoretical level that you are suffering recurring nocturnal hallucinatory experiences."

"They're called nightmares, Raziel." She glanced over her shoulder at him. "I haven't had one yet, but I'm waiting for it. I can't stop thinking about how close I came to dying. Do you have any idea what the odds were of me surviving that?"

Raziel spoke with zero emotional inflection. "Nine-hundred-sixty-two-thousand-five-hundred-and-forty to one... had I not provided assistance."

She sighed.

"You are not taking into account my adjustment of the position of the aircraft."

"What?" She stared at him.

Raziel lifted his head enough to reveal a subdued smile. "At the instant you leapt, I overrode the flight control system and moved the craft into your path."

Her gut churned. "So I would've been dead if..."

"I told you I would not let you come to harm. Perhaps someday you will believe me."

She paced for a moment. "I can't do it anymore. Angel, AI, synth, whatever you are... I'm the one who has to live with myself for the things I've done. I'm never going to feel happy again, no matter how long I live. There'll always be that guilt hanging over me, wondering how many innocent lives my bombs shattered." Her gaze fell to the floor. "It doesn't matter how wonderful Pavo is to me or how hard I work to try to do the right thing from now on... Every time I have a moment of quiet, I'm going to think about being a killer."

"There are casualties in war. Change of this magnitude requires it. You have been far more deliberate and mindful than most. Your conscience should be clean."

"Don't give me platitudes about war. You can try to take the high road, but I'm not buying it anymore. The whole time you led me along, you made me think you were an angel. All dustblow. You had me believing there was a Heaven... there was a God up there somewhere, and he *chose* me." She covered her mouth, close to tears, but anger won. "Don't you dare lecture me about a clean conscience. I was a vulnerable kid and you took advantage of me. You probably knew Garrison was my real father the whole time, didn't you?"

Her voice seemed to echo to the horizon and back.

Raziel bowed his head. "My knowledge is limited to that which is recorded or can be predicted. The odds of his parental relation to you were—"

"Fuck your odds." She whirled in a circle; the white-floored world appeared identical in all directions. "Where's the damn exit? Why can't I log off?"

"The people of Mars—"

"Don't even *want* us," Risa shouted, feathers ruffled. "You see the NewsNet. You know what they think of us. Everyone I see wants the MLF in prison or executed for killing babies. We're not going to win a goddamned war like that. You're so full of yourself with throwing out the odds... run a simulation of that. What are the odds the MLF can win a bullet-flinging war against two superpowers while living inside territory controlled by one of them and surrounded by people who all hate and fear them? Play that out a million times and tell me what happens. I bet they die every time."

Raziel's eyes glowed.

He's actually doing it. Literal bastard. "The MLF isn't even what we thought it was. It's C-Branch."

"I am aware. Still, they are useful."

She buried her face in her hands. *I don't believe this.* "Look. The only reason I'm not going off on you is because you saved my eyes. As much of my humanity as you stole, you gave me back a little bit of it."

His eyes, glowing amethyst gems, dimmed. "I can give you back the years you lost. It is a simple matter to create a record of a paid reservation at Reinventions. If you are willing to accept an eighteen percent risk of death having your body reverted to how it was when you were eight years old... A telepath can solve the rest. It can be as if nothing happened."

"You're missing the point!" She leaned at him, hands balled to fists. "That won't change anything. I'm lucky enough to have made it to being an adult once. I don't want to roll those dice again... especially as an orphan." *My luck I'd never wake up from the tank. Eighteen percent might as well be a hundred.*

"And that girl you've grown fond of."

"Leave her out of this." Risa narrowed her eyes.

Raziel smiled. "I understand why you cannot return to your past, but the citizens of Mars deserve a future free from tyranny as well."

Risa pointed at him. "Think about it. There aren't enough people on Mars to survive all-out war. Both sides are controlled by dishonest, greedy, deceitful prongs so far removed from the lives of real people they might as well be aliens. The only chance of anyone being left after the shitstorm subsides is to work *with* one of them and help it win. The UCF isn't *that* bad. They don't have pockets of armed resistance trying to overthrow it from within. You should ally yourself with them. If the day ever comes when the Corporates no longer infest Mars, *then* work to change the stuff you don't like about the UCF."

He glided off to the left, pacing.

She stalked after him. "A few adjustments to an existing regime is a lot easier to pull off—especially for someone with your power—than it is to start over from scratch. What guarantee do you have that the 'people of Mars' won't come up with a government worse than either side is now? Did you even consider that without a central government, they might devolve into sovereign cities at war with each other?"

Raziel made the sound of a deep breath. "Your argument is not without merit."

"The Pueri Verum Martis is committed to change from within once the ACC is out of the way. Talk to General Everett. He'd probably welcome your help. I've been lied to, tricked, and misled too much. I can't do it anymore. I'm done." She waited ten seconds, gazing at the blue sky, clouds, and distant snow-capped mountains. "Okay, let me out."

"I would still like you to be my hands out there. I've arranged to send some equipment for you to Pavo's residence. I can ensure you live comfortably without the need to waste your life at some rote office cubicle."

She examined her toes for a moment. "I don't think I'd really mind that... after everything. A boring job sounds nice. I don't want to take chances with my life anymore."

"You'll need to support that child of yours. I give you my word I will not ask you to do anything too risky."

The world faded to white. Seconds later, the perfect silence gave way to the distant sound of a shouting woman. A sense of falling over backward came over her, and the voice increased in volume. Her body shook and bounced, and the warm stickiness of sweat swam over her. Heaviness pressed down on her gut and shoulders. A fluffy-haired silhouette appeared in the blank everything. Within seconds, detail filled in to Tamashī, straddling her with a hand on each shoulder. The faux teen shouted a mixture of Japanese and English, neither one decipherable.

Risa moaned, and wiped her forehead. "Ugh. What happened?"

Tamashī blinked, looking stunned. She sniffled; her lip quivered, and she burst into tears for another minute before regaining composure. "I thought you got coreburn or something. The deck showed you as logged out, but you wouldn't wake up. I tried to pull the cord, but it shocked the piss out of me."

Risa gazed up at the beige ceiling. Her back ached where the guard construct stabbed her with the stunrod, even though it hadn't happened for real. The tiny woman climbed off her and sat nearby, crossing her legs in a yoga pose, ankles resting on opposing knees. Risa sat up and tried to rub the spot on her back.

"What did you see?" asked Tamashī. Though her cheeks streamed with tears, she grinned.

"Raziel wanted a word with me."

"And?" Tamashī leaned forward and unplugged the wire from Risa's head.

"He still wants me to work for him." Risa shivered from a twinge of fear, and drew her knees to her chin, heels hooked on the edge of the Comforgel pad. Damp fabric stretched tight on her back. *He could do so much damage if he wanted to.* "I'm almost afraid to say no."

19

LOGISTICS

R isa knelt on the floor behind Kree, washing the girl's hair in the stream from an old-fashioned showerhead dangling from a pipe on the wall of the locker room. The primitive arrangement, lacking even a plastic curtain, offered zero chance of cleaning the child without getting soaked herself, so Risa had decided to share the shower. She focused on scrubbing Kree clean first, then washed herself while the girl played in the water, running in circles and jumping in puddles.

After toweling off, she handed Kree a packet of new underwear she'd picked up on her way out of Elysium, as well as a new outfit: a plain black T-shirt and baggy grey pants. She remembered the fit the child threw at being given such 'girly' clothes upon first arriving. Kree demanded pants back then, but didn't react to them with the adoration Risa expected, rather a smile of gratitude, sans cheering or squealing.

Part of Risa envied the girl and wanted the comfort of normal clothes, but fear made her reach for the ballistic suit.

Kree tilted her head. "Why aren't you wearing underpants?"

Because I'm screwed up and wear this suit all day long. Risa fidgeted at the MolWeave fastener on the armor. "Uhh. This armor doesn't breathe."

"Breathe?" Kree furrowed her eyebrows. "That's silly. It's not alive."

"I mean, air doesn't pass through it. I sweat, and anything I wear under it sops it up. It feels squishy and nasty."

"Oh." Kree stepped into her moon boots, tapping the toes on the floor one after the next to get them all the way on. "Javier said it's 'cause you only get ten minutes to be with Pavo."

"Javier is going to get a fist in the nose the next time I see him."

Kree looked up with a confused expression.

Risa took the girl by the hand and walked her to the common area. She dialed up pancakes for both of them and flopped into a seat at the round table. Nine others, mostly new people she didn't recognize, smiled or waved at her, though none attempted to strike up a conversation. *Guess I'm still the scary, crazy bitch.*

Kree made silly faces at her while letting half-chewed pancake fall out of her mouth.

Risa laughed, but wrestled with fear and sadness inside. *Okay. Enough. I'm getting her out of here now.* She head-dialed Garrison. When his virtual image appeared hovering over the table, she whined at him.

<Something wrong, Bit?>

<Dad… wow, it feels so weird to call you that.>

She smiled at a warm rush racing up inside her chest. <I don't know what to do with Kree. I want to get her out of the safehouse before something happens… this is no place for a kid.>

He looked down. <Sorry.>

<I didn't mean me. I'm talking about Kree. I want to take her to Pavo's, but every time I try to bring up the idea of taking her out of here, she freaks out and I can't handle it. I cave in.>

<You've been *asking* her if she wants to leave, right?>

<Yeah.>

Kree made explosive noises while stabbing her pancakes with her fork.

"Eat them before they melt, hon. It's OmniSoy." Risa grimaced. "They're going to turn disgusting."

<Well. If you want me to say it. You'll need to do what I wasn't brave enough to do.> Garrison scratched his six-day old beard. <Put your foot down. Tell her you are leaving, and she's coming with you. Don't leave it up to her.>

Risa stared at the happy little face across the table from her, dreading the idea of it warping with terror and tantrum. <I'm not sure if I can.>

<You took her outside yesterday. How did that go?>

<Fine. Better than I thought. She seemed to like the sky. I don't know that she'd ever seen it before.>

<I have an apartment in Arcadia. It's on the thirty-first floor of a residential tower in the Tegea district. It's nice, not extravagant. I haven't set foot in the place. I rented it soon after we set up shop here, and never got around to visiting it.> He exhaled. The finger tapping on his desk remained out of the image, but the sound she knew well. <Look, it might be best if you moved in there. There's no way to know what's going to happen with the Front.>

<I can't ask you to pay for an apartment for me.>

<I'm not; the government is.> He winked. <And if you feel that bad about it, I can kick you out if I ever need to move in.>

She laughed, startling a few people. Kree gave her a quizzical look. <Come with us. Get out of here too.>

A fond smile tugged one corner of his mouth. <It's not that simple. I'm part of the command structure, Bit. Captain goes down with the ship and all that shit. Too many things are relying on me. Too many people counting on me.>

<Dad...> Her NetMini chirped and beeped.

<I'll be fine. I registered your PID to the apartment's security system so you can get in. Go make yourself at home and...> He sighed. <And live like a normal damn person. You deserve it.>

<Dad, don't talk like that. You make it sound like I'm moving out and I'm never going to see you again.>

He offered a wan smile. <Don't read too much into an old man's regret. I should've left years ago, when I had the chance. It's my fault you're in this position.>

<You tried to keep me away from it more than I ever realized. I'm sorry I didn't listen.>

<Don't repeat history.> He winked. <Get that kid of yours out of here.>

<Okay. Thanks.>

Garrison's image vanished. Kree picked up her plate. Risa leaned back, watching the girl seek out every trace of syrup with her tongue. *She looks so happy. I don't want to ruin it.* Her jaw tightened. *I'd rather have her alive and mad at me than happy and...*

"What's wrong?" Kree froze, staring over the top of the plate at her.

Risa stood and offered a hand. "I need to talk to you."

Kree's eyes widened. "I didn't do it. Kyle's lying."

"Didn't do what?"

"A tool cart got knocked over." Kree swished her boots back and forth.

After a few seconds of Risa's stare, she gazed into her lap. "I kinda sorta bumped into it, an' it went rolling."

"Thank you for being honest. I'm sure it's not a big deal. C'mon." She took Kree's hand and walked her out of the dining area.

Minutes later, she turned left into Death Row, and returned to the now-empty room she'd been using.

"I thought we got kicked out?" Kree looked up at her.

Risa smiled. "We did. But no one else wants to live in here. It's quiet, so we can talk."

"Why?"

In the room, she sat on the edge of the Comforgel pad and pulled Kree to stand in front of her. "Do you know why they call this hallway Death Row?"

Kree shrugged.

"There's a lot of people living in the safehouse. No one gets a private room but the people who work with bombs."

"I don't like bombs." Kree bit her lip and looked down.

"I know. I don't either." Risa hesitated until the emotion wouldn't affect her voice. "You know what bombs do."

Kree nodded.

"Sometimes they don't work right and they hurt the person trying to use them."

"Bombs don't hurt people. They kill." Kree trembled.

"Every time we go out there, there's a chance we won't come back. That's why they call this Death Row. Because everyone on it is waiting for the day they die."

Kree sniveled.

Risa brushed the girl's tears off her cheeks. "I'm not going to use bombs any more. That's why they kicked us out. I don't want to die."

Kree looked up, almost smiling.

"This is no place for a child to grow up. I've been asking if you want to go outside with me, and you always say no."

"I'm scared." Kree shivered.

"I understand. What happened to your mother is horrible. You should never have had to watch that. I don't want the same thing to happen to you. It's not safe here."

Kree's chaotic emotions leveled off in a perplexed stare. "Why do they call it a safehouse if it's not safe?"

Risa hugged her, taken by a sudden laugh. "It's, well… it's safe for grownups with guns. Not safe for little girls. Do you trust me?"

Kree nodded without hesitation.

"I'll do everything I can to keep that trust. Today, I'm going to do something you might not like, but I am doing it because I want to protect you."

Kree pulled back, but Risa held on.

"We are going to a real home. I'm asking you to trust me to protect you. Nothing will happen to us." *I hope.* "Look at me."

Kree stopped squirming, locking eyes with her.

"It doesn't matter how much you scream or carry on. I know you're frightened and worried about the bad men. I am taking you out of here before you get hurt."

Tears flowed in silence down the child's face.

"Hey. Do the bad men have speeware?" Risa winked.

A snot bubble formed at Kree's nose when she giggled. "No."

Risa wiped it with her fingers. "You know what I will do to the bad men if they try to hurt you, don't you? That's what you were drawing the other day."

Kree nodded.

"We're leaving. Together."

The child looked down, tapping her boot on the floor. "'Kay."

Risa picked her up as she stood, cradling her tight while walking without ceremony or farewell to the main door. The closer she got to the exit, the deeper tiny fingers dug into her back. Kali and Lancaster stood on either side of the front gate, armed with full-size assault rifles and night-vision headgear. One look at Risa's grim expression, and they got the hint.

Kali shook her hand while Lancaster patted her on the child-free shoulder.

"Take care of yourself," said Kali.

"It's not me I'm worrying about these days." Risa smiled. "Keep your eyes open. A giant ball of crap is rolling down Primus Mons. Don't be here when it lands."

"I hear that." Lancaster waved at Kree, who didn't react.

Risa walked across the large tunnel, boots *skiffing* in the dirt. She'd come back for her box of clothes… or hell with it, order new stuff. More important to get out of here while she could. Another moment of conviction strong enough to overpower Kree's fear might not happen.

The girl clung, occasionally trembling as they navigated a series of old driller tunnels at the bottom of Primus. After ascending three ladders and two stairways—the vents offered a more direct route up, but she wasn't about to risk some of those climbs with Kree—she forced open a plastisteel double door and stepped out onto Tier 8, where the air stank of fetid organic rot and metallic dirt.

Graffiti-covered metal walls lined a larger finished passageway full of tiny unused residences. As with most cities on Mars, the deeper one went in Primus, the greater the danger. Most people preferred to be homeless on Tier 5 than pay rent on Tier 8. At the sight of metal-covered walls, Kree's body shivered out of control. Risa cradled the back of her head in one hand and made soothing noises.

For once, she missed her metal eyes. The purple glow advertised her being a *ti-zhèn*, a badge that kept miscreants away.

"Let me know if anyone tries to come up behind me, okay?" Risa squeezed her. "I'll watch forward."

Kree buried her face in the side of Risa's neck, trying to sob while making as little noise as possible. Risa's heart felt as though a cyborg crushed it between mechanical fingers, but she clung to knowing she had to do this. *Dammit. I ran off too fast. I forgot the damn headset.*

Focused on the shadows, she marched forward, refusing to surrender to doubt. Food cartons crunched under her boots, the plastic crinkle echoed for what sounded like miles. Shadows emerged from side passages, tailing them before they'd walked fifty meters. Risa stared down one man after another, unsure if they were curious vagrants or ill-intentioned thugs.

Whether they had a spot of pity for a sniveling child or were taken aback by a slender woman giving them a 'go ahead and try it' glare, no one did more than look at her as she walked. Ten nervous minutes later, she reached the stairway up to Tier 7. Kree squirmed and tried to break loose when a handful of dosers on the steps sat up to check out who walked by.

Risa clamped her arms tight and hurried up the stairs. She'd never thought twice about walking through these areas before. Not even the denizens of Deep Primus were dumb enough to tangle with a *ti-zhèn*. Now, she looked normal. Normal, and terrified—a victim for the taking. Risa slowed as she neared the exit to the seventh tier. Fear attracted trouble. She adopted her old facial expression, daring the world to mess with her. *Whoever designed this place and put the stairways at staggered sides needs to be shot.* The fastest way to the next stairwell would be to head down a merchant concourse three lanes wide bisecting the middle of Tier 7.

Kree hyperventilated, and muttered, "I gotta pee."

Risa hummed the music from Colony Commando, which seemed to distract her.

A handful of gangers, Pantheon by their logo, emerged from the crumbling hollows of abandoned storefronts. One peculiarity of the gang took the form of a fondness for melee weapons. Broadswords, boarding party axes, and knives glinted in the yellow artificial light emanating from weak bulbs at the corners of the ceiling.

"Oi, tasty little bit of crumpet walkin' around," said a bearded man on the right.

Risa glared at a six-foot-and-change man with a long beard, a battered MDF helmet modified with Viking-like horns, and two rubber-handled axes. Tattered brown pants, old miner's boots, and a piecemeal attempt at armor made from inch-thick squares of plastisteel zip-tied to a leather vest put an image in her brain she wouldn't soon forget.

Kree wailed, convulsing as if on the verge of throwing up.

"It's okay, Kree. They won't hurt us," whispered Risa. "None of them have speeware."

A tiny giggle slipped out between the child's sniffles.

The giant walked out in front of her.

She strode up to within arm's length and stared defiance up at him. "Get out of my way."

He chuckled. "This ain't a safe place for a little woman to be walking alone."

"I was hoping to get through at least *one* day this week without having to kill someone."

A handful of men off to the right made patronizing 'impressed' faces, and gestured at her.

"Cute kid," said the tall man. "Come on." He nodded in the direction she'd been walking. "I'm guessin' you're headin' up?"

Five other members of Pantheon walked up behind her, bearing an assortment of vibroblades, katanas, and nunchaku. One man carried a sword as long as her height.

"There's people behind us," whispered Kree.

"Not for much longer." Risa glanced over her shoulder.

"Easy." The big man raised a hand. "We ain't no threat to you or the little one. The shitheads at the other end of that street are another story."

The longer I wait, the worse her nightmares are gonna be. "Fine, but I'm more dangerous than I look."

"I know." The Viking grinned. "Garrison said you'd be coming."

She gawked. "You could've said something!"

"Aye." He nodded. "I could'a. Havin' a li'l fun."

Risa grumbled, but followed him. By the midway point between east and west, wild-eyed dosers crept out of alleys carved between stores. The Pantheon drew their weapons, resulting in a mile-long moving staredown. Fortunately, none of the hollering maniacs did more than make noise. Risa nodded at the men despite her annoyance at being treated like a 'girl in need of protection.' However, given her current cargo, she didn't mind as much.

The stairway led up two levels to Tier 5, which for the most part, functioned as the demarcation point of civilization. Defense Force patrols occasionally set foot there. Something about the design of the metal-plated walls, the plasfilm posters, or the mixture of salty ramen scented air with body odor set Kree off again. She clamped on hard, whining and shivering.

Risa walked at a quick, but determined pace, avoiding places she knew to be riskier and taking the 'tourist path' down the least grungy passages to a wide-open mall concourse in the center of the level. In the last segment of tunnel between the city and the shopping area, Kree stuck her thumb in her mouth and whimpered.

I wonder if it happened here... "We're almost out. It's okay."

"Mmm," whined Kree.

Risa weaved among a crowd of citizens drifting from store to store, avoiding two beggars and one idiot rambling on about the End Times. Twenty meters from the primary elevator bank, a large column ringed with holo-panels blared with NewsNet feeds discussing politics, the conflict with the Corporates, and a handful of adverts for everything from colony jobs to the latest, greatest food reassembler, to custom 'fully living' penis replacements.

She shivered at the voice of Moht Daran rambling on about the 'eerie lull' in activity on the part of the Martian Liberation Front. He seemed worried because nothing had blown up recently, and took that to mean they planned something big. The old guy with crazy white hair in the next frame raised the possibility that the MLF had been responsible for the Bliss disaster. Of course, no one believed him. Too deep in ACC territory. Too high profile. Much to her amusement, the NewsNet pundits all embraced the notion that the explosion came as a result of ACC error, who then tried to blame the MLF so they didn't look foolish. In a roundabout sort of way, the disaster *had* been their fault. Risa only wanted to sever communication lines. Whatever idiot approved putting a Cryomil line across the Strand (and doing it as cheaply as possible) bore the guilt for the scale of the destruction.

A lump slid down her throat as she darted into an opening elevator. Fourteen other people shuffled in after, pushing her back to the wall. Kree stilled, staring out from beneath a veil of her hair at the people all with their backs turned. Being behind everyone in an enclosed space seemed to calm the child, and she squirmed, seeking a more comfortable position on Risa's hip.

Six agonizing minutes later, the elevator opened on Tier 1. The sight of the mall full of people sent Kree into a near panic. Risa kept a hand on the back of the girl's head to hold her close as she headed straight for the shuttleport. Once inside the terminal building, Kree's fear fell off like an abandoned coat.

"I gotta pee."

Risa set the girl on her feet and crouched to eye level. "I am sorry for scaring you, but I did it so you will stay safe. I will never let anyone hurt you."

Kree looked around while wiping her face, then nodded. "It's not scary here."

She took Kree to the nearest restroom, using her headware to book tickets for a shuttle flight to Arcadia while the kid ducked into a stall. On the way from the bathroom to the waiting area, Kree eyeballed a snack counter selling cinnamon sugar hot pretzels. The smell *was* rather appealing, though the C60 price tag on the non-OmniSoy snack made her wince. *I should treat her for being a good sport.*

"Hmm. Looks like someone wants a pretzel?"

Kree returned a rapid nod and a grin. "Yes, please."

Risa bought two. In the waiting area, they sat on blue-cushioned seats, square pads mounted to a forty-meter metal bar, munching. Kree seemed to have climbed out from under her terror, and gazed around at the massive room with the two-story ceiling, swinging her feet. She looked straight up, gaping-mouthed, as a shuttle passed over the geodesic dome window, a rumble of ion thrusters shaking the entire facility. Once it passed, Kree nibbled on the pretzel while watching people in civilian clothes. The child appeared to have little fear of anyone who didn't resemble a ganger. Wound up on sugar, nerves, and the aftereffect of terror, Kree kept shifting position between letting her feet dangle and sway to tucking them up and sitting on her moon boots.

Risa forced herself to peel her gaze away from the little smiling face beside her every few seconds to watch for threats. Four Mars Defense Force officers in full armor walked in formation across the center of the huge waiting area, in a constant state of observing everyone, but they paid Risa little mind. With her natural eyes and a little girl leaning against her, she had to look like any normal young mother.

I'm being paranoid. No gangs would dare do anything in a shuttleport. She surveyed the entrance, other people sitting on the long benches, and a small crowd by an assistance counter. *As soon as I relax, something will happen.*

Eleven minutes later, her NetMini pinged, and she led Kree by the hand to the boarding area to take their place in line. A couple of other children waiting to board glanced at her. One smiled, two gave her blank looks, and one boy younger than Kree responded to her gaze with a raspberry. None of them screamed or cried at the sight of her.

As wonderful as it felt not to be terrorizing small children with inhuman metal eyes, Risa couldn't help but keep looking over her shoulder. Everett, Raziel, Shiro, or who knows what might be waiting behind any shadow to steal her happiness yet again. The line edged forward person by person, each body accompanied by a soft *ping* from a wall panel as NetMini's scanned them in. Kree leaned to the right, her weight hanging by Risa's grip of her hand, so she could keep looking at workers and crew vehicles moving around on the false window displaying the tarmac on the surface.

They followed the flow of people into the shuttle and found their seats. Kree busied herself with a cheesy side-scrolling video game on the datapad tethered to the seat in front of her. Risa leaned back, watching her play. She let out a relieved breath and entertained the hope that maybe their exodus from the underbelly of Primus wouldn't leave permanent mental scars. Kree's lack of a complete freak-out didn't necessarily mean she handled it well. All too well, Risa knew a child could become too terrified to make a sound. Still, the girl's present state of calm-normal reassured her.

Garrison's got friends in Pantheon... Never would've thought.

Kree scrambled across the seats to the window, but soon got bored with the tarmac and resumed playing games on the tethered tablet. A while later, when the shuttle lifted off, she lost interest in the game and stared out the window. There, the child's attention remained for forty-one minutes, until the shuttle touched down at Arcadia Starport. Once the 'stay seated' light went out, Risa guided her along to the door and onto a moving sidewalk that brought them from the shuttle platform along a transparent tube to the baggage claim. Having no bags to pick up, she kept a firm grip on Kree's hand and headed across the concourse toward the escalators to street level.

The child swayed in a perpetual state of turning and gazing at everything, mouth open. Several times, she went to dart off, but Risa held her back. A thousand 'what's that' questions later, they emerged from the building into the fresh air of a surface city. Kree stared in wonder at two rows of living, green trees planted in strips between the shuttleport courtyard and the street... and started crying.

"Kree?" Risa dropped to a knee and grasped the girl's shoulders. "What's wrong?"

Kree sniveled for a moment before pointing at the trees and wailing, "They're pretty."

Risa tried to suppress the urge to laugh, and spent a few minutes explaining trees. She felt a bit foolish, as less than a month ago, she understood a tree to be a plastic thing covered in decorations that people set up once a year. She hadn't the first idea that these giant plants in front of her were 'trees,' or that the holiday decoration had been based on another type of tree, an actual plant. *The strange things people read about when they're bored.* Risa picked Kree up and carried her to the nearest tree.

"This is nice." Kree touched a leaf. "I like sky."

Risa ruffled her hair. "I'm glad you're happy. I was afraid you'd be frightened."

Kree bit her lower lip. "I don't like the tunnel streets. That's where the bad men hide. *Outside* outside is okay."

This might actually work. I wonder if Pavo will move here. He can get a transfer I bet. She frowned inside at the thought of his apartment. Kree wouldn't care that the whole district is full of Defense Force officers, the subterranean residential section under Primus was a classic example of the environment she feared most. Now, more than ever, she wanted to forget the MLF and all the dustblow that came with it.

Raziel, please let me be happy.

She paged a PubTran, fed it the address to the apartment Garrison mentioned, and leaned back. Kree crawled to the front of the little car to press herself to the windshield, still gazing around awestruck at a place with open sky. The ride came to an abrupt halt sixteen minutes later when the car pulled over to the side of the road in an area lined with bars and restaurants. Rapid braking bounced the child off the windshield; she landed on the floor.

Kree rolled up onto all fours, wide-eyed. "I didn't touch anything!"

"What happened?" Risa reached out an arm.

Kree climbed into a hug and whined, "I dunno."

"I'm asking the car." Risa patted her on the head. "Shh. It's okay. PubTran, what happened?"

"PubTran Corporation apologizes for the delay. There has been an unscheduled violence event in your trip route. You will not be charged for this delay."

"What's going on?"

"PubTran Corporation is unable to provide an answer to your question due to privacy considerations."

Shit. This thing's been hacked. She accessed the Arcadia City net and checked their position. They'd come to a dead stop one-point-two miles away from the apartment. It sat within a cluster of glittering skyscrapers visible from here. "End trip. We'll walk the rest of the way."

"PubTran Corporation cannot be held liable for injury or death due to a trip abort."

Risa grumbled. "Why would aborting the trip cause injury?"

"PubTran Corporation cannot provide details due to privacy considerations. If you would still like to end your trip at this point, your fare will be adjusted down by ₵11. Please acknowledge that you release PubTran Corporation of liability."

She spun in the seat, looking for people heading toward the car. Not seeing anyone only made her more nervous. "I accept."

The door opened. Risa hopped out onto the sidewalk, holding the girl's hand.

"Why did the car break?" Kree looked up, blinked, and pulled her hair away from her eyes. "Is someone gonna fix it?"

"It's not broken, just being annoying." Risa tried to seem confident.

One block forward, she turned right at a corner and skidded to a halt. Eight MDF cars formed a horseshoe around the front of a restaurant with blasted-out windows. A few steps from the wall, a man with a full-body cybernetic conversion held a pair of armored officers aloft by one hand each. Every inch of him gleamed in shiny plastisteel, a combination of armor plates, grey Myofiber muscle bundles and metal parts with a hint of human skeleton to their design. He may or may not have still had a live brain inside.

Both of his eyes glowed red, save for a gold 'O' hinting at an iris. Most of his shirt had been chewed off by laser fire; what fabric remained on his shoulders still burned. His chest gleamed in the sun, a darker shade of plastisteel than his arms and legs, dotted where it had laughed off shots from the officers.

Orange energy smears connected from various MDF pistols to his chest every few seconds, but the lasers only diffused into char marks. The man frothed at the mouth, screaming incoherent non-words. Exposed hydraulic actuators clung to the underside of his upper arms, a crude and cheap means of providing superhuman strength. Segmented metal hoses emerged from the back of his neck, connecting to the midpoint of his back, vibrating with the flow of fluid.

Well damn. Guess the car didn't get hacked after all...

Kree screamed.

Where does a cyberganger get energy-resistant plating? She squinted. *He's gotta be brain-fried private security or something.*

The psychotic aug hurled the female officer across the street where the crimson-armored figure struck the third story of an office tower and fell limp into a large cluster of bushes. Continued laser fire appeared to annoy the aug like a swarm of mosquitos. He held the male officer in front of himself as a shield, causing the MDF officers in the police line to stop shooting.

Risa yanked Kree off her feet and sprinted for the nearest MDF car, carrying her. Two officers, both women, noticed her approach and pointed their weapons at her.

"Halt!" yelled one.

"Get back! This is a Defense Force incident area."

Risa raised the hand not supporting Kree. "You don't have the hardware to crack that nut."

"Lady, get the hell out of here with that kid." The taller officer grabbed Risa by the left bicep. "What the fuck are you thinking?"

"Kree, stay with these officers. Keep your head down."

"'Kay."

"You nuts? You can't drop off an unwanted kid with us right now." The shorter woman lowered her weapon, no longer regarding her as a threat.

"She is *not* unwanted." Risa scowled. "Just keep her safe for a few minutes while I give you guys a little assistance."

The crazy cyborg raised the male officer over his head, looking about to smash him into the ground.

Risa shrugged out of the cop's grip and sprinted around the car, not bothering to draw her pistols. The aug looked at her, flashed a manic grin, and tossed the unconscious cop to the side like an overgrown boy done with an old toy after finding a new one.

MDF officers shouted, telling her to get back. A few called her a crazy bitch.

At fifteen feet, Risa kicked on her speedware, shoving the Japanese electronics to the edge of their performance envelope. The cyborg's already slow movements ground to a standstill. Her tactical processor couldn't pinpoint weak spots as effectively without the metallurgical scan mode, but did its best working from visual data it lifted from her brain. Flickering amber octagons appeared over his joints, the hoses, and the only skin left on him anywhere—the area around his nose and mouth. A flashing yellow octagon appeared over a discolored panel an inch below and left of his sternum.

His near-motionlessness ended with a punch that moved at the pace of a lazy wave. She leaned to the left, sprouted claws, and raked at the exposed hydraulics on the back of his arm. In the six seconds relative to her sped-up perception it took him to recover from throwing car-smashing force into a punch, she slipped around behind him, sliced all the cables on his back, and savaged the hydraulic cylinder on his other arm.

The man stumbled about to face her again; dark-green translucent fluid spurting from the severed hoses sprayed on the wall. A leak would shut down his crude mechanical muscles in about five minutes—not fast enough. She wondered what sort of components he'd had crammed inside his body to make him run those lines on the outside. Then again, Nano blades weren't the sort of weapon a street aug expected to run into. His armor would've laughed off metal claws. Dancing with this nutcase made her understand why some people carried swords. Claws forced her to get too close to a monster capable of killing her in a single punch.

He shook his head side-to-side, spewing foam and warbling nonsense from his lips.

With his lower arms useless thanks to the destroyed 'street boost' hydraulics, he proceeded to swing his entire arm at her like a club attached at the shoulder. Risa crouched low to let his attack pass over her head, then leapt up, thrusting her claws under his chin. Eight-inch transparent blades pierced with little resistance. A quick curl of her fingers pulled the blades through material too tough to be biological, likely the uppermost portion of spine, reinforced with metal. She yanked her hand back, leaving four tiny triangular holes in the front of his throat leaking a mixture of blood and milky white liquid, nutrient carrier for Myofiber muscles.

He shuddered on his feet, twitched, and collapsed over like a statue falling off its pedestal. Spasms conjured the image of a short-circuited android. Risa took three steps back and shut down her speedware. Threads of mild pain from hot wires in her arms and legs faded.

The MDF broke cover, except for the woman watching Kree, and ran up on him. Some diverted to check on the motionless officer lying on the ground near the restaurant wall.

One man approached Risa, laser pistol pointed at the aug, but his eyes on her hands. "What the hell did I just watch?"

Risa retracted her claws. "The spine felt like metal. His brain's probably not dead yet, though I think it was more or less mush to begin with."

"Who are you?"

"A concerned citizen who happened to have the right tools." She smiled and strode to the car where she'd left Kree. "Excuse me, my daughter..."

The officer followed. "You can't just walk into the middle of an active crime scene and... and... do that, and then walk away like you dropped off a cake."

"Your people looked like they were in deep shit. The guy had diffusive armor and I didn't see anyone whipping out a vibro-sword and going toe to toe with him. I have a soft spot for MDF officers, since I'm in love with one." Risa reached for Kree. The girl squirmed in the female officer's grip. "Thanks for keeping her safe. Do you mind letting her go now?"

No need to worry, said the voice of Raziel. *If they run records, they will find your daughter.*

She tensed.

"Not so fast, miss." The man who'd followed her held up his forearm and tapped at a holo-panel floating over it.

"Risa Tanais." She tapped her foot. "I can't answer your questions, officer. All I can say is I work for the government."

He raised an eyebrow. "What branch?"

Risa winked. "Logistics."

Understanding flashed in his eyes. He leaned back and waved at the other officer to let the girl go. "Thanks for the assist. That would've been a huge mess."

"You're welcome."

Kree held her hands up like claws and shouted, "Speeware!"

"Cute," said the female officer.

Risa held Kree's hand and walked across the street to add distance from the crippled psycho.

"What was that, Barnes? You just let that woman walk?" asked the woman, evidently thinking Risa couldn't hear.

"Don't worry about it. She's either Spec Ops or C-Branch. Nothing you want to stick your head into."

"You got all that from fuckin' 'logistics?' Seriously?" The woman sounded upset.

"Well that, plus military-grade reflex boosters, Nano claws, the surgical takedown. What's your opinion? Extreme babysitter?"

"Fuck you, Barnes."

"I thought you'd never ask, Gomez. Want dinner first or should we just get a room right away?"

A muted thud of armored fist striking armored body followed.

Risa laughed. They walked the last mile enjoying a beautiful day. When the building came into view, she turned her attention to the girl at her side. "See that tower up ahead? We're going to live there for a while."

"How long?" Kree kicked a small rock. "I don't ever wanna go in the dark again."

A lump formed in her throat. Risa squeezed her hand as she approached the main entrance. "Neither do I, kiddo. Neither do I."

20

NASCENT NORMAL

Bucking metal under Risa's boots swayed from side to side. Distant explosions pounded shockwaves along the disintegrating strand spanning the Melas Chasma. A small one-man fighter craft hovered ten feet away like some precarious platform in a video game. Without thinking, Risa leapt for it. Time froze, leaving her hanging in midair reaching for the arrowhead-shaped flying craft. The far-off buildings and spires of Bliss glimmered in the sun, like ice at the top of the ridge, lit blue by puffs of Cryomil flames blasting chunks out of the stone. Hundred-story buildings crumbled and fell, a mass culling of a plastisteel forest.

The crystal castle collapsed in slow motion.

Her refuge, the small aircraft, slid backward out from under her—of course, the pilot should have been able to avoid her with ease—and she fell into the open sky, windmilling her arms and screaming for an eleven-kilometer fall. Huge flaming metal chunks surrounded her on the way down. From her position far above the ground, the colony at the canyon's bottom resembled a scattering of ice cubes on dirt.

I'm dreaming! Air refused to enter her lungs. Eyes closed, she tried to gain enough control of her spiraling fear to imagine herself winged. Dreams could do that. As soon as a person realized they dreamed, they could take control.

At least that's what she'd read.

She opened her eyes to find a settlement of drop box buildings racing toward her, only seconds before she crashed into the crimson ground. Despite the tremendous *boom* of her body striking the canyon floor, it hurt no worse than if she'd fallen out of bed. Stunned relief lasted seconds before a massive hunk of debris smashed into the ground nearby. Risa curled into a ball on her side, screaming as pieces of the Strand came down like meteors on all sides. Buildings flattened like empty synthbeer canisters under the tires of a prowler. Shrieks from panicking citizens cut off to silence as they perished under a pelting rain of debris.

A gentle howl of wind broke the subsequent silence, accented by a fluttering of metal. She pushed herself up to sit and found herself at the base of a shallow crater. That she'd struck the ground with the force of a meteor and survived brought her mind to a stop. *I'm still dreaming.* Squinting at the sunlight shimmering on the debris, she gazed around at utter ruin. The twisted remains of drop box pods lay scattered around, half-inch thick plastisteel ripped apart as though an enormous dog had shredded giant takeout food cartons.

Moans emanated from the wreckage. Flaps of Epoxil boards, metal plates, and cloth curtains parted as bodies crawled free from the site of their deaths. A thousand bloody, mangled people dragged themselves toward her. Risa leapt to her feet and started to run, but stalled in her tracks as forty or fifty small glops of gore slid out from under a piece of crushed building and recombined into an almost-human shape. The man's right arm reached out, tipped with what had been his left hand.

Risa screamed, and backed away—into the grasping arms of the angry dead.

She snapped awake on the floor of her new bedroom. Cool air clung to a beige carpet shaded pale orange from the glow of the city outside. Heavy tint could only do so much. Covered in sweat, she shivered and wrapped her arms around her legs. Even with the windows as dark as they could go, years of living underground made Arcadia's night seem bright as day.

After a few minutes, the inhuman sounds of shambling corpses faded into the recesses of her mind. She slid one hand down her shin and covered her numb toes. Her hair clung to her back, sticky with perspiration. *Damn.* She rested her head against her knees until the shaking stopped, and stood.

"Climate, seventy."

A *chirp* sounded from nowhere in particular. Within a few seconds, the layer of cold over the carpet changed to a warmer breeze. For a while, she stared at the outer wall, composed of four window panels of half-inch-thick transparent aluminum between inch-wide plastisteel beams. Variable tint could make them as dark as sunglasses or so clear they almost vanished. Outside, Arcadia swam with advert bots, a smattering of hovercars, and millions of winking lights from windows, streetlamps, and holograms.

Do I belong in this place? She watched things fly around until the clammy wetness around her body became intolerable.

She peeled off her T-shirt and sweat-soaked panties on the way to the small, attached bathroom. Modern conveniences that even the lower end of middle class took for granted felt strange and extravagant, as if she'd stolen luxury from a world she'd disavowed. A boxy white appliance mounted to the wall left of the sink accepted her underthings via a hatch at the top. Soon, the scent of fabric softener filled the room as it cleaned them. She stepped into the autoshower tube to freshen up. A metal ring around the outside descended, spraying her with a hot water/soap mixture. She stood still, letting the machine work until the hot air dry cycle completed about fifteen minutes later.

The bottom end of the white box offered a clean, new, and plastic-wrapped set of panties, but she still hadn't gotten used to the feeling of wearing them. A handful of purchases on the spur of the moment provided some necessities to the unlived-in space, one of which had been underpants. Garrison hadn't even loaded the machine on the wall with briefs.

Risa headed back into the bedroom and claimed a knee-length black shirt from the dresser. After fluffing her hair out of the collar, she padded down the hall to Kree's room. The girl sprawled over an adult-sized twin Comforgel pad in a pose more befitting a college student after a late-night drinking binge than a six-year-old. Mouth agape, one arm dangling over the edge, more sheet on the floor than the bed, Kree elevated sleeping to an extreme sport.

Wow. The kid sleeps hard. *Guess she's making up for lost time.*

Risa clung to the doorjamb, smiling. How many nights had she been unable to sleep out of fear? For the first few months after Garrison took her off the street, Risa slept in the ventilation duct connected to his room. Kree's sanctuary of choice was a spot under the bed in their room on Death Row. Risa bit her lip, wondering if the child in front of her had found the streets as terrifying as she did. *It had to be worse for her. At least I was two years older.* Watching Kree sleep so soundly stirred a mixture of relief and guilt. They hadn't been living in the apartment for long at all, yet the girl felt safe enough to *truly* rest.

The smiling face she first saw in the mine tunnel had been hiding so much fear. *She knew the game. Act cute and happy and people feed you.* Unease fluttered in her gut at the thought of being responsible for a small life. *I hope you made the right choice picking me, kid.* Risa crept over and lifted Kree off the edge, setting her on her back under the sheets. She planted a light kiss on her forehead before backing out.

Two weeks in this place and we've traded places. She sleeps like the dead and I'm up all night with horrible dreams. She chuckled without making noise on her way to the kitchen. *Better me than her.*

The reassembler produced a no-caffeine mint tea, which she carried to her bedroom. There, she reclined on a cushioned bench running the length of the massive window, back to the plastisteel wall on the left. She covered herself to the waist with a fuzzy maroon blanket, tucking it around and under her feet before cradling the tea.

Her mind couldn't decide what to worry about most between a splinter faction of C-Branch hostile to the MLF, whatever Everett was gearing up to do, what Raziel would ask her to do, or if any of the hundreds of horrible things she'd done in the name of 'freedom' would come back to bite her on the ass. Not to mention, she still owed Heitzenroeder a favor... and had a feeling Raziel would expect her to continue doing whatever he demanded of her. Despite his impressive ability to influence the technological world, doing his bidding would make her an independent operator without the umbrella of protection afforded by technically being a government asset.

When the tea ran out, she leaned her head back against the wall and stared at the innocuous white box that had arrived via delivery bot her second day here. She hadn't ordered anything, but when she went to refuse it—suspecting an attack—Raziel whispered in her mind, reassuring her he had sent it.

Curiosity got the better of her. She set the empty mug down on a little glass table and clambered out of the blanket. The potato-sized box contained a block of black foam. She withdrew it and pulled it apart into unequal halves. Embedded within the larger chunk sat a black metal device about the size of her thumb in an aerodynamic style with a slight curve. A flat pad along one side and its general shape hinted the device should sit above the right ear. The front end had five tiny lenses: two clear, one yellow, one red, and one opaque silver.

"How the hell is this thing supposed to stay on? It'll fall off if I walk too fast."

She pulled her hair back and tucked it where it felt natural. A strange tingle, not quite painful but also not exactly pleasant spread over the skin it touched. The word 'calibrating' appeared midair, followed two seconds later by 'Charge: 18%.' Whatever it did, the device appeared to have adhered to her and auto-linked to her headware. A test pull convinced her it would take skin with it before it let go, likely the same micro-hook tech that kept those impossible (and impossibly expensive) dresses on celebrities.

"Ow. Son of a bitch."

Beep.

Text scrolled across her vision.

New component detected. Install?

"Sure, why not." She thought 'yes.'

Starpoint Corporation EVM-300 driver download complete.

All text vanished. A few seconds later, a large paragraph appeared, explaining the hardware was classified technology issued under license to authorized operators in the employ of various United Coalition Front agencies. Failure to secure the proprietary technology within would result in severe penalties... blah blah.

She thought-clicked the 'acknowledge' button.

IR Nightvision. After three seconds, *Online* appeared.

The mode, a short delay, and confirmation repeated four more times.

Metallurgical... Online.

Motion Sense... Online.

Optical Zoom... Online.

Thermal... Online.

Risa felt a twinge of excitement, then hated herself for it. Raziel had given her the means to return to full operational capacity, but she didn't want to do that. A couple hundred-thousand credit component stuck to her head felt like a ten-pound leash chaining her to a violent, unpredictable death.

She closed her eyes and thought about the Wraith. Grey wispy shapes appeared in the endless darkness as she moved. Her old friend, the electronics allowing her to see without any light, once again worked.

I guess if I'm going to be threatened into working for him, I might as well stack the odds in my favor. She scratched at her stomach, worrying what would happen if she said no. Would he piss and moan, but leave? Would he be spiteful and rearrange records so the government took Kree away? Would he arrange an advert bot to fall from the sky and crush her? She'd put her life in his hands so many times, such total trust thinking he was *of the divine,* but he'd lied to her from the start. Then again, he never directly claimed to be supernatural. She'd assumed that part. To be fair, he didn't say anything to rein in her flights of fancy, either.

A few virtual menus later, she located the release button. According to the help menu, thousands of nanofilament wires extended into her skin from the EVM-300, ensuring it would stay on even in the roughest battlefield conditions. A thought-click, followed by an 'are you sure' later, it shut down and detached. Risa rubbed the skin over her ear. Peeling it off didn't hurt, but a few seconds after she removed it, mild soreness pervaded the spot.

After setting up the charging cradle, she flopped back on her bed. Maybe she could test the waters. She didn't have to obey him slavishly anymore. If what he asked didn't involve bombs or assassination, maybe she would humor him after all. *Not like I've got any other real skills.* She sighed. *I hope he saves the risky shit for after Kree's old enough to look after herself.*

RISA MOANED AT THE PRESS OF A HAND ON HER BACK. SOMEHOW, THE WALL had gone from dim orange to bright white. She remained face down on her Comforgel pad in the same pose she remembered flopping in, though it didn't feel much like she'd slept.

"Rough night?" asked Pavo.

She smiled and rolled onto her back. Pavo hovered over her, dressed in a Defense Force uniform that looked too clean to be duty wear. "Dress reds?"

"I'm due at the Arcadia Command Barracks in about an hour and a half. Nothing to worry about; local brass wants to sniff me out before deciding on my transfer request."

Risa sat up and hugged him. "Maybe I'll be able to sleep through the night once you're here."

He held her for a moment. "You sure everything's okay? It's not like you to be the girl who needs a man to protect her. If I remember things right, it's usually you saving my ass."

"Heh." She slid to her feet and kissed him. "Nothing wrong with wanting to surrender for a little while. Hypervigilance is exhausting."

"Nightmares?" He threaded his arms around her and kissed her again.

"Yeah. I think it's all the stress. I'm dreading what's coming."

Pavo feigned hurt. "Well, if you don't want me to move in…"

She jabbed him in the side. "I mean with Everett."

"Well. Since you're feeling like a damsel right now…" Pavo picked her up and carried her out into the hall.

Risa kicked her feet and overacted the rescued princess. He walked her to the kitchen and set her in a chair by the table. Kree beamed as they entered. The huge grin on her face, and seeing her barefoot made Risa choke up. She'd gotten over her thing with those moon boots. Back in the safehouse, the child complained about having to take them off even long enough to shower. On their third day here, the girl seemed to lose interest in them entirely. She'd been stuck without shoes on the streets. Her possessiveness toward the boots made total sense: she likely feared one of the other kids would steal them if she didn't keep them on. Perhaps the apartment really did give her a sense of security.

Pavo caressed her neck, sliding his hand up to her jawline, and pulling her into another kiss. Risa couldn't find a voice, so she called him.

A smaller virtual Pavo appeared in front of her as the real one moved to the counter, where he opened a plastic milk-carton full of liquid syn-eggs.<You're calling me and I'm right here. Guess you wanna talk about stuff not meant for little ears.>

Kree grabbed the edge of the table and leaned close, whispering, "He's gonna make us breakfast."

Risa glanced at the window, waiting to see a sniper. She closed her eyes, cringing at Shiro's imagined voice telling her how she would always be looking over her shoulder. <She's not obsessing about those boots anymore. It's like she's healing. I can't really talk right now. My voice doesn't want to work.>

Pavo poured the egg fluid into a pan and set it on the stove. <Strange things turn into security blankets. You wouldn't believe some of the items we find kids clinging to out there. She probably feels safe now. Doesn't worry one of the other kids is going to steal them from her.>

<What are we doing?> Risa leaned an elbow on the table, head in her

hand, and smiled at Kree. <I mean as a society? So many orphans. If the war doesn't make them, the gangs do.>

He crossed to the small window over the sink to retrieve a loaf of bread from an arriving delivery bot. <Yeah. We should be spending money on our people, not on funding a shadow military to run false flag bombings.>

Risa shivered. <Wait a second; is that real bread? You did not just spend a hundred credits on toast.>

"It is, and it's fine." Pavo spoke aloud, dropping the call. "So, how are you liking Arcadia?" He winked at Kree before using the reassembler to produce bacon.

"It's pretty!" She bounced in her seat. "I did a painting of the sky, an' Miss Garr said it was good."

"She's in school," said Risa. "Started three days ago. Damn, how is it that bacon smells so good out of a 'sem, but everything else smells like melting plastic?"

"Bacon was the major selling point for the first gen assemblers when they hit the market. No matter what you make in one, it's still no-animal-had-to-die OmniSoy. People could have their bacon with none of the downsides. Billions of credits were spent on R&D to get it right." Pavo raised an eyebrow. "School?"

"Virtual." Risa chuckled. "I was expecting more of a fight."

Kree rambled on about her classes. Granted, being in Grade 0, the 'work' wasn't too complicated. Pavo set a plate of scrambled eggs, toast, and bacon in front of her and Risa, grabbed one for himself, and sat close.

"You okay?" he whispered.

Risa held his hand under the table. "Sometimes I wish I was half as resilient as that kid."

"You are. Most people who had your life wouldn't leave their bedroom closet." He set his fork down to pick up a strip of 'bacon.' "Oh, Gen decided to move in with Aurelia. They're going to take my old place. Lease is up in a few months."

"Because you're paying for it doesn't mean you *have* to live there." Risa half-closed her eyes.

He stooped closer. "True."

Their lips touched.

"Eww," said Kree. "I'm eating. No mushy stuff."

Risa laughed, and looked down. "You shouldn't be late for your review board."

Pavo kissed her again despite a long wail of 'eww' from across the table. "We can figure things out later, over dinner."

"Okay." Risa glanced at the wall clock. "Kree, time to go log in. Your first class starts in four minutes."

The girl hopped out of the chair and went to the living room. Risa walked Pavo to the door, got a proper kiss, and returned to help Kree with the Senshelmet. The round, grey disc at the other end of the wire amounted to a 'toy' version of a cyberspace deck, about one-hundredth of the power of the one she'd used to help Tamashī. It had been cheap though, barely five-hundred credits. Not a big deal if a kid broke it. Risa patted her atop the helmet and headed back to the kitchen long enough to print a cup of coffee before melting into the sofa. She sipped, made a 'blech' face at the reassembled java, and watched Kree act as though in a room full of students. Months ago, she'd been sure the girl would grow up like her, if she even got the chance to grow up.

Risa gazed around at the apartment, trying not to listen to the little voice telling her it wouldn't last. At what point did civilian life strike her as intimidating? *What deal with what devil am I going to have to make to hang on to this life?*

She scratched at the top of her foot, unsure if she should be thrilled or terrified.

A HIDDEN WAR

At 12:10 p.m., Kree started a one-hour 'lunch' period. With school being virtual, she logged out to eat. Engineers hadn't quite figured out how to provide nutrients over the net... yet. Risa decided to get some air and exercise. In matching black shift dresses over violet leggings—she embraced the cheese factor of dressing the same as Kree—they walked two blocks to an open-air shopping area with a food court. Risa splurged on an Ahi tuna salad.

Kree pointed at 'chicken fingers' with fries on the holographic menu. "Can I have that?"

"I didn't think chickens had such big fingers." Risa made a goofy face and pantomimed an ungainly wing flap. "Must make it hard to fly."

Kree giggled.

A twenty-something woman in tight black pants and a green apron walked over. She had features like Tamashī, but the same Marsborn white skin and black hair as Risa. "Hi, I'm Chloe. I'll be taking care of you today. Can I get you started with anything to drink?" She offered a conspiratorial wink to Kree. "You look like you're in the mood for a purple unicorn."

"Okay," said Kree.

Chloe let off a nervous laugh and glanced at Risa. The awkwardness grew at the cluelessness radiating from her. A thought, and four seconds later, MarsNet wiki appeared in a virtual window, explaining a 'purple unicorn' was a somewhat harsh mixed drink, a favorite of those who wanted to forget the previous eight or ten hours spent in a cube.

"Oh." Risa shook her head. "Not for her. Sorry, I'm still only on my first cup of coffee."

"Aww," whined Kree. "I wanna unicorn."

"She didn't mean an actual unicorn, sweetie. It's an adult drink."

Kree blinked. "Oh."

"Can we get two green teas, iced, please?" Asked Risa.

"Right away." Relieved, Chloe smiled. "Do you know what you want?"

Risa ordered. While her exposure to school learning had been limited, she'd read enough to talk with Kree about how the 'chicken' she ate was meat grown in a hydroponic tank. The already-open wiki page helped her sound like she knew what she was talking about.

"They used to keep real chickens in tiny little cages. In 2239, so many people protested the use of live animals for food that they made it against the law. Instead of raising animals, companies poured money into biotech and grew only the meat."

The article mentioned that live animals had become too expensive, and synthetically grown meat resulted in higher profit margins, so the food industry likely had a part to play in the 'social movement' necessary to convince a hesitant population to consume 'mystery meat.' That part, she left out. A six-year-old didn't need the cynicism.

Kree made a face, considered for a moment, and shrugged. "I like them not to kill animals."

Risa stared at the image of a real chicken; it looked nothing like what she imagined it would.

"It's bad to kill animals. Why were they made out of food?" Kree tilted her head.

"Animals are made out of animal." She bit her lip. Too juvenile. "Animals are made of different parts. Meat, bones, blood… other squishy bits."

Kree giggled.

"Meat is a food. Many animals eat other animals. *They* didn't make animals out of food, we figured out we could eat them a long, long, long time ago."

"Oh." Kree seemed satisfied, and gnawed on a piece of chicken.

Risa scanned the article about the 'food revolution,' which mentioned bombings at processing plants and murders of industry executives by a fringe group calling for animal rights. Toward the bottom, one of the 'benefits' of vat-growing the meat the article mentioned included formerly controversial food sources like dog or cat could be synthesized without guilt.

Oh. Ugh. She closed the article, trying to force that thought out of her head.

After paying, they headed back home.

"What are you looking for?" asked Kree.

Risa hesitated, not wanting to lie, but also not wanting to damage the girl's newfound lack of fear. "I'm staying alert."

"Are there bad men here?" Kree glanced sideways up at her, a hint of worry in her eyes.

"Not in this part of the city." Risa assumed Kree meant gangs. "Even if there were, they are less interested in someone aware of their surroundings."

"Okay." Kree smiled, twisting to watch a flashing advert bot bearing holograms of plush toys sail overhead.

"We're going to be late." Risa tugged her along, moving up to a brisk walk.

They made it to the apartment with two minutes to spare before Kree was due back in the virtual classroom. As soon as Risa helped her put the helmet on, her headware beeped with an incoming call.

Major General Donald Everett.

Shit. Ice filled her veins.

She backed up, sat on the sofa, and answered, covering her mouth with both hands as the image of the grandfatherly dark-skinned man appeared. His short afro seemed more grey than before. Not a great sign.

<Lieutenant,> said Everett. <I'm sure you've not exactly been looking forward to my call.>

Ahi tuna swam circles in her stomach. <Yeah. I hope the anticipation is worse than the reality.>

He chuckled. <The problem with C-Branch is too many chiefs. In theory, I'm in command of the whole mess from a military perspective. However, I've got to deal with a cabinet of sub-commanders each responsible for different areas of operation. Surveillance, cyberspace, international operations, internal affairs, Mars... And if that wasn't enough of a clusterfuck, there's a bunch of civilians directing policy at a level over my head.>

<How is that possible?> Risa hugged a small throw pillow to her chest.

<Politicians, Miss Black. Politicians,> said Everett. <Most of the

cabinet wants to pull the plug on the MLF and disband it. Only a handful of personnel have the requisite training to be absorbed into official intelligence operations. The shiniest idea on the table right now would be to quietly shut things down, give everyone a chance to reorganize and disperse, and then claim 'victory' over a known terrorist organization.>

Risa shivered. <I... don't really like the sound of that.>

<Relax. No one is going to face actual charges or any nonsense like that. The world will forget who you were in a matter of months. Any news reports of 'senior terrorist personnel' being sent to prison are talking about fictional characters made up for PR purposes.>

<Are you sure it's a good idea to entirely shut things down?> Confidence infiltrated her voice. <The Front has a major intelligence network established throughout individual cells of ACC resistance. Maris once said we know stuff before the UCF did. If that's true, why waste that capability?>

General Everett scratched at his chin. <Don't think I haven't considered that. We're looking at a nuclear option here... proverbially speaking. I've been trying to maneuver things in such a way as to protect our people.>

<You mean PVM.> She fidgeted with the blue satin pillow. <What about the others?>

<Disbanding the MLF and scrapping the project is the only thing I can order and implement fast enough to possibly avoid problems. Even doing so, some of the 'lower-value' personnel may be scapegoated by the political fallout.>

Kree raised her hand and waved it around.

Risa glared. <You're dancing around something I won't like.>

He pursed his lips. <Observant. Fair enough. I'll give it to you straight. I'm sure you are quite sick of all the smoke and mirrors.>

<Quite sick.> Risa grumbled.

<General Maris has, as you know, refused several missions against internal assets.>

<Yeah, I heard. He didn't like the idea of false flag ops, especially when they killed civilians. That's not what the Front was about.>

<The Front was never about anything but enabling us to strike at the ACC in ways that would minimize worsening an already disastrous war. Some damage was necessary on both sides to keep the Corporates from figuring out the MLF dangled on puppet strings.>

<Dustblow, General. No offense, but that's not true. The guy who

almost killed me at Arden told me exactly what this was about. Money. The Senators weren't scared of the MLF anymore and we needed to stir the shit pot so they could keep their defense contract kickbacks.>

<Maybe you won't dislike what I'm about to ask you to do as much as I thought you would.>

Risa set the pillow aside so she didn't shred it.

<Our problem has a name.>

General Everett's virtual avatar shrank and slid to the side, allowing room for a silver-haired woman with caramel skin to appear next to him. Nothing about her seemed military in the least; a little heavy, a lot pampered, and she had cruel eyes.

<This is Senator Marta Nur, age fifty-three. Her family has been involved in politics for six generations. Her father was a senator, as was his mother. The rest of them are up to their elbows in a firehose of credits flowing through the entire military-industrial complex. Everything from weapons to cyberware to starship construction.>

Risa looked down at her shoes, basic black flats that left most of the tops of her feet exposed. <You want me to assassinate her, don't you?>

<Senator Nur is the driving force behind this forty-ton ball of shit rolling downhill. She is the one responsible for Shiro's team being sent to Mars. She is the one who greenlighted the operation at Arden, as well as others you aren't aware of. As long as she's in power, there is a real danger to everyone who's ever touched the MLF project. She will burn everyone she can to keep her hands clean. Without her, we can continue. And I assure you, no more false flags.>

<I'M OUT OF THE GAME, GENERAL. I'VE COME TOO DAMN CLOSE TO DYING too many times. I've got a chance at a stable life now.>

General Everett's grandfatherly charm hardened into the quiet drill sergeant demeanor capable of making new recruits too frightened to speak. <What chance do you think you'd have if Nur gets her way? You, Pavo, Garrison… everyone involved in the MLF would be trotted out to the public as a spectacle. She *is* that vindictive. Your face isn't unknown on the NewsNet, though our people have kept it distorted enough. We *do* have real data, and she *would* use it.>

"Fourteen!" yelled Kree. A second later, she clapped, and whispered, "I got it right!"

Risa grasped the front of her throat, envisioning military police kicking in her door, taking Kree away, arresting her, and then being forced to stare out at a quad full of angry citizens while some holographic judge pronounces a death sentence for treason. *I'm not an assassin...*

She stared at the little girl on the rug ten feet in front of her. To protect that child, she *could* kill a total stranger... but it didn't mean she had to like the idea. <You're the military director of C-Branch. Why are you coming to me for this? Don't you have people?>

Everett shook his head. <I'm too close. With the pissing contest I've started in boardrooms, if an assassination gets traced back to the agency, they're going to come right to my door. If Senator Nur doesn't get her way, and by that I mean Maris dead and replaced by someone who doesn't care *who* he blows up, you and the rest of the MLF are going to get swept up in a shitstorm of interplanetary proportions, and either killed or treated as the 'terrorists' you pretended to be.>

Risa flattened her hands on her thighs, white fingers stark over violet leggings. The calm eeriness of her voice reminded her of the old Risa, the woman everyone thought to be Cat-6. <I suppose I don't have much choice then, do I?>

'Grandpa Everett' returned as his affect softened. <I'm sorry to have to put it to you like that. If out is what you really want, I'll do everything I can to give it to you. But there are asses that need to be covered before anything can happen. I have reports here that tell me your attitude aligns well with certain groups. You do not derive pleasure from the taking of life. As much as I agree with you, sometimes the removal of certain individuals proves necessary. You are far more precise than bombs.>

Kree leaned forward and waved her arm back and forth as if coloring or painting.

<General, are you sure killing Nur is going to have the effect you're hoping for? You said it would cause blowback if they traced it, and you also said my face is out there. If her death is linked to the MLF, wouldn't that be the same as pointing to you? Assassinating her is messy. I have a better idea.>

Everett's eyebrows drew close, twitched, and returned to neutral. <Alright, let's hear it.>

<A corpse is a hornets' nest of problems. Too many people asking too many questions. Someone up to their tits in corporate money, even UCF corporations, is going to have dirt. If we can find anything proving her connection to Arden... or anything similar, we can engineer political

death. Better to have everyone looking at what *she* did rather than who did what *to* her.>

<Hmm. I'm not sure we have the time to engineer something like that.> Everett glanced to the side, pondering. <If there is anything to find, it would be on the 'shadow net.' The Senate and the highest reaches of government keep most of their secrets on an isolated network with no physical connection to the GlobeNet on Earth or the MarsNet.>

<Can't C-Branch jockeys get in there?>

<No. When I said there's no physical connections from outside, I meant it. We'd have to put an operator in the facility, and all our people are in the system already. I could authorize a wipe and turn someone into a ghost. I'd have to make it look related to events going on in Europe, and slip it past eight pairs of eyes. That would take longer than we have.> He tilted his head down a half inch, and leaned forward. <We'd need someone who *already* doesn't exist.>

<I'm not a deck jockey. I couldn't... and I'd have to leave Mars.> She tried not to sound as scared at the thought as she felt. <I... don't want to go to Earth.>

<Not Earth. The Moon. The Senate chambers are on the Moon. There is zero official ACC presence there.>

Risa flared her eyes wide and rolled them. <Never thought they'd pay attention to an ancient flag.>

<They didn't.> Everett flashed a proud smile. <We kicked their asses off that rock. Somehow, we wound up agreeing to say it was them doing 'the honorable thing' and respecting that old claim. The same thing that's going on around you on Mars now happened on the Moon a long time ago, only then it was a lot more messy.>

<Oh.> *More lies. Why am I not surprised?* <Still.>

<You don't need to do the network part of the job. That we can handle from remote. All you need to do is build a bridge.>

The tuna threatened to erupt all over the floor at the idea of leaving Mars, even for only a short time. Thinking about what a privileged senator with a vengeful axe to grind would do to Kree, Pavo, Garrison, Gen... and everyone else she'd bled and suffered with tamped it down. She'd already braced herself to accept killing the woman. Now, it seemed she might not have to. Sneaking in there to plant a device bothered her significantly less than murder.

<How much time do we have?>

Everett's nostrils flared with a sigh. <About three days.>

THE DARK SIDE

R isa stared at the floor in the back seat of a nondescript beige hovercar. The man and woman up front wore civilian clothes and looked like ordinary middle-class citizens, but they picked her up on Everett's instruction. She felt like they carted her off to prison, a notion made worse by her lack of weapons (other than her claws) and armor. Risa, too, had dressed in a nondescript fashion. Baggy white blouse and loose black pants similar to fatigues, though without pockets on the legs. Sneakers felt strange in their comfort.

A mental poke opened a virtual holo-panel, in which she played the recording of her conversation with Kree. Genevieve came by to babysit. Risa explained that someone far away wanted to do something bad. If Risa didn't go deal with it, people might make her go away forever. She took deliberate care to reinforce she did not intend to blow anyone up or even hurt people, just sneak some electronic device into an office. The girl took the news well; of course she cried, but she didn't scream, tantrum, or beg Risa not to go. If everything went well, she'd be back in a few days.

She froze the image on Kree's face, and stared at it until the hovercar landed fifteen minutes later at Fort Vanguard. Arcadia City had two starports, and this one belonged to the military. She peered out the window at a wide variety of aircraft. Lava Wasps, light recon fighters, in both green and Mars camo schemes dotted pads wherever the tiny ships could squeeze in. Larger DS2 dropships clustered to one side while a few DS4s, which looked almost identical but several times the size, parked a quarter-mile away on the far north end.

The dropships had a basic design aesthetic: an aerodynamic box with retractable wings, and a long tail boom with trefoil fins, one up, two down at forty-five degree angles. The cockpit on the DS4 looked like the same modular component as the DS2, which made it seem tiny compared to the rest of the ship. Armored personnel carriers—wedge-shaped things with six wheels two feet taller than the vehicle—lined up in front of the smaller ships. The cargo hold on the DS2 appeared designed around the APC, perfectly sized to hold one.

The DS4, on the other hand, was a true starship capable of carrying four DS2s in its hold.

"This way, lieutenant," said the woman.

Her escort walked her across the blinding glare shimmering on the plastisteel tarmac. Here and there, black and yellow lines defined taxiways or boundaries where ion thrust remained at safe levels and the occasional red square labeled 'NO STEP' broke up the silver monotony.

They led her to a DS4 surrounded by puffs of smoke and fog, clearly in the midst of takeoff prep as opposed to the ones sitting idle. Its cockpit sat so high up, she couldn't even see the pilot from the ground. The ship perched on three legs: two massive forward struts tipped with pads, and a smaller one, which folded down out of the tail boom.

"This is as far as we go." The man stopped, turned, and seemed unsure if he should salute or shake hands. He opted for neither and gestured at a ladder formed by dozens of small recesses in the hull. "Your chariot awaits."

"Thanks."

Risa grabbed the hollows, noting scratches along the inside suggesting the bottom of the recesses moved forward to close flat while in flight. At the top of a two-story climb, a man in green fatigues offered her a hand in a door-sized hatch. She accepted, glancing at his chest as he pulled her inside. His nameplate read 'Meeks, J.' Risa followed him down narrow metal corridors, past several staterooms with officer rank insignia on the doors and a room full of bunk beds.

"Everett wants you on the Moon today... Normally, the trip takes about sixteen days. You ain't got that kind of time." Sergeant Meeks looked her up and down. "You ever jump before?"

"I've never left Mars."

"Oh, boy." He sighed. "Please tell me you're not going to have a freak-out at a gel tube."

Risa laughed. "No, I'm quite familiar with them."

"Good. Okay, noob time. The jump from here to the Moon will take about two minutes. Unfortunately, even that short, we gotta tank up. If you're thinking of cutting corners, don't. G-forces involved with wormhole spelunking will tear you apart from the inside out. The gel absorbs the stresses and protects the body."

"I read there's rumors about interdimensional creatures too. Some people have seen wild shit."

Sergeant Meeks waved her off. "Don't go talkin' bout any of that nonsense on my ship. We're a superstitious lot, and that's bad juju. It's similar to a medical tank. You'll be sedated for the duration of the jump. You probably won't even realize you went out."

"Right. Where's my room?"

"This way." Sergeant Meeks grinned.

After cutting across an area with a few tables, a food reassembler, lockers, and showers, he opened the door to a long chamber with twenty-four clear cylinders—and no privacy among them. Already, four men and a woman stood around naked, grumbling about the 'bogus assignment.'

"Nice. Everett booked me first class." Risa sighed, and pulled her top off. "What locker should I use?"

Disappointment radiated from Sergeant Meeks. A few of the others sighed as well.

Risa glanced from them to Meeks. "I can act embarrassed if you guys were that desperate for the lols."

He shook his head and laughed, pointing at a small metal door marked '0020.' "That one."

She, and the soldiers, sat around nude for a little while as the ship lifted off and flew out to Mars orbit. Two men sipped coffee, one tried to sleep, and the woman munched on something from a silver packet. Aside from the deep rumble of heavy-duty ion thrusters, the DS4 felt like riding a PubTran bus over a crappy section of road. About twenty minutes after takeoff, two women in green jumpsuits walked in and proceeded to strip in front of lockers. At their entry, the rest of the soldiers approached their tanks and got in. She eyed the pilots with unease for a few seconds before it hit her.

Oh. Right. Autopilot... everyone's gotta be in a tank for the wormhole.

She stepped into her assigned tube and felt a little odd at going into one without a medical or cybernetics problem. Everyone else tubed up. Except for one pilot, they all watched her expectantly. With a trace of a smile, she let all the air out of her lungs as the peach-colored goop rose up to cover her head. Again, the crew appeared mildly disappointed at not getting a 'show,' watching a newbie lose their mind during the air-to-gel transition. Hanging weightless in the syrupy breathable liquid, she waited. Eventually, the room lights dimmed.

Less than a minute later, she felt a touch drowsy, but the lights came back on before anything noticeable occurred. Mechanical whirring filled her ears from the pump removing the fluid.

In the blink of an eye, here we are.

———

RISA PACED BACK AND FORTH ACROSS A GREY CARPET IN A GREY ROOM, looking out the window at a grey landscape with a black 'sky.' The Earth, a blue and white gem, lurked at the left edge. *Great. I'm in the world that color forgot.* Not being able to call Pavo or Kree twisted at her guts. C-Branch had been adamant about that point, forcing her to leave her NetMini at home.

She wandered to the hotel bathroom, stripped, and spent an hour cycling her CamNano among various skin tones and hair colors. At a knock, she slipped back into her blouse, the garment long enough to cover the criticals as long as she didn't raise her arms, and padded to the door. A blond man outside in a shimmery black suit glanced from side to side in an impatient manner, bouncing from foot tapping.

"Who are you?" asked Risa, via the intercom.

"For what you charge per hour, you ask a lot of damn questions."

I'm going to hurt someone for these code phrases. "You're older than you're supposed to be."

He banged on the door. "Come on. Let me see what I'm paying for."

She hit the button to open it, and he swooped inside.

"Nice," whispered the man. He brushed past her and set a black briefcase on the bed.

Risa closed the door. "So, you're Berkeley."

"I was expecting someone older. Are you even eighteen?" His thumb tinted green from a code panel as he keyed five digits into buttons beneath the handle. The briefcase popped open with a *click.*

"Thanks, and I'm twenty… something. Five maybe."

"Okay." He took out a plastic packet. "Underwear. The waistband has a concealed garrote."

She caught it. Black lace. "Great. Killer panties. What's the bra do?"

"Covers breasts." He reached back into the case and set out a black skirt, white blouse, and a matching black woman's suit jacket with silver bands around the sleeves and military markings on the shoulders, a silver field with two black squares.

"Right. I can't say I mind the hurry. The sooner I get back, the better." She clutched carpet with her toes. "I'm really hoping no one is going to screw something up due to rushing."

He retrieved a small spray can from the case. "We're good. Would you mind taking your shirt off?"

"I thought the call girl bit was a cover?"

"Trust me, I'm not interested." He raised the spray can. "This coating lasts approximately five hours and will create a barrier on your skin capable of blocking scans from picking up your neuralware and installed components. It may erode from your hands with abrasion, so be careful."

Risa pulled her shirt off and stood like a child being sprayed with sunscreen by their parent.

"Turn."

She did. Cool mist settled on her skin, and soon became a maddening embrace of tiny tickling pinpricks *everywhere*. Risa squirmed, feeling as though she'd been shrink-wrapped in thick plastic. "Shit, that's weird."

"Give it a minute to dry off and you won't feel them anymore."

Risa walked back and forth until she felt dry, and put on the clothes provided. She whined at gloss-black dress shoes with one-inch heels. "Those look uncomfortable... and impractical."

He handed her a thin NetMini. "You are Warrant Officer 2 Rebecca Ann Marsh. You are twenty years old, live alone, have two living parents in East City. Your oldest brother Dorian was killed in action with the Division 0 police in West City four years and five months ago. Your surviving brother Adam is finishing up a Master's degree at the Mars Academy of Engineering."

Risa checked the NetMini, noting photos of a family who appeared dark skinned. Well, dark skinned to someone used to living among Marsborn. They'd be pale next to Osebi.

Berkeley pointed at one woman who resembled Risa with a heavy suntan. "That's you."

"Is that spray-on stuff going to interfere with CamNano?"

"Shouldn't."

Risa eye-traced a little box around the woman's picture to sample the color, and sent it to the control software for the CamNano. Within twelve seconds, she had a Mediterranean complexion.

He reached over and pinned an ID tag on her breast pocket. "You're a recent graduate, assigned to the Senatorial Chambers as an Information Technology worker. We have already implemented an event that will cause Senator Nur to place a request with the help desk. You will examine her terminal, run a diagnostic, and conclude that a recent update on the public network caused a .087-second offset between her terminal's internal clock and the network clock, triggering a security lockdown."

Risa thought notes into words in her headware, and saved the file. "Got it."

He held up a light pen. "While you are working on the terminal, your primary objective is to employ this device."

"What am I supposed to write on, or is that some cleverly concealed intelligence tech?"

Berkeley chuckled. He demonstrated twisting the top, causing a nozzle to pop up. "The spray is silent, so you should only need a minute or so of the Senator not looking at you. Based on her personality, it is unlikely she will remain in the area while you are 'working' on her terminal."

Risa frowned. "She doesn't like being near peasants."

"So you *did* read the briefing." He shook his head. "I never know what to expect from outside contractors."

She took the 'pen.' "I'm not that far outside. More like living in the basement. So what is this?"

"It contains a carrier medium infused with nanobots and an atomic suspension of pure silver. Start the spray into the M3 port on the side of the terminal, and trail it to a nice, flat surface... like the bottom of the desk. The nanobots will construct a wafer antenna from the silver. The larger the area you can cover, the better."

"That's the bridge." She tucked the pen in her blazer's left outside pocket.

"You ready?"

Risa nodded. "What's the worst-case scenario?"

"The Senator catches you spraying, calls security, and you get shot dead while fleeing."

"Umm." She gathered the blazer tight around herself. *This won't stop a damn thing.*

"Well, you did say *worst.*" Berkeley grinned. "If you get compromised, surrender. Everett will protect you… though it might take a few weeks. Then again, Senator Nur might fall for some weak line about it being an air duster and you're cleaning the port."

I don't want to be away that long. Right. Don't fuck up. "Got it."

"I'll leave in forty-five minutes so we aren't seen together. If this goes smoothly, we won't see each other again." He reached out a hand. "Nice working with you. Good luck."

She shook. "Thanks."

Risa left the hotel room, thankful to escape the 'house of drab.' Of course, so far, everything she'd seen on the Moon had been colorless. Someone once mentioned that many centuries ago, entertainment holos weren't even holos, mere two-dimensional images. At the early stages of those, they'd been devoid of color. She had a harder time believing movies had ever been 2D than they'd been all black and white; sometimes, they still used greyscale for artistic effect. The Moon made her feel like she'd been pulled into an old film.

They hadn't been able to terraform it either. Instead, Paramount City relied on a dome. Unlike the Mars domes, a break here would be catastrophic. If this one cracked, the vacuum of space would claim everything inside. Fragments of something she'd once read came back to her, about the moon not having enough geomagnetism to hold an atmosphere.

At the hotel exit, she summoned a PubTran car using 'Rebecca's' NetMini and gazed off in the distance at a massive emerald spire of glass jutting out from the center of the city. Anyone who looked like a tourist wound up mobbed by rag-clad children begging for food or credits with which they could buy something to eat. Her uniform seemed to keep them away. Risa checked 'Rebecca's' finances and frowned at a meager ₡5,582. She also didn't have a spare credstick, and the beggars didn't appear to have NetMinis.

One passing pedestrian commented about how the beggars were part of an MLF ploy to destabilize the government. *Dustblow.* She scowled, wanting to correct him, but held it back. *The MLF doesn't operate anywhere but Mars. Those kids really* are *starving.*

When the little self-driving car skidded up to her and opened its side-hatch door, she got in. A boy of about twelve locked stares with her. At first, his chocolate-brown eyes brimmed with hate, but at the guilt on her face, he softened.

"Thank you for choosing PubTran Corporation for your transportation nee—"

"Senate Chambers." She swiped her NetMini over the console to her left before it could tell her how much it cost.

The door closed with a soft *hiss.*

"Thank you for choosing PubTran Corporation. Your estimated arrival is six minutes twenty-four seconds."

She couldn't pull her gaze away from the boy until the car drove too far away to see him. Most of the buildings on either side of the black plastisteel streets resembled larger, more primitive versions of drop boxes she'd seen on Mars. The Moon had colonies centuries before Mars, so these had to be the ancestors of modern temporary structures. None retained their spring-loaded legs, having long ago been built up into permanent emplacements. Many looked to be composed of stacks of six or seven, fused into a single tower.

Fortunately, she didn't see any more desperate waifs on the ride. Before long, the surroundings improved from deep grunge to well worn, and after another fifteen minutes, the Senate Chamber came into view. The high-rise had a sharp, faceted design similar to an immense green crystalline shard stuck into the Moon at the center of a circular park full of trees, benches, and a grand reflecting pool.

The boxy PubTran car squealed to a halt at the stairs leading to the front entrance. An emerald glass archway bore the carved words 'E Pluribus Unum' at the end nearest the street. She hopped out of the taxi and made a passable show of looking like she knew how to walk in one-inch heels. Nine heavy doors, imitation jade with tall faux-bronze bars as big as quarterstaffs for handles, sat below more 'carved' letters, which read: *'Robur, Prudentiam, Aequitatem.'*

Risa shook her head—and walked straight into the door. Fortunately, she hadn't been going too fast and it hurt her pride more than her nose. *Shit. They're not automatic.*

A few people laughed. Fighting the blush response, she backed up and hauled the door open, feeling weak when she needed a two-handed grip to move it. *Oh, great. I look like a complete noob. At least any security people watching would never expect I'm a spy.* When she lifted her head, she forced an embarrassed laugh. On the far side of a large atrium, a curved wall at least twenty-five-meters wide contained a bas-relief of mountains and clouds with eagles soaring in the sky. Twelve men and women in green camouflage armor stood post at even intervals along the curve, each with a compact assault rifle. Black visors concealed their faces, though at least two quivered with silent chuckles at the idiot who'd walked into a door.

Four people in civilian dress suits staffed an information desk a distance ahead, nearer the middle of the room. On either side of the counter, heavy security barriers offered four scanning lanes, two per side, staffed by a handful of Military Police armed with pistols.

One MP in green camo fatigues trotted over. Barely restrained contempt simmered in his gaze, though he saluted her before glancing at a portable computer wrapped around his left forearm. "Ma'am. Is there a problem?"

"First day. I'm so used to automatic doors…"

He smiled. "We get that a lot. Looks like you're headed for ITC." The MP pointed at one of six hallways. "That way."

She walked with him to the security station. Her throat constricted at the worry the spray-on stuff wouldn't conceal her cybernetics from the machinery. Even these low-ranking soldiers would question why an IT worker had top-of-the-line speedware, Nano claws, and a predictive target-analysis system. *It better be worth feeling like I'm shrink-wrapped.* Risa squirmed at the sensation of the spray chemical tugging on her skin everywhere.

Risa flashed a nervous smile. At least the 'first day on the job' cover allowed her to show some of her anxiety. A square-faced woman with cornrows and thick muscles waved her through with a pleasant nod.

Once clear of the scanner, Risa hurried down the indicated corridor and followed signs and arrows until she reached one labeled 'ITC,' with 'Information Technology Command' in smaller letters under it.

Inside, ten people lounged about in flagrant disregard of military decorum. Most had their feet up on their desks. One snored, two played video games, and one orange-haired woman who bore a strong resemblance to a shapeless young teen seemed to be stuck with the laborious task of reinstalling an operating system on the terminals. She had six of the silver bars set up on the table in front of her. Holographic panel screens displayed progressively further stages of the process. A pushcart behind her held seventy or so more.

"Hey Simp, looks like you got some help," said the nearest man. "New blood." He waved over his shoulder. "Go give Simp a hand with the update, she's been whining all morning about it."

Risa swallowed the urge to snap at him, since the majority of them screwed off while they made the WO1 do all the work. Unfortunately, the guy barking at her had lieutenant's bars on his sleeve and outranked her cover persona. "Sir."

She went to the desk in back, where the skinny woman looked up with hope in her eyes. According to the badge on a near-identical black blazer as Risa wore, her name was Simpson, K. Nothing about her said military. She looked fresh out of high school... if not still in it.

"Looks like I got a cush assignment." Risa pulled up a chair.

"Yeah, these are older TD-92s from Media Relations. Some jackass opened a flagged message, and a virus monkeyfucked the entire network segment."

Risa lost her composure at the language coming from such an innocent looking girl, and laughed.

"Oooh." Simpson seethed. "Sometimes I think they should make these idiots pass an IQ test before they're allowed to take government jobs."

"They do," said a deep-voiced man in the middle of blowing up a screen full of strange organic-looking space ships. "If they get too high a score, they don't hire them."

Chuckling spread over the room, except for the snoring woman.

"It's not as bad as it looks," said Simpson. "Most of the time we're on standby unless something breaks. It's the tier-two guys... the security wonks who are on call."

Risa looked at the cart full of silver plastic terminal bars, each oval in profile, about twenty inches long, four inches wide and three inches tall at the widest part. "I guess I'll get started on some."

While two of the 'veterans' dragged a folding table out of storage for her, Risa opened a connection to the GlobeNet via her headware. She searched using an image of the terminal unit and the phrase 'OS reinstall.' The system came back with over thirty-eight-million hits. *Crap. I don't think there's that many posts on all of MarsNet. Uhh, shit.* She mind-clicked on one at random while grabbing a unit from the top layer.

"Get one started before you put another on the table. That way you don't have multiple steps occurring at the same time." Simpson pointed at a three-inch black box tipped with an asterisk-shaped M3 prong. "The OS is on this. Since we're doing a low-level reformat of all the neural memory, there's no net drivers. Gotta reinitialize via a physical connection, but you know that already. We've got a whole bunch of custom tweaks to the OS for this facility. The process is mostly automated. All you have to do is click past the prompts."

Risa chuckled. "So all they need us for is plugging in the box."

"Geez, Marsh… Not so loud or we'll be out of a job." Simpson winked.

"Right… or reassigned to a post where we'd need to do actual work." Risa sat on a backless chair and connected the box to the first terminal.

Sure enough, the level of automation allowed her to sit back and watch progress bars. Every so often, she had to click a holographic button to acknowledge security protocols. By the time she had six terminals on her table, she stared at the clock. *Come on… come on… I don't want to spend all day here.*

"It's not afraid of you," said Simpson with a grin. "Giving it the evil eye won't make time go faster. Thanks for the help with this… Might actually finish them all in one day now."

"No problem." Risa smiled.

Over the next hour and change, she limped through small talk with WO1 Kellie Simpson. She learned the girl was eighteen, from the southern end of East City on Earth, and wanted an education paid for by the military. Her parents had forbidden her from taking a combat role. Not that she had to listen to them, but she wasn't too keen on getting shot, either. Risa passed along tidbits of her constructed persona, making things up about her family quietly emigrating from Egypt when her grandfather's parents realized their three-year-old was a telepath. This, of course, started a discussion among everyone in the ITC room about how outside of the UCF, psionics tended to be shot on sight, even in the more 'enlightened' countries.

GlobeNet to the rescue.

"Actually," said Risa, while skimming an article floating in front of her on a virtual display. "It's not that bad where I'm from. Psionics are registered and monitored. As long as they don't use their abilities for criminal purposes, they're fine."

"You're spewing the same dustblow they paste all over the media," said the lieutenant. "It ain't your fault 'cause you obviously didn't grow up there… but what they tell the world and what they do when no one's watching are different. If we weren't so busy worrying what the ACC was up to, we'd go in there and show them how democracy works."

Risa suppressed a tremble of anger. "You think it's that easy? Just sweep right in, replace a regime, and suddenly everyone's smiling and all their problems go away? You can kill leaders, you can hunt down dissidents, but you can't *force* people to be happy or to change how they live. You can bust your ass for years, even die for them, and the citizens probably won't even notice or care."

The lieutenant raised a hand. "Whoa. Slow that down a bit. I meant diplomacy."

Yeah, sure you did. "Sorry."

"Wow," whispered Simpson, scooting closer. "You okay?"

"Yeah. I have a few friends who've been on the receiving end of the government 'happiness cannon.'"

Deep-voice muttered under his breath, wondering how 'Marsh' made it through security screening since she sounded like a fanatic. The man nearest him chuckled. 'Rebecca Marsh' shouldn't have been able to hear him, so she tried not to show a reaction.

Beep.

Her first terminal showed complete. She carried it to a different cart and added it to the bottom row of finished installs, then replaced it with another one from the overloaded cart and started the process over again. *Damn, this is boring.* She gazed into the warped reflection of the ceiling lights on the mirror-finished plastic terminal bars, and smiled. *But I'm not getting shot at.*

"Hey Marsh," yelled the lieutenant.

"Sir?" She sat up tall in her seat, peering over the holo-panels.

"You up for a desk call?" He looked like a used-hovercar salesman.

"I don't like that smile. This is some hazing rite-of-passage crap, isn't it?" She folded her arms. "I'm not falling for that 'go get a bucket of steam' thing."

"No way. Total serious request. Senator Nur sent in a trouble ticket, her desk terminal's acting up."

Everyone found something to look busy doing, even Simpson.

Don't sound too eager. "That guy's playing a damn video game. Send him. What's the big deal?"

Simpson looked at her like they'd scheduled her new friend for execution. "Nur's a bitch. You do one tiny little thing wrong in there and she'll get you reassigned to custodial services or booted to Mars." Fear made the girl look even younger. "And I don't mean actual 'wrong.' I mean 'wrong' according to an unreasonable intergalactic megacunt."

A few of the guys chuckled.

Risa frowned. "I get the feeling I don't get a lot of choice in this."

"I could order you to," said the lieutenant. "But then I'll feel bad if you wind up cleaning latrines."

"No you wouldn't," said the formerly sleeping woman.

"Fine." Risa stood, faking defiance. "She's probably just a misunderstood busy person who senses your lack of respect." She walked around the table full of terminals, heels clicking on the white-tiled floor. "What's the issue?"

"Her terminal's frozen up. She sent this in from her NetMini. In her technical opinion, 'the terminal is completely fucked.'"

Risa laughed. "Love a diagnosis from a paper pusher."

"Good luck." The lieutenant leaned back and laced his fingers behind his head.

"You're not picking on me because I'm a woman, are you?"

"Nope. If that were the case, I'd have grabbed your ass by now, and I don't feel like going through another sensitivity e-learn. You're getting it because you're the FNG."

"Right." Risa snagged a datapad as well as a case of delicate tools, and headed out. *Finally.*

The door slid shut behind her. Her augmented hearing picked up Simpson's sigh and mutter of, "Pity. I was just beginning to like her. Shame she'll be gone tomorrow."

Relief at getting away from the monotonous reinstallation procedure kept her nerves at bay as she made her way out of the ITC room, down the hall, and crossed in front of the long sculpture and Marine guards. In the main foyer, the echo of her shoes carried with such volume she wondered if Pavo could hear her walking back on Mars. A few of the guards checked her out. One gave her an inviting wink. She returned a flirty smile, but didn't slow down.

The trouble ticket showing on the datapad's clipboard-sized screen provided a navigation assistant, which led her to the elevator and to the sixty-second floor, down a curving hallway of muted-blue carpet. Dark-brown wainscoting covered half the corridor wall, topped with slabs of faux jade. Brass light fixtures every thirty feet held a trio of flower-shaped glass shades. *What is it about government that makes them like old-looking stuff?* Her shoes made no noise on the carpet here, for which she felt grateful. For most of her life, first as an orphan hiding in the tunnels and later with the MLF, stealth and silence had been tantamount to life. She *still* hated loud noises, especially ones she made. Hope she could spare Kree the same mental scars pushed aside her unease.

Two men in fancy suits passed by, not even affording her a glance. She ignored them and kept walking. Rectangular silicon wafers jutted out from the wall by each door, bearing various Senator's names. A short dark-skinned woman in an expensive-looking suit slowed and glanced at her. Her hair resembled some manner of prehistoric bush, an explosion of inch-thick braids. Risa's attention gravitated to a pearl broach surrounded by gold filigree over the woman's breast pocket. *That's probably a camera.*

"Good afternoon"—the woman leaned closer—"Miss Marsh. You're new here, aren't you? I don't believe I've seen you before."

"Yes. First day. ITC."

The woman shook her head, flashing a weak grin. "Welcome to the madhouse. I hope you turn out different from the rest of your compatriots. Seems all they want to do is sleep."

She's gotta be a senator. "No, ma'am. I'm here to get the job done, not sit around."

"I like your attitude. If you manage to keep it, you'll do well here." The woman smiled and walked on by.

Risa kept going until she spotted the nameplate for 'Senator Marta Nur.' The door handle rattled in her grip, locked. She swiped 'Rebecca's' NetMini near the reader on the wall, but it didn't do anything. *Shit. What am I supposed to do now?* She raised a hand to knock, but thought better of it. A flash of white on her black blazer caught her eye, and she tried swiping her dangling ID badge.

Beep. A small red light turned green.

She entered an enormous office, its blue carpeting flecked with black diamonds. Heavy green curtains gathered at either end of a window that ran the length of the far wall, offering a drab-grey view of the Moon. It seemed as though the Senate Tower was the only item of color anywhere in Paramount City.

Behind an imposing desk of burgundy-hued 'wood,' a dour older woman in a pale-grey skirt suit hammered her fingers into the tiny screen of a NetMini, hard enough to make her puffy cheeks tremble. Senator Nur couldn't be called 'overweight,' but she definitely wanted for nothing. She looked older than the image Everett provided, and made Risa think of the villain from a cartoon she'd watched with Kree a few days ago. Add black dragon wings and they could've been sisters.

Risa stood in place feigning awkwardness for almost two minutes before the Senator looked up.

"Well, one of you finally decided to show up. I suppose I should consider myself grateful I managed to get someone here the same day." She waved a long-nailed hand at the lump of silver plastic on her desk.

"Yes, ma'am. You're having a problem with your terminal?"

"You can read, can't you?" Senator Nur rose from her chair. "Why do they make us fill out those silly forms if you people are too lazy to even look at the system?"

"I'm sorry; I was just trying to be friendly."

The woman drew a breath, likely ready to blast her with another rant, though Risa's 'sent-to-the-principal's-office' posture seemed to placate her need to feel important. "Fix it… if you can. What's your name?"

"Marsh, ma'am. Rebecca."

"Humph." Senator Nur walked to the left, away from the desk to the wall of swirled wood texture. A previously invisible door became apparent when she touched a spot and it popped open. The room beyond contained a bed, smaller desk, and a six-person conference table. "This place is unbelievable. Do what you have to do and get out."

"Yes, ma'am." Risa stared at the rug as if she were in trouble. *Okay, maybe I wouldn't feel so bad about assassinating this bitch.*

The senator slipped into the concealed room, pulling the door to but not closed. Risa rounded the desk, not daring to sit in the woman's chair, and dragged her fingertip over the terminal housing. Blank indigo on the holographic panel changed to a desktop view, displaying an error about a security lockdown.

A glance to the left confirmed the senator had her back facing the main office, while muttering at the NetMini. She tuned out the complaining about idiots working for the support staff, how someone incompetent is costing her time because her terminal is dead, and so on.

She reached into the blazer pocket and withdrew the pen, twisted the cap, and pointed the nozzle at the M3 port. Two seconds of spray saturated the plug before she trailed it off across the desk to the edge. Risa took care not to allow any gaps, moving her arm like a careful painter. Twenty-eight seconds later, she'd covered the entire underside, and the canister went dry.

"What's wrong with it?" asked Senator Nur, head poking in.

Risa froze, squatting in front of the desk with her arm in the hollow. She pivoted the pen in her fingers, and slipped it into her sleeve before pulling her arm into view. "There was an update with our neural memory cluster last night. Your terminal detected a time shift in the clock of eighty-seven-hundredths of a second and locked itself down as a security precaution."

"Why are you crawling under my desk?"

Risa flashed an embarrassed smile. "I didn't want to sit on your chair; I lost my balance."

"Use the damn chair. I don't have crabs… and next time tell Hoffman that I require notice of updates like this." Senator Nur whirled away from the door and disappeared inside the hidden room.

Holy shit. Risa's heart raced. She poked the little-used spot on the terminal housing that created a holographic keyboard, and typed in the sequence of meaningless letters and numbers Berkeley gave her to disable the fake lockout.

"Nur," said the senator.

Risa glanced at the door. The woman remained out of sight. A mental nudge eked up the setting on her augmented hearing.

"Ahh, Andreas… so nice to hear from you."

Alas, from the NetMini's tiny earpiece, Risa could only make out a man's voice warbling in an upset tone. The urge to record this gripped her. As soon as she wanted to, a little panel appeared at the top-right corner of her vision displaying an equalizer graph.

"Don't fret over it," said Nur. "The delay will be minimal. Our underground friends will soon be playing by the rules they were meant to." A pause. "Of course, you dear, sweet, nervous boy. Fear is money."

The male voice warbled, somewhat calmer. Risa picked out the words 'defense spending,' 'fortune,' and something about investments. The last bit went up in tone at the end, a question.

"That was their damn fault for putting a bleeding heart in control over there. Can you believe he legitimately believes in the principles of the UCF?" Nur emitted a haughty laugh. "The military forgets the *people* are in charge, not their generals… and I am the people."

Mumbling came out of the NetMini, something about 'that problem.'

"Oh, I wouldn't worry about her, Andreas. It seems our wayward daughter has gone all soft and mushy. I'm not sure. The intel I've seen says she's plucked a Scrap off the street and decided to raise it as her own child."

At the woman referring to Kree as an 'it,' Risa scowled, and flexed her fingers. *She'd never know what hit her.*

The man muttered a longer response.

"Oh, yes… Touching, really." Nur sighed, an eye roll clear in her tone.

"Probably full of all sorts of diseases. Anyway, it suits our purposes. That one has been unstable for years now, talking about angels and so forth. Probably just cracked. It's less complicated for us if she removes herself from the equation. Everett doesn't have the balls to challenge me in an open inquest, and he's certainly not going to risk getting more directly involved. You, and your fortune, have nothing to worry about, my dear."

The NetMini warbled with the unintelligible male voice.

"I assume the others as well. Everyone profits from a little planetary skirmish, no?" Nur chuckled. "Grand. I'll see you then."

Risa stopped staring at the door and typed feverishly at the holographic keyboard. She triggered a system restart, which should clear the disabler soft as well as allow the system to recognize the newly 'installed' wireless connection. A sheen of metallic silver appeared and spread over the sprayed area. She stopped breathing as the concealed door creaked open.

"Are you done yet? Don't they train you people?" Nur frowned.

"Yes." Risa sprang from the chair, hoping her fast motion would distract the woman from noticing the desk. "I re-synced the system clock with the network, but it had to restart. It should be fine now, ma'am."

The senator stormed past her. Risa pivoted in place, paralyzed with dread. The metallic luster in the spray path had vanished. Silver wires thinner than human hairs had become invisible, sealed to the fake wood by the formerly liquid substrate. Her heart resumed beating.

"You're still here?" Senator Nur sat at the desk. "Do you need to do anything else with this thing or are you wasting taxpayer credits?"

"Making sure it reboots okay before I leave so you don't have to call us back up here, ma'am."

Nur's expression remained unreadable. She could've been amused at someone not eager to run away from her, or annoyed at the intrusion. Her face shimmered from cyan to white as the holo-panel reinitialized and rendered into a desktop. The older woman tapped an icon, which opened a black and green login prompt.

She's going right for the shadow net...

"Good. It's working. You know where the door is."

Risa rendered a slight bow, and walked out.

OPEN DOOR POLICY

Risa watched the deep-brown melt out of her skin in her reflection on the gel tank. One minute later, Rebecca Marsh was gone. Two of the soldiers in facing tubes stared at her, though she got the sense her chameleon act interested them more than her nakedness. Anyone who'd gone through boot camp lost sensitivity to group nudity. Between showers and jump tanks, privacy was too expensive to worry about, not to mention barriers between soldiers and their weapons lockers could kill.

The full-body tingling of the gel's nanobots devouring the spray-on coating faded. Anything not living or metal exposed to the tank fluid seemed to disintegrate, considered 'contamination' by the life-support system. Risa let a long sigh of breathable gel out her nostrils, reveling in no longer feeling as though she'd been plastic-wrapped.

She hung weightless in the viscous skin-temperature goo, ticking down the seconds until the DS4 would take her home. Everett could've made her take a civilian ride back to Mars, anywhere from fourteen to twenty days' travel, but he didn't. The military transport seemed like quite a bit of bending over backward for someone who wanted to walk away.

Much to her amazement, she'd made it out of the senate chambers without incident. Having to finish her eight-hour shift hadn't been too bad after all. Simpson reacted with surprise to her return from Nur's office. The girl figured 'Rebecca' would wind up escorted out of the building, exiled off to some 'remote listening post on Mars'. That Risa wound up going to Mars on purpose struck her as ironic. Maybe she could get used to the whole 'day job' thing. Simpson sure needed the help, and the company. A twinge of guilt came on at leaving the woman to face the mountain of installs alone... but she'd rather be home.

Raziel?

Clanking made her open her eyes. The two pilots rushed in, peeling off their flight suits as they hurried over to waiting gel tubes. *Guess they finished programming the jump.*

Change your mind? asked Raziel, a voice in her head.

Gel flooded her lungs with a deep breath, streaming out her nostrils on the exhale. *I have information. You say you want to help the people of Mars. Have you thought about what I said? About fighting two wars at once?*

I have.

Risa shivered as a pump kicked on, creating a current down her back. *The problems we've been having are all coming from Senator Marta Nur. She's involved in some kind of back-room deal with a man named Andreas. That woman is the one sending the false-flag operations.*

Raziel's *hmm* washed over her brain. *I don't see you anywhere.*

I'm in a military dropship about to jump. There's a temporary nano-antenna on the senator's terminal. You can get into an island net full of secrets. 00EE.18AD.158F.FFFC.989E. I don't trust Everett's people to finish this the right way. Please go digging. Find something to bury this bitch before she kills everyone I've ever known... for money. I mean bury in a political sense, by the way.

Raziel remained quiet. Lights outside the tube flickered on. Risa started, realizing she'd slumped from unconsciousness. A mechanical *clunk* shook the gel an instant before the whirr of pumps chewed on her eardrums. She waved her hands, pushing herself down to kneel on the base of the tank, still aspirating gel. One of the worst mistakes newbies made was to attempt breathing air as soon as their head breached the surface, before they could bend down to clear it all. Few things hurt like *half* a lungful of gel, even if a person could overpower the primal fear of drowning.

The soldiers did the same, crouching low and waiting for the *slurp* of pumps sucking on an empty chamber before coughing up the peach-colored liquid. Risa earned a few respectful looks at her blasé response to going from gel to air breathing.

She kept her face near the floor, huffing and coughing until nothing other than air came out. Of course, the soldiers finished getting their uniforms on and tromped out of the room before she finished clearing her airway, a product of routine. Risa slipped in the gel, pulled to her right by the ship executing a turn. She managed to steer her fall to a flop on an ice-cold metal floor, and crawled to the towel rack, not even trying to stand up while coated in slipperiness. Once there, she pulled a towel down and rolled into it.

Interesting, said Raziel. *I am grateful for your trust in providing me this information.*

She huddled on the floor, hugging herself in the embrace of warm cloth. *I know it's not the perfect world you want, where there's no ACC or UCF on Mars. Happy anarchy isn't going to work. Look at human nature. Maybe we can change things, but we can't do anything dead.*

Risa waited a moment, but he didn't reply. Worry swam around in her gut as she dried off and dressed. Minutes later, beeping in her head announced a re-established connection to the MarsNet. As soon as the login process ended, she called home. By the third ring, she'd stopped breathing. When it went to vidmail, anxiety brought her to the verge of clawing a hole in the ship's hull so she could jump out and run home faster.

No! dammit. What happened!

She dialed again, and again it rang to vidmail. After a moment of staring at the wall and shaking, she sprang to her feet and dashed down the hall. Three soldiers in the ready room looked up as she raced past. Twenty feet later, she stopped herself by grabbing the sides of the cockpit doorway and leaned through, peering down a narrow stairway on the left of two pilot chairs. The more distant helmet hovered at boot level.

The canopy, which she hoped was solid metal with an electronic display, tinted mostly brick red. Mars filled it, though remained far enough away to appear like a 'planet' rather than the landscape.

"How long 'til we land?"

"About half an hour," said the woman in the higher seat.

Risa tried to make sense of the controls, but her pilot skill chip didn't include spacecraft. She whined. "Any way to hurry it up? I think something's happened."

"We are hurrying." The pilot in front glanced back at her and shook his head. "You should go sit before you get thrown into something painful."

Sick with worry, Risa forced herself back down the narrow connecting passage between cockpit and a forward storage room full of weapons lockers. After returning to the gel tank area to trade the towel for her clothing, she walked into the ready room, where she fell into a corner chair. One of the soldiers had 'semmed an egg sandwich, which flooded the entire area with the smell of breakfast.

"Hey, ell-tee," said the soldier with no food. "Something you wanna tell us? You look like someone got shot."

Her heart pounded in her head. Her brain tormented her with ghastly things she'd see when she got home. Blood. A too-small body. Or worse— an empty apartment with no answers. She covered her face in her hands and rocked in the seat. "I don't—"

Beep.

Genevieve appeared floating in front of her. <Hey.>

<Don't do that to me!> screamed Risa. Though her voice remained in cyberspace, the soldier quirked an eyebrow at the look that must've been on her face.

<Whoa!> Genevieve held up her hands. <Something wrong with a girl taking a shit? I was in the bathroom when you called.>

Risa melted into the chair, staring at the ceiling. Genevieve's apparition rose, appearing to float horizontal over her. <Sorry. I'm a little wound up.>

<Ya think?> asked Genevieve.

"I'm good. Just a little paranoid." Risa smiled at the soldiers. "How's the coffee out of that thing?"

Both soldiers laughed.

The one eating the egg sandwich shook his head. "The same as any other military-issue java. Strip the paint off a DS4."

"That's what I'm used to." Risa trudged over to the reassembler. <Shit. I thought something had happened. I'm in orbit now, should be home in about an hour. How's Kree?>

<Adorable. She's worried about you, but being a trooper. Logged in to her classes right now. Oh, you should've seen how red Aurelia turned last night. Kree asked if she could be the flower girl at our wedding.> Genevieve blushed, giggled, and bit her lip. <I hope she proposes, but I don't wanna rush things. Aura almost fainted.>

Risa breathed a sigh of relief and took a sip of the most brutal black coffee she'd ever tasted. <You two make a beautiful couple. Damn, this stuff is strong.>

<Thanks, and what?>

<Coffee. See you soon.>

<Oh.>

Genevieve made the face she used to make whenever she'd forgotten something big. <Oh, some Asian guy stopped by here looking for you. Said he needed to discuss something important.

<Shiro?> Risa scowled. <What's he up to?>

<I have no idea what his name was. Looked like a sales weasel, if you ask me.>

<Wearing all white?>

<No.> Genevieve's red hair flopped about in a wild tangle as she shook her head. <Cheap black suit.>

Her sense of relief died a withering death. Dark clouds of worry circled like buzzards overhead. The need to get back to Kree before something happened got her hands twitching with adrenaline. She drifted to the corner and sat on the edge of the chair, forearms across her knees with the coffee cradled in two hands.

<Stay alert, okay, Gen? Please. Something feels wrong. I'll be there as soon as I can.>

TWELVE HOURS

For three days, Risa kept the blinds drawn and the windows at full tint. Whenever Kree looked over, Risa smiled and acted upbeat. A Hotaru-6 was never more than two feet from her hand at any time, except in the shower. Her first night back from Earth's moon, she'd brought Kree to bed with her like a living teddy bear. The girl didn't mind, but Risa didn't sleep. Hours passed, alternating between paranoia, fear, and the heart-smashing thought she needed to distance herself from Kree before something happened. She'd stared at the clock until it read 24:39:35 and jumped to the next day.

Day two she spent pacing the apartment from front to back, checking the hallway cam on one end and staring out the windows of the main bedroom on the other. Nothing seemed out of place, yet the quiet bothered her more than a strange Asian man showing up unannounced. Tamashī couldn't find anything on him. Whoever it had been didn't show up on any image feeds. Her friend suggested either someone better than her at electronic manipulation altered the video, Genevieve saw a ghost, got victimized by a psionic, or experienced a vivid dream.

On day three, Kree gave her odd looks every so often, but said nothing.

The scuff of bare feet on carpet broke the silence in Risa's bedroom. She angled her eyes down, peering over herself at a little head of black hair passing by the foot end of her Comforgel pad.

Kree walked up alongside her and leaned on the gel mattress. "What's wrong?"

Risa sat up and slid over to sit on the edge. "I'm okay."

Kree crawled up next to her. "No. You're not. You have the windows closed, the lights off, and you carry the gun all the time." She looked down. "You don't even smile anymore."

I'm going nuts. Shiro said it, and I'm doing it. "I don't know why I'm jumping at shadows." She put an arm around the girl. "You're right. It's not good to stay inside all the time. When you're done with school, we'll go to the park."

Kree smiled. "It's Saturday."

Risa wiped her eyes. *Damn. Week gone already?* She chuckled inside at 'Saturday,' at how she once viewed the imposition of Earth's system on Mars to be an instrument of domination. At nineteen, she'd gotten into a shouting match involving calendars. According to 'true Mars' time, she had been 10.09 years old. At the time, she didn't want to be called nineteen, especially around her boyfriend. *Damn, what was his name?* She pictured a grime-stained face, a man with wild hair and beard. She wanted to say Robison… Robinson… Roberts…

He'd died four months later. Legged by an ACC sniper and used as bait, he'd bled out before anyone could get to him.

I'd install a million operating systems on a million terminals to spare Kree from that life.

"Saturday. Okay." Risa stood. "Window, clear."

The windows lightened until they all but vanished, so transparent the bedroom didn't even appear to have a wall anymore. Risa raised a hand to her face, squinting at the invasion of daylight into her personal space. The sun, distant as it was, glared from a cloudless sky over shimmering silver buildings.

She left the laser pistol on the nightstand and walked Kree to the kitchen, where they both had cereal. After tossing the bowls in the machine, she ordered a pair of short dresses, one for herself and one for Kree. Same style, though white for her and yellow for the child. On a lark, she also picked out matching foam sandals. Going outside without heavy boots felt almost as awkward as streaking, but she wanted to try experiencing the whole 'grass in her toes' thing.

The atmosphere field kept Arcadia at a comfortable summer temperature this time of year, much more pleasant than the near-freezing wind outside the dome. In flagrant disregard of Mars, Arcadia City maintained an Earthly sense of season, simulating winter, spring, summer, and autumn regardless of where in orbit they happened to be. She found the adjustment to 'weather' annoying, having spent most of her life in underground cities where they didn't bother. Beneath the surface, every day was 'room temperature'. In some ways, living in a subterranean city felt a lot like being a crewmember of an immense starship that had nowhere to be and eternity to get there. Terraforming had done much to warm the planet over several centuries, though it remained too cold for comfort most of the year.

As far north as Araphel, the winter could hit -160°F or worse.

However, the whole 'going outside on a summer day and running around barefoot in the grass' thing did have a certain charm to it. Perhaps she could get used to 'seasons,' though already knew she'd hate the winter.

Beeping distracted her from her mental wandering. A delivery bot hovered by the front door. Fear welled up, but she kept it at arm's length. To her relief, the hovering box merely dropped off what she'd purchased and didn't bother with complimentary explosives or poison.

The new dress hung a touch less than halfway down her thigh and left her shoulders bare. *Nowhere to hide a gun.* She grumbled. *Guess I'll have to be all normal and stuff and carry a bag.* While Kree played with her sandals, Risa ducked into the back and rummaged drawers she hadn't touched since moving in. A silver purse, the same one she'd taken to Shiro's apartment, lurked under a stack of folded T-shirts in the fourth one she checked. Risa had cheated. Rather than fold them herself, she'd sent more or less her entire floordrobe off to a delivery-bot laundry service and put them away still in the individual plastic wrap.

Her Mems, moddable shoes that could go from flats to high heels in a few seconds, remained inside. She pulled the blue plastic slabs out and dropped them in the drawer. *Not going to let that son of a bitch ruin this. I need to wear them out somewhere with Pavo.* She grinned, thinking of teasing him by wearing *only* the Mems one night when he showed up.

Fortunately, the bag had enough room for one pistol as well as her NetMini. She slung it over her shoulder and started toward the living room, but froze as she passed the bathroom. The woman in the full-length mirror attached to the inside of the door didn't look like anyone she knew. She looked like a normal person.

Risa let slip a nervous laugh on the way to the living room. *Maybe the forces of darkness won't recognize me.*

Kree secured the Velcro strip of her spongy sandals around her ankle and bounced to her feet. Risa clasped her hand, took a deep breath, and walked out. A few neighbors passed them in the hall. Two women hurried by without making eye contact; one older man smiled at them, but didn't stop to talk.

They had the bubble elevator to themselves on the way down; Kree pressed against the transparent shell, mesmerized by thousands of little advert bots flying around an open-air city, darting between buildings. A momentary feeling of being a sniper's dream target, helpless in a clear capsule, passed. She resisted the urge to pull Kree in and shield her from the outside.

Dammit, Shiro. Why did you have to say that? No. I'm fine. Lars is ACC intelligence and he didn't recognize me. They have no idea who I am.

She couldn't help but eye the crowd as they exited the ground-floor lobby and caught a PubTran car in front of the building. The nearest park with 'stuff to do' for kids required an eleven-minute ride. On the trip, she talked with Kree about school. The girl's only complaint was the helmet hurt her neck after wearing it for so long.

"I wanna plug." Kree poked a finger at the socket behind Risa's ear.

"No cyberware until you're eighteen."

"But..." Kree made a face. "You can't do *anything* without a port. *All* the good games require them. I'd like school more if it didn't look fake like a holo-vid."

Risa held a hand to her chin, tapping a finger at her lip. "Well, there is one implant we can do that'll make it seem more real."

"Really?" Kree's eyes widened.

"Yep." Risa grabbed her in a one-armed hug. "We could implant you into a real classroom."

Kree flattened her eyebrows. "No one goes to *real* school anymore."

"Sure they do. It's just easier and cheaper to do it online."

Kree shrugged.

Hmm. No immediate protest. Maybe it would be good for her?

The PubTran let them off in a small lot full of cars. A wide field of grass and trees stretched out ahead of them, a recreation of Earth. Some people played with dogs, others lounged in the shade, lost in their NetMinis. A man passed jogging, trailed by a fist-sized orb-bot spouting off like an angry old man coaching the next great kinetic boxing champion.

Kree gravitated to a playground area with low-impact rides and stuff to climb. Risa followed the cue and went over. She took a seat on a bench where a few other parents watched their kids as Kree ran into the mix. Three fences boxed in the play park, offering a small feeling of security that the only way in or out was past the benches full of parents.

Unlike most of them, Risa didn't pull out a NetMini, sleep, or try and hit on the guy next to her. She locked her attention on Kree, sparing the occasional left–right glance. The girl went straight for the climbing bars, and seemed to insert herself into a group of like-age kids within minutes.

After an hour or so, Risa relaxed—a little. The children had moved on to a rotating platform after getting bored of the 'horses-on-springs,' even if they were shaped like space motorcycles and had harmless laser 'weapons' consisting of holograms; typical holovid-style blasts of red or green light in distinct streaks.

"… an update on the latest goings-on with Senator Marta Nur. Moht?"

Her consciousness snagged on the name. Risa swiveled her head around and up at a car-sized bot flying overhead. A too-pretty Marsborn woman smiled from a fifteen-foot square holographic panel suspended beneath it. She vanished, and in her place appeared a youngish man with short, curly hair that appeared wet and lopsided to his left.

Text at the bottom of the image read: 'Moht Daran, Mars Media Corp Political Correspondent.'

English, Chinese, Japanese, and Spanish subtitling scrolled beneath him at various speeds.

"Thank you, Aimee." He smiled. "Senator Nur has recently come under fire amid a series of disturbing allegations involving under-the-table deals with Aegis Industries, a prominent defense contractor." An image of the sour older woman appeared at the top left, looking much less intimidating behind a podium during a full-panic-mode press conference. "Information which has come to public light via an unidentified source implicates the senator in numerous ethical violations involving the awarding of government spending contracts to Aegis. In addition, the Senate Ethics Committee is investigating allegations that recent terrorist action, specifically the destruction of Arden Settlement, came at her direct order and was not, in fact, the actions of the terrorist Martian Liberation Front as previously reported.

"Senator Nur has vehemently denied involvement, however, the number, scope, and variety of the files released to the public by the as-yet-unidentified cyber vigilante have stirred a veritable wasps' nest on Earth's moon and thrown almost one-third of the entire UCF Senate under the spotlight."

Risa smiled at the fish-out-of-water face the old bitch made. *Much better than assassination.*

"Nice work," said Shiro, right behind her.

She froze. Her gaze shifted to the purse, and the almost-recognizable outline of a laser pistol under the thin, silvery material.

"The girl seems to have come out of her shell."

Tears gathered in her eyes, but didn't fall. "Please don't."

Shiro, hands in the pockets of his white suit pants, walked around the right side of the bench. He sat about a person-width away, leaning back with his sunglasses pointed at the NewsNet bot. "I didn't come here to threaten you, Risa. You've no reason to be frightened."

"I'm supposed to believe that?" She wanted to go for the weapon, but who knows how much backup he had watching her. A slow gaze from right to left couldn't find any snipers or anyone hiding in a nearby bush. "You tried to have Pavo killed. You don't hesitate when you're given orders to murder innocent people. Innocent people who trust the government you work for."

"The government I work*ed* for and the government you work for aren't the same thing." He reached up to his face—she tensed—and pulled off his sunglasses. "Few things can drive a man to foolishness like love."

Risa lowered her voice. "Killing a man to steal his girlfriend isn't love, it's psychotic. It's possessive."

"I suppose." He folded the glasses and tucked them in the inner pocket of his suit jacket.

"No katana?"

Kree jumped from the moving merry-go-round, tumbled, and sprang upright. Risa shifted her weight forward to stand, but the child popped up giggling rather than crying. She grabbed a slightly taller girl by the hand and dragged her to the swings.

"I didn't want to spook you."

"You being here spooks me. Why aren't you back on Earth?"

"I am surprised you didn't kill Nur. If I was in your position, it's what I would have done."

"I'm not an assassin."

He smiled. "You're beautiful when you're angry."

Risa narrowed her eyes. "You're making me prettier."

Shiro held up a placating hand. "My associates have located your safehouse under Primus. Senator Nur is not yet completely out of the picture and still retains significant influence over the actions of C-

Branch." He locked eyes with her. "Listen to what I am about to say carefully."

"W-what?" She leaned closer to him.

"A team has infiltrated your old home. Demolitions charges have been placed all throughout the ventilation system."

Senator Nur's voice echoed from the sky, flinging around words like 'spurious' and 'smear campaign.' Most of what she said melted into meaningless babble in Risa's mind.

She grabbed her purse, fumbling for the NetMini.

Shiro put his hand on hers, holding it down. "They are watching what goes on. The charges are set to detonate in approximately twelve hours. If they see alarm, or signs of an evacuation, they will set them off early."

"What are they waiting for? Why the delay? You're here to torture me, aren't you?"

He shook his head. "No, Risa. The MLF has two event teams out in the field, currently finishing up operations. They are waiting so they can catch as many fish as possible with one net."

"Everett can't stop this?"

Shiro sighed. "It's over his head. Internally, Senator Nur is blaming the MLF for 'constructing lies' and disseminating the information to the NewsNet. She has convinced enough people that Maris has gone rogue and is plotting a coup to overthrow the whole Senate. I am not even sure Everett is aware of this operation."

"That's so far from reality 'dustblow' isn't a strong enough word." Risa shook her head in disbelief.

"By the time they figure out she's lying, it will be too late. You, however, might be able to get in there and shut down the bombs. You did well at Arden."

"If that's doing well, I'd hate to see what you call a pooch screw." Risa rubbed the back of her neck.

Kree squealed and giggled on the swings.

Shiro watched her for a moment before smiling at the ground between his shoes. "I never worked for Starpoint. I didn't come to Mars because I was a concerned executive willing to donate money to a cause I believed in. When I said I would keep things between us strictly professional, I meant it... at the time. I never planned on falling for you."

"They sent you here to kill me. Getting the target in bed is one of the easiest ways to assassinate." She squirmed, feeling unclean at the mere thought of it.

"I was sent here to evaluate your intention and threat level. If you were willing to follow orders, I wouldn't have had to do anything."

"But I don't kill innocent people."

"Admirable of you." He sighed. "However, you wanted to quit. They wanted me to get rid of you as a risk, but I believed you really wanted out."

"I do." She teared up again at the massive smile on Kree's face. "I do."

Shiro clapped his hands on his knees and sat straight. "I regret attempting to kill one man you love, so I wanted to help you save the other one."

Risa glanced at him, the comment he'd made about how her father should have forbidden her from getting cyberware echoed at the back of her memory. "You knew?"

"Your father?" He flashed a grin two parts smug, one part rogue. "Of course. Why do you think they call it military *intelligence*? Granted, I wasn't a hundred percent sure. I did run a comparison of Andriy's DNA to yours."

"No match." She let her NetMini slip out of her hand into the purse.

He took his sunglasses out and put them on. "Not even close."

"How do I know you're not trying to get me to go down there to get caught in the explosion, too?"

"You don't." He peered over the sunglasses, holding steady eye contact. "I am not betraying you. I don't expect you to forgive me for Pavo. This is my attempt at apologizing. If you do decide to go, you've got twelve hours." Shiro stood and watched Kree. "I hope you find what you're looking for." He stood silent for a little while, bowed his head, and started to walk away, stopping after only one step. "Kurasawa."

"What?" Risa blinked.

He bowed his head. "My real name. Jun Kurasawa."

She sat in silence, watching him walk off into the crowd. A gleeful squeal from one of the kids distracted her for an instant. When she glanced back to her right, Shiro had vanished. Risa traced her thumb over the screen of her NetMini, shivering from worry. Trap? Genuine warning? Something about the tone of his voice made her believe him. Her throat tightened at the sight of Kree's grin, trailed by her waving hair as she went around and around on the spinning ride.

Shit.

AN IMPOSSIBLE CHOICE

R isa rushed in the door of her apartment, tugging Kree along by the hand. She'd given a brief explanation, 'someone is going to hurt Garrison,' which stalled the tearful protest at having to go home early. On the elevator ride up, she'd tried to call Pavo, but got his 'on duty' immediate punt to vidmail. She sent a text-only message after that, which the Defense Force allowed since they could be read whenever and did not demand instant attention: 'Emergency. Need you here asap.'

The child followed her to the bedroom. Risa stripped, kicked off the sandals, and retrieved her ballistic suit from the closet.

"Are you gonna kill people?" Kree stood in the doorway, twisting side to side.

"No, sweetie. I'm trying to stop people from dying."

"When can we go back to the park?" asked Kree.

"Tomorrow, we'll spend all day if you like." *If I'm still alive and this isn't a trap.*

Kree wandered to the nightstand and brought Risa her weapons harness, sans pistols.

"Thanks." Risa patted her on the head and slipped into the black nylon rig.

"Who's babysitting me?" Kree squatted and ripped open the Velcro on her sandals. "Is Aunt Gen coming over? She left a popsicle on the floor last time, but it didn't melt."

"What?" Risa blinked.

Kree shrugged. "A purple popsicle. It was big, and it didn't smell like grape. She screamed at me to drop it like it was gonna burn me or something."

I'm going to slap the shit out of her. "Oh, I'm sure it was just a bad popsicle. Food goes bad sometimes. When I get back, I'll get you a nice one."

"Okay." She tilted her head. "Are we gonna have lunch before you go?"

No way can I eat right now. "I'm not hungry... I'm too nervous. Come on." Risa grabbed the wearable electronics suite Raziel sent her, and pressed it into the skin over her right ear. Her stomach clenched at the thought of metal threads weaving into her skin. Indicators flashed by as the scanning modes synced up with the computer in her brain.

Risa jogged to the kitchen and dialed up macaroni and cheese from the reassembler for Kree. Within a second of the plastic bowl hitting the table, the doorbell rang. She sprinted over, spotting Pavo in a black shirt outside.

"Thanks for coming so fast. That was umm... fast." She pulled him inside.

He smiled. "You sent a hell of a text. What happened?"

"I'll explain when I get back. Can you watch Kree?"

"Sure."

Risa ran to get one laser pistol from her purse and the other from the drawer in the nightstand. Pavo stood in the center of the living room, hands in his pockets. She raced for the door, but skidded to a halt near him, regarding his plain black outfit.

"Your message said you were on duty. You doing undercover work now?"

He rolled his eyes. "I was already in Arcadia. They've sent me to see a 'stress therapist.' I got a little rough with a shoplifter."

Risa thought back to watching him manhandle a cupcake thrower. "Maybe I should go with you next time."

"That would be nice." He smiled. "You're not going to get shot at again, are you?"

"No. Damn, I hope not." She wanted to kiss him, but that would lead to more than a kiss and she didn't have any time to waste. "Sorry. I'll be back."

"Call me if you need anything. I can drop her at the station and come in, guns blazing."

"Kree, I'll be back as soon as I can," she yelled.

The girl came zooming in and leapt into a hug. "Don't die."

Risa nearly changed her mind about going, but she couldn't leave her father—or anyone else down there—to get caught in a massive explosion. One tear ran down her cheek. "I'm not planning to."

After a brief squeeze, she set the girl down on her feet and ran out. Instead of seeing herself falling to her death from the Strand, her brain tortured her with nightmare images of the safehouse filled with smoke and body parts. She paged a PubTran car on the way down the elevator, and it arrived within forty seconds of her reaching the street edge.

She jumped in as soon as the door opened. "Shuttle port."

"Thank you for choosing PubTran Corporation for your transportation needs."

"Skip it. Hurry."

"Expedited trips are available for an additional"—the electronic male voice dipped an octave lower—"fifty-two credits."

"Fine." She waved her NetMini again.

The little car with eight-inch fat wheels burned rubber. Sudden acceleration slammed her into the back of a hard plastic seat covered by a thin layer of cloth bearing a repeating pattern of teal squares. She found herself clinging to the 'oh shit' handle on the corner of the roof as the demon-possessed AI used a combination of streets and sidewalks to navigate. Whenever they approached a red signal, the auto-driving car leapt the curb to get around traffic. Several pieces of food, coffee cups, and at least one pedestrian bounced off the hood. At the end of the next block, the PubTran car cut off a giant cargo truck and slid sideways around a ninety-degree turn.

All the shit I've been through, and I'm going to die at the hands of a damn Pub car.

It spun around a right turn, slapping her into the left wall. Something *ka-thumped* under the vehicle. She twisted to peer out the thin strip of transparent plastisteel serving as a rear window, hoping not to see a child lying maimed in the road. A terrified woman in a white business skirt suit pushed herself up out of a puddle away from a smashed suitcase. Clothes danced in the wind.

Only luggage.

Damn. She exhaled.

The PubTran car squealed around a hard left; this time, Risa braced for it and got her boots on the opposing wall to avoid another body slam.

Two minutes and nine seconds after it got underway, it stopped in front of the Arcadia Starport entrance.

"Trip complete. Thank you for choosing PubTran."

With a *hiss,* the hatch door, most of the right side of the car, whirred up like an awning. Never had she been so happy to get out of one of those things. Risa sprinted up the moving stairs to the second-story platform where the doors stood like some kind of ancient temple and ducked into the over-tuned air conditioning.

After booking a ticket to Primus under her 'Raina Aum' alias, she flopped on the front row in the seating area to wait for the boarding call, unable to stop her leg from bouncing.

Beep.

She jumped. A round-cornered square appeared in her vision courtesy of her headware. Pavo's smiling face from his contact tile.

Risa answered. <Hey. That was quick. What happened?>

Several days without shaving caused his cheeks to blend seamlessly into his super-short hair. <You sent me a scary sounding text, so I got here as fast as I could… and the place is empty.>

She stared at the Mars Defense Force duty armor, visible on his shoulders at the bottom of his virtual image. <What's going on?>

Pavo raised both eyebrows. <You did text me, right?>

Risa leapt to her feet, screaming, "Dammit! No!" before bursting into tears.

"You got bumped to the next flight too?" asked a phlegmatic man in the row behind her. "Damn RedEx. Damn monopoly. Think they can treat us like shit."

<Ri?> Worry creased Pavo's forehead.

<They got her…> She sobbed. <They got her and I fucking handed her to them.>

<Who got her?> Pavo turned his head to the side and muttered, "Unknown individuals have abducted my daughter. I need a team here, stat." He looked at Risa again. <Calm down. Tell me everything that happened.>

Risa was too furious to be sad, and too despondent to be angry. Hearing Pavo say 'my daughter' hurt as much as it made her heart swell. *He probably only said that to make the MDF respond faster.* She stood in a daze for a moment before gravity took her back into the seat.

<Risa. Hey.> Pavo snapped his fingers in midair. <Come on!>

<You showed up at the apartment. Dammit, I thought that was too

fast. I'm such a damn idiot. I... explosives at the safehouse. I can't warn anyone or they'll set them off early.> She blinked. *Did Shiro help them set me up?* Again, she pictured that somber look on his face when he'd told her his true name. As much terror and anger as that man stirred within her, the final stare he'd given her didn't feel right. No... Shiro, Jun, or whoever he was hadn't done this.

<Who is 'they?'> asked Pavo.

<Senator Nur's people. C-Branch. The bad ones. Shit, they probably have Kree.> Risa punched herself in the thigh twice. <I'm going to kill that bitch. Damn, I'm such an idealistic moron. I *had* to talk Everett out of doing things his way. I should've just dealt with the problem like he wanted me to.>

A beep filled her head as the words 'incoming call' flashed. No identification displayed for the caller, only a blank grey generic person silhouette. Risa thought-clicked over and muted Pavo, but let him listen in.

Pavo's image shrank to a six-inch video tile, replaced by a larger virtual screen showing a close-up of beige carpet. Before Risa could venture a word, the image panned up. Kree, still in her yellow dress, sat on a frilly white bedspread over a Comforgel pad. Black cords bound her hands behind her back and her ankles together. A strip of dark tape covered her mouth. The little girl glared hate at whoever held the NetMini, not a trace of fear in her eyes.

Pavo's expression hardened to plastisteel as he muttered to someone nearby, probably Aurelia.

Risa guessed she looked into a hotel room, though whoever called took away any object with an identifiable logo. Kree struggled, making furious 'mmm' sounds in defiance of the tape over her mouth.

The image blurred from a rapid swivel, and a smiling Pavo appeared in a dark suit. His face shimmered and took on a telltale holographic glow before it melted into a broad-faced Chinese man with a wide grin. He looked older, past forty, with a thin streak of white in his hair over both ears.

<So sorry I was unable to meet you the other day, Miss Black.>

Kree 'mmm'ed past the tape again in the background.

Risa drew in a breath to scream, but held it at his raised finger.

<My employer wishes to secure your services in the elimination of a criminal who has stolen a great deal from us. We know you have an arrangement with the Syndicate that will let you get close. You have two

hours to kill the one who calls herself Tamashī. Refuse, or do anything other than travel immediately to Elysium... well, you can use your imagination what will happen.> He shifted his grip on the NetMini to allow a squirming Kree into the frame.

Terror gripped Risa's heart. Three seconds later, anger erupted like a volcano, followed by the most painful sense of sorrow she'd ever known. After ten seconds of silence, she felt like a dead woman still standing.

<If you've done any research at all on me, you know what I'm capable of.> The cold detachment in her voice stalled the real Pavo into staring at her. <I don't believe for a minute you're going to let her go, even if I do everything you ask. She's seen your face. You're going to kill her anyway.> Risa stared at his virtual avatar for a second. <You listen to me now. This is what's going to happen. You tell me where you are. I recover my daughter, alive and unhurt. We all forget this happened. If not, within forty-eight hours, not one person on the executive board of Míngtiān Corporation will still be breathing... and they won't die easy. And then I start on the rank and file employees. Everyone. Right down to the cafeteria staff.>

The Chinese man showed little emotional reaction. <We are tracking your NetMini. You'll have to trust us.>

His call dropped off, allowing Pavo's avatar to expand to full size.

Risa stared at the blank, black slab of technology in her hand.

<Don't do anything stupid,> said Pavo. <We're trying to trace that call. We'll find it in the 'net.>

A status window in the middle-right of her vision provided a timer until her booked flight to Primus boarded: 04:09. *Four minutes.* She flipped the NetMini over and over in her hand. *Garrison is going to die... Everyone in the safehouse is going to die... If I go to help them, that motherfucker will kill my daughter.* She pressed the device to her forehead and cried tears of rage. *Two hours. I can go there and back in time to maybe stop the bombs. But... Tamashī.*

<Risa. Stay put. The team is here. We'll find them. Supervisor just walked in. They're going to ask me to step aside if I can't focus. I gotta go. I'll call you as soon as I can.>

Pavo hung up.

Tears splattered onto the dark screen of the three-by-five-inch device. Faces danced across the bleakness of her mind. Garrison, Osebi, Javier, Kendrick, Kali... everyone she'd grown up with would die in a touch less than eleven hours. If she tried to save them, a piece-of-shit corporation would kill her child. *I never should have let her get close. It's my fault.* She pictured Tamashī giggling at her with those silly cookie sticks hanging out of her mouth. Pink T-shirt, pillow fights, video games. A forever-teenager. Even at forty-whatever, life continued being little more than a game to her. Maybe the woman never quite grew up mentally. Genevieve had been like an older sister, but Tamashī was her first true friend, even if she was weird as hell. If Risa tried to stop the explosives that would kill her father and everyone else in the safehouse, Kree would die. She had no way to know if the Chinese would keep their word and let her live. If she raced to Elysium and killed Tamashī, she might be able to get to Primus fast enough to stop the bombs. But, how could she kill her friend?

She slipped from the seat, landing on her knees in the middle of the starport waiting area, and cried. *Raziel? Help me, please. I don't know what to do. Please...*

Risa listened to the echoing sound of boarding and arrival announcements over a distant loudspeaker and the din of people moving through a cavernous building. She leaned back, staring up at a ceiling three stories over her head.

White-painted metal offered the same answer as Raziel: silence.

RATS IN THE WALLS

No one paid much attention to Risa crying into her hands.
They all had places to be. She thought about the time she'd walked into Tamashī's room at the Orbital Hotel and found her sprawled half off the bed, naked and apparently dead. She sniffled, gripped by the same grief she'd felt at the sight. Telling a cyberspace jockey apart from a corpse when they were jacked in usually required medical scanners. Finding her friend dead was bad enough, but the idea of being the one to cause it brought bile up to the back of her throat.

One minute, ten seconds left until the Primus shuttle opened for boarding.

She tried to imagine how Kree felt at that moment. The child looked angry, far from frightened, but she'd been on the street for months. She knew appearing terrified only invited problems. As much as she resembled one, Tamashī was no child. The woman could've easily been Risa's mother by age. The Sword of Damocles over her friend's head was one of her own creation. Kree had done nothing but attach herself to the wrong person.

They're tracking my NetMini. If I call Tamashī, they'll kill Kree. If I don't go to Elysium, they'll...

She snarled. No matter what happened in the next few hours, Míngtiān Corporation would need a new board of directors. Nothing on Mars—or Earth—would contain her vengeance. She bowed her head. The thought of betraying her friend cut deep, but the wound didn't ache as much as the idea of finding Kree's tiny, lifeless body stuffed inside a delivery bot at her window.

I'm sorry, Tamashī. I hope you can forgive me. She opened a connection to the Starport system, and switched her flight to Elysium. The boarding timer adjusted to eight minutes. Nine rows away, a man cheered. He'd been bumped up to the Primus-bound seat she relinquished.

Risa found herself attempting to pray to Raziel, or the god she once believed him to serve. The more she thought about walking into the room at the Orbital Hotel, the smile Tamashī would give her, and the horrified expression of betrayal that the girl would use her last scraps of life on, the more Risa cried. *She's never going to expect me to be able to kill her.*

She lurched forward, vomiting. Pale-yellow liquid splattered on the thin blue-grey carpet between her boots. Her body convulsed again. A memory of Tamashī giggled and hurled a pillow at her. *I... can't do it. But Kree will die if I don't.* Risa threw up more.

A round, flat bot zipped across the room, halting in the midst of the puddle she'd made. It wound its way back and forth over the stain, scrubbing the carpet. When it finished, it backed up and pivoted to 'look' up at her. Two dark spots, likely cameras, seemed so much like eyes she imagined the thing being 'hungry' and wanting her to throw up again so it could eat.

She obliged.

All manner of justifications swam around in her thoughts: *Kree's only six. Tamashī is forty... whatever. Kree's innocent, Tamashī isn't. Okay, well, she looks innocent. She is a thief. Every time I ask her for help, she helps me. She's my friend. Kree's my... daughter. They're going to kill her anyway.* Risa took and released a slow breath. *I'll call them before I kill her, demand they let her go.* She growled. *They won't. They didn't blindfold her. Would the Syndicate play along and let me fake it?* Her stomach knotted. *Walsh would want me to do a hit for something like that.* Her body trembled. *Total stranger's life or my kid's? Yeah, no choice there. Sorry pal.*

When the notification for Elysium boarding vibrated her NetMini, Risa stood like an automaton and trudged down the concourse hallway to the terminal gate. By the time she got there, the line had grown to fifty people deep. She took her place at the end, feeling like a piece of shit for what she contemplated doing to her friend. *She's going to smile or giggle at me, and I'm going to shatter. Kree's going to die.* Risa closed her eyes and pictured the only way she could possibly murder her friend: speedware into the room and kill her before she even realized anyone had walked in.

A twinge in her head felt like a caterpillar crawling down her brainstem. Risa shivered at the unscratchable itch, grasping the back of her head. *Great. A brain tumor too.*

However, she fully expected Míngtiān to kill Kree no matter what she did. For all she knew, her child could already be dead. Perhaps she should forget Tamashi and buy a ticket to Xīwàng dà, the first city established by China on Mars. She'd start there and refuse to rest until not a single person employed by that company remained alive. Revenge dominated most of her adult life; it would be a fitting end to be consumed by it in death.

White moved in her peripheral vision. Expecting Shiro, she whirled. At the sight of Raziel, she wound up crying again. People in the line around her glanced back, a few muttered about crazy, though someone pointed out she was probably on a phone call.

<I apologize for the delay. I will confess to being curious what you would do given the parameters of your current situation.>

<Asshole.> She covered her mouth. <Shit. Sorry. Please… help me.>

He strode up alongside her; his white feathery wings looked solid, until they passed through waiting passengers without effect. Raziel, the hallucination created by electronics inside her skull, reached out and ran his hand over her head. She twitched at feeling his touch—sensory input fed to her brain.

<Be at ease, child. I am ghosting your NetMini's positioning signal. As far as the Míngtiān people are concerned, you are going to get on this shuttle and fly to Elysium City. Then, walk on foot to the Orbital Hotel. You will 'arrive' in Tamashi's room in thirty-four minutes.>

She sniffled, wide eyed, trembling. <But…>

<The call you received from the Míngtiān agent originated from here in Arcadia.>

All traces of weepiness vanished. Her sudden shift to an aggressive pose and a fatalistic glint in her eye made several passengers step away. <Where?>

<The Hotel Presidium.>

Risa ran for the exit.

Raziel, despite not moving his legs, remained at her side, seeming to glide along the floor. <There is a PubTran car waiting for you outside. I took the liberty of borrowing one.>

<Thanks.>

Risa hit her speedware, surging up to a forty-mile-an-hour dash across the waiting area. Air in the wake of her passage tore drinks from people's hands and knocked at least three toddlers over. She slowed for the stairs, and headed right for an idle grey-and-cyan auto-car with a man pounding on its roof.

She launched herself at him, driving a knee into his back and drilling him into the side of the car. He let out an *oof* and started to fall, but she shoved him aside before he could collapse. "Sorry, this one's taken." The door popped open. She leapt in, braced her boots against the wall on either side, and grabbed both roof handles. <Okay, go.>

While the little car spat smoke from all four tires, Risa opened a headware call to Genevieve.

An apologetic redhead appeared floating before her. <Sorry, Ri. I know I shouldn't have left the dildo where—>

<Forget it. I need your help.>

Genevieve blinked. <What? Damn girl, you sound pissed.>

<You have to go back to the safehouse. Don't walk in the front door. Don't tell anyone you're going there. Don't call anyone. Just go.>

<What?> Genevieve shook her head. <Are you crazy? I can't go back there… I'll get sucked right back into…>

Risa sighed. <I'm not gonna blow dust up your ass, Gen. C-Branch is splitting in half. They found it. Hah, *found…* they knew where we were all along. Bombs in the vents. About eleven hours left.>

<Oh, shit.> Genevieve looked down. <I'd, umm, love to help but… Aura left me handcuffed naked to the bed.>

Risa smirked. <The bed ten feet behind you? Come on, Gen. Garrison's my father. You know those people, too. They were our family. There are kids in there because of me. I know you're scared, but you have to believe me. No one tried to assassinate you personally. The rigged detonator was aimed at the Front. It could've gone to anyone. You don't even have to show your face. Go in the vents. Disable the charges. Leave without being seen.>

<Okay…> Genevieve sucked in a breath and let it out with a shuddering exhale. <You're sure about the timeframe? I dodged a bomb with my name on it once… not sure how many of those I got left. You know how bad my luck is.>

<As sure as I can be given the circumstances… if you think it's sketchy, get out, but please try.>

Genevieve nodded. <Okay. If you get me killed, Aurelia's going to kick your ass.>

<This is all your skill. No luck needed. Just skip the Indian food.> Risa cringed as the little car went up on two wheels to take a turn at seventy-something. <I'll come help as soon as I deal with some Chinese take-out.>

<You're sending me to defuse bombs and you're going for food?> Genevieve's face went red.

<No. I'm going to take out a couple of Chinese guys who kidnapped Kree before they can kill her.>

<Oh, shit.> Genevieve went bug-eyed. "What the—?"

Risa flinched as something heavy enough to sound like a body bounced off the front of the PubTran car. <I'll call you back in a few minutes.>

<Okay.>

She hung up and called Garrison. His face appeared eight seconds later. <Lieutenant Tanais reporting in, Sir. Sitrep uneventful. Johnson's dog keeps shitting on the floor. Awaiting orders.>

Garrison nodded. <Understood. Tell him to change food brands.> He fiddled with something off screen. A band of static descended over his hallucination. <Line secured.>

Risa took a breath. <Dad... Do not react visibly to what I am about to tell you. The safehouse has been compromised. There are explosives. C-Branch has eyes inside. If they sense alarm, they'll set off the bombs.>

Oh, shit. What if he's the inside man? Fuck it... no way in hell could that be true.

<Are you inbound to disarm?>

RISA'S HEART FLUTTERED. IF HE WAS THE TRAITOR, HE WOULD HAVE TOLD her to stay away to remain safe. <Negative.>

He paled.

<Gen is. I have something to deal with.>

<What kind—?>

<Kree's been kidnapped.>

<Say no more. You can fill me in later.> Garrison shot a hard stare at his desk. <Who do you trust?>

<You.> Risa wasn't on speaking terms with smiles at that point, but she got close.

<Someone else. I can't leave.>

<Osebi.>

Garrison nodded. <Very good. Deal with your issue, then check in.>

Risa cringed during another violent swerve, shuddering as the little car bashed through a decorative hedge and bounced down a long staircase in the middle of a huge park. Garrison's illusion disintegrated into pixels, leaving the cabin dim.

Raziel's driving made the PubTran AI feel tame, but at that moment, Risa didn't care.

THE PUBTRAN CAR SLOWED TO A NORMAL, UNSUSPICIOUS SPEED A QUARTER-mile away from the Presidium Hotel. The hundred-and-thirty story building looked like a sleek wedge-shaped starship landed nose down. Three prominent towers rising about twenty stories higher than the rest of the building resembled engine nacelles. Sixteen clear-capsule elevators glided up and down outside the walls.

Risa exited the car when it stopped by the delivery entrance in the back. She leapt up to the loading dock and strolled in an open garage-style door to an enormous room where a series of gargantuan delivery bots dropped off cargo pallets. A handful of workers paid her no mind, too busy unpacking caviar, snacks, and other overpriced luxuries.

Raziel's assault on the hotel network provided her a virtual trail of pixie dust to follow. She hurried along the path, ignoring an interior door and hurrying down a corridor to an employee break room. The wispy light went straight past it and hooked a left at a four-way intersection. Soon after taking the corner, the thrum of industrial equipment grew loud. Security doors opened on their own as she jogged up to them, allowing her into a room full of server towers. The glimmering thread spiraled and plunged into the slats of a large air-intake grille between a pair of computers the size of industrial refrigerators.

Once she slipped inside and pulled the cover closed, she stared up at a long, arduous climb. *Vents. Great. Nothing I haven't done before.*

Around the time she reached the fourth floor, Genevieve called. Risa answered, though she shut off the virtual avatar. A tiny 2D image floated at the top-left of her view. The redhead had packed her voluminous hair into a visored cap, and had a dust mask over her mouth and nose.

<I'm in,> said Genevieve. <No one saw me. No contact in the tunnels.>

Risa suppressed a chuckle. <I'm surprised you remembered the back way in.>

<Aww, come on. Who are you talking to?>

<Thanks.>

Gen grunted. <I got fat in my old age. Some of these ducts are hard on the hips.>

<Gen, you are not fat. When you were twenty, you didn't have a shape. And you're not old. You're what, thirty-one?>

<Meh, something like that.>

Risa hauled herself up the vertical shaft, bracing her boots on the quarter-inch ridges between sections of duct. <Oh, this is... I'm going to kill that bastard slow.>

<You sound tired already. What's up?>

She glanced at Raziel's waypoint. <Climbing forty-three stories straight up.>

<Oh, no thanks. I'll take squeezing my fat ass sideways along a vent any day. Oh, hello.>

<Rat?> Risa mentally smirked over the comm channel. <And you are not fat. You're normal. I'm a twig.>

Genevieve shook her head. <Nope. Spicy Pop Tart. Ooo. This one's new. I don't remember this model.>

Sweat got into Risa's eyes and stung. *Ow. Shit.* She couldn't wipe her eyes; letting go of the wall would send her plummeting. Metal eyes didn't have that problem. She blinked and tried to ignore it. The twisting square tunnel in night vision green overhead seemed endless. At least she had the ability to see in the dark again thanks to the pod Raziel sent her. An image of Kree, tied and struggling, fueled her. Risa's fingers stopped aching. Her eyes ceased burning.

<Okay. You said they're live-monitoring this shit, right?> asked Genevieve.

<Yeah.> Risa wished the vent was a little smaller. She could've made better time if her arms were long enough to wedge her back against the far side. Climbing tiny ridges like a ladder sucked. <There may be an inside person... or maybe it's only cams.>

<Right. I'm going to bypass the detonator here then... that way, the charge will look like it's still online. This is some intense hardware. Tamper sensors out the ass.>

<You're way better at demo than I ever was.> Risa smiled. <Next time,

just say you don't wanna teach me anymore instead of faking your own death.>

Genevieve stifled a shout of alarm. <Gah. Don't make me laugh right now.>

Risa climbed for three minutes in silence. *Ten more floors.*

<Got it. One safe.> Genevieve stashed her NetMini on her belt. The little 2D window now displayed a black square rather than her face. <Do you have any idea how many charges there are?>

<No. Probably enough to collapse the entire safe house.>

<Fifteen at least then. They're not very big. Uhh... yeah, probably fifteen. I can estimate where I'd put them. Sorry it took me so long on the first, was figuring it out. The rest should go quick.>

<Gen, don't use the phrase 'go quick' when talking about bombs.>

A laugh hissed past clenched teeth. <Sorry. Ugh. You know, even if I survive this, Aura's gonna kill you. And probably me too for agreeing to do this.>

<Yeah. I'm glad you two have each other.>

<Thanks.> Genevieve smiled. <I'm glad you found Pavo.>

At the forty-third floor, the trail of pixie dust bent ninety degrees into a side duct. Two feet from the vertical, a fan grille blocked her.

Raziel, please tell me you're there.

Faint tingly energy swarmed down her limbs, soothing rather than paralytic.

Thank you. Can you mask this fan from the building's network? I need to cut it out to get past it and I don't want anyone noticing.

It ground to a stop two seconds later.

His voice seemed to whisper from right behind her, "Can you fit through?"

An X-brace held the fan motor to the four corners of the tunnel. Each somewhat-triangular segment looked too tiny, even for someone as thin as her. *Not without greasing my hips. There's gotta be a release. I don't see a manual switch. Probably on the other side.*

"You are correct," said Raziel. A heavy *click* echoed in the shaft.

The fan assembly swung open like a door. Risa pulled herself up and into the horizontal shaft, taking a ten-second breather. *My arms are jelly.* She pushed past the fatigue, thinking of the little girl 184 meters away according to the dot on her mini-map.

<Ding,> said Genevieve. <Two down. Same make and model. I don't think this was any of our people. This unit is way more high-tech than

anything I've ever seen come from Denmark. I'm going to guess you're right about it being C-Branch. She grunted with the effort of crawling. <Sounds calm in there except for... who had kids?>

<Don't you remember me telling you about them? I found them in a tunnel I was about to demo. Group I found Kree with.>

<Shit. Why'd you bring kids to the safehouse? You know most crazy people collect cats, not children. Who in their right mind would bring children to the safehouse?>

<You mean other than Garrison?> Risa laughed in her head.

<Ouch. Yeah, good point. We were both kinda young, weren't we?>

Risa sighed. <I didn't want to blow them up. I couldn't leave them on the street either.>

<You adopted Kree, but left the other ones? Like kittens I guess; you took the cutest.>

<That's not fair. She's the only one of them who isn't afraid of me. The other ones think I'm Cat-6 too. Or at least terrifying.>

<Wait, you're not?> Genevieve shushed her before she could reply. Twenty seconds later. <Three down. Go.>

<No, I'm not Cat-6. Raziel hacked my headware. He's an amazing... entity, but he's not a supernatural being.> Risa suppressed a grunt while pulling herself past a narrow spot.

<So you gave up on that whole mythology thing?> Genevieve hummed. <Oh, nasty, I didn't need to see that.>

<Do I want to know?> Risa squeezed around a ninety-degree turn left, crawling faster and faster the lower the distance counter got.

<Kali's diddling herself with the handle of a combat knife. She's kinda hot, but that thing is filthy.>

<The dagger or the other thing?> Risa smirked to herself.

<Dirty mind. The knife. Silence! Bomb.> Eighteen seconds passed. <Got it.>

As Risa neared the targeted vent grille, she even thought in a whisper, as if the people inside might hear that. <Gen... I'm on target. I gotta go. I'll call as soon as I'm secure.>

<Copy. Kill those bastards.>

The call dropped.

Risa edged up to the slats. Fortunately, the angle of the light kept any from entering the vent... and she no longer had glowing eyes capable of giving her away.

Kree sat on the same bed she'd seen in the call, still bound and glaring as if her anger might kill. A slender Chinese woman in a slinky black dress, black tights, and soft shoes approached and sat near Kree, who tried to scoot away.

The woman spoke in Chinese. English text scrolled across Risa's vision. "This is cruel. What are you afraid of? She is so small. We do not need to tie her."

Another female voice answered, too far right in the room to see. "No mistakes. You are too gullible. Mister Liào will not tolerate any errors. The contractor is twelve minutes away from Elysium."

The woman near Kree reached toward the child's face. "I will give her water."

Kree ducked away, emitting an angry grunt.

The woman pantomimed drinking and spoke English. "Water? Thirsty?"

When she reached again, the child remained still. The woman peeled the black tape away from Kree's mouth.

The nicer woman rambled in Chinese, as another, taller woman strolled into view. She, too, wore all black. Text translation scrolled by as fast as she spoke. "If she runs away, I will bring you to Mister Liào myself. Give her water, then cover her mouth, and blindfold her. I am sick of her staring at me."

Kree narrowed her eyes. "When my mommy gets here, you're all gonna die."

Risa's heart swelled.

"Cute kid," said a man, in English.

Risa drew her legs up, balancing her weight on the balls of her feet. *Raziel, if you're there... I need a favor.*

Ask, my child, said a silken voice in her mind.

Ten Nano claws slid out from Risa's fingertips. Seven small segments per digit locked together to form rigid curved blades with triangular cross sections, cutting edge on the underside.

Hit the lights.

27

GAME OVER

Dark.

"You're gonna die now," said Kree, sounding far too calm.

Risa activated her speedware, raked her claws down the sides of the vent grille, and leapt out into a slow-motion fall. The component on the side of her head provided night vision even sharper than her old metal eyes, leaving the room bright as day despite being monochromatic green. She tagged three adults as well as her child, the combat processor in her skull providing a constant awareness of their relational position.

The cruel woman swiveled toward her, bright green spots shone from her eyes. Her motion appeared sluggish, but still fast enough to be a threat. To her right, the man who contacted her over the vid stood frozen in time near a doorway. Nearer the bed, the woman holding a cup of water to Kree's lips had also become a statue. She headed for the man out of pure contempt, the boosted woman following.

The tip of her right boot touched carpet. Risa let gravity pull her into a forward somersault, ducking a reverse spin kick and a ten-inch blade sticking out from the toe of the woman's shoe. Risa sprang up from the roll and thrust her right hand out, plunging four claws into the man's back between his shoulder blades. A flick of the fingers severed his spine, causing instant paralysis.

The woman recovered from the missed kick, planted her foot on the rug, and charged. A trio of long, thin blades slipped out between the knuckles of both fists, followed soon by the screech of a hypersonic oscillator. Electronics in Risa's ears filtered out the noise, reducing it to a weak sense of a presence in the air rather than a conscious realization of sound.

She twisted sideways. Two thrusting arms tipped with vibroblades passed around her, one in front of her stomach, one behind her back. Risa smashed her elbow into the woman's face, knocking her reeling backward, then raked her claws down in an effort to sever her opponent's limbs, but the woman pulled away, suffering only shallow slices on each forearm.

Fear showed plain on the woman's face. She backpedaled, but made the mistake of moving closer to Kree. Risa lunged. A telegraphed leaping swipe scored another shallow flesh wound on the woman's gut. Her opponent faked with her right hand, going for Risa's head with the vibro claws, and twisted the other way, kicking at her thigh. A single vibroblade sprouted from the front of the woman's shoe.

The inferior quality of the Míngtiān woman's speedware made the fight seem more as if Risa sparred with someone demonstrating moves instead of trying to kill her for real. She caught the incoming ankle before the implanted blades could draw blood, then shoved the leg up to the side, stared into the woman's artificial eyes, and swiped her other hand's claws through the shin, cutting the limb as easily as slashing a standard knife through soft cake.

Blood sprayed. Horror spread over the woman's face as she hopped backward on her one intact leg. Risa tossed the severed limb aside. In the monochromatic green of night vision, the two women stared at each other, existing on a level of time apart from the rest of the world. The 'nice' woman, on the bed, only now showed a hint of reaction to the lights going out by glancing up. Her cup pulled millimeters away from Kree's lip.

The man's knees bent forward at a slight angle, his fall starting.

Her opponent flailed her arms in an effort to retain balance. Blood gushed from her severed leg. She raised her hands in a gesture of surrender. Risa looked down for six-tenths of a second, and lunged in, thrusting both arms forward.

Ten Nano claws speared into the woman's gut; Risa lifted her off the ground in a jerky motion that shredded a half-inch or so at a time upward. The woman convulsed and thrashed until her own weight pulled the insanely sharp edges high enough to reach her heart. Risa held eye contact as the Chinese woman gurgled and gasped away her last few seconds of life before falling limp.

She leaned forward and let the body slide off her hands, then disabled her speedware.

A *thump* sounded from behind as the man hit the floor.

Light please.

Raziel obliged; the lights flickered on, shifting the room to full color. The shorter woman on the bed yelped at the blackout that had occurred four seconds ago. She looked back, presumably to ask her associates what happened, and screamed.

Kree narrowed her eyes, no longer fighting the cords. "I told you my mommy would find me."

The remaining woman scooted over the bed, back to the wall, and screamed again, cowering away from Risa as though she were a demon brought to life. Chinese streamed out of her too fast for the translator to turn into text. A line of question marks flickered by in a marquee.

Risa strolled to the edge of the bed. "Hold still."

Kree sat patiently while Risa flicked the tip of one claw at the binding between her ankles. When the cord sprang away, the child hopped off the bed and turned her back. Risa cut the knot between her wrists.

"Is there anyone else here?"

Kree shook her head. "No. Just these three."

Risa stared at the whimpering woman. She held up a hand, watching blood drip from her claws. "You took my daughter."

The woman shrieked, cried, and whimpered, clutching her fists to her chin. A metallurgical scan, courtesy of the device stuck to her head, showed minimal cyberware: NIU, skill chip board, some other headware, but no body wiring or implanted blades. *She's helpless.*

"Please…" The Chinese girl bowed her head. "I am not wanting to do this. I have no authority."

Kree clutched the carpet with her toes, and looked down.

"Sweetie… go to the bathroom and close the door. Don't look to the right."

"Yes, Mom." Kree walked off, careful not to step in blood with her bare feet.

Risa froze. *She called me Mom…*

The woman cringed, trembling. Twelve seconds later, the *click* of a door lock broke the silence.

"Get lost." Risa turned away from the bed, and approached the moaning man.

She squatted next to his head, arms draped over her knees, claws dangling. Transparent blue Nano gleamed. The soft *thump thump thump* of the surviving woman sprinting for the door passed behind her.

"H-how..." wheezed the man.

"You should've listened to me. I told you how things were going to happen, and you chose to be a hardass. It takes a weak, weak man to threaten the life of a child." Risa held her right arm out and sank her claws into his back, around where she estimated his kidney to be. He didn't react. "Oh, darn. You can't feel a damn thing because I severed your spine."

"You—"

Risa stood, hesitated a few seconds, and kicked him in the side of the head as hard as she could, launching a spray of blood from his mouth. When he attempted to murmur again, she repeated the kick. After a brief pause, a surge of anger came out of nowhere. She kicked him twice more, and again until he passed out. *Kree's already seen too much.* Risa let her rage bubble up, and struck out with a surgical stab to the back that pierced the heart. In and out in under a second. The kind of strike a *tì-zhèn* could deliver to a target in a crowd, invisibly fast with speedware. Gone before anyone noticed the dead man falling.

A male voice emanated from a few feet to her left, speaking Chinese over the barely audible thrum of a holo-projector.

"Zhū, what is the status of your—?"

The face on the shimmering screen, grey-haired, wrinkled, froze. A tiny amount of color drained from his cheeks for a second before they reddened with fury.

Risa stepped in between the holo-panel and the dead man, adopting the posture of a broken marionette. "You shouldn't have threatened my daughter, Liào." She held her hands up, bringing bloody Nano claws into view of the camera. "You wanted an assassin?" She stepped closer. "You got one. I'll be seeing you... and the rest of the board very soon."

Liào's eyes went wide.

She jammed her claws into the Vidphone unit, killing the call and sending a shower of sparks and smoke upward.

Risa walked to the bathroom. "It's me."

A *click* came from the lock.

She stepped in.

Kree sat on the closed toilet, covering her eyes with her hands. In the solace of a private room, she'd started crying. She sniffled to a state of quiet calm as Risa approached the sink and held her hands under the faucet. A sensor tripped the flow and she rinsed away the blood, retracting her blades a few seconds after no trace of red remained.

"I'm sorry." Risa bowed her head.

Kree pulled her feet up and stood on the toilet lid. "Why are you sorry?"

Risa didn't bother to dry her hands—that would take too long. She swept Kree into her arms and hugged her. "For letting them take you."

"He tricked us both with a Pavo head."

She laughed despite her body surging with too much unspent adrenaline and rage. "Yeah."

"Did you kill them?"

"Not the one who wanted to give you water."

Kree squirmed. "She wasn't mean like the others."

"I know. That's why I let her go. Close your eyes."

"'Kay." Kree snuggled. "You did just like I drawed?"

"Yeah. Just like you drew. I won't ever let the bad people hurt you." Risa kissed her on the head. "But I still don't want you looking at it."

Risa carried her across the hotel room, down the hall to the elevator, and held her the whole way to the ground floor. She seethed to herself. *She'd been acting like a normal kid. This is going to give her nightmares... she's going to hide under the bed again. I'm going to tear that company apart.* Guilt at what she'd been almost willing to do to Tamashī sent a sniffle into the crook of Kree's neck.

"Don't cry. I knew you would find me." Kree kissed her on the cheek and rested her head on Risa's shoulder.

You would not have killed Tamashī, said Raziel. *Think of it as a theoretical question. You would choose the life of your child over the life of a non-relative. Do not feel shame for following a decision branch most biological creatures would select.*

The elevator door slid open. The Presidium Hotel lobby flashed blue from the lights of at least fifteen MDF cars. Risa crossed the fancy room, exiting the main doors as the first line of Defense Force officers reached the top, Pavo at the lead.

He waved the others in and stopped, grasping her arms. "What the hell happened in there?"

"Míngtiān wants Tamashī dead. They tried to pay off the Syndicate, but they didn't go for it. As long as she works for them, they'll protect her. Somehow, Míngtiān found out about me… knew I could walk right into the Orbital, thought she'd never see it coming." *She never would have.*

Pavo pulled them both into an embrace.

"Raziel spoofed my GPS going to Elysium. He backtracked their call and led me here."

"How many dead?" asked Pavo.

"Two. One had a soul, so I let her go." She narrowed her eyes. "I'm going to China. I have an appointment with a Mister Liào… and the rest of their executive board."

Pavo shook his head. "Leave them to the Defense Force."

"China's a sovereign state. They're not UCF or ACC. What are your laws going to do? I told that old bastard he's going to get the assassin he wanted."

"Mommy, please don't go away again." Kree sniffled.

Pavo gestured at Kree as if to say 'how can you argue with that?'

"Míngtiān has a presence here, as well as UCF Earth. Offices as well as merchandise going into stores. We can deal with it. It probably won't result in the death of their executives, but it'll hurt them more… in the wallet. Let us deal with it."

"You better…" She fired back an 'or I will' look.

Pavo's NetMini chimed a second before Risa's rang with an incoming call. Noticing the call came from Garrison, she patched it to her headware for privacy.

His bust appeared in midair, coated in grey dust. <Risa. Do not return to the safehouse. Situation critical.>

<WHAT? NO. I JUST FOUND OUT YOU'RE MY FATHER FOR REAL… I'M *NOT* going to let you die a month later.>

<Wait what?> yelled Genevieve. She leaned into the frame with Garrison. <Father? What!>

<I'm sorry, Bit. I love you. The most important thing to me is that you stay alive. I'm sorry. You have to stay away. It's too late.> Garrison lingered for a second, and ran off camera.

Genevieve stepped in, gazing off to the side. She pulled a filter mask down, exposing a patch of clean skin around her mouth and nose, the rest grey with dust. <What the hell?>

A massive explosion overloaded the audio channel.

Risa screamed. Kree slipped from her arms as she grabbed the sides of her head, cringing from the volume. The child landed on her feet and clung to her side. Her brain quivered from a roar that would've blown eardrums out had it not been mere electrons being fired into nerves, making her swoon to her knees. Genevieve's floating apparition vanished in a cloud of smoke.

The line went dead.

"Risa?" Pavo grasped her shoulders and shook her. "What the hell was that?"

She stared at him, wordless.

He shook her again. "Risa."

"Bombs..." She shuddered. "They blew it up."

"Blew what up?"

"Everyone." She jumped up. "I have to go..."

His grip slid down to her forearms and he yanked her back. "Go where? The safehouse? Why? If they blew it up, it's gone. It's done. There's nothing there for you now. What are you going to do?"

She used an aikido technique to reverse his grip, grabbed his wrists, and pulled his arms around Kree. "Gen said she disarmed most of the bombs. There's gotta be survivors. He's my father, dammit. I have to try."

Kree reached up, put her hand on Pavo's cheek, and squeezed. "He doesn't feel fake."

"Risa, don't." He grabbed for her, but she evaded with a backward leap.

"Please watch her. I... can't not know."

He growled. "You're not going alone."

"Does the MDF know the way through the vents?" Anxiety made her bounce on her toes.

Pavo scooped Kree into his arms. "Risa..."

Dad. No... Dad. The emotion in Garrison's eyes before he disappeared from the comm looked too resigned, as if he knew his time was up. She ran to the curb, and a taxi obelisk. Before the automated voice could say, "Thank you for using PubTran," Pavo grabbed her arm and pulled her around to face him.

"No way. We'll make better time in mine."

He dragged her back to his patrol car, pulled the door open, and let Kree slip down. The girl crawled into the back seat. After bodily lifting Risa into the passenger seat, he slammed the door.

Risa dug her fingers into the cushion. Endless attempts to call Garrison's vidphone and NetMini all failed, as did Genevieve's. She tried

Osebi, Lancaster, Ralek, Huang... all went to vidmail without even ringing.

Please... Please... Please... Her head snapped around to the left as Pavo got in. "They're not answering. No one is answering."

Pavo gripped the wheel with a grim, determined stare. The tires squealed as the car whipped around, the rapid turn bouncing Risa off her door. A half-second later, the car got a grip and rocketed forward. She twisted to peer back at Kree huddled in the back seat. The child appeared frightened, but gave her a grateful smile.

Pavo muttered under his breath while plotting a Nav pin for the shuttleport.

"I'm okay," whispered Kree. "Little scared."

Unable to think of anything to say, Risa squeezed her hand and stared at the tiny person peering back over her knees. The tiny person that meant so much to her.

"Can we still go to the park tomorrow?" asked Kree.

"Yes... of course." Risa smiled, despite the tears rolling down her face. She had made a choice, Kree over everyone else that mattered in her life.

She could have peace with that, but not unless she at least *tried* to help them, however futile it might be.

28

BLACK SWAN

The thirty-six-minute flight from Arcadia to Primus may as well have been an eternity. She'd given up her endless rotation of trying to call anyone only after the landing pad came into view. Between Pavo's police ID and the look in her eyes, the flight crew hadn't given them too much of a problem when she got out of her seat before the shuttle touched down. He'd taken an MDF car from the regiment based out of the shuttle terminal, but Risa insisted she could get there faster on foot. Primus City's congested subterranean streets did not tolerate vehicles well. Even in places where the stone had been cut wide enough, too many people and too much junk had clogged them over the decades.

Tears streamed out of the corners of her eyes as she ran through the crowd, ducking large people, shoving smaller ones out of her way, and jumping over the occasional child. She'd spent a few minutes trying to explain to Kree—who did *not* want to be separated from her so soon— why she had to go underground. Still, the agonized look in the girl's dark-blue eyes as she left her with Pavo haunted her the entire way down to Tier 4. Kree's composure finally crumbled when Risa sprinted out of the elevator on Tier 1 and yelled, "watch her."

The farther down she went, the thinner the crowd got. Speedware pushed her to about thirty miles per hour on a dash across the lower reaches of civilization. Fortunately, she only sent one person flying into a window.

Risa slowed as she approached the familiar dead-end alley where the huge ventilation intake offered the best entry to the unpopulated deep tiers. A moan emanated from the waist-high trash as she slogged past it, raking her hands side to side to displace food cartons and cups. One vagrant sat up with a plastic ramen bowl for a hat.

"Spare a couple creds?"

She pulled the vent open. "Bit of a hurry. I'll get ya on the way out."

Eighteen meters in, right turn. Forty-five meters, right turn. Sixteen feet, vertical shaft down. Risa didn't rush to enable any vision modes; she knew this section of duct like the back of her hand. While easing her way down, counting each time her right palm pressed against the cold plastisteel, she activated the Wraith. A weak hum, out of the range of normal hearing, emanated from the little device clinging to her head above her ear.

The grey-on-black world she'd spent five years in returned.

Her boots hit the floor thirty meters below her entry point. In total darkness, the Wraith surrounded her with walls made of shimmery ethereal vapor that shifted around, appearing stronger whenever she moved, fading if she kept still. She dropped to all fours, once more crawling into the life she blamed on the UCF: darkness, tunnels, and bombs.

Already, the stink of NE6 explosive hung in the air, settling on her tongue with the flavor of acidic metal and a trace of dirt. Unfamiliar shapes glided toward her on the floor, things that should not be here. Risa stopped crawling and switched to active IR night vision, which illuminated an opaque wall in front of her.

Smoke, something the Wraith did not 'see.'

Chunks of debris had skittered into the vent; a fragment of black plastic housing, likely from one of the charges, sat near a pile of small rocks. She forced herself onward, clinging to her anger as a lifeline, knowing the second she let go, she'd break down with it. She feared what she'd find in the safehouse... if a safehouse even remained to be found.

Two minutes of crawling later, she headed left at an intersection. After thirteen meters, she slipped into another narrow vertical, which ran the rest of the way down to what would have been Tier 8 had the city not stopped developing. Coughing started as soon as she breathed. She collapsed on her knees in dust too thick to see beyond the length of her arm. IR didn't show her anything but haze, so she switched back to the

Wraith. Grey-on-black ductwork became visible, but the passage she'd once thought of as home looked foreign.

A noticeable twist warped what had once been a sixty-meter-long straightaway connected to an intake duct feeding the safehouse, which ultimately led to Garrison's office. The passage in front of her stopped after only twenty-three meters, according to her targeting system. Dirt and rocks, ranging from pebble to bigger than her skull, had caved in. What little fragments of her childhood she'd hidden there, burned dolls and toys, lay buried out of reach.

No...

She ran over the tunnel map in her memory. At fifteen, she'd gotten General Maris unusually enraged at her ability to sneak past all their sensors unnoticed. He'd ordered Huang to double down. At the time, she lacked the expertise to disable them... so she'd gone around. Risa knew ways into the safehouse that even Maris didn't... though two of them wouldn't work now that she had grown up. The old water mains made for a tight squeeze even at ten.

She climbed up one tier and scurried along another duct to a twelve-foot-square fan chamber. The massive air mover hadn't seen power since probably before she'd been born, and looked no closer to working. A mild contortionist dance got her past a gap in the blades and into a crouch on the soft, springy bed of silt below it. Few things on Mars made Risa's spine lock up from disgust, but stepping barefoot in whatever lived at the bottom of this chamber as a kid had been one of them. Even now, wearing boots, the squishy/springiness of walking on it made her sick—or maybe the heavy feeling in her gut came from nerves.

The shaft ahead was twice as wide as most ducts, but had a low ceiling, forcing her to move in a tight hands-and-knees crawl. She gave serious consideration to repurposing her panties—the only fabric she had—into a face mask given all the dust, but didn't want to waste the time it would take to get them out from under her armor. Instead, she reduced her breaths to shallow sips of air. Even with a Tox Filter in her trachea, she coughed. Her grasping hands found more loose rocks as she dragged herself forward, following a path that would take her into the safehouse vents in a little over a hundred meters. If she remembered correctly, this path would lead to a grille at the right-angle corner in Death Row, where she'd played 'speeware' with Kree and the boys.

Her hope died less than fifty meters later; she expected a vertical descent, but found a solid mass of dirt in the passage. Four times, she grabbed handfuls, refusing to believe what her senses told her. Her father, her 'older sister,' and a crew she'd trust with her life lay somewhere down that shaft, buried under thousands of tons of Martian regolith. Genevieve wouldn't have even been there if not for her.

Risa lowered her forehead to touch her arm, and cried. *It's not fair.*

Minutes later, she quieted, lying limp on the bottom of a ventilation duct seven stories below the surface of Mars. Amid the stillness, Garrison's voice whispered in her memory.

You chose your child over everyone else. That's what a real mother would do.

He didn't sound as though he minded she let him die. She gasped, sniffled, and wiped her face. Every angry thing she'd ever screamed at him came to haunt her in the silent dark. A slow breath filled her throat with the flavor of dirt. *I can't stay here. Kree...*

A pitiful wail echoed in the tunnel. Risa blinked, sure she'd imagined it. When it happened again, she sprang up to all fours.

"Hello?" yelled Risa.

When no response came, she sighed. *It's in my head.*

"Help!" The voice sounded distant... and female.

"Hello? Where are you?" yelled Risa.

"Ri?"

"Gen!" Risa shouted and scrambled forward. "Where are you?"

A weak reply echoed back a few seconds later amid coughing. "Motor pool vent. Trapped. Can't breathe."

"Save your air. I'm coming."

Risa crawled as fast as the tunnel would allow. Burrs and bolts in the wall and ceiling nipped at her back and butt, though couldn't cut the ballistic suit. If Genevieve had gone into the vents from the garage, she'd be in another section of passages one level up. That part was closer to the cave exit and built higher into the underground.

Four minutes later, she emerged in the fan chamber, disregarding the clammy, spongy muck oozing between her fingers, and slithered up past the dead turbine. She climbed onto the blade, bypassing the side channel she'd come in from, and went out an opening in the top. The inter-tier shaft sucked air down from exterior vents, and offered a straight shot up to a surface building. An impractical exit, as too many still-functioning fans blocked the way.

She ascended another eleven meters before slipping into a square lateral duct. Though it offered enough height to duck walk, she opted for a faster crawl. In her head, she visualized the path she'd take if she were trying to leave the safehouse via vent from the garage. After clearing three turns and one short vertical drop, her Wraith picked up motion ahead, rendering it as a grey blur fluttering near the floor.

"Gen?"

"Ri!" Something soft thumped on metal three times. "I'm here! Holy shit. You found me… Help."

Risa crawled forward, ignoring sharp rocks under her hands. Detail crept into the grey form, which solidified into a woman's hand sticking out from between inch-thick square bars. She hustled over and grabbed on.

"Gen!"

"I can't see shit." Genevieve coughed. "Too much dust. What is this?"

Risa looked around, moving her head in a shallow side-to-side bob to keep 'the environment' in motion and visible via the Wraith. Genevieve's upper body stuck out from a pile of dirt that had come down from an opening in the chamber above her. The bars between them were most likely the grille covering fallen off the junction, knocked loose by the avalanche and wedged.

"Gen… you're buried up to your waist. Can you feel your legs?"

"Yeah. I'm fine. I can wiggle my toes and shit. I just can't get this cage out of my way. I hate my luck. Fell in on me. Something heavy slammed into the floor real close to my head."

"Sounds like your luck isn't as bad as you think." Risa let off a nervous laugh. "Pull your hand back. I'm going to cut the bars out."

Genevieve raised her hand, pivoting her right arm at the elbow—the only way she could move.

Risa popped one Nano claw from her right index finger and used it to slice the grille. Lacking the strength to force the Nano blade through a square inch of plastisteel, she resorted to a sawing motion.

When the first bar snapped free, the entire grille moaned and buckled, as if the frame no longer had enough strength to resist being crushed.

"What was that noise?"

"Uhh, nothing." Risa set her claw on the second bar and sawed.

"Ri." Gen grumbled. "Sand hit me in the face. That wasn't nothing. If that damn thing is gonna cave in, you get out of here."

"No. I'm not leaving you. You're only here because of me." Risa sniffled. "I'm not losing anyone else. I'm not having you die on me twice!"

"Oh, no…" Genevieve choked up. "Kree… I'm so sorry."

"She's fine. I mean Garrison and everyone else who was in there. I'm sorry I didn't listen to Everett and just kill that Nur bitch." She grasped her finger in her left hand, dragging the little blade back and forth, gaining a sixteenth of an inch on each motion. "I thought you said you disarmed them."

"Oh, I did. Maris and Garrison decided to demo the safehouse since it was compromised. I rigged the detonators onto one of our control frequencies... only something went wrong and they maybe detonated a wee bit early."

"Great job." Risa smirked, not that Genevieve could see with all the dust... and utter lack of light.

"It wasn't my fault!" Genevieve yelled, sounding like a bratty teen. "C-Branch got back into them somehow and set them off early."

"Gen." Risa stared at a quarter inch of bar remaining and set her boots against the sides of the grille against the wall. "Listen to me carefully. When I cut this bar, there's a damn good chance there's gonna be some more dirt coming down. Stick both of your hands as far forward as you can."

"D-don't risk yourself." Genevieve held her hands out anyway. "I don't wanna die."

"Okay. On three."

Risa kicked on her speedware and cut the last sliver of metal, retracting the blade as she flicked her hand around, seized Genevieve by the wrists, and pulled with her entire body. Her 'older sister' slipped from the dirt mound, flying toward her. Cracks raced around the square frame of the grille; the weight of dirt and rock crushed it closed thirty-two hundredths of a second after Genevieve's boots cleared it. She landed on top of Risa, face to face.

Speedware off.

Genevieve let out a yelp of surprise.

Dirt continued to seep into the tunnel, covering them both up to the knees.

"Aurelia's going to be jealous." Risa wrapped her arms around Genevieve and squeezed.

"Eww. You're like my kid sister. That's wrong in every way imaginable."

Risa couldn't tell if she comforted Gen or clung to her like a little girl in need of an older sibling. Genevieve, trembling, returned the enthusiastic embrace.

"Ri, can I make a suggestion?"

"Yeah." Risa sniffled.

"I just spent the past… oh, hour praying to six different major religious figures that I don't die down here."

"But sane people don't believe in that stuff…"

"Beside the point. Anyone is ready to believe in something when there's forty tons of dirt about to fall on their head. Look. My suggestion? We shouldn't stay here. This whole place is about to come down."

Risa squirmed over onto all fours. "Crap."

"Already did."

"Ugh."

"Kidding," Genevieve tried to laugh but wound up choking on dust. "Can you see?" A hand grasped Risa's left butt cheek.

"Hey," said Risa. "What happened to sisters?"

"I can't see a damn thing." She squeezed. "Leg?"

"Ass."

"Oops." Genevieve slid her hand up and grabbed Risa's belt. "Sorry."

"Follow me."

Risa crawled forward, retracing her route. She dropped into the fan chamber, balanced on the blades, and reached up. "Air pump room. Lower yourself slow."

Genevieve rotated to descend boots first. Risa started to guide her down, but Genevieve let out a startled cry and lost her grip. A butt to the face knocked Risa over. She fell backward, landing draped over two sections of fan. An instinctual activation of speedware allowed Risa the reaction time to get an arm up and prevent Genevieve's skull from smashing into her teeth. Still, she crashed down on top of Risa, driving the edge of a fan blade into her upper back.

For a moment, they both lay still, gasping for air.

"You missed your calling. You should've become a ballerina." Risa winced.

"Ow." Genevieve groaned in pain. "Nah, I'm too graceful for ballet."

"Can you move?"

Genevieve squirmed. "Yeah, but I can't see."

Risa guided her off the fan to the chamber floor and dropped down next to her. After crawling a few feet into the horizontal duct, she stopped. "How many died?"

"I don't know. We didn't have a lot of time to move, but they'd already started evacuating when they thought I'd gotten control."

"Did the kids…?" Risa choked up.

"They're okay. Garrison sent them out with Osebi before I even got there. He made a big deal of announcing he wanted them going on a 'camping trip' to learn some survival skills so it looked normal. He'd been hoping C-Branch didn't care about missing them. Hell, the way he talked, even I almost believed we weren't in any danger."

Risa chuckled. *Yeah... Garrison's a good liar.* She sighed. "I hate spies."

"Me too."

Everything rumbled and shook.

Genevieve screamed and lurched forward in a panic. Risa took the hint and crawled for a few seconds with a hand pushing on her butt. A tremendous onrush of dust and silt blasted over them from behind on a short but powerful wind.

"Okay, okay." Risa coughed and spat out dirt. "I'm going as fast as I can."

Risa decided to change course, heading for another common feeder duct that would take them all the way up to Tier 2, a faster path than the one she'd followed in. Oddly enough, she thought of the vagrant who tried begging from her. *Poor guy, he's gonna be waiting on me for a while.*

Nine minutes of crawling and climbing later, Genevieve gasped. "I see light ahead."

"That's an intake. Maintenance workers go in there sometimes, so it's got lights."

Risa switched the Wraith off, returning to night vision, and headed for the near-blinding orb. Dust still swirled in the air, but not enough to blot out her ability to see. After crawling for a little while longer, she pushed open a grille and peered into a giant vertical shaft large enough to house a cargo elevator: the primary air intake.

Intense wind from above whipped her hair around and forced her to squint. A howling gale tore down past her, swallowing any effort to talk short of screaming. The opposite wall ranged at ten meters. She peered up at the shaft, lit every ten meters by a brilliant glow, LED bricks turned into small dying stars by her night vision. The way up looked clear, and even had a ladder for maintenance workers. Risa switched to standard vision, turned around, and backed in boots first, stretching one leg to the ladder. When Genevieve climbed after her, Risa eased herself lower.

"No pressure, but there's a thirty-meter fall if you lose your grip," shouted Risa.

"Thanks." Genevieve wobbled onto the ladder, putting all her weight on her right foot. Char and smears of black grease covered her dull-red fatigues, as well as her breathing mask. Blood ran in trails down her face from a scalp cut. Four bloodstains decorated her left leg.

"Shit, you're hurt." Risa patted her on the calf twice to get her attention, and yelled the same thing again.

"I've had better days, but I'm good. Little banged up is all." Genevieve heaved a grunt and climbed.

The wind grew stronger the higher they went. Risa huddled close to the ladder, jumping whenever a piece of plasfilm or an empty take-out carton drifted by. Anything light enough for the ventilation system to inhale often wound up collecting in a fan chamber somewhere. Primus City's ducts offered plenty of things for an orphan to make a nest out of. She didn't like how Gen favored her left leg, but her heart ached for Garrison. If the tunnels collapsed that high up, the whole safehouse had to be caved in. Without heavy equipment, she'd never get to anyone… and even if she had a digging machine, she'd be recovering bodies.

Silent tears of grief ran down her face; only the worry Gen might lose her strength and fall kept her from giving in and sobbing. She kept close, ready to catch her 'big sister' if she fell. Every rung seemed a great exertion, and after thirty feet, Genevieve started taking short breaks between each step. Long minutes passed in the deafening howl. She didn't waste energy on talking until they drew close to Tier 2 and she spotted a door above them marked with yellow and black diagonal stripes and a small square window.

"There," yelled Risa.

Genevieve clamped on to the ladder and peered down at the pointing finger, then up to the door. She shuddered and climbed five more rungs, pausing to catch her breath after the last one. Eventually, she reached up and slapped a red rubber-covered button on a wall panel. Flashing amber lights erupted, filling the tunnel with blinking. The overbearing downblast of wind died off. Genevieve pushed the door open and stumbled through, favoring her left leg, before collapsing on the floor of a hallway.

Risa leapt in behind her. A man in a grey jumpsuit bearing a PCMA logo emerged from an office a short distance ahead. He pointed a pistol at them, looking more annoyed than afraid.

"This is a restricted area. On the floor. Now!"

"I already am, asshole," said Genevieve.

"There's been a collapse," said Risa, gesturing at the thick layer of dust on both of them. "We're trying to survive, not break in."

The man hesitated for a moment, but put his weapon away. "Where was the collapse? I didn't hear anything."

"Tier 11." Risa pulled Genevieve to her feet. "Can you stand? Walk?"

"Yeah, yeah. I'm exhausted. Lying down seemed like a great idea."

"Tier 11? What on Mars were you doing that far down? Those tunnels aren't even finished." His hand drifted closer to his sidearm.

"That gun comes out of the holster again, I'm going to beat forty points of IQ out of you with it." Risa put an arm around Genevieve and helped her forward. "I'm not at liberty to discuss what's going on. All you need to know is this is a military operation."

"Oh, yeah, like I haven't heard that before."

Speedware on.

Risa closed the distance to the guard, yanked the pistol off the man's belt, and aimed it at his forehead in about one real-time second. No trace of reaction to her motion showed in his expression until after she turned off the boost. His fingers grabbed at empty nylon.

"Gah!" He jumped back.

She pivoted the gun sideways and held it up. "Look familiar?"

"Fuck." He put a hand on his chest, gasping for air. "Okay, okay, fine. I believe you."

Risa tossed his weapon back to him. She helped Genevieve up, supporting her on the walk to the end of the corridor, and a door that led out onto the street. Above, a bland white holographic sign read: Primus City Municipal Authority.

"How did a hand trick convince him you were military?" Genevieve snickered, then winced from pain.

"Punks don't have boosts like that." Risa opened a vid call to Pavo, who answered in one ring. <Hey.>

<Shit. I've been trying to call you... no signal.> Pavo wiped his forehead.

Behind him in the image, Kree leapt between the two front seats of an MDF car. <Mommy!>

Warmth bloomed in Risa's chest. <Hi sweetie. I'm okay. I'm coming back now. I'm going to the Tier 2 Mall, medical pavilion. Genevieve got banged up a bit.>

<Meet you there,> said Pavo.

<See you soon. I love you both.> Risa forced herself to end the call. "Come on. Little walking."

Risa went to the right, guiding Genevieve among a thick crowd of people, none of whom seemed to notice or care that they looked like refugees from a war zone. Genevieve pulled the mask down from her face and spat dark grey. Her limp seemed to worsen as they went on.

At the end of the next sector, they emerged on a huge subterranean passage. The corridor, as wide as a six-lane highway, carried a smattering of vehicle traffic as well as hundreds of people moving in and out of the various storefronts on either side. The scarcity of cars allowed people to saunter back and forth across the road at will.

"Oh, that smells awesome." Genevieve leaned towards a place named 'Q-Gasm.' A holographic pig in a cowboy hat held a plate of baby back ribs in one hand, and barbecue chicken in the other. She reached at it like an infant demanding a bottle. "Want. Food. Now."

Risa pushed her forward. "After you get patched up. I promise. I'll even pay. Least I can do."

Genevieve overacted being upset, but surrendered to insistent pushing. They walked for another few minutes until the street widened into a great courtyard in the general shape of a plus sign. The Tier 2 Mall's western end had a multi-leveled effect with several garden platforms. Benches and pseudo-plants sat on one side, a food court on the other, and a walk path threaded through the middle around obelisks containing electronics that put on a virtual tour of the building and history of Primus.

Total tourist magnet.

A few families meandered along the trail, shadowed by holographic AI tour guides in dark-violet tunics with a row of buttons down the middle, who narrated about life in the early days during the initial construction. Secundus City had a similar attraction. The people who dug these cities out sure were proud of themselves. As a child, Risa had thought the tour guides to be some kind of monks. One of the other street kids had convinced her they were magic, and would beat her up if she did something wrong. Of course, 'magic' had meant holographic, which also meant appearing out of thin air and scaring the hell out of nine-year-old Risa.

Motion drew her glance to a well-dressed man in a soft cloth hat walking toward her. A thin face, silver goatee, and bushy eyebrows gave her the impression of a university professor or some other intellectual type. The way his body filled in under a blue satin Chinese-inspired shirt didn't fit the way his face looked. Bodybuilder chest, intelligent face, impossible man. *Damn guides.*

"Thanks, we're not tourists."

He placed a solid hand on her shoulder.

She froze for a second, then glared at him. "Back off."

"Risa..." He lifted his grey caterpillar eyebrows a quarter-inch. "Don't you remember me?"

Genevieve pointed. "Bench... Good."

She stared at him. A haunting specter of familiarity danced around, but refused to land on her brain. "I... no, not really."

"I'm sorry I never got you that doll."

Scenery behind him seemed to drag itself away while the man drifted closer to her. The ambient sound of people milling about faded to a warbling rush like a waterfall. She gazed into his eyes; her mind peeled away the years from his face, and a cloud of fire engulfed him from behind. A man's scream reverberated at the edge of memory. The scream she had dreamed every night for years.

Dad? She blinked hard. *No. Andriy.*

He smiled. "You remember."

"You're dead."

"News to me." He smiled.

"Andriy." Risa pushed Genevieve behind her, and took on a protective posture. "What the hell do you want? How... how are you even still alive?"

He clasped his hands behind his back. "I know you've been lied to constantly for many years. What I'm about to tell you is going to sound unbelievable, but that is exactly what *they* want." He looked down, pursed his lips, and fired a sharp exhale out his nostrils. "I am Colonel Darren Black. The man you know as Garrison is an ACC special operations soldier by the name of Andriy Voronin."

Risa's eyes flared wide. "I don't believe you. You're Andriy... you somehow got out alive."

"I'm sorry, hon. I would've made contact sooner, but I wasn't able to get through the Front's damnable tight net. Voronin is part of the same operation as Lars Staanek. Why do you think 'Garrison' got the charge from Heitzenroeder? They're all working together."

"But." She pointed at him. "But..." She jabbed her finger in the air at him and huffed, unable to come up with anything to say.

"Your mother may not be dead either." Colonel Black stared at a square LED light overhead, pain clear in his eyes. "When you were two, she left you with me while undertaking an assignment to infiltrate Bliss. C-Branch had been grooming Andriy to be a defector for months. He used his position in their intelligence community to gather valuable secrets. Her mission was to extract him from enemy territory. Something went wrong. He made it out, but she never did."

Risa shook in her boots. *D-did I kill my mother when Bliss went up? No...*

"I'll be over here." Genevieve stumbled a few feet to the side off the shiny silver walkway, stepped over the curving light band at the edge, and flopped onto a cushioned bench. "Ooh. Yeah. This is much softer than pointy rocks."

Colonel Black folded his arms. "It didn't take Andriy very long to realize that the woman he believed to be Marissa Donnelly didn't really love him. Once he knew he was a mere 'assignment,' he came after me. That little fire show you had a front row seat for was a simple case of petty jealousy."

Risa's legs wanted to give out. As much as she didn't want to—*couldn't* —believe what she was hearing, her somatic response system didn't pick up even the smallest trace of deceit. All the lines, graphs, and fluctuating meters around his head showed truth.

"W... what about Genevieve? Was that a lie too?"

Colonel Black shook his head. "The sabotaged device was not targeted at Genevieve personally. They intended indiscriminate disruption of the MLF operations. However, because she was so beloved by everyone down there, the attack which they all believed to have killed her backfired. It cemented resolve and made the Front stronger rather than weakening it... so they did not repeat the process. At least not until you took out that bio weapons facility. Fortunately, Pavo's a lot better at demolitions than anyone expected. He fixed the unit before planting it on that Cryomil tank."

"Dustblow. Garrison wouldn't have knowingly sent me on a mission with a bad detonator. He... loved me." *He's down there under all that rock.* Two tears raced each other down her cheeks.

"I suppose it may be possible." The colonel reached up and picked a crumb out of the inner corner of his right eye. "The man no doubt took a great deal of pleasure in stealing Serena's daughter. To take from her what she refused to give him."

Risa squeezed fingernails into her palms inside shaking fists. "Why are you telling me this?"

"I still have a few loyal friends in C-Branch." Colonel Black smiled. "We don't believe Andriy was killed in the demolition operation. He's still out there somewhere, and we *need* you. You can get close to him. He would never expect I've made contact with you. It may be that he even believes his assassins succeeded in killing me. I've spoken with General Everett. He's agreed to give you what you want. A clean slate. New life. Even a pension if you want it. Use your advantage. Get close to Andriy, and take him out."

Risa's brain chewed on the words. As unlikely as it seemed, her soma indicated she should believe this man. She contemplated how angry she might be if she confronted Garrison with this truth and he admitted it. His sad expression, the same one he'd given her every time she got a new piece of cyberware or hurled insults at him, formed in her thoughts.

She visualized the look on his face in the infirmary, once the shock had worn off.

"I can't." Risa looked away. "I don't care."

"Sorry?" Colonel Black raised an eyebrow. "Did you say you don't care?"

"That's exactly what I said." She locked stares. "It doesn't matter who he is. I know he's my biological father. Hannah ran the test right in front of us."

Colonel Black grasped his chin and rubbed his goatee. "Poor girl. That's rather underhanded of them. Do you honestly believe Garrison to be your father? Doesn't that strike you as a little too good to be true?"

Dozens of moments replayed in her mind of the way Garrison had been throughout the years. If he didn't know he was her father, he'd sure hoped. "I don't believe you."

"Think about it." He glanced to his left, tracking the motion of a curvy blonde in a bikini top walking past stores on an elevated terrace one story up. "You had a test run on an electronic device by a medtech who is in the employ of C-Branch. Do you not think they can make it say whatever they want?"

No... no. She suppressed a tremble. Her eyes tingled from tears fighting to emerge.

"Your entire life has been defined by your concept of having a father. When you learned General Everett's version of the truth, your reason for serving the MLF evaporated. You were no longer useful to them. Giving you the father you always wanted was their way to control you." He put a hand on her shoulder. "I know it's difficult to accept, but your real father did not die in that apartment sixteen years ago. I'm right here."

She lifted her head to make eye contact. Her gut wanted to run to Garrison and cry, but her brain twisted over the logic. The somatic system still showed zero indicators of falsehood. "I… don't know if I can kill him."

Colonel Black let his arm drop to his side. "There is not much of a window of opportunity. He will make contact soon. When he does, you must do what needs to be done. For Mars. For the UCF. For the people."

Her gaze dropped. The thought of killing Garrison so close to her readiness to murder Tamashī felt like a cybernetic hand squeezing her heart. *So much deception.* She looked up again, hoping to find some trace of untruth in his expression. *I can't do this. But what if he's right? What if Garrison is Andriy? No. It can't be. You can't fake something like that.* She pictured herself at nine or ten, sitting in Garrison's lap after he'd wedged himself into the vent and crawled to her sanctuary. Rather than try to drag her out, he'd spent two hours in there reading to her.

She stared up at blurry overhead lights; closing eyelids forced out a waterfall of sorrow.

Risa, said the voice of Raziel. *The man before you lies.*

Rage exploded in her chest. Time slammed to a stop. Before Colonel Black could twitch, Risa swiped a handful of Nano claws through his throat. The stroke of her arm happened as a reflex, faster than conscious thought. A noticeable hesitation in the cut struck her as strange. *The spine's too hard.* For two seconds to her perception, no noticeable sign of injury appeared, then milk-white fluid seeped out of four slices. One second later, it sprayed like a fountain from the stump of a neck. His head tumbled in slow motion; Colonel Black had been fast. He'd managed to look startled before she'd taken his head off. If he'd expected an attack, he may have even been boosted enough to duck.

The body fell to its knees, wobbled a second, and collapsed backward.

Risa glared at the twitching body and the pool of white artificial blood expanding out behind him. Glowing rectangles shined on the surface, a reflection from lights overhead.

A fucking synthetic… No wonder the soma didn't pick up the lies. Who would bother making an artificial version of Andriy? Her throat tightened. *Or was Andriy a synth all along?* Before her thoughts could fall down that particular bottomless pit, a bright dot settled on her chest.

She whirled to the right and jumped back. Six thin luminous lines converged on her out of a sea of oblivious shoppers and sightseers, infrared targeting systems invisible to the naked eye, but detected by her electronics. From between an elderly couple, a man in a dark coat advanced out of the crowd. He knocked the old man down with an elbow shove and pointed a rifle in her direction. Risa flung herself into the air, a sideways flying tackle that took Genevieve over the bench. The redhead's mouth hung open in her normal time state, the first breath of a scream at the decapitation of the synthetic.

They hit the ground amid a cluster of bushes. Bullets slid by in the air overhead, followed by a quartet of orange laser pulses, which melted a channel into the bench where Genevieve had been under a second ago.

Risa drew one of her pistols while dragging her 'sister' up against the base of a wide metal planter box holding a tree. Demonic wails and growls rose from every direction, the effect of accelerated perception on terrified tourists only now reacting to the gunfire.

While half of her brain focused on aiming her laser pistol, the other half hunted for targets. She peeked around the edge of the box and spotted a man in civilian-normal clothes stationary against the tide of fleeing people.

She pushed her speedware to the limit and popped up in a world suspended in time. A bullet as big around as her index finger crawled past her arm. She raised her pistol and lined up the virtual crosshair with the man's heart. The targeting computer in her head estimated overpenetration, and drew a line out from the man's back, which entered the face of a little boy being carried by his mother. Risa changed angles, putting a laser blast into the man's right shin, two inches below the knee; the beam continued into the floor behind him.

Wirepaths in her muscles heated, but she kept the speedware pegged and turned sideways to allow another bullet to spiral past her chest. The man she shot reacted at long last to the hit and crumpled forward and to the side. Risa moved her aim point over his head; the nanosecond empty spaces between the tangle of shoppers behind him lined up to give her a clear shot, she fired.

A streak of emerald light connected the clear tip of her Hotaru-6's barrel to the man's cheek, a finger's width below the eye, and traced over the head of a tween girl a few paces behind him, who had been dragged off her feet by a man trying to pull her out of the path of bullets. The child hung suspended in midair, half-wrapped in her protector's arm. The laser continued between the astride legs of a sprinting woman, threaded the needle through the crook of the arm of a teenage boy, who had twisted around to watch the show, and fizzled into the wall of a consumer electronics store.

The beam winked out, its quarter-second pulse glowing for almost three to her. Steaming blood shot out of two small holes in the man's head. Risa flung herself to the ground fast enough to change a crippling shot from a laser to a grazing pass on the crown of her hip.

She landed on her back next to Genevieve. Gritting her teeth, Risa picked at a narrow strip of exposed skin where the laser melted a narrow slash into her ballistic suit. She stifled a scream. *Shit, that burns.* Her speedware throttled back to protect her nerves from damage. A brief mental command activated a tactical map, displaying the estimated position of six more hostiles in an approximate horseshoe around her.

"Did you just seriously cut that guy's head off?" Genevieve went to sit up, but Risa pulled her down. "Why am I on the ground?"

"Ambush," yelled Risa over the sound of a panicking crowd.

More bullets and laser blasts kicked dirt out of the two-foot-tall planter. She head-dialed Pavo. The electronic ring dragged down to a noise like giant kettle cauldrons bouncing down stairs. The combat analysis computer ramped up her speedware as the hostile contact on the far-right tip of the horseshoe came sprinting around.

She looked to her left and up; a skinny platinum blonde in a white bikini top and wraparound skirt ran across the elevated platform past small tables of abandoned food. The woman's rifle had a clear plug for a barrel tip. Oversized octagonal sunglasses glimmered with orange light, a combat visor disguised as tourist wear. The too-beautiful woman aimed to the side as she sprinted, training her laser rifle on Risa. At the sight of it, the stinging wound on her hip flared.

Bitch.

No innocent targets posed a risk behind the woman on the second story. The upward angle would send any misses into the rock ceiling. She rolled away from Genevieve as another bright orange beam connected the woman's rifle to the ground behind her. Risa raised both pistols and put two shots into the woman's chest. Emerald streaks flickered in the air, hanging for a hundredth of a second drawn out to feel like two. The assassin's run became a fall, and she crashed into four tables, landing out of sight on the floor of the upper patio. An explosion of milky white liquid spattered the storefront behind her.

More Synths? What's going on? Her mind raced with panic. The ACC feared synths, and as far as she knew, wouldn't use them. *C-Branch? Mingtiān?*

Another hostile contact on the opposite side advanced a second behind the downed female synthetic. Already, three bullets cruised toward Genevieve. Risa rolled to her right and covered her 'sister,' putting herself in the path of all three slugs while raising her pistol out over her head. A floating targeting reticle did not require sighting over the weapon; she traced laser blasts into his chest, neck, and nose. The man spun into a death whirl, spraying boiling blood in a wide arc.

Three wads of lead crushed into the material of her ballistic suit.

One struck her left shoulder, another skidded down her back and slapped to a halt along the upper curve of her butt with the force of a heavy punch, and the third slug Charlie-horsed her in the back of the right thigh. A gelatinous layer sandwiched inside her suit hardened in microseconds, preventing penetration.

For a second and three-quarters, small areas became tougher than steel.

<I'm almost there,> said Pavo, sounding far too calm.

She screamed in pain, both over the head comm as well as aloud.

<Shit! What's going on?> yelled Pavo.

<Ambush. I'm pinned down,> wheezed Risa. <Four unknown hostiles.>

Genevieve helped herself to Risa's second Hotaru, pulling it out of the harness. "Who's shooting at us?" In the 'idle' phase of Risa's speedware, her voice sounded two octaves low.

Ngh. Ow. She winced, unable to decide if she wanted to grab her shoulder or brace her backside. She yelled again when Genevieve plucked the bullet off the small of her back. *That's a bruise.*

<I don't like those noises. How bad are you hurt?> asked Pavo.

<Left shoulder might be cracked. Bunch of bruises. Small laser burn on my hip. I think the suit's melted to my skin. That's gonna hurt coming off.>

The not-too-distant sound of squealing tires made her smile, despite the fusillade of bullets slapping into the ground and gouging the plastisteel on both sides. A constant pelting of planting soil, splinters, and leaf bits rained on her.

They're not trying to hit me; they're trying to keep me still.

Expecting a hand grenade, or something equally excessive, Risa pushed Genevieve down, maximized her speedware boost, and sprang upright.

Headlight glare flashed behind a guy in a blue-and-white Hawaiian shirt, pink Bermuda shorts, and sandals over white socks. He stood next to the kind of enormous bag carried by awkward tourists who pack enough gear for a ten-day safari when taking a four-hour walkabout. Except, rather than sandwiches to feed fifty, he'd brought an over-the-shoulder rocket launcher. Two 60mm 'soda can' missiles pointed at her. He flashed the kind of placid 'I win' smile that made her want to rip off his testicles.

Pavo's patrol car slammed into him from behind a half-second before he fired, raising the trajectory of his missile such that it went high, cruising over the planter box instead of hitting the ground right behind it. Risa swayed to the right, cringing out of the way of the snub-nosed rocket spewing acrid fumes and fire. Four seconds later to her perception, it exploded far enough behind her not to be a threat.

Brilliant orange flashed in every reflective surface around the courtyard.

Risa righted herself, staring down the length of a smoke trail at the black windshield of an armored maroon car with a flashing blue MDF light bar on the roof. Launched by the impact, the man who'd fired the missile crashed through the tree and bushes, landing face down close enough to kiss Genevieve on the head. Risa raised her pistol, and shot him point blank in the back.

Five times.

Pavo's little floating apparition growled. The patrol car door opened; he dove out and kicked it closed. All the civilians had fled at this point, leaving only three remaining hostiles. He opened fire with an assault laser rifle on the two on the right. Rapid streaks of dark-crimson light flickered, chasing a pair of armed men behind benches.

A tiny hand waved from inside the dark vehicle.

"Pavo!" screamed Risa. "What the hell are you doing? Is Kree in that car?"

"She's perfectly safe. The thing is armored. Nothing they have can touch it."

"They have a missile launcher!" shouted Risa.

Pavo glanced at her for a second, then resumed firing off to his left. "Which is on the ground in front of you."

Risa shrieked as the man on the opposite side of the car from Pavo riddled it with bullets on full automatic. Sparks snapped and danced off the armor plating, shredding the emergency lights, but failed to scratch even the windows. Kree dropped out of sight inside the car. Pavo whirled around and fired a short burst over the roof. A puff of bloody steam spat in two thin trails from either side of the attacker's arm. The man grabbed the wound and collapsed behind cover.

Pavo fired at random into the area where the man hid. "Shit. Only winged him."

Nine more MDF cars converged at the archway where the western strut of the Tier 2 Mall met the central terrace. They screeched to a halt, doors flew open, and a crimson-clad army sprang out. Seconds later, an intense barrage of laser fire from eighteen Defense Force officers chewed up the silvery plastisteel benches and planter boxes by where the last two had taken cover. The man Pavo clipped risked popping up to take a shot, and went down in a hail of bright-orange and dark-red lasers.

Pavo's voice came over a loudspeaker. "This is the Mars Defense Force. You are under arrest. Drop your weapons and step into view with your hands in plain sight. You have four seconds to comply."

Two near-simultaneous gunshots launched gore into the air.

"Clear," yelled an unknown woman.

Risa swallowed hard. She glanced down at the pistols she clutched, realizing she'd sat there and watched the last few seconds of the fight play out without doing anything. The odd feeling of being 'saved' made her laugh. Motion from laughing burned on her hip.

"Ri," wheezed Genevieve. "Is Aura out there?"

"I don't know. I'm not into that new-age stuff."

"Jackass." Genevieve closed her eyes and cringed, despite chuckling. "If she is, I'm going to tear her armor off right here."

"You need medical—"

Boom. A series of rapid rippling *clacks* followed the roar of an explosion.

Risa snapped her head up.

Pavo sailed backward through the air, smoke peeling from the front of his body. He crashed onto the bare plastisteel floor tiles and skidded for another six meters before halting, motionless.

Risa let out an unintelligible scream, the product of her brain trying to combine 'no' and 'Pavo' into one sound. She leapt the planter box into a full fortyish-mile-per-hour dash, covering the distance to where he'd landed in seconds. Other than his face hiding behind an intact helmet, the charred, bloody armor looked too much like what she'd seen in that room when she thought she'd found his body. One-inch square metal bits stuck to where they'd partially melted into his chestplate.

She collapsed over him, bawling.

Other figures in MDF armor gathered around him. One man yelled something about the suspects having implanted bombs, ordering the others to stay away from anything dead.

Risa grabbed at his helmet, twisting and yanking on it in a futile effort to open it. Tears rendered the world into a total blur. She gave up on the helmet and pounded her fist into his chest, yelling, "No!" four times before succumbing to sobs.

"Stop being an asshole," said Aurelia.

Risa froze, sniffled, and leaned back to look up at an armored woman. "W-what?"

"Not you. Him." Aurelia kicked him in the leg. "His vitals are fine. He's being an asshole."

Pavo groaned. "Huh? What?"

The gore all over him belonged to someone else.

"Or, maybe it knocked him loopy." Aurelia took a knee and hit a tiny button on the side of his helmet that caused the faceplate to open.

A little blood trickled out between Pavo's teeth. "Oh, hey." He coughed. "Damn, I love this armor."

Risa fell on him, hugging, crying with elation, and not wanting to ever let go of him.

"How'd I wind up on the floor?" asked Pavo. His breath smelled like smoke.

"LADs," said Aurelia. "That shithead blew up when his heart stopped… and you were too close."

"Last act of defiance," muttered Genevieve. "At least"—she coughed into her fist—"that's the unofficial name for those implants." She fell into Aurelia's arms. "I wanna do you right here."

"Medic," yelled Risa, then muttered, "For all three of us."

Pavo raised his hand, pointing at the ceiling. "I second that."

A dull *whump* came from the far side of the square, seconds before a rain of smoking electronics and melting plastic 'flesh' pelted the area.

"Stay away from the bodies," barked a man. "Medical unit's three minutes out."

The fast pattering of small bare feet on metal ground grew louder.

"What idiot brought a child to a gunfight?" asked an unknown man.

Kree ran over and leapt onto Risa.

"That would be this idiot," said Aurelia, pointing at Pavo. She picked Genevieve up as if to carry her over the threshold. "You, young lady, are going to the med center."

"Hey," wheezed Genevieve, pointing at Risa. "You owe me 'cue."

"Right." Risa pulled Kree and Pavo close. "As soon as I can move."

Pavo grunted, sat up, and kissed her. "You're bleeding."

Stinging pain in her hip worsened. "So are you."

He licked at his upper lip. "Yeah, I s'pose I am."

Risa squeezed Kree and Pavo tight, no longer able to hold back her need to cry for Garrison.

29

RETIREMENT PLAN

F ive blue dragons flew in formation against dark clouds lit by intermittent flashes of lightning on a 130-inch screen. The new holo-bar synthesized fragrances as well, making the living room smell like rain, ozone, and someone's best guess at a fire-breathing lizard's breath. Risa, in a white tee and sweat pants, sat at the left end of the couch with her bare feet tucked under a pillow to her right. Kree lay at her side, resting her head on Risa's thigh. She hadn't bothered changing out of her pajamas, a soft powder-blue top and pants covered with cartoon vampire bunnies. Stretched out, the child rested her heels on Pavo's leg. Tamashī sprawled in the middle of the floor on her stomach like a teenager, swinging her pink-socked feet back and forth.

Pavo had one arm across the seatback, close enough for his hand to occasionally tease at Risa's hair. He'd taken full advantage of finally getting a day off, skipping both shower and 'outerwear.' He lounged in charcoal-grey sweat shorts and tank top, a synthbeer in his fingers, dangled over the armrest.

Genevieve sat on the loveseat to Pavo's right, jumping and clinging to Aurelia at scary parts in the video, even ones Kree didn't bat an eyelash at. This, of course, caused Pavo to joke she was the youngest in the room. Aurelia laughed; Genevieve replied with a raspberry. The two of them had been as giddy as schoolgirls since making 'the announcement.' *They* were pregnant. Each carried an embryo consisting of their own egg fertilized with genetic material constructed from the other's DNA. In essence, both were mother to the embryo they carried and father to the other.

Pavo made a lame joke that humanity had no further use for men, argument bait Risa, Genevieve, Aurelia, and Tamashī all refused to bite on. Granted, two men could also have a child via a similar process with the help of an artificial womb in the med center.

On the giant holo-panel, the dragon flight circled a castle built into the peak of an impossibly high mountain, bombarding it with streams of blue fire. Men and women riding them either held on for dear life or added magical spells to the attack, streamers of scintillating blue (lightning) or red (fire). Risa hadn't been paying enough attention to the vid to understand who they were or why the dragons tried to chew on each other; she'd spent more time watching Kree's reaction. The child thrust her arms into the air and kicked her feet into Pavo's leg in an alternating jackhammer motion when one of the castle towers broke off and fell into a deep fog-filled chasm.

"Monwyn's gonna save the prince!" Kree squealed.

A *ping* came from the door.

Risa's chest constricted. She looked around for a weapon.

"Want me to get it?" asked Pavo.

"I'm fine." She grasped Kree's shoulders and lifted her to sit upright. "Be right back."

The front door, across the living room from the small sofa, stood in perfect view of everyone. She held back the worry of what might wait outside and padded up to the console. At one finger's touch, a hologram of the hallway appeared at eye level.

A white and red delivery bot bearing the logo of 'Q-Gasm' hovered outside.

"Oh." *I am an idiot.* She slouched, giggling. "It's the food." Her smile ran off. *It could be a bomb. Damn you, Shiro. Why did you have to say that?*

Tamashī paused the movie and switched to a net station playing a kid-safe game show involving a real-life recreation of a platform jumping game. Ion suits let people leap as though gravity didn't apply to them.

Risa pushed the door open button. The wondrous fragrance of barbecue sauce filled the outer hallway. A white-haired man from two apartments over stared at the bot as he passed, sniffing. He had his NetMini out after three steps.

Risa laughed. The bot dropped off a massive red-and-white striped box, which Risa carried in and set on the coffee table. Beneath the 'Q-Gasm' logo, a faux yellow warning label jokingly cautioned that the contents were considered legally addictive. Inside, one large bucket of chicken and two of baby back ribs, one regular and one with 'Nashville hot wildfire' sauce.

Kree scrunched her nose. "What's a Nashville?"

"I dunno," said Genevieve. "Maybe some mythological creature?"

"You both need to go to school." Pavo shook his head. "It's a prewar location in what used to be the United States. Badlands now."

"I knew that," said Tamashī in sing-song.

Risa rolled her eyes. *Earth. Who cares?* "What does that have to do with hot sauce?"

Pavo shrugged. "I dunno. Maybe just a catchy name? Lots of places name stuff after the old world. Some kinda retro thing."

Aurelia fished out smaller buckets of mashed potatoes and another full of little yellow bits.

"Those peas don't look right," said Risa.

Genevieve threw a pillow at her. "That's because it's *corn.*"

After fetching plates from the kitchen, Risa handed them out and helped herself to two pieces of chicken, a glop of the mash, and a small 'test portion' of corn. Tamashī loaded up a plate with ribs and sat cross-legged by the end of the coffee table; Kree scooted to the floor and knelt next to her, gnawing on a rib. After a few minutes, their faces had more sauce on them than the food.

Risa glanced at Pavo out of the corner of her eye, and winked. He smiled. Aurelia held up some ribs and licked them in a suggestive manner while giving Genevieve a meaningful look. Since Kree had moved to the floor and couldn't see, Risa traced her tongue around the end of a drumstick while making the same face at Pavo. He shifted.

All the adults laughed.

Kree looked back, confused. When no explanation was offered, she frowned, and went back to gnawing on a bone. "You guys are weird."

For about twenty minutes, Risa felt... normal.

Doorbell.

She jumped again.

You'll always be looking over your shoulder, said Shiro's voice.

"Die in a fire," she muttered.

"Uhh." Pavo fidgeted. "What...?"

"Not you. I got it." She jumped up, holding her barbecue-sauce-covered hands up like a surgeon as she walked across the living room. An elbow tap on the console turned on the camera. "Who is it?"

The figure outside resembled a vagrant; shredded green coat, loose fatigue pants, unshaven, hands in his pockets and gaze down. *He probably smelled it from outside. Oh, whoa, did that dude from the vent track me down for the money I promised him?* Risa glanced back at the buckets, and sighed. Before she could offer him food, he looked up at the camera.

Garrison, slightly charred.

Risa yelped, and mashed her sauce-covered hand on the console. She dove into him, wrapped her arms around, and made a noise into his shoulder halfway between screaming and cheering. The scent of metallic soil and burned cloth filled her nose.

"Hey, Bit."

She squeezed hard and took a step back. Relief and anger got into a catfight on her face. "I... thought you were dead."

"Oh, wow," muttered Tamashī.

"I'm sorry. I would've made contact sooner, but..." He walked in. "I had to go into a comm blackout until they assessed the level of threat remaining after that assassination attempt."

"I'm still not sure I believe it came from the ACC. I didn't think they allowed synthetics to exist." Risa walked to the kitchen. "Sit. I'll grab you a plate."

"Only ones they make and can control. They're not sentient. Wash your hands while you're in there." Garrison approached the couch, but didn't sit.

"They do that on purpose." Tamashī licked sauce from her fingers and picked up another rib. "Use synthetics so people think it's *not* the ACC."

Garrison smiled at her. "You didn't tell me Kree's got a sister."

"That's Tamashī," said Risa.

He blinked in disbelief. "I thought she was... quite a bit older."

Tamashī stuck out her tongue, then giggled.

Risa hurried to the sink, rinsed the sauce from her hands, and returned with a clean plate for him.

Garrison reached into his green military jacket and pulled out a familiar pink princess doll. "You left this behind."

Risa covered her mouth. Her lip quivered and tears gathered. "Y-you ran off to grab that... You could've gotten killed."

"I... knew what I was doing?" He smiled and took her spot, near the left armrest.

She sank between him and Pavo. "I... I'd been begging my fa—I mean, Andriy for it when I was little. I couldn't tell if he was going to get it for me. He... didn't live to see my ninth birthday."

Garrison put a hand on her leg and squeezed her knee. "Your father *did* get that for you."

"You..." Risa sniffled, thinking back to the strange delivery bot that brought her a birthday cake and a doll while she hid near the ceiling on her favorite vent cover. "How? Tamashī said the order came from Araphel."

"An angel told me you once wanted it." He looked down, guilty. "I asked him to send it because I didn't want you taking it as me trying to manipulate you."

Risa clung to the doll and leaned into him, sniffling. "Yeah, you're right... I probably would have. Thank you for the doll." She stared at him. "But you shouldn't have risked yourself for a toy."

"It's more than a toy." He kissed her atop the head. "It's a memory. One of the few good ones you have."

She sniffled, but smiled. "I've got more than you think... and you're in most of them."

Tamashī gnawed on a rib. The noises Genevieve made while eating sounded like they belonged in a bedroom.

Garrison raised an eyebrow at her. "Well, these must be some damn good ribs." He fixed himself a plate.

Before long, everyone moaned or rubbed their stomachs, though it looked like enough food remained to feed everyone a full meal all over again. Pavo got up to toss the leftovers in the fridge, making a comment that they were living on the 'high end' because the place actually had one.

Kree walked off down the hall. "I'm sticky."

Risa shivered and curled in a ball, clinging to the doll.

"What's wrong?" whispered Garrison.

"I keep waiting for the bad news... the bomb to drop... something." She collected herself and sat up, planting the doll in her lap.

"Things are under control." Garrison set the plate of picked-clean remains on the table. "I never did understand why they make bones in vat-grown meat."

"They skipped them at first." Pavo chuckled. "You try eating ribs... with no ribs. No one liked it."

"Under control?" Risa grabbed carpet with her toes. "What does that mean? Usually that phrase makes me think someone's about to go boom."

"Beer?" Pavo glanced at Garrison, and stood.

"Yeah," said Tamashī.

"Not 'til you're older, kiddo." Pavo winked.

Tamashī gave him the finger.

"Great idea." Garrison leaned back in the sofa. "We have the NewsNet scaling down their coverage of MLF activities. In a few months, most people won't even remember what the Martian Liberation Front was. General Everett has taken back the reins, though Maris is still the OIC for the field. There's no point using a hidden safehouse anymore; that's why we decided to blow it."

Risa tried to swallow a lump in her throat. "I can't believe it's gone... it's like watching my childhood home burn down."

"You might have grown up there, but that was no home." He accepted a silver synthbeer canister from Pavo, transferred it to his left, and stroked a hand over her hair. "I'm sorry for taking you there. I didn't want you to wind up on the street and I wasn't strong enough to walk away from the agency."

"I'm not angry with you, Dad." She fussed with the doll's dress. "I... Yeah, I would've been a completely different person if I'd grown up with dolls and cute clothes and who knows what else. I don't blame you for the way my life is. I'm just terrified it's going to end."

"Senator Nur has officially been charged with a number of financial crimes related to the way she moved money between the government and certain corporations. They're keeping treason on the back burner for now, and threatening to press murder charges for everyone who died in Arden as well as two other operations you're too young to remember if she puts up much of a fight. The head of the inquest commission has even gone after Andreas Beyer with the information you"—he chuckled, shaking his head—"blasted all over cyberspace. Aegis Industries isn't going to want a long media frenzy. I'm sure he'll quietly disappear. Everett wasn't too happy about that leak."

"Oops." She shrugged. "I didn't leak anything. Raziel found it." Risa examined her fingernails. "Worked, didn't it?"

Pavo returned, handing out beers. He teased Tamashī for a few seconds, holding it too high for her to reach before she gave his crotch a meaningful look. Laughing, he handed her a canister and flopped back in his seat.

"That it did. I told him Raziel was so deep in your head he helped himself to it and you didn't know." He sipped his beer. "Damn, boy." He leaned forward to glare around her at Pavo before settling back. "Buys the cheap stuff."

"Tell your friends in Paramount City to raise Defense Force pay." Pavo held his beer up in mock toast.

"Did anyone tell you what they're going to do to me?" Risa shuffled her feet back and forth.

Kree walked back in, smelling of autoshower soap and wearing a coral-hued knee-length dress. She crawled into Risa's lap and rested a damp head on her shoulder.

"Everett wanted to keep you on the payroll. I told him you weren't at all interested. He asked how you'd feel about intelligence gathering missions. Spy stuff, minimal risk."

"I have a daughter to think about." Risa threaded her arms around Kree, holding her close. "I can't see myself agreeing to anything he asks me to do. Maybe I'd be up for testing domestic security... nothing where I'd be shot at for real."

Garrison chuckled. "I'll tell him to check back when she's in university."

"Shame to waste all that hardware," said Pavo, grinning.

"Oh, I'll find some use for it." Risa's smile faded to a flat line. *Raziel's going to call in that favor eventually, and who knows what Heitzenroeder is going to ask me for.* "I was thinking of getting an office job." *I'll probably wind up spying for Everett anyway... he's got too much on me, but I have to at least try to walk away.*

"Dustblow." Pavo choked on his beer, coughed, and poked her. "I don't believe that for a hot second."

"She's an expert at reinstalling operating systems now." Tamashī winked.

"So what happened to everyone else?" asked Risa.

Kree pointed at the holo-panel. "Put the movie back on."

"Well," said Garrison. "The Martian Liberation Front is done. The people we could salvage—not criminals, I mean—are being brought on board as official staff. Right now, most of them are on their way to Earth for proper training. If the Corporates are ever given the boot off this rock, I suspect the PVM will take a good hard look at our government and figure out what to do."

Risa fussed at Kree's hair. "Think I need to tune up the dry cycle. Her hair is so thick it's still wet." She looked sideways at her father. "What are you going to do?"

The giant ethereal screen shimmered from gameshow to a still image of a castle swarmed with dragons. A second later, the magical battle resumed.

Garrison sighed, fluttering his lips. "I'm getting too old for this shit. With things shaping up to be all official now, I'm not too interested in slogging through all the usual bureaucratic dustblow. Guess sixteen years of playing fast and loose made me lazy. I might retire. Ehh, know anyone looking to hire a babysitter?" He winked and sipped his beer. "Oh, General Everett wanted you to call him. Said he needs to go over a few points with you. I'm sure he plans to repeat all the same things you've already got an answer for."

"Are you going away?" Kree looked up, a hint of worry in her dark-blue eyes.

"No, sweetie." Risa kissed her on the forehead. "I'm not going anywhere."

---

fin

ACKNOWLEDGMENTS

Thank you for reading the Daughter of Mars series!
  I'd like to thank Kate Bystrova and Lee Sheridan for editing.

ABOUT THE AUTHOR

Originally from South Amboy NJ, Matthew has been creating science fiction and fantasy worlds for most of his reasoning life. Since 1996, he has developed the "Divergent Fates" world, in which *Division Zero, Virtual Immortality, The Awakened Series, The Harmony Paradox, and the Daughter of Mars series* take place. Along with being an editor at Curiosity Quills press, he has worked in IT and technical support.

Matthew is an avid gamer, a recovered WoW addict, Gamemaster for two custom RPG systems, and a fan of anime, British humour, and intellectual science fiction that questions the nature of reality, life, and what happens after it.

He is also fond of cats.

Visit me online at:
Facebook: https://www.facebook.com/MatthewSCoxAuthor
Pinterest: https://www.pinterest.com/matthewcox10420/
Goodreads: https://www.goodreads.com/author/show/7712730.Matthew_S_Cox
Email: mcox2112@gmail.com

OTHER BOOKS BY MATTHEW S. COX

Divergent Fates Universe Novels

Division Zero series

- Division Zero
- Lex De Mortuis
- Thrall
- Guardian
- Harbinger
- The Shadow Fixer

The Awakened series

- Prophet of the Badlands
- Archon's Queen
- Grey Ronin
- Daughter of Ash
- Zero Rogue
- Angel Descended

Daughter of Mars series

- The Hand of Raziel
- Araphel
- Ghost Black

Virtual Immortality series

- Virtual Immortality
- The Harmony Paradox

Prophet of the Badlands Series

- Prophet's Journey
- Prophet's Mercy

Divergent Fates Anthology

(Fiction Novels - Adult)

The Roadhouse Chronicles Series

- One More Run
- The Redeemed
- Dead Man's Number

Faded Skies series

- Heir Ascendant
- Ascendant Unrest
- Ascendant Revolution

Temporal Armistice Series

- Nascent Shadow
- The Shadow Collector
- The Gate to Oblivion
- The Queen of Discord
- The Burning Alchemist

Vampire Innocent series

- A Nighttime of Forever
- A Beginner's Guide to Fangs
- The Artist of Ruin
- The Last Family Road Trip
- The Phantom Oracle
- How Not to Summon Demons
- Ordinary Problems of a College Vampire
- A Vampire's Guide to Surviving Holidays
- An Introduction to Paranormal Diplomacy
- A Vampire's Guide to Adulting
- How to Stop a Vampire War in Six Easy Steps
- Ancient Vampire Death Cults and Other Annoyances

- Hunting Vampires for Fun and Profit

Standalones

- Wayfarer: AV494
- Axillon99
- Chiaroscuro: The Mouse and the Candle
- The Spirits of Six Minstrel Run
- Sophie's Light
- The Far Side of Promise anthology
- Operation: Chimera (with Tony Healey)
- The Dysfunctional Conspiracy (with Christopher Veltmann)
- Of Myth and Shadow
- The Girl Who Found the Sun

Winter Solstice series (with J.R. Rain)

- Convergence
- Containment
- Catalyst
- Catacombs

Alexis Silver series (with J.R. Rain)

- Silver Light
- Deep Silver
- Silver Quarrel
- Silver Crucible

Samantha Moon Origins series (with J.R. Rain)

- New Moon Rising
- Moon Mourning
- Haunted Moon

Vampire For Hire series (with J.R. Rain)

- Moon Master
- Dead Moon

- Lost Moon
- Vampire Destiny
- Infinite Moon
- Vampire Empress
- Moon Elder
- Wicked Moon

- The Devil's Eye
- The Drifting Gloom
- Dark Mercy
- Primal Wrath

- Blood Moon

- Broken Ice

- The Elementalist
- The Black Rose
- The Wakefield Curse

- The Witch and the Hangman

- The Beast of Devil's Creek
- Wanted: Undead or Alive

Young Adult Novels

The Eldritch Heart Series

- The Eldritch Heart
- The Cursed Crown
- The Sapphire Soul

Evergreen Series

- Evergreen
- The World That Remains
- The Lucky Ones
- Nuclear Summer
- The Nuclear Frontier
- The World We Make

Progenitor Series

- Out of Sight
- Out of Mind

Diary of a Teenage Fey

(Short story series)

- Elder Horror
- The Hag of Barrow Falls
- Babysitter's Nightmare
- Lharakki
- Bauble for a Soul
- Simulacrum
- Amorphous
- Manticore

Standalones

- Caller 107
- The Summer the World Ended
- Nine Candles of Deepest Black
- The Forest Beyond the Earth

Middle Grade Novels

The Adventures of Ubergirl series

- My Dad is a Mad Scientist
- Aliens Ate My Homework
- The End of all Halloweens
- Dr. Infinity and the Soul Smasher

Tales of Widowswood series

- Emma and the Banderwigh
- Emma and the Silk Thieves
- Emma and the Silverbell Faeries
- Emma and the Elixir of Madness
- Emma and the Weeping Spirit

Standalones

- Citadel: The Concordant Sequence
- The Cursed Codex
- The Menagerie of Jenkins Bailey